What Readers Are Saying about *The Guardian*

Faith should be an adventure, and yet many times we as believers avoid adventure, risk, and sacrifice for the illusion of security and safety. The Guardian is a powerful story of pursuing God's calling in spite of fear, danger, and uncertainty. It's a compelling read that entertains while also reminding us of the reality of the battle that we're all a part of every day.

—Jenni Catron, Executive Director of Cross Point Church,
Nashville, Tennessee

Up-and-coming authors Robbie Cheuvront and Erik Reed nailed it with this entertaining, first-rate-thriller. The action never stops—I simply couldn't put this book down!

—Mindy Starns Clark, award-winning, bestselling author of
Shadows of Lancaster County and *The House that Cleans Itself*

I haven't read a book front to back in a long time but *The Guardian* was one that I just couldn't put down! I knew Robbie Cheuvront was a very creative person from writing songs with him over the years. But as a novelist, Robbie has, without a doubt, taken his craft to a whole new level! Robbie and Erik have outdone themselves!

—Richie McDonald, former lead singer of LoneStar
and award-winning songwriter

Having been privileged to work with Robbie cowriting songs and recording in the studio, I'm certain anything with his and Erik's names on it deserves a closer look—he is the definition of multitalented.

—Chris Waters, Grammy Award-winning songwriter
and food critic columnist

The plot is captivating. The characters are believable. The pace is fast. You absolutely must read this book.

—Ben Stroup, writer, blogger, and consultant,
TheContentMatrix.com

Well congratulations, Pastor Erik and Pastor Robbie, for writing such a thrilling first novel. I picked up *The Guardian* and could not put it down. It had me on the edge of my seat from the first page, and I couldn't stop turning. The writing is fresh and relevant, and the storyline is incredibly gripping. You'll be taken in right away and immediately invested in the characters and their phenomenal, perilous, life-threatening quest. A definite must read."

—Pete Wilson, author of *PLAN B*,
senior pastor of Crosspoint Church, (Nashville, Tennessee),
and host of the blog *Without Wax*

THE GUARDIAN

ROBBIE CHEUVRONT
AND ERIK REED

BARBOUR
PUBLISHING

DEDICATION

For our wives, Tiffany and Katrina,
who have sacrificed more than anyone would know
so that we can minister and write.
We love you and thank God for you.

© 2011 by Robbie Cheuvront and Erik Reed

ISBN 978-1-61626-278-5

For more information about the authors, please access the following Internet address: http://www.thejourneytn.org/

Published by Barbour Publishing, Inc., P.O. Box 719, Uhrichsville, OH 44683, www.barbourbooks.com

Cover design: Faceout Studio, www.faceoutstudio.com

Our mission is to publish and distribute inspirational products offering exceptional value and biblical encouragement to the masses.

ecpa Member of the
Evangelical Christian
Publishers Association

Printed in the United States of America.

A NOTE FROM THE AUTHORS

Thank you for taking the time to read mine and Erik's first novel, *The Guardian*. We hope you will be edified and enjoy the story. And that's just what it is: a story. Erik and I do not, never have, nor will we ever proclaim to be scholars of the book of Revelation, prophets, or anything of the like. We simply were intrigued by a passage of scripture in Revelation that mentioned a little scroll and took note that there was never any more mention of it throughout the rest of the book. Being scatterbrained and creative (to a fault sometimes!), the story almost wrote itself. We do not intend for anyone to read into the story for some cryptic meaning or solution to the book of Revelation. It is merely a fictitious story, one that is focused on Anna Riley's journey of faith. Nothing more. The scriptures are clear: no one knows the hour except the Father. We'll leave the decoding of Revelation to others, if they wish. But ultimately, we just yearn for the return of our Savior, whenever God chooses that to be.

—Robbie and Erik

Then I saw another mighty angel coming down from heaven,
wrapped in a cloud, with a rainbow over his head,
and his face was like the sun, and his legs like pillars of fire.
He had a little scroll open in his hand. And he set his right foot on the sea,
and his left foot on the land, and called out with a loud voice,
like a lion roaring. When he called out, the seven thunders sounded.
And when the seven thunders had sounded, I was about to write,
but I heard a voice from heaven saying,
"Seal up what the seven thunders have said, and do not write it down."
Then the voice that I had heard from heaven spoke to me again, saying,
"Go, take the scroll that is open in the hand of the angel
who is standing on the sea and on the land."

REVELATION 10: 1–4, 8 ESV

PROLOGUE

Patmos Island Prison, 60 years after the Crucifixion

John came to, finding himself still in his cell—still lying on a cold slab of rock, which sent stiff, cold pain through his lower back. His old age had begun to betray his once healthy, strong body. He was sure that his frail frame would soon give out completely and leave him an invalid. His head throbbed with a mighty headache from the vision. It was the Lord's day, and he had been praying when it happened. He remembered the last image, as if he were standing there yet, standing at the top of a great mountain, beside a beautiful angel, looking out over a new Jerusalem, with Christ at the throne. His hands trembled and his brow was soaked with sweat. He was both terrified and overjoyed at what he had seen, the beauty of a redeemed creation, the Christ sitting on His throne. John didn't know how long his vision lasted. All he knew was that he had to write it all down. He had been commanded to do so.

He stood from his bed and walked over to the parchment lying on his table. He took the pen and ink and began to write:

The revelation of Jesus Christ, which God gave him to show his servants what must soon take place. He made it known by sending his angel to his servant John, who testifies to everything he saw—that is, the word of God and the testimony of Jesus Christ. Blessed is the one who reads the words of this prophecy. . .

As he wrote, he lost track of himself. The words flowed from his pen like water. Indeed, just as Christ had promised, the Holy Spirit was bringing remembrance of all that had been shown to him.

. . . Then the voice that I had heard from heaven spoke to me once more: "Go, take the scroll that lies open in the hand of the angel who is standing on the sea and on the land."

John immediately stopped writing. His stomach started to churn. What was it? What was this sudden sickness he was feeling? Then he remembered. The angel had told him to eat the scroll. He had. The angel told him it would be sweet like honey to his lips, but would turn sour in his stomach. It had. And now he was feeling the sickness of the scroll in his belly.

John stood and walked back to his bed. He lay down rubbing his stomach which was now violently churning. He felt a moan well up from deep inside of him. He fell to the floor, bent over holding on to the wall and began to cough. Violently cough, and gag. And then he felt it.

John was now scared. He couldn't breathe. Something blocked his airway. He reached inside his mouth and felt his fingers touch something. He latched onto it and pulled it out. He heaved and gasped for breath as the obstacle dislodged from his throat and fell to the floor below. He knelt down to see a tiny scroll, covered in mucus and stomach acid.

John continued to suck in deep breaths, his lungs burning as the fresh air came in. He tried to stand. He held the tiny scroll in his hands, his fingers trembling as he grasped the corners to open it. Suddenly, the room was enveloped in a blinding white light, causing him to stumble backward. He stopped when he reached his bed, but only because his legs were kicked out from under him by the slab. He found himself sitting again and trying to focus on this great light.

"Do not fear me, John, servant of Christ," a voice that emanated from the light spoke. "I am Micah, a messenger of the Most High."

And with that, the bright light dimmed. John removed his hand that shielded his eyes. He recognized this being. It was the angel who had given him the scroll in his vision.

"Greetings from our Lord and Savior, Jesus, the Christ," Micah said.

"Th–thank you," John muttered. "And also to you."

The angel continued. "I have been sent here to explain the gift you have been given, John. Its purpose is great."

"Do you mean this scroll?" John asked.

"I do," Micah answered.

CHAPTER 1

New Orleans, Present Day

"Let's do another shot!" The young woman strained her vocal cords to get above the music and noise in the nightclub. She and her friends had been there nearly four hours.

Outside, the streets were filled with the raucous noise of thousands of tourists and locals, all celebrating the year's most anticipated event. Mardi Gras. Everyone wore their beads and gaudy masks in celebration of the festival. It was almost midnight and the last of the partying was at hand.

"Come on, Anna," the girl pleaded to her companion. "Just one more! It's almost midnight. You know they're gonna kick us out at twelve."

"Are you crazy?" Anna protested. "My head is swimming. I'm looking forward to midnight."

"You're a prude! We travel all this way to come to Mardi Gras, and you wanna wuss out on me thirty minutes before it's all over? You're kidding me, right?"

"Look at that, Jane." Anna pointed to the middle of the room.

The rest of their friends were in the middle of the dance floor, bouncing up and down like they had pogo sticks for legs. "I'm sure they will all do another shot with you. I'm going to bed. We have a nine a.m. flight back to Nashville, and I don't intend to be throwing up on it!"

Jane chuckled at Anna's remark. She knew that Anna wasn't much of a drinker. It practically took her twisting Anna's arm just to get her to come down here in the first place. "Okay," she said, "but I'm not leaving yet. So you're gonna have to just sit here and wait on me."

"You know what? I think I'll just walk back," Anna said.

"No you will not! This is New Orleans, girl,—the French Quarter—not Nashville. Not to mention, the biggest freak fest in the whole world is going on outside those doors!"

"It's literally two blocks. There are cops every nine feet out there. I'm going to be on the main street. I'll be fine."

"More like seven blocks, and no you won't."

"I have my mace, my cell phone, and my police whistle. I'll be fine. I promise. I'll even let you know when I get there. Okay?"

Jane hesitated. She didn't like the thought of her friend out there alone, but she wasn't ready to leave yet. "All right. But when you get there, you text me."

"I will."

Anna Riley stood from her stool and hugged Jane. She grabbed her jacket from the seat and walked outside. The cool night air felt good at first, but after a few steps, she felt a slight shiver. At least her vision wasn't as blurry as it had been an hour ago. She had only had two margaritas, but being the lightweight drinker she was, they had exacted their revenge. She sucked in a deep breath and let it out. Maybe that would clear away some of the cobwebs.

As she passed the bars and nightclubs one by one, she turned her head and looked into the windows. She had heard as a little girl the outlandish things that went on down here during the festival. Seeing them for herself, she was both stunned and embarrassed as women passed her on the street exposing themselves to passers-by. Men shouted obscenities at the women from the sidewalk. The women yelled back propositions.

Anna continued walking until, little by little, the noise became fainter and the people became fewer. She hadn't realized that she and her friends had come this far down Bourbon Street. The alcohol made her less aware of the time she had spent hopping from club to club as well as how far they had gone.

She finally made it to Canal Street where she turned to head to her hotel, the Fairmont. The streets were a little more deserted outside the French Quarter. As a matter of fact, there didn't seem to be much of anyone around. She picked up her pace. Suddenly, walking home by herself didn't seem like such a great idea. She reached into her pocket and felt for her can of mace. That eased her a little bit.

As she passed a dimly lit alleyway, she thought she heard a child crying. She stopped, listening. There it was again. It was definitely someone crying, although she wasn't sure now that it was a child.

"Hello?" Anna half whispered. "Is anyone there?"

Nothing.

"Hello?" she said again, a little louder this time.

Still nothing. The crying had stopped.

"Do you need help?" Anna now asked full voice. "I have a phone with me. I can call for help if you need it." She pulled her mace out of her pocket. Still nothing.

Anna waited for a few seconds. Maybe her mind was playing tricks on her. Maybe she should just quit drinking altogether.

She turned away from the alley, ready to run the rest of the way to her hotel. But standing in front of her was a little boy who looked to be about ten years old. She almost knocked him over.

"Holy freakin'—Good grief!" she screamed as she jumped back. "You scared the life outta me! What are you doing out here this late?"

"Maybe *you* should watch where you're going," the boy said.

"I'm sorry. It's just. . .well. . .you scared me to death."

"That wasn't my purpose."

"Well, you did."

"I'm sorry, Anna." He really did look sorry.

Anna couldn't stay angry at him. "Don't worry about— Hey! How do you know my name?"

He only lifted an eyebrow in a manner that seemed far too old for such a young boy. "I have a message for you."

A shiver ran down her neck. "From who? How do you know my name?"

"You need to go home."

"What? Who are you?"

"You need to go home." His expression looked compassionate, almost pitying.

Anna found it hard to breathe. She didn't want to show she was frightened of this strange little boy. Anger seemed safer. "I am going home. Tomorrow. What is it any concern of yours?" She meant to take a step toward him, but her feet moved backward instead. "How do you know my name?"

"You need not fear me."

"What? Who talks like that?" she asked. "Especially some little street punk! I asked you a question. Who are you and how do you know who I am?"

"Anna, listen to me. I am a friend. It doesn't matter how I

13

know you. All you need to know is that you need to go home. Right now. This instant. Get into a cab and go to the airport. Take the late flight out to Pittsburgh and go home."

"Hah! I'm from Nashville, you little twerp! You aren't as smart as you think, huh?"

"No, I do not mean where you grew up with your parents. I mean where you are from. Pittsburgh. That is where you were born."

Anna's mouth dropped. No one knew that. She'd never told anyone. She and her parents had moved to Nashville when she was six, after her grandparents had died tragically. Her father couldn't handle the grief. Or at least that's what her mother had told her.

Anna had never really known her grandparents. They were always gone. Constantly traveling. The last time she remembered seeing her grandfather was in a church. She could barely remember. She had been kneeling down in front of the altar. The church was empty except for her, her grandfather, and the pastor. She remembered a prayer being said over her. And that was it.

"Pittsburgh?" she finally responded. "My grandparents were from Pittsburgh."

"Yes, and so are you."

"You obviously have me confused with someone else."

"I don't think so," the boy said. "You are Anna Riley. Daughter of James and Elizabeth Riley. Granddaughter of Thomas and Olivia Riley."

"Okay! That's enough!" She shifted her purse higher on her shoulder and took another step away. "Who put you up to this? Jane? Alex? Did they do this?"

"Neither Jane nor Alex have anything to do with this," the boy said. "Anna, your grandfather needs you."

"My grandparents died when I was six, you idiot!" This entire conversation was ridiculous. Why was she even talking to him?

14

"I know that's what you were told," the boy said.

"What are you, some little voodoo psychic or something?"

"Actually," he said, "I'm something quite different."

"Yeah, like crazy. I'm outta here." She started to walk away.

"Your grandparents did not die when you were six," the boy called after her. "Your grandmother just died recently, and your grandfather is still alive."

She looked over her shoulder and found him smirking at her. "Actually, your grandmother is very much alive, too. Just in a different way."

Anna whirled around set on ending this ridiculous conversation. "What are you talking about? Who are you!" she demanded.

"Anna, give me your hand," the boy said.

"I'm not giving you anything!"

The boy grabbed her hand with such grace and speed that Anna didn't even notice until she felt his little hand squeezing hers. All at once, the street disappeared. So did the buildings. She couldn't see anything except a great white blinding light coming from behind the little boy. She tried to pull away, but as he held on, a strange sense of calm came over her. She felt warm and safe and an unbelievable sense of euphoria. The only thing she could think of was she didn't want to let go of this little boy's hand. She wanted to hold onto it for the rest of her life. She could only describe it as complete and total peace. She didn't know who this little boy was or why he was talking to her, but for some reason, she knew she had to listen to him. And then the boy let go.

Anna fell backward and caught herself just as she was about to land on the sidewalk. "Wh—what was that?"

"Anna," the boy let out a long sigh, "I have said more than I was sent to say. Go to Pittsburgh. Your grandfather needs you. He has something for you. It is yours by right. It is to be your charge for the remainder of your life. He will explain all of this. Go to him. Go now. He is in Mercy Hospital. His time is short. You must hurry."

Anna stood there in complete disbelief. The world, as she knew it, had just changed. Her grandparents hadn't died when she was a child? Why? Why would her father and mother tell her that? Why would they do that to her? She always envied her friends in school at Thanksgiving break who said they were off to their grandparents' for the holiday. She and her parents never did anything special. They cooked a big meal and watched football, but other than that, it was an ordinary day in her household. And what about Christmas? Of course, her parents weren't religious, but they still exchanged gifts. Had she missed out on all of the fun times at Christmas with her grandparents?

"Why?" Anna asked the boy. Suddenly tears filled her eyes. "Why would you do this to me? My grandparents are dead!"

"Yes, Anna," the boy said, "your grandmother has passed away, but your grandfather is alive."

"How do you know this?" she asked again, now crying.

"Go to him. He needs you. It is your destiny."

"I don't understand!" Her words were choked with sobs.

"You will, soon. Now go. The time is short."

And then there was no little boy, only an empty alley filled with the sounds of Anna's tears.

CHAPTER 2

New York City

Father Vincent Marcella sat in prayer in the Cathedral Church of St. John the Divine on Amsterdam Avenue, just one block off Broadway in Manhattan, New York, in the fourth pew back from the altar. He hadn't felt much like praying these last few days. He had failed.

A long time ago, Father Vin, as he liked to be called, was given a proposition, an opportunity that he'd been told was only given to a select few. So select, in fact, that he was only one of four people in the world who would know about it. The other three were the priest who was offering him the deal, the man whom he would be assigned to, and the pope himself.

"This is the opportunity of a lifetime, Vincent," Father Giovanni had told him. "Understand that if you say yes, you can never change your mind. You will be making a covenant with God Himself."

And *there* was the catch! There was always a catch. He wasn't allowed to know what the assignment was until he said yes. But that created a whole new set of problems. What if he said yes and then was unable to do this task? What if after hearing about it he had no interest in it at all? Father Giovanni had said it would be the ride of a lifetime. He had always been an adrenaline junkie. Hadn't he? Ever since he was a child he would do anything and everything he could to get that rush. That's partly why he became a priest in the first place. He was so afraid of what he could become out on the streets as a teenager that he gave his life over to God. He looked to God for his strength. That was the only thing that kept him out of trouble. And he was grateful for it.

That's why when Father Giovanni brought this proposition to him, he barely hesitated before saying yes. If God had given him this need for action and adventure in his life, then maybe it was for God's purpose. "Yes! I'll do it!" he had said. And he never looked back.

That was forty years ago. He was an old man now. Slower. His mind wasn't as quick-witted as it used to be, and physically he couldn't beat up a dustcloth, let alone his many enemies he had running around the earth. Times had changed. Technology had changed. He was out of date. And for all he knew, he had failed.

"Hello, Vincent."

Father Vin whirled around in his pew to see who it was. Caught off guard, he also came around with a backhanded fist.

The speaker quickly ducked the roundhouse punch aimed at his head. "I see you still have something left in you, old man."

"Sammael! I really wish you wouldn't sneak up on me like that."

"After all these years, I still catch you off guard."

"I was praying. You of all people, or. . .whatever, should know that."

"Ah. . .but you weren't really praying. Were you? You were

just going through the motions. If you had been, I would not be allowed to disturb you. Would I?"

"No, I guess not." Father Vin hung his head. "I've failed, Sammael."

"Actually, you didn't."

Father Vin lifted his head. "What do you mean?"

"He's alive."

"But. . .but. . .I saw him! Surely he couldn't have survived that. I was too late. When I got there, they were. . .they were. . .stabbing him. I got scared, Sammael. I could see the beasts hovering above, circling over him like vultures. I've never actually seen them before. It was awful. Their faces were grotesque and distorted. And some kind of foul grunting noise was coming from their mouths. They were just waiting for the men to finish him. I shot at the men, but Thomas was already down. I waited until the ambulance got there, and then I ran. I think I was more afraid of the beasts than the human attackers. I've never seen anything so terrifying in my life—and that's saying a lot."

"Some would say I am frightening to look at."

"Yes, but once someone knows who, or I guess I should say *what* you are. . ." Father Vin waved his hand at him, pointing out his unique appearance.

"Still, I have this uncanny ability to unnerve some people."

"Is that why you show yourself as 'the boy'?"

"It is, at least until they get to know me."

"Well, I must say those beasts were a hundred times scarier than anything you could ever appear as." Father Vin stood to pace.

"My friend, I see those foul creatures everywhere I go. Do not be afraid. It seems you have been given the gift of protection."

"What do you mean? Look at me! I'm as frail as a brittle piece of paper!" Father Vin flung out his arms.

"I mean by being able to see them, you have been given a gift. You can protect yourself from them now. And if you know that they're there, then you may well be able to protect—"

"Yes, yes, I see what you are saying." He continued his trot back and forth. "But still, I abandoned him! I ran." He sank down into the pew and ran his hand through his hair. "I am old, Sammael. I think it's time I found an apprentice."

"I would hardly say you are old, my friend. I've been here since. . . Well, let us just say you are not that old. Nevertheless, I understand your concern. That's why I am here."

"So, it's time then?" A hint of disappointment colored his voice.

"Yes, I believe it is."

"You know, every time you and I talk, inevitably someone comes in here and thinks I'm talking to myself. Maybe someday they'll just commit me!"

"They could see me, too, if they would just open their eyes. All of your kind could. Don't worry though. We won't let them commit you until you find a suitable replacement!"

"Thanks! That's just what I needed to hear!"

Sammael let out a chuckle. "Oh, and one other thing. . ."

"What's that?"

"She's been found."

"What! Are you kidding me! Where?"

"She's on her way to see him."

"Does she know?"

"I think that's going to be left up to you and him."

"It doesn't matter. We've found her."

Sammael tilted his head and said, "She will not be that easy to convince. You have your work cut out for you."

"She has to. She's next in line. If she doesn't, then who?"

"She will. It might just take some time."

"How do you know that?"

"Because, my friend, God has purposed it. It will come to pass."

CHAPTER 3

Pittsburgh, Pennsylvania

Anna got out of the taxi, paid the driver, and then faced the sprawling old building in front of her. Mercy Hospital. This was it. This was where the boy told her to come. This was where he said her life would change forever. He said it was her destiny. Not to mention, she was about to talk to a man she thought had been dead for fifteen years.

After a stop at the information desk, she arrived in the intensive care unit where a nurse greeted her. "Can I help you?"

"I'm here to see Thomas Riley."

"Are you family?"

"Ah. . .yes. Yes I am. I'm family."

"And who would you be?"

"I'm Anna Riley, his granddaughter."

"Granddaughter, huh?" the nurse asked hesitantly.

"That's right," Anna said.

The nurse softened her face and sighed. "Ms. Riley, I'm afraid your grandfather has passed away."

Anna felt as if someone had punched her in the stomach. What little bit of hope or anticipation that she'd allowed herself in coming here had been stripped without warning. Suddenly, she felt alone.

"When? I don't understand," she said. "The boy—he told me to come. He said it was— I don't understand."

"About an hour ago. I'm sorry, Ms. Riley. We've been looking for any family. Trying to get in touch with someone."

"What happened?" Anna asked. "How long has he been here?"

"You don't know?"

"We haven't kept in touch." Boy, was that an understatement.

"He's been here for about a week." The nurse walked behind her desk and grabbed a manila folder. The tab on the top had the words "John Doe" scratched out and "Thomas Riley" written under it.

"John Doe?" Anna was confused. "What's that mean?"

"When they brought him in, he had no ID on him and no one was with him. He was unconscious, and we didn't know who he was. Just a formality."

"How did he get here?"

"Ambulance."

"Okay. Let's back up." Anna ran her hands through her hair. The long night, the flight, and lack of sleep were beginning to take their toll on her. "I haven't seen my grandpa since I was six. To be honest, I didn't even really know he was still alive." She put up a hand to forestall the questions forming in the nurse's face. "Don't ask. Long story. Anyway, I have no idea what's going on. All I was told is that he was here. So, can you just. . .fill me in or something?"

The nurse nodded with a soft smile and offered her a seat. "I'll tell you as much as I know, but that isn't a lot."

Anna sat down beside her and waited to hear what was going on.

"About a week ago," she said, "a man came in here in an ambulance. No ID. They said they picked him up in Point Park. He had been beaten and stabbed numerous times. A witness called an ambulance, but no one but your grandfather was there when the EMS got there."

"Oh my gosh!"

"He was rushed here and immediately taken into surgery. The trauma team worked on him for a while, and then he flatlined. He was gone for nearly four minutes before they were able to revive him and stabilize him. They brought him out of surgery and sent him up here. He's been in and out of consciousness since then. And then a little over an hour ago. . ."

"But I thought you said they stabilized him."

"Ms. Riley, your grandfather suffered some very traumatic wounds. To be honest, it's kind of surprising that he was able to hold on as long as he did."

Anna nodded. "So what now? What's going to happen to his body? Can I see him?"

The nurse patted her on the hand. "Sure you can. I'll take you to his room." She stood and motioned for Anna to follow. "His body is being released to Rome. There is a man here from the Vatican right now filling out the proper paperwork. The body should be ready for transport in just a few minutes."

"Rome?" Anna asked, as the nurse opened the door to her grandfather's room. "Why Rome? That doesn't make—"

As she entered the room, a man writing on a clipboard and wearing a priest's collar looked up and smiled.

He stepped close and extended his hand. "Hello, Anna. I've been looking for you. My name is Father Vincent Marcella."

CHAPTER 4

The Vatican

Cardinal Louis Wickham sat in his study drinking a warm glass of brandy. Actually, Cardinal Louis Wickham sat deep inside the shell of a body that was once his.

Many years ago he had been a prominent member of his order. He was on the fast track to becoming pope. The only problem was, he lacked something very important: faith. He believed in the Almighty, sure. He even believed in the Holy Trinity. That was not the issue. The issue was that he couldn't control his ambitions. He had a very weak spirit and refused to give the control over to God. And because of that, he found himself involved in things that the church could never agree with. He constantly gave in to temptation. He was full of pride. He only thought of himself and how *he* benefited in every situation. Quite simply, he was a lost soul.

One evening when he should have been in a prayer session with the rest of his brothers, he drank himself into oblivion, where he was approached by a strange man. The man was very sophisticated.

He spoke eloquently and wore a fine hand-tailored suit. He had warm, deep blue eyes and a smile creasing his lips that would invite anyone to talk to him. He made Louis feel comfortable just sitting there talking, telling him his life story. Before long, they had switched from scotch to champagne, and he and the man were entertaining three ladies. It was that night that the cardinal became someone, or something, different.

The man spoke of unlimited power and control. He convinced Cardinal Wickham that if he worked for him, he would be rewarded in a way that the church could never do. This man literally promised him the world, a world that was here and now, not some fantasy of something promised by the church. The cardinal, being drunk and loose of his senses, readily agreed. The man took him outside the pub and into the alley. He told the cardinal to get on his knees, bow, and call him Master. The cardinal did. And at that moment, a shockwave of energy ripped throughout his body, like a lightning bolt had coursed through his veins. The man that was once Cardinal Louis Wickham seemed to fall into a deep pit inside his own body. He could see out, but it was like watching a movie. He was no longer able to control what happened on the outside. He had been imprisoned. The saddest part of it all was that he knew it. And he realized that he did it of his own free will. The ice consumed him and became who he was. And he had let it happen.

Now, thirty years later, he sat in front of his fireplace a vile, corrupt man. And he was upset. He was more than upset. He was furious. And rightly so.

He'd spent the better part of ten years trying to find Thomas Riley. Well, actually his men had. He did nothing more than give the orders and finance the work. But the call finally came. They had found him. Years of following the man around the globe, always two steps behind him, and where do they actually get him? His hometown of all places! And after all the years of searching, what do they find? Nothing! A big, fat nothing! Those stupid idiots!

They had been told time and time again that the old man had something he needed. He told them not to harm him until they had it. Bumbling idiots! That's all they were. The old man was dead, and he still didn't have the scroll. And now he would have to answer for his—their—incompetence.

The phone rang and startled him. He set down his glass of brandy and reached for the receiver. "Hello?"

"I need to speak to you."

"I told you to never call me on this line."

"It's about the old man."

Cardinal Wickham's grip tightened on the phone as he sat up in his chair. "Meet me in twenty minutes. You know where." He hung up the phone and stood, his back rigid. He walked out of his study and into his private chamber. Ten minutes later he had changed clothes and was on his way out the door.

Mad Jack's Irish Pub, Rome

Cardinal Wickham made his way to the bar and ordered a Guinness. He paid the bartender and turned to find his usual table in the back of the room. He took off his hat and began to sip his drink. Less than a minute later, a tall, slender man wearing all black scooted in beside him.

"Hello, Cardinal." The man set down his beer beside the cardinal's.

Cardinal Wickham squeezed the man's arm as he spoke in a hushed voice. "Do not call me that in here!"

"Relax, Louis." The man removed the cardinal's hand from his arm. "This isn't exactly the type of place where people go looking to make friends. They couldn't care less if you were the pope!" He laughed, taking a big gulp of his ale.

"So you have news for me?" Wickham looked around to make sure no one was listening.

"He's alive." The man held his arms out in a "Go figure!" gesture.

"What happened?" asked the cardinal. "And I mean everything! You and your goons have put me in a very dangerous position." Wickham took a long pull from his beer and waited for his associate's answer.

"Well, you see, Louis. I *can* call you Louis, right?" Wickham rolled his eyes at the use of his first name. "Like I said, we just happened to run into him. Literally!" The man laughed again at his own humor. "I mean, we're walking out of his apartment. He had his head buried in some newspaper, walking down the street, and *boom*! I walked right into him. Or rather, he walked right into me."

"That's very interesting," Wickham snapped. "When do we get to the part where you almost killed him without getting me what you were sent to get in the first place?"

"I think you need another Guinness, Louis." The man's tone was threatening. "You know, you should really watch how you talk to people. One of these days, it's going to get you in trouble. Remember what I do for a living?"

"Go on," Wickham said. He tried to relax a little bit as he shifted in his seat.

The man let his last statement hang in the air for effect before continuing. "As I was saying, we ran into him. Of course, he had no idea who we were, and we were so shocked it was him that we just kept walking, so as not to draw any attention to ourselves." The man took another drink. "So we saw him go into his building. We decided we'd just keep an eye on him. A few hours later, he left again. We followed him to the park. That's when we tried to take him."

"What do you mean tried?" Wickham asked.

"When we approached him, he freaked out. We tried to subdue him, but he kept yelling. One of my men pulled his knife to try to scare the old man into shutting his mouth. Somehow the situation got out of control. One of my *former* employees, and I stress *former*, accidentally stabbed him. He kept yelling, 'They're trying to kill me! They're trying to kill me!' About that time, that priest showed up. He pulled a gun and started shooting. We had to abort. We couldn't risk getting caught. Anyway, the next time I see him, I'm gonna tape his mouth shut."

"And when do you think that is going to be?"

"Soon. He's in the hospital right now."

"So go to the hospital and get him."

"I can't."

"Why not?"

"There are guards."

"Dispose of them. You have my permission."

"These are not normal guards."

"How do you mean?"

"I mean, they are about seven feet tall, and they are wearing some weird kind of armor. Not to mention, they're extremely fierce-looking, like special forces or something. It would take a small army to take them out. I have no idea how this man rates having that kind of security. I've never seen anything like them before."

"No, I imagine you haven't. I'm surprised you can see them at all."

"Come again?"

"Never mind. They'll be gone as soon as he has recovered. You just be there when that happens. He can't stay in there forever."

"Don't worry. I will be."

"See to it you are. Oh, and Jonathan. . .don't disappoint me again. *My* boss is much scarier than anything you've *ever* come across. Unfortunately for me, he rather likes you. He thinks you have potential!"

CHAPTER 5

Mercy Hospital, Pittsburgh

Hello, Anna. My name is Father Vincent Marcella. Father Vin."

"Who are you?" Anna demanded. "Why are you taking my grandfather's body? And why is he going to Rome? Shouldn't I get a say in that?"

Father Vin let out a long, deep breath. "Anna, there is much to tell you. And I will. But not here—"

"No," she said defiantly, "you're going to tell me now. I just flew all night to get here. I haven't seen my grandfather since I was a six, and now all of this—"

"Anna, please—" He turned to the nurse. "Could you give us a minute, please?"

The nurse nodded and ducked out of the room.

"Anna," Father Vin continued, "the men who did this to your grandfather will be back. We need to leave, or you, too, will be in danger. Your grandfather's body will be ready for transport in just a few minutes. There is already a plane waiting to take him back to Rome. Please, come with me. There is a diner across the street. I'll

31

buy you some coffee. Give me ten minutes to explain. If you still want to leave after that, I'll understand."

Anna stared at the old priest, trying to get a read on him. He seemed genuine. But she wasn't taking any chances. "Give me a minute," she said and walked out the door. She found the nurse she had spoken with earlier sitting at the nurses' desk a few feet away. "Excuse me, again."

"Yes, dear?"

"That priest. Do you know who he is?"

"Yes, Ms. Riley. Well, sort of," the nurse replied, almost questioning her own response. "I mean, we got a call just before you got here from our administrator, telling us that he would be coming in. He's from the Vatican. All of his credentials check out, and the body—I'm sorry, your grandfather has been released to him. It's all legit."

Anna turned around and walked back into the room. "Okay, priest. I'll give you ten minutes. But I want some answers."

"Thank you, Anna," Father Vin smiled. "Let's go."

"Just a minute," Anna said. "Can you give me a minute alone with him?"

Father Vin looked at Thomas's body. "Oh yes. I'm sorry," he said. "I will be waiting outside the room when you're ready."

CHAPTER 6

Spumoni Brothers Diner, Pittsburgh

They sat across from one another in the small diner. They had found a table in the back for privacy. Aside from the two older gentlemen sitting at the far end of the bar counter deep in conversation, they were alone. The waitress brought them coffee and took their order, then left them again.

"So why Rome?" Anna jumped right in. "Why can't I take his body back to Nashville? And why did my parents tell me he died when I was a kid?"

"Anna." Father Vin held up his hand to interrupt her. "Let me try to explain what's going on here. And then if you have any questions after that, I'll be happy to try and answer."

She folded her hands on the table and nodded.

"Okay." He drew a long breath and let it out again. "Anna, I've known your grandfather, and your family, for more than thirty years. I actually married your parents, if you can believe that. Anyway, your grandfather and I have been like brothers for a long time." He stopped and shifted in his seat. He glanced around the room then leaned closer. "Anna, what do you know about the book of Revelation?"

"You mean the Bible?"

"Yes, Anna. The revelation of John, the disciple of Christ."

"Not much," she admitted. "Isn't it like some freaky, weird code about the end of the world?"

"Yes," he said. "And no." He reached inside his coat pocket and pulled out an old, worn leather-bound Bible. He flipped to the end. "Let me read something to you."

He began with chapter 10, verse 1 and continued through verse 8. When he finished, he closed the book and stuffed it back inside his coat.

"Yeah, so?"

"A lot of people believe that the book of Revelation is symbolism. That the things John saw were not actual visions, but manifestations of his mind, symbolizing the fall of Rome."

"Okay."

"No. Not okay," Vin said. "Anna, the Bible is the true, inerrant word of God. John was not a crazy person. He was led by the Holy Spirit to write and give an account of what God had actually shown him concerning the return of Christ. Just like any prophetic text, there are things in there that John wrote that did concern the people of his time, and even perhaps the fall of Rome. But none of that matters. People have been trying to decode Revelation, or put their own spin on it, for two thousand years. What really matters is that it is a prophecy of Christ's return to redeem this world and return it to its rightful state. And that is not symbolism."

"What does this have to do with my grandfather? Me?"

"I'm getting to that," he assured her. "The passage that I just read you—it holds great significance for your life."

"How? What do you—?"

"Anna, please," he pleaded with her.

"Yes, go on. I'm sorry."

"It's all right. Now," he said, continuing, "while some things in the book are symbolic, that scroll definitely is not. The angel actually gave the scroll to John. When John awoke from the vision, he got violently sick and vomited the scroll up out of his belly. An angel appeared to him immediately afterward and explained what it was and why it had been given to him. John was told that it was not for him to keep. He was to pass it down through his family so that one of his ancestors would one day be the one to unlock its secrets."

"C'mon, man." Anna laughed, and then her laughter died away. "You're serious?"

"Anna, your grandfather is dead. I'm most definitely serious." He paused and let the weight of it sink in. "Anna, the keepers of this scroll are known as guardians. They are and have been the descendants of John, the disciple. Your grandfather was one of them. And so are you."

"What? How is that possible?"

"How it's possible is not important. What is important is you. You are a direct descendant of the disciple John. That scroll has been in your family for two thousand years." He stopped and rubbed his forehead. "Well, technically, it's been in your family for that long, but it's been missing for most of it."

"What do you mean?"

"After the fall of Rome, the world was chaos. Nations warred against one another on a daily basis. One of the guardians, fearing for his life and not knowing what to do with the scroll, hid it. On his deathbed, he revealed the location to his son, the next in line. But he, too, feared the danger that the scroll would bring, and so he hid it again. And he never retrieved it. The legend has been passed down ever since. The details of where and how it was hidden got fewer and fewer over time. There were only a couple real clues to go on. The scroll had been locked away safe until your grandfather came along. Thirty years ago he came across a piece of information that set him, and me, on a journey around the world in search of it. And two years ago we found it."

"That's a pretty unbelievable story," Anna said. "Where is it now? Show me."

"I can't."

"Why not?"

"I don't have it."

"What do you mean? If what you're saying is true, then show me. Prove it."

Father Vin smiled. "You remind me a lot of him."

"What's that supposed to mean?" she asked tersely.

"Nothing, dear." He chuckled. "That's a good thing. Anyway, I don't have it. Your grandfather hid it again." He held up his hand to keep her from interrupting again. "But I know how to get it. Anna, I was your grandfather's protector. Or at least I was supposed to be," he said solemnly. "And for the last thirty years, we've been chased around the globe by someone who wants it. About a month ago, we had an incident and got separated. We kept in communication, and then last week we were supposed to meet here to go retrieve it. Unfortunately, he found us again."

"Who?"

Father Vin pursed his lips, looking reluctant to speak. At last he cleared his throat and spoke. "Lucifer."

"As in the devil?"

"Yes."

"Okay," she said, standing up. "Thanks for the coffee. I'll be leav—"

Father Vin grabbed her arm. "Anna, please!" Desperation tinged his words. "Please sit back down. This is not some joke! Your grandfather died for this. Please, at least let me finish. After that, if you want, you can go."

Anna glared at him for a moment and then sat back down.

"Anna, I know this is hard to believe, but I swear to you. It's true. Lucifer is real. He, too, was an angel in service to God, until his pride made him think he was God's equal. This started a war in heaven. The scripture says that he and about a third of the angels in heaven were cast out. And now God allows Lucifer to reign on earth until the appointed time. And he is very powerful. But make no mistake. He is not God. And he doesn't know everything. But he does know, just as the first guardians and your grandfather did, that that scroll has something to do with the second coming of Christ. And he believes that if he can get his hands on it, then he can stop it."

Anna shook her head. "This is all—I don't know what to say." She bit her lip. "How do you expect me to believe all of this?"

"Anna, God has always used imperfect people to complete His perfect will. You can see this all throughout scripture, from Abraham to Joseph, to David—even the disciples of Christ. They were ordinary men and women, trusting in what God had called them to do. You have to trust that this is what God has called you to do. And your grandfather always said that if he didn't finish, you were the one. And the work is almost done."

"What do you mean?" she asked.

"There is a riddle on the scroll, Anna. And your grandfather believed he had all but solved it."

"A riddle?"

"Yes."

"What is it?"

"I don't know."

"You want me to believe that you and my grandfather have some scroll, given to my family from God, with a riddle on it, and you never saw it?"

"Anna, I've never wanted to know. That's not what God called me to do. Sure, your grandfather offered. But I've always felt it was not for me to know."

"I can't believe I'm listening to this."

"Anna, taking on this task—protecting the scroll and solving its purpose, is ultimately up to you. But know this. What God has willed will come to pass."

"What, so you're saying I actually don't have a choice?"

"Not at all. What I'm saying is that it's your choice. But there are real consequences for our choices. And no matter what we choose, we cannot thwart the plans of God. You may say no, but God will pursue you relentlessly. And you will live with the regret of not having done what He's asked of you. That I can promise. Go read the book of Jonah. You'll see what I mean."

Anna stared at him. She had a million reasons to get up and walk out. She should—she really should.

Father Vin sat back, rubbing his neck. He looked tired. Old. "Let's do this," he said. "You need to get back to Nashville. I have your grandfather's plane."

"He had his own plane?"

"You have no idea what all he had." He shook his head. "I'll take you back. You can ask any questions you want on the way. I and the flight crew will do our best to answer. But when we get to Nashville, we won't have much time. I'll need an answer."

There was silence for more than a minute while she stared at him. Finally, she spoke.

"I'll go to Nashville with you. But let's get one thing clear. That doesn't mean that I believe what you've told me. I'll take the ride home. After that, we'll see."

CHAPTER 7

Pittsburgh International Airport

Anna ran up the steps of the Gulfstream 5. Impressive. It looked like one of those fancy tour buses that the big rock stars rode around on. She had never flown private before. Just commercial like everyone else, herded like cattle by airlines that overbook and charge too much for bags. This—this was a whole different world. Calm, dignified, comfortable. She could definitely get used to traveling like this.

A pretty young lady greeted her in the main cabin as she walked in. "Hello, you must be Anna. My name is Marie."

"Nice to meet you, Marie." Anna shook the woman's hand.

"Good day, Father Vin," Marie greeted the priest. "Can I get you anything before we take off?"

"No thank you, Marie, I'm fine. Tell Hale and Miles we are ready as soon as they have clearance, would you?" He turned to Anna as they both sat in luxurious recliners. "Not too shabby, huh?"

"Not at all," Anna replied. "Do you always travel like this?"

"What? You mean in your plane?" Father Vin said.

"*My* plane?"

"Yes Anna. Your plane. All of this is yours now. Your grandfather has left it to you."

Unbelievable. Aside from the jolt of pleasure at being the owner of an entire plane, it did lend credibility to Father Vin's story. Her grandfather must have been involved in something important to have such a luxury item. The plane began to move. Marie came through the main cabin again to make sure that Father Vin and Anna were seated and ready for takeoff. In just a few minutes, the plane had taxied onto the runway and was at full throttle. The G-5 lifted off seconds later, and they were in the air.

"The answer to your question is yes. *We*, Anna. *We* will always travel like this. Not because it's a life of luxury either. We will travel like this because it's private, it's quick, and it's the safest way for you to move around, if need be. Marie, Hale the pilot, and Miles the copilot, will always be with you. They are all specially trained. If you are ever headed up the stairs of this plane and you don't see all three of them, do not get on board. They are instructed always to be together when you travel. There will never be any personnel substitutions. They are it. If you don't see them, you don't go unless I, or the pope himself, has told you it's okay. Understood?"

"The pope? Are you kidding me?"

"No Anna. I'm not. The pope is just one of the more interesting people you are about to meet. Only he, Sammael, and I know about the scroll. Well, and you of course. Oh yes, and the demons. Ah, and Lucifer—"

"Yes Vin, I get the picture."

"Oh yes. Sorry. Anyway, the flight crew knows a little about it, that it exists and you are its rightful guardian. But that's the extent of it. They have taken an oath, like me, to protect you at any cost. That includes their own lives."

"Why would they do that? They don't even know me."

"It' doesn't matter. They are devout Christians. Like you, at some point in their lives, they were contacted by Sammael. He informed them that they, too, had been chosen by God to take on this role of protection. They accepted. Now they are here. And they will be a part of your family from now on."

"Sammael?"

"Oh yes," he nodded. "I forgot, you don't know. Sammael is an angel. I believe he appeared to you in New Orleans."

"You mean the boy?"

"Yes, but that's not who he really is. He only appeared to you that way, so as not to frighten you."

"So I was talking to an angel?"

"Yes Anna. As I said before, all of this is very real. You will more than likely see him again."

She sat there, as if letting that sink in. "Tell me about my father and Grandpa. Why did my dad take me from him and my grandmother? Why did he lie to me?"

"I think that would be best if you asked him that. Right now, you should rest. We will be in Nashville in about forty-five minutes. Meanwhile, I'll be thinking of a way to make you disappear. If you decide to do this, you need to be a faceless person no one remembers. That's how you stay alive."

"That's nice. I'm just supposed to completely detach myself from my life and everyone in it? Perfect!"

"I do have some good news for you though."

"Oh yeah? What's that? Did my grandfather leave me this enormous fortune and I'm rich beyond my imagination?"

He grinned. "Yes, actually."

"I was being sarcastic."

"I know. But I'm not. The Catholic Church has power of

attorney over your family's fortune. When your grandfather passed away, the church passed the assets of your family into your name. Yes Anna, you are one of the five wealthiest people on the planet."

She began laughing and couldn't speak for several moments. This couldn't be real. Finally, she let her laughter trail off. "Wait. . . You're serious! How is that possible?"

"Your grandfather holds some rather interesting patents. On top of that, he was a brilliant businessman and a good investor."

It couldn't be real. But there was evidence all around her that it was. Either that, or it was the most elaborate scam in the world. But she studied Father Vin's face and saw honesty and compassion in his eyes. And she knew—it was true. No more scraping together money to pay rent or to save up for a trip. No more bargain hunting at department store clearance sales. No more living like a college student on macaroni and cheese. She had never longed for money—it had never even occurred to her to wish for it. But now she felt flooded with possibilities, and a pressure she didn't even know she'd been living under lifted.

"I'm rich!" She punched the air over her head. Marie came running out of her private quarters to see what was the matter. Anna assured her everything was fine. Marie just smiled and left again.

"Calm down, Anna," Father Vin chuckled. "You *are* rich, but there are some rules that go along with it."

"It figures."

"We can go over all of that later. If, I mean, you decide to go."

"Yeah. If," she said, her words trailing off. Then, "What if I say no?"

"Well, I suppose it's still yours. All of it. We would just have to go to Rome and sign the proper documentation to transfer the estate into your name."

"This just gets crazier by the second. You know that. Right?"

"Yes, I know."

BNA Airport, Nashville

The G-5 came to rest in the private terminal just a few hundred yards from the main airport. A car was waiting for them as they stepped off the plane. A man who introduced himself to Anna as Nick ushered them into the backseat and asked, "Where to?"

"Get back on I-65 and head south," Anna answered. "Take the Brentwood exit. I want to go see my father. He should be at his office. I'll call my mom and tell her to meet us there."

Father Vin shut the door. "Anna, are you sure that's a good idea?"

"I've got a lot of questions that need answers. They're the only ones who have them. I'm not making any decisions until I talk to them."

Father Vin nodded. "Nick, take us to Brentwood."

"Right away, Father Vin. How was your flight?"

"Fine, Nick. Thank you for asking."

"You know him?" Anna asked, pointing to the driver.

"As I told you before, your grandfather and I have traveled all over the world. Nashville was a regular stop for us. I meant it when I said I know your family very well. I've practically watched you grow up."

She supposed that should creep her out a little, but it didn't. For some reason, knowing that her grandfather had been there, even if she hadn't known it, felt kind of nice. And even more strangely, she felt drawn to this priest. She couldn't explain it, but for some reason she wanted to believe him and everything he

44

had told her. All of it. She stared out the window as they merged onto I-40, trying to rehearse what she was going to say to her parents.

Third Financial Mortgage, Brentwood

"Hey, baby girl," James Riley stood from behind his desk, giving his daughter a peck on the cheek. "How was New Orleans? You and the girls have a good time?"

"New Orleans was fine, Daddy. Listen, I don't have a lot of time. I called Mom, and she's on her way here. We need to talk."

"Honey, I'm very busy. I've got three closings and a refinance today. And what is the meaning of this?" James Riley looked at his daughter with a scowl as Father Vin entered the room. "Your mother? And why is *he* here!" He pointed to the man wearing the white collar.

"Daddy, sit down for a minute. I will answer all of your questions, but first I have some of my own," Anna took a stern tone with her father, something she had never done before. She halfway expected him to point his finger at her—as he'd done so many times previously—and give her what for. Her father was someone who always took charge of any situation. This time, however, he just stood there looking confused. It was almost as if he knew what was coming.

The door to her father's office opened, and in walked her mother. She was already midsentence, asking what was going on, when she noticed her husband and daughter standing nose to nose, staring each other down. It was then that she saw the old man in the corner of the office.

"Come on in, Mom," Anna said, still looking at her father.

"We were just about to get started."

"What's going on, Anna?" her mother asked. "I thought you were in New Orleans." Then to Father Vin, "And what are you doing here? I thought we told you to stay away from our family!"

"That's enough!" She faced both her parents. "I'm gonna talk, and you all are going to listen. I don't want to be interrupted until I finish. Understood?"

"I don't know what this is about, Elizabeth," James said to his wife. "She just barged in here and started taking over."

"Daddy! I'm talking now! Pretend, just for once, that I'm more important than some stupid real estate deal, and listen to me."

James held his hands up in surrender. "I'm just trying to figure out what you're so upset about. And why this man, who has tried to destroy this family, is with you!"

"I'll get to him in a minute." Anna watched as her parents' expressions changed from a look of impatience and disgust to absolute worry in an instant. "Now," she continued, "who would like to tell me about my grandfather?" Again Anna watched her parents' expression shift. Now they looked like little kids who had gotten their hands caught in the cookie jar. "Anyone?"

"I don't know what—"

"Stop it, Daddy! Just stop it! I just flew here from Pittsburgh, where I might add, I just saw his dead body. For real this time!"

Anna's parents stared blankly at each other. They seemed to be waiting for the other to respond. Finally, Anna's mother started to speak. "Anna, I think we need to explain—"

"Really, Mom! You think? How about this for an explanation? You lied to me! For fifteen years I thought my grandparents were dead! Dead! Do you understand that? Who does that? I mean, really! Who lies to a little kid and tells them that their Grandpa and Grammie died in an accident?"

46

Anna stopped all of a sudden as the tears welled up inside her. She didn't care anymore. She let them come. Her parents came to her and put their arms around her.

"Anna," James rubbed her shoulders. "We can explain, honey. Just listen for a second. Okay?"

"No." Anna pushed her father's arm away and wiped her cheeks. "I came here to tell you that I know everything. There's nothing to explain."

"Anna, I'm your father, and you are going to listen to me, young lady! Is that clear?" James pointed at Anna. "Your grandfather was a crackpot! He was *my* father. I knew him better than anyone. All of this bull about '*the scroll.*' Anna, no one has ever seen the stupid thing, including him!" He pointed at Father Vin. "Yes, I'm talking about you. And when I'm done with my daughter, you and I are going to have a private conversation, sir." James turned his attention back to Anna. "He's made it all up, Anna. There is no scroll. There is no secret mission from God. There are no bad guys chasing him all around the world trying to get their hands on it! Don't you understand? It's all a big myth!"

"Anna, don't be foolish!" her mother interjected.

Suddenly, Anna wasn't so sure of anything anymore. What if her father was right? What if this priest was a crackpot luring her into some kind of Indiana Jones crusade to find a fictitious artifact that a bunch of other crazy people would try to kill her over. But that couldn't be, could it? After all, she had seen the boy—the angel. There was the plane. And the flight crew. And her grandfather was definitely dead. For real this time. Truth be told, everything Father Vin had told her, while perhaps a little hard to believe in some instances, so far proved to be true. Her father, on the other hand, had lied to her for most of her life.

"No Daddy," Anna finally replied, "I think you're the one who doesn't understand." Anna held up a hand. "You've always been one of these people who has to see it to believe it. Well, let me tell you. I was the same way. Daddy, I've seen things in the last eight hours that you can't even imagine. And it's not going to do me any good to tell you about them either. You'll just think I'm some crackpot, too! But let me assure you. There were men after Grandpa. That's why he was in the hospital. They tried to kill him."

"Anna, listen. . ." Her mother tried to calm her down. "We only did what we thought was best for you."

"No Mom, you listen. I'm leaving here with Father Vin. I've decided to take Grandpa's place. We know where the scroll is. It's real! I know it. And from now on, I'm going to be the one in charge of it. This is not up for discussion. It's my decision."

And there it was. She didn't know why, but in that moment she had made her choice. Probably out of her own defiant nature, but mostly because she really believed that everything Father Vin had told her was true. And for whatever reason, the moment she had said it, she knew it was the right thing to do. She turned around and headed for the door. "Come on, Vin. We have a plane to catch."

Anna was silent for the first few minutes after leaving her father's office. What had she just done? This was crazy. How could she just pick up and leave her life behind? She could ask the driver to pull over and let her out. She could call one of her friends to come and get her. She would go home and sleep. For the next two days. Then she could call her parents and tell them that everything was okay. She hadn't run off after all.

But that wasn't going to happen. No, she had made her decision. And that decision meant she needed to go home immediately.

"Nick," she finally said, breaking the silence. "I need you to take us to Elliston Place."

Father Vin frowned. "We need to get to the airport."

"I understand that, but that's where I live. And if I'm going to leave my life behind, there are a few things that I need, as well as a couple things I just want to take with me. Don't worry," she said, seeing the concerned look on Father Vin's face. "I can be in and out in thirty minutes."

Another hesitation. Then he shrugged. "Thirty minutes. Then we're headed to Venezuela."

Venezuela. Just going to hop on a plane for South America. Anna slumped down in the seat and wrapped her arms around herself. She'd done it now. Everything would change. From this moment on, she would be hopping on planes for who knew where. Running—possibly, at times, for her life.

CHAPTER 8

The Vatican

Hello?" Cardinal Wickham looked at his bedside clock as he answered the phone: 3:30 a.m. There was only one person he could think of who would call him at this hour.

"Is this the Capriatti residence?" The voice was pleasant and quick.

"I'm sorry, you have the wrong number," the cardinal answered. He hung up the phone and got out of bed. He turned on his light and fumbled around until his eyes adjusted.

Earlier, after their conversation at the pub, the cardinal had given his associate, Jonathan, a new instruction. "From now on, if you have to contact me at home, use this code." He didn't think, however, that Jonathan would have reason to use it so quickly.

He dressed and quietly slipped from his chamber. He made his way into a dark alley. Hidden from the view of the main street was a pay phone. He stepped inside, pulled the door shut behind him, and punched in the number. He waited for the other end to pick up then spoke into the phone. "This better be worth getting me up in the middle of the night.

"Good morning to you, too, Louis. What's the matter? Bit of a hangover?" Jonathan didn't wait for a reply. "The old man is dead."

"What do you mean he's dead?"

"No need to shout, Louis. My guy called me a few minutes ago."

Cardinal Wickham slammed his fist against the glass booth. "This is unacceptable! You'd better have something better for me than 'He's dead'!"

"My guy was paying off a janitor to keep him posted on the old man's condition. He called me a little while ago and told me the janitor called him and said the old man had checked out."

"This just happened?"

"Earlier today. He didn't call me until just now."

"What kind of crew are you running over there, Jonathan? Do they think they can just sit around and check in whenever they feel like it? This is precisely why I wanted you there! And yet you're still here. Explain to me again why I'm paying you?"

"Calm down, Louis. He couldn't call before. He's been busy. It seems Riley had a visitor today. A girl. A young girl, about twenty or so. After checking it out, my guy tells me it's his granddaughter. Immediately after Riley died, she and that priest that's always with him left outta there and headed to the airport. It took my guy awhile to find them, but he did. They had a private plane waiting for them."

"So Father Marcella is with the girl now?"

"Yeah, and from what I hear, they were in a big hurry. Barely stayed long enough to sign the release papers."

"Where did they go?"

"Nashville, Tennessee. That's where she's from."

"So you're on your way to Nashville, then?"

"No, I'm on my way to Venezuela."

Cardinal Wickham pinched the bridge of his nose and let out a long sigh. "And *why* are you going to Venezuela, Jonathan?"

"Vacation, of course," he snapped. "Because *they're* headed to Venezuela. Why else?"

"So you're leaving now?"

"I'm at the airport as we speak."

"Find her, Jonathan. If she doesn't have it yet, she will. He couldn't just die and not leave it with somebody. She and Marcella know where it is. You get it from them at any cost. You hear me?"

"I hear you."

Cardinal Wickham hung up the phone without saying good-bye. He pulled his hat down over his eyes and walked back to the Vatican. With any luck, he would have his prize soon.

CHAPTER 9

Caracas, Venezuela

Anna and Father Vin stepped off the plane into a sweltering heat. It was almost nine o'clock in the evening, and the temperature still hadn't let up for the day. It was a far cry from what they were used to this time of year.

They grabbed their luggage and exited the terminal to hail a cab.

"I'm starving, Vin," Anna said. "You know anywhere around her to get some good food?"

"I'm afraid I have only been here twice in my life. Both times were for missionary work. We ate at the homes of the people we were working with. I'm sure the hotel will be able to help us find something good."

"I hope so. I'd hate to know that I have all this money and can't get a decent meal anywhere!" Anna nudged Vin in the arm. They both laughed at her joke.

"I was very proud of the way you handled your parents earlier today." Vin patted her arm.

"I don't know what made me do it. I just felt like I was supposed to tell them that. But I still have a lot of questions myself. You and I are going to have to have our own heart-to-heart here pretty soon."

"I can't wait!" Vin showed a big smile. "How's breakfast? Tomorrow."

"Sounds good. So, where are we going?"

Vin raised his eyebrows and looked at Anna intently. "Ever hear of the Cathedral de St. Anna?"

"St. *Anna*? You're kidding me. Right?" She preened. "Well, I *have* always been rather saintly."

"Yes," he said dryly, "a paragon of virtue." He held out a piece of paper with the address written on it.

"That's just a number and a street name," Anna said, examining the paper. "How do you know it's here in Venezuela?"

"Because I know Thomas came here after we got separated."

"So what do we do when we get there?"

"That's the big mystery, isn't it? I have no idea. Your grandfather only left me the address. I guess it's up to us to figure it out."

The cab twisted and turned along the roads and through the Plaza Bolivar, a historical and touristy area of town. When they reached the hotel, the driver got out and helped them with their bags. Father Vin pulled out a twenty and gave it to the man. "Keep the change," he said. They walked inside and checked in.

At the top floor, Father Vin turned the key to their room and stepped inside, holding the door for Anna behind him.

"Wow!" Anna looked around the room. It was furnished like a New York penthouse. Two steps led down from the foyer into a living room area. Off to the left there were two bedrooms and a computer station. Toward the back of the room there was a small kitchenette. A fully stocked pantry was off to the side. There was a note on the coffee table. She picked it up and read:

> *Welcome to La Casa de la Belleza, Ms. Anderson. If we can be of any service to you during your stay, please let us know. Your personal hotel staff will be available to you in the morning. Just call the front desk, and we'll send them up.*

Anna placed the note back on the coffee table and smiled. "Hey, Vin, did you know that we are in some chick named Anderson's room, and she has her own butler service?"

"Just one of the perks, Anna." Father Vin came out of the bedroom where he had been putting away his luggage. "You're Ms. Anderson. You'll find that a lot of times when you stay somewhere, you will have a different name. It's one of the ways you can keep a low profile on the outside. Keeps you from having to watch over your shoulder so much. You will have to get used to it. And always remember the name you're using. You don't want to arouse suspicion if someone calls out that particular name and you don't answer."

"Sounds like James Bond stuff to me." Anna shrugged her shoulders and walked to the pantry. "I'm fixing something to eat. You want some?"

"Speaking of James Bond—here." He took off his shoulder bag and set it on the counter. Reaching inside, he pulled out four passports and handed them to her. "Now, give me your wallet."

Anna was stunned. All four passports had a current picture of her, originated from four different countries, and had stamps from a bunch of countries she had never been to. And each one bore a different name.

"Your wallet please, Anna." Vin stood there with his hand held out.

"How did you get these?" Anna marveled at the fake documents.

"You'd be surprised what you can do with a digital camera, a laptop, and as much money as you have. Your grandfather has had at least four identities for you ready to go since you were eighteen. Your wallet, Anna. Please."

She held up the third passport, an Australian one. Inside the name read Maggie Anderson. "So I guess this is me. . .Ms. Maggie Anderson."

Father Vin reached across the counter and grabbed Anna's purse. He took out her wallet and began emptying its contents on the counter.

"Hey!" Anna objected. "What are you doing?"

Continuing to empty the leather pouch of its credit cards and identifications, Vin replied, "Anna, remember what I said? You are a ghost now. There can be no trace of your former life. You are no longer Anna Riley as far as the world is concerned. From now on you are one of these four people." He held up the passports. "And when these four have been used up, there will be four more waiting."

He grabbed the small pile of plastic and paper now scattered on the counter and carried it over to the trash can in the kitchen area. Placing the contents inside, he carried the small metal basket out onto the private balcony. He struck a match he had retrieved from one of his pockets and set the pile on fire, erasing Anna's identity.

Anna stood there staring at the small fire. This was just one more reminder of how crazy all of this was. She knew she should feel cheated or violated in some way, seeing her identity literally go up in smoke. But for some odd reason she didn't. The truth was, she was okay with it. If anything, it was kind of exciting. And scary. But mostly exciting.

"Okay. Well, I guess that's that," she said. She picked up the new passports again and thumbed through them once more.

Father Vin sat down on the couch. "I need to make a phone call. When I'm done, I think I will retire for the evening. We have a busy day tomorrow." He reached into his shoulder pack, retrieved the satellite phone he had used on the plane, and started to punch in the numbers. "Ah yes, Martin. I need to speak to him. It's important." There was a pause then, "Hello, Your Holiness. . . . Yes, everything is fine. . . . I am safe. . . . Caracas, Venezuela. . . . I'm afraid Thomas has gone to be with our Lord. . . . Yes, I am with her now. . . . What's that? . . . Oh yes, of course! Hang on one second." Father Vin cupped the mouthpiece of the phone and turned his head toward her. "Anna, you have a phone call."

She reached for the phone and noticed that Father Vin was smiling from ear to ear.

Anna grabbed the receiver, still cupping the mouthpiece. "Who is it, Vin?"

"Someone very important." Father Vin seemed almost giddy.

Anna put the phone up to her ear. She could hear rustling around on the other end. She looked at Father Vin as he was giving her a "Go ahead and say something" look. "This is Anna Riley. Who is this?"

The voice that echoed through the earpiece was soft and gentle. At the same time, it was also authoritative and tough as nails. "Anna, this is Pope Paul VII. I have been eagerly waiting to talk to you."

Anna's eyes went wide as she dropped the phone. Father Vin was horror-stricken at her reaction. Quickly, he leaped at the phone lying on the floor and picked it up. "Hello? Hello?" The line had gone dead. "Anna, you just hung up on the pope! What were you thinking?"

"Me?" Anna replied in shock. "What were *you* thinking! How about a heads-up next time? I mean you could've at least told me who it was, Vin! How am I supposed to know it's the pope? I mean it's not like we're buddies or something. I don't just go around talking on my phone, 'Oh hey, Pope! How's the weather over there? What's been going on? Seen any miracles lately?'"

Father Vin picked up the phone and began to fumble with the numbers when it started ringing. "Hello. . . . Oh yes, Holy Father. I'm sorry about that. There must have been a bad connection. Hold on. She's right here." Father Vin cupped the mouthpiece once again and handed the phone back to Anna. "Anna, it's the pope," he said sarcastically. "How's that for a 'head's-up'?"

Anna took the phone and smiled at Father Vin. "That's a little better." She winked at Vin, took a deep breath, and put the phone to her ear. "Hello, ah. . .sir."

"Your Holiness!" Father Vin hissed.

"Sorry. . .Your—Your Holiness."

"Hello, Anna," came the reply. "I've long been looking forward to this moment. Your grandfather spoke of you very highly."

"He did? He didn't even know me."

"You were not able to know him, and it grieved him every day of his life. But he knew you, and he loved you."

Anna blinked back sudden tears. "Thank you."

"My child, it's a heavy burden you've taken. I wanted you to know that I, too, mourn the loss of your grandfather, and I pray for his soul to be in safe-keeping with God. Thank you for taking his place on this vitally important journey."

The pope was thanking her? Suddenly, her reluctance and fears seem small, petty. Larger, more important things were at stake. "You're welcome."

"We will meet soon, and we will talk more."

"I would like that. . .Your Holiness." And she realized she actually meant it. There was something gentle and wise about this man. Like a grandfather. Her throat tightened, and she swallowed hard. "Do you need to talk to Father Vin again?"

"No, that will be all. Just tell him to check in again in the next couple of days. May God bless you, dear child."

She handed the phone back to Vin and walked into the kitchen to fix a snack.

"So, what did he say?" Father Vin stood and followed her into the kitchen. "You two didn't talk very long."

If she tried to explain how she really felt, she'd end up crying. She blinked back tears and put on a teasing smile. "Ah, you know." Anna shrugged her shoulders. "He just wanted to see how the weather was over here, that sort of thing!"

"Anna." Father Vin stood there with his arms crossed.

"I'm just kidding, Vin! He said that he looked forward to meeting me and he was glad that I am doing this." Anna took a bite of her toast. "You know, this could be kinda cool. I mean, hanging out with the pope!"

Father Vin didn't look fooled by her superficial joking. He walked over and kissed Anna's forehead. "Good night, Anna. I'll be in the next room if you need anything. Don't stay up too late. We are getting up at six o'clock."

"Six o'clock! What's the hurry? We just got here."

"Six o'clock, Anna," Father Vin said matter-of-factly. He held up a street map of the city. "It says here that our address is indeed St. Anna's. They have a Mass starting at seven thirty. We need to be there and talk to the parish priest before then. Maybe he can help us. We can stay for Mass if you like."

"Jeez!" Anna put down her fork. "I guess we'd better get some sleep then, huh? And I was all excited about having our 'personal hotel staff" come up here and spoil us!"

"Don't worry, *Ms. Anderson*, there will be plenty more opportunities." Father Vin laughed and patted her on the shoulder. He turned around and headed into his room.

Caracas Airport, Venezuela

Roberto stood at the head of the taxi cab line directing traffic and whistling for the next car in line to pull forward. He had a good eye for big tippers, so it was no coincidence that the man in the black leather jacket thumbing through a wad of American cash while exiting the terminal caught his attention. Without missing a beat, the young Latino chirped his whistle and waved to the man. "Over here, sir!"

The man in the leather jacket quickly moved to the front of the line without acknowledging the displeased glares of the other patrons, some of whom had been waiting in line for more than ten minutes.

"You look like a man who is ready to get somewhere. Do you need taxi?" Roberto hated that his English was a little broken, even after several years of practice.

"Um, yes," the man said, flashing his wad of bills. "But I was wondering. . . . I have a niece who got here a little while ago. We are all here for a family vacation. Unfortunately, I have lost all my contact information. I'm afraid I don't know how to get in touch with her. Her hotel and the rest of the information was written down. I've gone and lost the paper." He shrugged and shook his head, looking foolish. "Hey! Wait a minute! I have a picture of her. Do you think if I showed it to you, you would recognize her?"

"Yes. Perhaps." There was something not quite right about this *gringo*, but with so much money, who was Roberto to judge? "If she pretty American girl, I remember her."

"My name's Jack, by the way." The man stuck out his hand.

"I am Roberto."

"Well, Roberto, nice to meet you. Here's the picture." He reached into his coat pocket and took out a snap shot of a very pretty *Americana*.

Roberto didn't believe for a second that the girl was related at all to the man, but he'd learned to keep his mouth shut and his eyes closed about such things.

He thought he recognized the woman. "How long ago she come here?"

The man called Jack shrugged his shoulders. "Ah, I don't know. Maybe an hour or two? She was on the earlier flight. That's all I know."

"Wait here." Roberto turned and walked to the end of the taxi line and peeked into the window of the first car. He showed the driver the picture. The driver shook his head no, and Roberto moved on down the line. He worked his way to the end of the line, stopping at the next to last cab. The driver nodded. "I remember her. She was with a priest."

Before he could motion to Jack, the man had flung open the taxi door and climbed into the backseat.

"Mr. Jack." Roberto exchanged a glance with the cab driver. "I find your niece." He and the driver both rolled their eyes. Americans were so impatient.

"Yeah, I saw him nodding when you asked." He reached up over the backseat and handed Roberto a crisp one-hundred-dollar bill. "I know I'm jumping in line, but since he"—he pointed to the driver—"drove my niece, I'm just gonna let him drive me, too." He pulled out another crisp one-hundred-dollar bill and waved it at

Roberto. "That all right with you?"

Oh, more than all right. Roberto could overlook anything for that much money. "Sure, Mr. Jack. Whatever you want."

"Let's go." The man took off his hat and threw the cabbie another hundred-dollar bill. "Don't know why your friend there keeps calling me Jack. I told him three times my name was Bill!" The man called Jack, or *Bill*, leaned over the backseat and pulled the stack of bills from his pocket once more.

Pulling out three crisp one–hundred-dollar bills, he leaned into the front seat. "So where did you take them?"

"Downtown," the cabbie quickly answered, eyeing the cash. "You want to go there?"

"Yes I do."

Roberto walked away, shaking his head and fingering his cash. He hoped the girl would be fine—there was something suspicious about the man. But as he slid the bills into his pocket, his mind filled with how to spend the windfall. The Americana would just have to look after herself.

The driver took "Bill" to the same location he had brought his previous passengers. He pulled around to the side of the hotel as Bill instructed him to do and put the car in PARK.

Bill got out of the cab's backseat and opened the driver's door. "Get out."

"Please! I am just cab driver. I know nothing. I don't want know anything," the driver said with a nervous twitch in his voice.

Bill swallowed his rage. Third world cab drivers were all as dumb as dirt. "Calm down, chief. I'm not stealing your cab. I just want to show you something."

The cabbie reluctantly opened his door and stepped out.

Bill stood against the cab, hiding his face from the street and passersby behind them. He pulled out another stack of bills and began to peel them off. "This is two thousand American dollars." Predictably, the cabbie's eyes lit at the sight of the cash. "Tomorrow, I have a friend who's coming into town. It's very important that he find me. Do you understand?" The cabbie's head bobbed up and down. "Good. He will arrive at gate 6. He will be looking for a cab driver wearing this hat." He pulled a brown baseball hat out of his bag. "Tomorrow, put the hat on and wait for him. Only him. No other fares. You understand?" Again the cabbie nodded. "Good. Gate 6. Pick him up and bring him here, and there's another two grand waiting for you." He closed the gap between them and poked his finger into the cabbie's chest. "And if you want to keep that money or get the rest, you'd better keep your mouth shut! You got that?"

The cabbie stretched out his hand and took the cash. "Your friend. . .I will pick him up. I say nothing to nobody. I drop him off right here!"

"Good." Bill turned to walk away. "Make sure you wear the hat."

CHAPTER 10

Caracas Airport, Venezuela

Jonathan stepped off the jetway and into the airport, feeling the assault of the ridiculous humidity that plagued this part of the world. He hated foreign countries, especially third world foreign countries.

He made his way out to the taxi stand and looked for the driver wearing the familiar baseball hat. He had a stiff neck from trying to sleep on the plane, he was tired, and he hadn't had his breakfast yet. Only one of those things was, in itself, usually enough to get anyone who looked at him crossways a one-way ticket to the afterlife. Today, however, he was on a tight schedule. He didn't have time for pettiness.

For that reason, he ignored the fat Latino man who continued to give him a piece of his mind as he cut his way through the line. The fat man had more bags than he could carry and was trying to get into the cab that Jonathan knew was reserved for him.

"I'm sorry, sir." Jonathan spoke pleasantly to the man. "I'm afraid I've called ahead to reserve this particular taxi. See there?"

Then to the driver, "Nice hat. A friend of mine has one just like it. Name's Jonathan." He grabbed his hand and shook it, passing the driver a few crisp bills.

The driver immediately began loading his things into the trunk, his hands sweating profusely. This must be the man the American agent told him about. He turned to the other man and said, "Sorry, sir, this cab already paid for."

"I don't care if you've bought the whole *coché*!" The fat man continued. "I was here first! And unless you want me to call airport security, I suggest you get in line like the rest of us!" His English was very good. The man sounded educated.

Jonathan leaned in close and whispered something to the fat man. Instantly the fat man's eyes widened and he stepped back a step. The fat man looked horror-stricken. He moved out of the way and didn't say another word. Jonathan got into the cab and waited for the driver to pull away.

"What did you say to him?" The driver asked.

"I asked him if he believed in the devil."

"What did he say?" The driver asked.

"He said yes. I told him I *was* the devil." Jonathan laughed. He no more believed in the devil than he did in Santa Claus, the Easter Bunny, or God Himself. He only believed in here and now. He would take what was here and enjoy it now. Money talked with Jonathan. That was his deity.

He didn't care about any scroll. All he cared about was getting paid. And the cardinal did just that. Handsomely, too. Maybe this would be his last job. He had enough to go away and live like a king for the rest of his days. All he had to do was find this stupid scroll and he would be doubling that amount. *Yes*, he thought, *this might just be the last job*.

"You should not make light of *el diablo, señor*." The driver looked hesitantly at Jonathan through the rearview mirror. "The devil, he is very powerful."

"Well, then it's a good thing I don't believe in him. Huh?" Jonathan mumbled back at the driver.

"Sorry? What you say?" The driver asked.

"Nothing, chief. Why don't you just drive me to where you dropped my partner off. Okay?"

The driver did as he was told and didn't say another word the rest of the short drive into town. He pulled around the side of the hotel and waited for his passenger to get out. "Here you go."

The alley was deserted. Jonathan looked behind him to see if there were any passersby. No one. He leaned his head out the back window and moved his head around in a circle. Nobody looking out of the windows. No one out on any balconies. Very good!

"You know, chief, my partner wasn't entirely truthful to you." Jonathan pulled his head back inside the cab.

"He wasn't?" The cab driver looked confused. "How do you mean?"

"Well, I know he promised you another two thousand for bringing me here. But I'm afraid this is all I have for you." Jonathan brought his arm up to rest on the back of the driver's seat. He leveled his silenced 9mm pistol and fired off two rounds into the back of the driver's head.

CHAPTER 11

St. Anna Cathedral

Father Ruiz." Father Vin extended his hand. "I am Father Vincent Marcella. This is Anna Riley."

Anna shook the priest's hand. She was a little taken aback at being in the private chambers of the priest. There were a lot of robes and Catholic artifacts hanging on the walls. It all seemed kind of spooky to her.

Father Ruiz greeted his guests. "It's nice to meet you, Anna, Father Vincent. To what do I owe this pleasure?"

"We are just visiting your lovely country." Father Vin smiled. "We thought we would take in a Mass. Your sanctuary is amazing."

"Thank you," Father Ruiz humbly bowed. "It is very old. A lot of history in this place." The priest scrunched his eyebrows and turned his attention to Anna. "Riley. . . I seem to recall a Riley. I think I met a Thomas Riley once."

"That was my grandfather," Anna said. "He's passed away."

"I'm sorry, dear. I didn't know." Father Ruiz seemed genuinely saddened.

"That's actually what we came to talk to you about, Father," Father Vin explained. "I must be honest with you. While we really look forward to seeing Mass in your native setting, we are anxious to talk to you about Anna's grandfather."

"Yes, I see." Father Ruiz studied his visitors now. He looked at them skeptically. "Well, perhaps I'll have a few minutes after our service. I'm afraid, though, I must get ready right now. Mass starts in three minutes." He studied them intently as if he wanted to say something. It seemed he'd changed his mind. "Father Marcella—"

"Please, call me Father Vin. Everyone else does."

The priest smiled. "Would you like to assist me with our Mass this morning? It would please me greatly to worship side by side with you."

"I would be honored," Father Vin bowed his head and accepted the invitation. "I'm afraid, though, my Spanish is pretty rusty. You'll have to forgive me."

As the two priests prepared for the start of Mass, Father Vin leaned in to speak to his colleague. "You're still trying to figure out what to do with us, aren't you?"

Father Ruiz smiled wryly. "I have forty-eight minutes, my friend."

And with that, Mass began.

CHAPTER 12

The Vatican

Cardinal Joseph McCoy had dreamed of becoming pope ever since he had become a priest. He would lie in his bed each night planning, thinking about all of the things he needed to do. He had studied every papal election for the last one hundred years. He knew what it took. And he knew how to get it. And he would be pope. Why? Because he was the best con man the Vatican had ever seen.

If they only knew half of his past, what he was before he became a priest, they would probably hang him in St. Peter's Basilica. Forget his life before being a priest. If they knew what he'd done as a priest, they'd probably just bury him under the jail.

Cardinal Joseph McCoy wasn't as saintly as most people thought him to be. He had secrets. A previous life. His real name wasn't even Joseph McCoy. He changed it to fit the profile he had created for his application to the seminary.

When Joseph Sikeston—his real name—was young, he got into a lot of trouble. It was always about power with him. He needed to feel the power of being in charge. His need eventually got him thrown into a juvenile center for boys. That's where he met Father Ryan.

Father Ryan would tell him, "Joseph, if you don't watch out, you're gonna be the devil's own personal instrument!" Joseph would just ignore the pompous old man, until one day he heard Father Ryan talk about a man called the pope.

The pope. Now there was a man of power. An entire body of people, an entire religion, at the beck and call of one man. And Joseph decided then and there that he wanted to be the pope. He didn't care about all of the religious stuff. He just wanted that power. He started planning that day. With Father Ryan's help, he was on his way.

Now, some forty years later, Joseph Sikeston was Cardinal Joseph McCoy. He set down his drink and checked his watch. Eleven forty. It was time to go. He was expected for a meeting. He would be early, of course. He always was. Punctuality was one of his strongest characteristics.

He walked out of the outdoor café and headed for his car. He could already taste the bitterness of the next hour. He wasn't looking forward to his appointment. Really and truthfully, he thought it was a waste of time. All they ever did at these meetings was talk. He had yet to see any kind of action. A bunch of tired, old windbags, he thought.

Rome, Just Outside the City

Cardinal Wickham sat alone in a high-backed mahogany chair. He sat at the head of an eight-foot-long, antique table. The room in which he sat was in the back of a historic, old country house. Technically, he owned the house, though one would have to do a major investigation to find any trace of a document with his name on it. Not that there was anything wrong with owning a property like this, but the kinds of activities that took place here on a somewhat regular basis were not the kinds of things that a prominent cardinal should be associated with.

The house was used for regular get-togethers. Many of the rich, prominent, definitely *not* Catholic community of Rome found themselves here on most weekends drinking and partying. It was more or less an extremely upper-crust, high-end, invitation-only nightclub. Cardinal Wickham found that he could make a substantial amount of money leasing out his place to these people who would rather have anonymity than be associated with the everyday nightclub scene. These people, different ones from time to time, would rent the house for two, sometimes three days a week. The usual going rate was five thousand dollars. That also included a cleanup fee.

Today was one of those days. A "client" had just left. There would be a get-together tonight. The arrangements had been made over the phone several weeks ago. Today was payday. The client, an attractive brunette in her late fifties, showed up, paid the bill, got the keys, and left just as quickly as she came. She extended an invitation to him and promised him more fun than he had probably ever had in his entire life. He politely declined, although a night of old-fashioned, worldly fun sounded good to him right now. He thanked the woman and showed her out. He apologized for the hurry, but he was expecting more guests any minute.

The first of his guests had just walked through the archway that led into the dining room where he now sat. The younger, gray-haired man said nothing as he entered. He simply walked into the room and took a seat, the same one he usually took at these meetings.

"Good day, Joseph," said Cardinal Wickham.

"Hello, Louis," Cardinal Joseph McCoy answered. "Who was the hottie in the Porsche that I passed on the way in here? One of your extracurricular activities, I assume?"

Cardinal Wickham dismissed this with a wave of the hand. "Not that it's any of your business who I visit or spend my time with, but no. Not this one."

"Too bad," said Joseph. "She was pretty easy to look at."

"So, Joseph, how are things in the archives?" Cardinal Wickham smiled as he said this.

"Enchanting." He scowled. "Where is everyone else? I have other things to do today."

"Books to shelve? Manuscripts to catalog?" It was nasty to tease the younger man like this, but it was so entertaining to see the red flush of anger darken his face.

Joseph was a very prominent, highly respected cardinal at the Vatican and had spent the last three years of his life stuck in the Vatican library. He was by no means a historian. Nor did he have a love for books or the Dewey decimal system, for that matter. He simply was the newest man in the order, and that's where Wickham had stuck him.

Joseph glowered at his superior but didn't respond. Wickham flicked his fingers in the direction of the door. It was no fun if they didn't take the bait. "They'll be here. Don't worry." He checked his watch. It was only twelve thirty, six thirty in the United States. Jonathan should be taking care of some business right about now. "Besides, Joseph, once again you are early. You're always early. I don't particularly have a problem with that. But you really must stop complaining about no one else being here when you show up thirty minutes before you're even supposed to be here."

"Why don't you like me?"

"I'm sorry, Joseph, I don't know what you mean."

"It's not a hard question. Why don't you like me?"

It was like talking to a petulant schoolgirl. "Joseph, my brother, it's not that I don't like you. I do. If I didn't, you wouldn't be here. It's just that. . .well. . .you whine a lot."

"Whine? What do you mean, I whine?"

"There! That's exactly what I'm talking about. You're whining. Right now."

"I hardly see how asking a question or two is whining."

"Call it whatever you want. The fact of the matter is we need you in the archives. Information is power. I know it's not glamorous. I know it's boring. Long before I was headmaster of this brotherhood, I was in the archives myself. Believe it or not, there is a ton of good that can be done from there. You just have to assert yourself. Be creative. Look for things that aren't there. That is precisely how I got to where I am today. I spent several years in those archives. Don't you realize that if the scroll isn't found before my time, someone else will have to head up this task? You, being in a place where all the information is, are the prime candidate. I didn't just sign you on to this order. I recruited you, not Harold, or Ibrahim, or any of the others. I just sent them after you."

Joseph stared at Cardinal Wickham, speechless.

"You see, Joseph. I know more about you than you could ever imagine." Wickham placed his elbows on the table and rested his chin in his hands. "For instance, I know that your real name isn't McCoy." He watched as Joseph shifted in his seat. "I know that you aren't from Ireland. You're from Canada. I also know that one night when you were sixteen years old you got drunk with some of your friends and decided to rob a liquor store." He watched now as Joseph's face turned pale. "I also know that it was *your* gun that went off. Oh, I'm sure it was an accident like you told the police.

Still, a woman and her little girl lost their lives that night. Didn't they, Joseph?"

Cardinal Joseph McCoy sat silent, suspicious. Wickham could almost imagine what must be going through the man's mind. What was the angle? Was he in trouble? What did Wickham want?

It wasn't so much a matter of what he wanted, but what he knew Joseph wanted. And that would make all the difference. "You desire the papacy."

Joseph shifted in his seat again and started to speak. Wickham gave a sharp shake of his head. He'd heard a noise. Someone else was here. The rest of the Brotherhood had arrived. This would have to wait.

"Don't worry, my friend." Cardinal Wickham smiled. "Your secrets are safe with me. And like I said before, information is the key to power."

CHAPTER 13

St. Anna Cathedral

". . .And so My brothers and sisters, let us not neglect the poor and needy, but rather sacrifice ourselves to help them, just as our Lord and Savior, Jesus, did. My peace I give you. Go in peace. In the name of the Father, the Son, and the Holy Spirit. Amen."

Father Ruiz made the sign of the cross and finished Mass as he waited for the procession that began making its way out of the sanctuary. The altar boys led the way down the center of the cathedral. Father Ruiz and Father Vin followed behind.

Father Vin motioned his head toward the back door to her as he passed. She waited until the other parishioners began to leave and then stood.

Her knees were stiff from kneeling during the service. Being a soccer player definitely was not conducive to Catholic worship.

She thought about what she'd just witnessed. It was her first Mass. It was beautiful. Most of the Mass was spoken in Spanish. Some, however, had been in English. Father Ruiz explained to the congregation that they had some American visitors and he did it for them. No one seemed to mind. Most of them spoke English anyway.

Given the few times she'd been to church in her life, Anna never experienced anything like a Catholic Mass. She didn't know really what to think. It was night and day different from the Baptist church where she and her parents went on the occasional Easter or Christmas. Still, it was beautiful.

Fathers Vin and Ruiz were waiting for her at the back of the church. She stood off to the side until the last little old lady made her way up to the priests. She gave Father Ruiz a hug and a kiss on the cheek. Then, she turned to Father Vin and said, "It was a pleasure having you to worship with us Father Marcella."

"My pleasure, miss. . ."

"Ruiz. Isabella Ruiz. I am Manuel's mother." She nodded to Father Ruiz.

"Ah yes, Mrs. Ruiz. So very nice to meet you." Father Vin stooped down to give the lady a peck on the cheek.

"Mamma, I am afraid I have some business to attend to with Father Vin. Please excuse us. I will be home for our brunch in a little while." Father Ruiz helped his mother down the front stairs of the cathedral and said good-bye. Once she was on her way, he turned his attention back to his mysterious guests. "We can go back to my chambers if you wish."

Father Vin nodded his appreciation. "That would be best, I think."

Father Ruiz led Anna and Father Vin back down the hallway they came from and into the rear of the church. They entered the private chambers where Father Ruiz offered them some pastries and coffee. Though neither was very hungry, they both accepted. Once they were all seated, Father Ruiz began.

"Father Vin, I must say I am impressed with your adapting

to the Spanish so quickly."

"Well, I must admit I did take several years of it in school, and in seminary. It's just been awhile. I thought it would come back to me quickly. At least I hoped!" Father Vin chuckled.

"You did well! I enjoyed ministering with you." Silence hung in the air for several seconds before Father Ruiz spoke again. "This other matter you mentioned earlier. . ."

"Well," Father Vin began, "I know Thomas spent several days down here. I was a very special friend of his. You might even say that I was his protector. Right before he came here, we got separated. Unfortunately, I was unable to meet him here. I don't know how much you and Thomas talked, but I do know that right before he passed away, he gave me this." Father Vin reached inside his pocket and pulled out a piece of paper that had one line scribbled on it:

Father Manuel Ruiz, St. Anna Cathedral, Caracas, Venezuela

"I don't know why he would have us contact you, but I *do* know what it's about. I assume you do, too."

Father Ruiz studied the face of the man sitting across from him. He looked over at Anna. "How do I know for sure you are who you say you are?"

Anna quickly reached for her purse to pull out identification but stopped suddenly, remembering she no longer had any. "Please, Father Ruiz, if you have any information for us. . ."

"You do understand," Father Ruiz continued, "Thomas was in fear for his life. He only confided in me as a priest. We talked. I counseled him with his spiritual walk. Nothing more. I am afraid he made no mention of the two of you."

"Are you sure?" Anna asked. "He didn't say anything to you about a scr—"

"Anna—" Father Vin quickly cut her off.

"Father, I'm sorry we've wasted your time. Anna and I will be going." He stood to leave.

"Just a second, please." Father Ruiz motioned for him to be seated again. "Anna, your grandfather did talk about a grandchild. He said she was a little girl, and he told me about the last time he had seen her. Do you know what I am speaking about? Perhaps you're the grandchild he spoke of?"

So here it was. A test. If she passed, they'd get what they needed. If not, so much for the scroll.

"Well, let's see." Anna tried to remember that day with her grandfather at the church. Unfortunately for her, it wasn't a memory that she thought about often. "I think we had gone to church that morning. It was kinda weird though. Grandpa said he wanted to stick around after the service and talk to the preacher."

"And did you?" Father Ruiz asked.

"I think so," Anna said. "I mean we talked to *someone*, just not the preacher."

"What do you mean?" This is what Father Ruiz was waiting to hear.

"Well, we waited for about thirty minutes after the service. We just sat there talking. I remember Grandpa saying that we were going to meet someone very special. I wanted to know who. He said it was a dear friend of his and he wanted to talk to me. Then I remember the preacher coming back inside where we were sitting. He told my grandfather that 'he' was here. I remember the preacher telling my grandfather that everything was 'all clear.' He told my grandfather that he and the elders would be outside, surrounding the sanctuary. I thought that was weird. So I asked

78

my grandfather what that meant. He told me that those men, the preacher and the elders, were going to go outside and say a special prayer for us because I was very special and 'it never hurt having people pray for you.' That's what he said."

Anna couldn't believe the details she remembered now. She hadn't thought of that day for years. She was amazed at how much she was actually recalling.

"So what happened then?" Father Ruiz leaned forward, an eager light in his face.

"Then a man in a white robe, kinda like yours," she pointed to the priest's robe hanging on the wall, "came in through a side door. I remember that as soon as he came in, a storm must've moved in. I could see shadows passing over the stained glass windows. I asked my grandfather if those were clouds. 'Cause if so, we needed to hurry up. I wasn't getting my new dress rained on. He told me not to worry. He said they weren't clouds, but we did need to hurry. Then the man that had just walked in came over to us and shook my grandfather's hand. He bent down and stuck his hand out to me. I remember not looking at him because I was still worried about those clouds. I kept my eyes on that stained glass. The other man saw me staring at the windows and told me not to worry. 'They' couldn't hurt me. I remember thinking, *What's that supposed to mean*? I finally took my eyes off the windows and looked at the man. He had such a friendly voice. I remember now. He had this crooked smile—"

Anna stopped midsentence. She looked at Father Vin, who was smiling the exact crooked smile she had just been talking about. "Oh my— You gotta be kidding me! It was you! You were there! Why didn't you tell me?"

Father Vin spoke for the first time since Anna started telling her story. "I would have eventually, Anna. I just needed to let you commit to all of this before I said anything. That's all. I couldn't influence your decision."

Anna was almost laughing now. She knew as soon as she had met Father Vin there was a connection there. She just couldn't put her finger on it. Now it all came back to her.

"Please, Anna, go on," said Father Ruiz.

"Okay. Well, like I said, Father Vin told me that he and my grandfather wanted to say a prayer for me. They asked if they could do that. Grandpa just said it never hurts to have someone praying for you. Besides, I was nervous about those shadows. So we went up to the ah. . .altar? Is that what you call it?" Both priests nodded in affirmation. "Yes, the altar. We knelt, and Vin took out some kind of oil and put it on my forehead. I particularly remember not liking that. It was going to get in my bangs, and Mom really made my hair look nice that morning. Then the weirdest thing happened. After we prayed, Father Vin stood up and started talking in some different language that I didn't—"

"Latin." Father Vin interrupted.

"Yeah, Latin. And all of a sudden, the clouds went away. The sun was shining through the stained glass like it was when we got there. I told Father Vin I thought it was magic! I remember he told me that it wasn't magic; it was truth. That's it. After that, Grandpa and I went home."

Father Ruiz smiled and said, "Your grandfather and I spent every night talking about the exact story you just told me. Please forgive my hesitancy. I need to make sure the information your grandfather gave me doesn't get into the wrong hands."

Father Ruiz stood up and walked to the little desk sitting against the far wall of his chambers. He moved it away from the wall. He reached behind the back of the desk and pulled an envelope from a slot hidden in the back of the desktop. He handed it to Anna.

"This is from your grandfather. He told me someday he would try to come for it. He said, however, that if something happened to him and he didn't return, he explicitly forbade me to give it to anyone other than you."

Anna took the envelope. It was light. There couldn't be more than a single sheet of paper inside. She looked at Father Vin with anticipation. "Should we open it here?" She asked.

"I think you should," Father Ruiz said. "Your grandfather told me to burn it after you read it."

Anna opened the envelope and pulled the piece of paper out. She unfolded it and began to read out loud.

Dear Anna,

I am sorry you are reading this instead of me telling you personally. I hope before you see this we have already been united. Unfortunately, you reading this means that I have fallen short of the task and have returned home to our Father. If we haven't talked yet, Father Vin will have explained everything. Either way, you now know what is going on.

What you seek is not here. It has been hidden for protection. I never carried it with me. Too dangerous. It's also too dangerous for me just to tell you where it is. You are going to have to do a little detective work. You have always had a brilliant mind. (Fortunately, you take after your grandmother!) I have the utmost confidence that you will be able to find it.

When your grandmother and I got married, it was a surprise to her where we held the ceremony. She was so excited. The place where we said our vows, she said, reminded her of her own grandmother.

*Go there. There is a basement. In that basement there
is a stone wall. Study the wall carefully. What you seek you
will find.*

> *I love you with all of my heart,*
> *Your Grandpa, Thomas Riley*

"I have no idea what in the world he is talking about here."
Anna looked defeated. She hung her head and handed the paper
to Father Vin.

Father Vin studied the note for a long time. Father Ruiz and
Anna watched him intently, hoping that he could make something
of it.

"I think I have an idea." Father Vin stood and grabbed his hat.
He handed the letter back to Father Ruiz. He shook the man's
hand enthusiastically, with great joy. "Thank you! Thank you, so
much, Father Ruiz. You have been most helpful." He turned his
attention back to Anna. "Come, Anna. We have to get to the
plane. Immediately!"

CHAPTER 14

Rome

Brothers, it's good to see all of you." Cardinal Wickham greeted the rest of the brothers as they each took their seats. All eight chairs at the antique table were now filled.

Cardinal Wickham rarely called a meeting of the Brotherhood in the middle of the day. Today was different. He had been thinking a lot these past several hours. For too long he'd sat at the head of this table scheming and plotting, unfortunately to no avail.

The members of the council each took his seat. The pleasantries were over. It was time to get down to business. Cardinal Wickham opened a manila envelope that was lying in front of him on the table and passed out a paper-clipped stack of papers to each person. "What we have here is the answer to our problem." He held the top sheet of his packet, a photo, up for all to see. "This," he said, wiggling the photo, "is Anna Riley." A few eyebrows shot up. "Good. Now that I have your complete attention, let's begin."

He spent the next ten minutes updating everybody on the

whereabouts of Anna Riley and Father Vincent Marcella. He assured them that everything had been going smoothly—a lie— and he should have access to the scroll very soon.

"How do we know she has it?" one priest asked.

"Because she's Thomas's granddaughter," Cardinal Wickham explained. "And she's running all over the place with Marcella. If she doesn't have it now, she will."

"But what if she doesn't? What if this is just Vin's way of throwing us off?" another brother asked.

"Trust me, Ibrahim. I have it all taken care of."

Finished answering petty questions, Wickham turned the conversation back to his original statement.

"Like I said, she is the answer to our problem. I have a man on her right now. As soon as he's confident she has the scroll, he'll take possession of it."

The members nodded their approval. There was a little murmuring among the other cardinals. The excitement of possessing the scroll was too enticing.

"Now," Cardinal Wickham continued, "on to the reason why we're here."

"You already stated this was our reason," Ibrahim said.

"No, unfortunately not." Wickham placed his hands on the table. He was going to have to be delicate with this matter. While each of the cardinals here shared his greed for worldly pleasures and power, he wasn't sure they would be committed to what he was about to suggest. He cleared his throat and began.

"Gentlemen, I believe we have a great problem. You all know of the scroll. You all know that this scroll was given to John during the Revelation. We all know that it has been protected for almost two thousand years. Why? Why hasn't the church been allowed to keep it here, in the archives? Why does some half-wit get to carry it around and never let anyone see it? I'll tell you why. Because that scroll contains information that leads to unfathomable knowledge. It must. Why else would it be kept secret from the Holy Church? Let alone the rest of the world? Obviously, John was afraid of that scroll falling into the wrong hands. While we don't yet know what is on that scroll, we are soon to find out. That, in and of itself, becomes our problem."

There were mutterings of confusion and impatience. Wickham raised his hands for silence.

"Let me ask each of you a question." Wickham stood from his chair and walked around the table. "We all know why we're here—in this brotherhood, I mean. That's obvious. We don't like the way our pontiff runs things around the Vatican. We all think he is weak. He has no backbone. Always blessing this and blessing that. Bah! Who cares! The man has unlimited power at his disposal and refuses to use it, for good or bad. Most of you don't even know the true purpose of this brotherhood." He watched as the inquisitive looks settled upon him. "I bet none of you know that this brotherhood was actually started by a pope for the sole purpose of finding that scroll. Pope Leo XIII to be exact. Yes, I will admit that our motives were somewhat different then. But our objective still remains."

"I remember hearing this," Ibrahim said. "But is it not true that Pope Leo XIII also disbanded this brotherhood several years later. So how is it exactly that we still exist?"

There were several people in the Brotherhood that Wickham had grown to dislike immensely. Ibrahim was at the top of that list. He knew that his colleague loved to goad him into bickering. He was always having to put Ibrahim back in his place. He fixed an icy stare on him. "Well Ibrahim, we haven't found the scroll yet, have we?"

Heads turned and followed Wickham as he walked around the table.

"So," Wickham continued, "the question is this: How far are you willing to go to get the knowledge of that scroll. . .and keep it? The pope, in all of his glory, happens to be one of three people in this world who 'supposedly' knows about the scroll. We know of course, but he doesn't know that. The moment we take that scroll, he'll be notified. Then, my brothers, our problem becomes serious. We will be hunted down like dogs. Probably by the Swiss Guard or whoever he decides to sic on us. I, for one, don't want that."

"So, what is it you suggest?" Ibrahim asked.

"I *suggest*, quite simply, that we remove the pope."

Instantly a cacophony of noise broke out. Everyone in the room stood up and began attacking him with, "What?" or "You have completely lost your mind!" or "Insanity!"

"Everyone, sit down!" Cardinal Wickham shouted, slamming his fist on the table. "Sit down and shut up!"

The room restored itself to order with a few cardinals still mumbling their objections. Everyone retook their seats.

"The bottom line is this: we are about to be in possession of a piece of paper that John was given during the Revelation of Jesus Christ. It has been kept secret for two thousand years. No one, especially the pope, is going to allow us to have it. Now we have two choices: either abandon our work right here and now or get rid of Pope Paul VII. Period. Those are our choices. I, for one, am not willing to quit when we are this close. I refuse!"

The room was silent for several seconds. Each cardinal sat in his seat thinking over his options. Finally, the silence was broken.

"How would this be done?"

That was Father McCoy. He actually had a smirk on his face. Wickham smiled. He had one on board. Six more to go.

Again Ibrahim stood up. "Joseph! You cannot be serious!"

"I am. You listen to me, Ibrahim. Louis is right. This scroll is going to give us power beyond our wildest imagination. We have to. It's the only way."

Once again the murmurs started. Wickham held up his hands to halt the chatter. The room settled down once more.

"He *is* old," Cardinal Bracken spoke for the first time.

"Yes he is," said Wickham. "His health could fail at any time."

"And how do we proceed once he has been *removed*, as you said?" one of the other cardinals asked.

"Well," Wickham said, "I would be temporarily in charge, of course. But Conclave would have to take place. I think we have enough pull between all of us to put whoever we want in that seat. We can discuss who later." He looked to Cardinal Joseph, whose eyes had lit up like spotlights. "Right now, let's just worry about getting him out of the way."

Wickham and the rest of the cardinals talked at length about what their options were. It was finally decided that getting rid of Pope Paul VII was their only option. One by one the brothers began to come around. A little over an hour later, Wickham had all seven votes. Yes. It would be done.

CHAPTER 15

Plaza Bolivar

There they go. Come on." Jonathan and Larry watched Father Vin and Anna exit the church and hail a cab. They hurried to the street, found their own taxi, and told the driver to follow the cab up ahead.

Minutes later they pulled up in front of the hotel. Anna and Father Vin had already gone inside. Handing the driver a fifty-dollar bill, Jonathan told him to pull over to the alley. He didn't want to be seen. The young man excitedly stomped on the gas and nearly ran over an older couple as he whipped into the adjacent alley.

"We're not going in?" Larry asked.

"Did you see them come out of there with anything?"

"Maybe she stuck it in her purse," said Larry.

"Did you see her holding a purse?"

"Maybe she hid it!"

"You're an idiot. You know that? It's a two-thousand-year-old piece of paper. What? You think she just folded it up and stuck it in her jeans pocket?"

Larry decided not to answer. Instead, he just shrugged his shoulders and looked away. This was the second time Jonathan had yelled at him today. He was making a habit out of getting himself in trouble. He figured it would be best just to do as Jonathan said: keep his mouth shut.

"Trust me," Jonathan said. "When she has it, we'll know. Until then we just follow."

"You're the boss, man."

"Anna," Father Vin shouted from his bedroom. "We must hurry. The car service will be here in five minutes. I've called the plane. They'll be waiting for us."

"That's kind of fast, isn't it?" Anna yelled back.

"Money talks, dear. And you've got a lot of it. Remember?"

"Yeah." Anna walked into the bedroom where Father Vin was finishing packing up his toiletry bag. "I keep hearing about it. But I haven't seen it!"

"In due time, Anna. Are you ready?"

"Yep! I only brought this one bag. So, explain all of this to me again. We're going to Europe, but we don't know where in Europe?"

"That's right."

"Then why are we going?"

"Because Thomas and Olivia were married in Europe."

"But you don't know where?"

"No, I'm afraid I don't. But we are going to find out."

"How?"

"That shouldn't be too hard. All we need is Olivia's grandmother's name. We should be able to find that on the Internet."

"I suppose we have Internet access on the plane?"

"As a matter of fact, yes. Satellites are amazing things, you know. And you own three of them."

Father Vin and Anna left the room and headed downstairs. They stopped by the front desk and checked out. Their car was waiting for them when they walked out of the lobby.

As soon as the cab had gotten inside the airport grounds, Jonathan told the driver to forget about following the car in front of them. That was pointless now. "We're gonna have to find out where they're going."

"How much money you got?" The driver asked.

"Excuse me?" Jonathan asked.

"I know guy at airport. You got enough dough, he tell you where they go." The driver smiled confidently.

"I'll tell ya what, chief," Jonathan chuckled, "you find out for me and I'll pay you enough you can take the whole next month off if you like." He turned to Larry. "I like this guy. Maybe we should give him your job."

"I be right back, man," he said. He took off at a dead run into the terminal. Ten minutes later, he was back.

"My guy say France." The cabbie was still sucking air into his lungs.

"Okay," said Jonathan. "Where in France?"

"He not know. Just France. That all he say," the cabbie said, still breathing hard.

"They had to file a flight plan." Jonathan was now getting annoyed. "What does the flight plan say?"

"That just it!" The cabbie seemed to finally get his breathing back to normal. "They do make ah. . .what you call it?"

"Flight plan?"

"Yeah, flight plan. It only say they go to France." The cabbie looked at Jonathan as if he was as confused about it as they were.

Jonathan pulled a wad of hundred-dollar bills out of his pocket. The cab driver's eyes lit up. Jonathan peeled off eight of them and handed them to the man.

"Thanks for your help," he said. He stood there for a moment. A thought hit him. "Say, slick, how'd you like to make another stack of those?" He pointed to the bills he'd just handed him.

"Jess! Jess! What you need? Private plane? I know other guy!"

"No. I've got my own plane. Here's the deal." Jonathan put his arm around the driver's shoulder. He wanted to make sure he had his attention. They started to walk toward the entrance to the terminal. "Eventually that plane is going to have to call back here and tell your tower where it's going. When they do, I want you to call me."

They were inside now. Jonathan walked over to the far wall. It was lined with lockers. He opened one and stuck another eight hundred dollars in it. He closed the door and pushed the lock button. A printed receipt ejected from the slot in the door. He tore the receipt in half, keeping the half with the combination written on it. He took out a pen and wrote down a phone number on the other half. He handed it to the cab driver.

"When you call me with the information I need, I will tell you what the combination of this locker is. You will just have made another month's salary. Take a vacation, move, whatever you want to do with it. I don't care. Just whatever you do, don't ever call that phone number again unless you hear from me first. Got it?"

"What phone number? I don't remember any phone number!" The driver smirked at Jonathan.

Jonathan looked at Larry again and jerked his thumb at the driver. "I mean it. I really like this guy!"

CHAPTER 16

Somewhere over the Atlantic

Jonathan checked the chamber of the 9mm again for the fourth time. It was still loaded. It was one of the perks of having your own plane. You could sit in your seat and fiddle with your gun.

As the private jet soared high above the ocean, he sat there toying with the weapon. It made him comfortable to have it in his hands. He hated flying. Playing with his gun was one of the few things he could do to occupy his time. It kept his mind off of the fact that he was forty thousand feet above the ground with nothing between him and a bottomless ocean except a few thousand pounds of metal and two roaring engines.

Larry was snoring in the seat across from him. He had already nudged him twice. The only thing he hated worse than flying was someone who could sleep on a plane. He had never been able to.

He got up and holstered the pistol. He unfastened his seat belt and headed for the lavatory. At least the weather had let up. For a while there, he thought they were going down. The captain kept blabbering over the intercom that it was only a little turbulence and that they would be clearing it soon.

Not soon enough.

He finished his business and washed his hands. As he made his way back to his seat, he felt the vibration in his pocket. He pulled the satellite phone out and pushed the SEND button.

"This is Jonathan."

"Ah, jess. Dis is your cab driver. I find out where your plane go!"

"Yeah, well, let's have it." Jonathan sat down and grabbed his little notebook and a pen from his jacket.

"Pau, France." The cab driver waited.

"Okay, slick. Good job. I'll get in touch with you if I need anything else."

"Ah. . .what about da money?" The cab driver asked hesitantly. "I stick my neck out for you, remember?"

"Oh yeah. Sorry about that, slick. Here ya go."

Jonathan read the six-digit combination to the young man. When he was finished, he simply ended the call. He didn't say good-bye or any other pleasantries. He leaned over to where Larry was again snoring, rather loudly now, and nudged him again. A little harder this time, just for fun. Nothing. The big, muscle-bound idiot hardly moved.

"Get up!" Jonathan smacked him in the back of the head. Apparently Larry was a heavy sleeper.

Larry smacked his lips and sat up, looking confused. "What? Are we there?"

"No, not yet," Jonathan said. "I just found out where we're going. I need your laptop."

"Dude! You woke me up for that?" Larry was agitated. "It's right here." He pointed to the seat beside him.

"No, you idiot. I woke you because when we get there, it's gonna be bedtime. If you sleep now, you won't be tired. I can't take the chance of you being jet-lagged. So do whatever you need to do to stay awake for the next couple of hours until we land. Besides, you sounded like a chain saw over there. You were getting on my nerves."

Larry mumbled something to himself and reached across the seat to grab his computer bag. He handed the laptop to Jonathan then got up from his seat and headed to the lavatory. As he walked to the back of the plane, he began to wonder why he took this job.

The Vatican

The dining hall was filled with people. Groups from the media, the ambassador's entourage, a few select Vatican employees, many prominent cardinals, and the pope were all seated among the beautifully decorated tables in the hall.

Once everyone had arrived, the pope asked everyone to take their assigned seats. He wanted to make a few announcements and say a blessing over their fellowship time and the meal that was to be served. Once he was finished, he informed everyone they would all be excused to mingle for the next thirty minutes. Dinner would be served promptly at seven thirty.

The pope had barely finished his prayer when Cardinal Wickham stood from his seat and made a beeline for the other side of the room. He nonchalantly wiped the bead of sweat that had formed on his brow as he pushed and excused his way through the crowd. The man he was headed to see stood talking to a group of people with his back turned toward him. Before he even reached his target, the man turned to face him with a big smile.

"Hello, Louis! So nice to see you."

"Excuse us, please." Cardinal Wickham led his guest by the

arm outside the main dining hall.

"What's the hurry, Louis?"

"What are you doing here?" Cardinal Wickham looked petrified. "I mean, how can you be here?"

"Louis, please," the man said calmly, "don't make a scene." The man nodded to a few guests walking past them.

"Again, what are you doing here?" Louis whispered frantically. "How am I supposed to explain who you are if anyone asks?"

"Not my problem! Make something up. I do love a good lie!" The man gave a giddy smile.

"I don't understand." The cardinal was dumbfounded. "How can you be here? I mean, in this place. I mean—"

"Louis, contrary to popular belief, I can go just about anywhere I want. I mean, this is practically home for me! Except for"—he paused for a second—"a few minor details."

"Minor!" Louis half shouted.

"Look, Louis. Calm down. You are only drawing attention to yourself. I'm here because I understand you have found a new recruit."

"I have no idea what you are talking about."

"Yes you do. He's one of your order."

"You mean Joseph?"

"The one and only! I do like him, Louis. He's very goal oriented. My kind of guy!"

"What about him?"

"Well, when you put your little plan into action, you're going to need someone to take ol' fatso's place over there." He pointed to Pope Paul VII. "Aren't you?"

"Yes, I suppose I am."

"Yes you are."

"And I suppose you've decided you would like it to be Joseph?"

"Louis, you're *so* good at this! Yes. I would like it to be Joseph."

"Why? Why him?"

"Oh, come on, Louis. You've thought about it. You know his background. You know that ever since he became a priest, all he's ever thought about was being the pope. And since you make such a good secretary of state and all, I think Joseph would be perfect!"

"Well, for your information, I don't know that he's the right guy."

"Now you're just being petty, Louis. Don't be such a child. And for *your* information, I think he's perfect. Seeing as how it's me who gets to make those kinds of decisions, I say it's Joseph. Understood?" The man stared Cardinal Wickham down with a menacing look. The cardinal didn't say a word. "Good! Then it's settled. Bring him to me. I would like to meet him."

"What, you mean now?"

"No. Not now. After dinner. Bring him to Mad Jack's. That's that pub you like to hang out in, right?"

"Yeah, I guess."

"Good. Then I'll see you later. Say around eleven?"

Louis nodded.

"Good. I think I'll go take a walk around the place. It's been a *really* long time since I've been here!"

The man turned around and was gone. Louis stood there, leaning against the wall. He pushed himself off and headed to the restroom. He needed to splash some water on his face. Suddenly, he didn't feel all that well.

A few minutes later, just as everyone was taking their seats for dinner, Cardinal Wickham reentered the hall. He made his way over to a table that was situated just to the left of his and placed his hand on the shoulder of Cardinal Joseph McCoy.

Joseph turned to see who it was. "Cardinal Wickham! Nice to see you. This is Raul. He is part of the ambassador's party."

Cardinal Wickham exchanged pleasantries with the man seated with Joseph. After doing so, he leaned in over Joseph's shoulder so he could whisper. He cupped his hand over Joseph's ear so no one else could hear and whispered the words he knew Joseph McCoy had longed to hear for most of his life.

"Joseph, how would you like to be the next pope?"

CHAPTER 17

Somewhere over Spain

Anna had finally given up on the big, soft blanket she'd been wrestling with. She tossed it over to the side of the couch and decided to find something to do. That didn't work out that well either. At thirty-seven thousand feet inside a small jet, there wasn't a whole lot one could do. She had grown tired of watching the satellite TV. She got bored with the book, the same one she'd been trying to read now for almost six months. And she was getting agitated at the pecking sound that was coming from Father Vin's computer. There was a magnetic chessboard sitting on the little coffee table in front of the couch. She moved the pieces around until she got tired of that. She opened the fridge, saw there wasn't anything there she wanted, and then closed it again. She opened the two or three cupboards, got the same result, and then closed them. She opened the fridge again. Still nothing there. She let out a long sigh and just decided to pace back and forth throughout the cabin.

"You're gonna wear out a path right through the bottom of the plane if you keep that up," said Father Vin, not even looking at her.

"I can't help it, Vin. I'm bored to death! There isn't anything to do on this plane."

"I'm afraid you'll just have to get used to that, Anna. You'll probably spend a lot of time on this plane over the next few years."

She settled back on a seat. "I shouldn't complain. I'm going to France—who would have thought? I still can't believe it was so easy to find my grandparents' place of marriage."

Father Vin smiled indulgently. "Checking that online genealogy site was your idea. And it was a good one."

"How much longer till we get there?"

Father Vin looked at his watch. "About another hour and a half."

"Aghh! I'm gonna go stir crazy!"

Anna threw her arms up in the air and started pacing again. She was definitely going to add some things to this plane once she had access to her money. She couldn't think of anything at the moment, but she was absolutely going to make sure she had things to keep her occupied from now on.

Father Vin closed the lid on his laptop and slid it into the leather pouch of his computer bag. He stood from his chair and walked behind Anna into the kitchen area. He fixed himself a cup of coffee and grabbed one of the cookies on the counter. He watched as Anna now picked up a magazine and flipped through it for the third time.

"Anna, let me show you something." He finished his cookie, brushed the crumbs off of his chin, and stepped around the leather chair into the sitting area. He walked over to the wall of the plane and sat down on the couch. "Sit here with me." He patted the cushion beside him. He leaned forward and reached his arm up under the bottom of the couch. "Give me your hand." He reached out and took Anna's hand with his free hand and pulled it under the couch to where he was already reaching. "There. You feel that?"

Anna's fingers felt a bump on the underside of the couch. "Yeah. What is it?"

"Push it."

"What do you mean, push it?"

"It's a button, Anna. Push up on it."

Anna pushed the button and heard a *click*. Nothing happened at first. She thought Vin was playing some kind of joke on her, when suddenly she felt something move under her fingers. Some kind of hidden panel was concealed under the couch. As she reached her hand inside the small chamber, she felt the touch of cold steel.

"Careful, girl. It's loaded." Father Vin gently placed his hand over Anna's as it rested on the gun. "Feel this?" Father Vin moved Anna's hand over a canvas-type material.

Anna nodded and said, "Yeah, what is it?"

"That is a specially designed holster," said Father Vin. "It's tilted at a forty-five-degree angle so you can grab it and pull it straight out from under this couch. To release the strap, you just do this." Vin grabbed Anna's fingers again and moved them over the canvas holster to the locking strap. He used her fingers to unsnap it. The snap gave way and the pistol slid out into Anna's hand."

"Whoa! That's way cool!" Anna said, amazed.

"Now, gently, just bring your arm out like this," said Father Vin.

Again he moved her hand with his. The gun came out from under the couch. Anna could see it for the first time. It was a little Remington .380. It was black and had a rubber grip. She could see the little red dot on the side where the safety had been moved into the *on* position.

"So, what's this thing for, anyway?" Anna asked.

"Hopefully, nothing." Father Vin raised his eyebrows. "It's not the only one in here, by the way. There are four more hidden. We've never had to use them. Thank the good Lord. They are merely for protection. If something should ever happen, well then, we have them."

"Show me the others." Finally, something exciting.

"Anna, have you ever shot a gun?" Father Vin had a concerned look.

Anna snorted. "My dad's the biggest hunter in the entire state of Tennessee. With this peashooter"—she held up the .380—"I could shoot the wings off a gnat at fifty yards. What else you got?"

Father Vin smiled. He placed his hands on his knees and pushed himself up off the couch.

Anna followed him. She had left the .380 back on the coffee table with the safety still on. She watched the priest open the lavatory door and step inside. She peeked her head around the corner to see what he was doing. He sat down on the seat and placed his hand, palm flat out, on the sheet of marble that was the front of the sink and then pushed against the marble. Again Anna heard a faint *click*. A six-by-nine-inch piece of the marble popped out. He pulled it to the side. It was fixed to the rest of the sink with hinges that allowed it to move back and forth like a sliding glass door.

Father Vin reached in and pulled out another pistol. This time it was a revolver, a .38 Special. Again it was in a holster with the strap locked and the safety on.

Anna took the pistol. The weight of it felt good in her hands. It was one of her favorite handguns. Her father had one just like it. She could remember the first time her father let her shoot a gun. It was a .38 just like this one. She handed it back to Father Vin and watched him place it back in its hiding place. He moved the marble door back to its position and snapped it shut.

"Here," he said, "you try to open it."

She took his place in the lavatory, placed her hand on the marble slab, and pushed. Nothing. No *click*. She tried again. Still nothing. She tried smacking the side of the sink. Still nothing. "I think it's broken," she said.

Father Vin gave her a sly grin. "Why don't you try sitting down and doing it?"

"What's the difference? Standing, sitting—what does it matter?" She continued to knock at the side of the sink.

"Really, Anna. Try sitting." Father Vin gave her a nod.

She sat down on the seat and placed her hand in the same position it had been ten seconds ago. This time, however, when she pushed on the marble, she heard the *click*. The little door popped open, and she was able to move it back. "Okay. What gives?"

Father Vin laughed for a few seconds before letting her in on his little joke. "It's weight activated. You have to be sitting on the seat. There has to be at least sixty pounds of weight sitting on that seat before that compartment will open. It's a safety feature."

"Well, let's hope I have to go to the restroom if I ever need to use this gun," Anna said sarcastically.

The plane touched down at the airfield in Pau, France, and rolled to a stop in a private hangar. Marie was already finishing up her postflight checks and gave the all clear sign. She pulled the lever and allowed the air-locked door to open, releasing the stairs to the tarmac below where a car was already waiting for them.

Father Vin was about to follow Anna out the door when Hale stopped him. He tapped Father Vin on the shoulder and asked if he could speak to him for a second in private. Father Vin stepped back into the main cabin and placed his shoulder bag on the seat.

"What is it, Hale? Is everything okay?" Father Vin asked.

"Well, it may be nothing, Vin." Hale had somewhat of a frown on his face. "I just wanted to tell you that we had a blip on our radar. It was about two hundred miles back."

"What do you mean a blip?"

"Another aircraft. It may be nothing, like I said. It just kind of popped out at me. You know?"

"Yes, Hale. I appreciate your being on top of things. Do you think it was following us?"

"It seemed to be. I even changed course a couple of times to see if it would follow."

"And?"

"And. . .it seemed to just stay with us. I don't know how they would be tracking us. I certainly don't think that they could have radar as sophisticated as ours. You know our stuff is NASA level. It's probably just a coincidence. I wouldn't worry about it."

"Thank you, Hale. Whether or not it was, it's good to know about it. I'll make sure that Anna and I are careful." Father Vin shook Hale's hand and headed off the plane. He told Hale that they may, or may not, be leaving tomorrow. Hale said they would be ready either way.

Father Vin hurried to the waiting car. He tossed his bag to the driver, who put it in the trunk with Anna's, and then got in the backseat.

"What was that all about?" Anna asked.

"Nothing. Hale just wanted to know when we would be leaving. That's all."

Anna looked at Father Vin dubiously. "You know, it's a good thing that you became a priest."

"Why's that?" Father Vin was puzzled.

"Because you can't lie worth a darn!"

The car pulled away from the tarmac and headed toward their hotel. Father Vin had used the satellite phone to book them a room at a hotel in Pau for the night. Tomorrow they would make the short drive to Oloron-Sainte-Marie.

CHAPTER 18

Mad Jack's Irish Pub, Rome

Cardinal Joseph McCoy hadn't stopped asking questions since they got into the cab and headed away from Vatican City. It reminded Cardinal Wickham of a child asking, "Are we there yet?" Only Joseph kept asking, "What do you mean, a friend? Who is this guy? What does he want with me?"

Finally, Wickham had had enough. Thank goodness he had never had children. "If you don't shut up, we're going back home!" That seemed to keep the young cardinal quiet for a few moments at a time. Inevitably, though, Joseph would start back up with his questions.

When the cab finally stopped in front of Mad Jack's, Louis told him that this was their stop.

"What are we doing here?" Joseph asked. "Louis, we can't be seen in here! We'll be excommunicated! They'll throw us out! What will we do then?"

"Joseph," Wickham said, "shut up. Do you honestly think the type of people that frequent this establishment are going to recognize you? Look at you!" He held his hands out in front of him. "You're wearing a baseball cap and blue jeans. You've got a sweatshirt on that looks like you slept in it last night. You're not exactly looking like a man of the cloth. Wouldn't you say?"

"Yeah, I guess. But still—"

"Still, nothing! I come in here all the time. No one has ever said anything to me. That's why I come here. No one says anything to anyone. It's a safe place."

"Okay. I just think we should be careful."

"Why don't you let me worry about that. Come on. We're going to be late. Believe me, you don't want to keep our friend waiting. He can be very impatient."

The two cardinals walked into the pub and made their way to a table in the rear of the bar. No one was there waiting for them, even though it was the table they were instructed to be at. Louis told Joseph that they should just wait here. He assured Joseph that the man would be along momentarily.

The waitress asked them for their order. Louis ordered for them both—two Guinness drafts. She wrote the order down on her little note pad and disappeared as quickly as she showed up.

A tall, good-looking man wearing a dark pin-striped suit walked through the door. He made his way over to the bar and spoke to the bartender. The bartender handed him three drinks, two Guinness drafts, and a brown-looking liquid in a tall glass. The man laid a few bills out on the counter and picked up the drinks. He turned and walked toward Louis and Joseph. He set the drinks down on the table and took a seat.

"Gentlemen, and I use that term loosely, how are you this evening?" He pushed the frothy beers at the two cardinals. "I went ahead and picked up our first round. I hope you guys are thirsty. Cheers!" He held up his glass, waiting for the others to do the same. Joseph and Louis picked up their beers and clinked them against the man's glass. "Here's to the future!"

Louis chugged his beer. Being around the man made him nervous, and he needed to take the edge off. After he set down his empty glass, he gestured toward the man and said, "Joseph, this is my, ah, friend."

The man stuck out his hand. "You can call me Prince."

"Your name is Prince?" Joseph lifted an eyebrow.

"It's more of a title, so to speak." The man smiled and shook Joseph's hand. "It's nice to meet you."

The men talked and drank for the next couple of hours. Louis explained to Joseph that Prince was responsible for the start-up of the Brotherhood. He told Joseph that he and Prince were basically working together. Prince laughed and cheerfully corrected Louis. "You work for me, my friend."

Louis felt a bit ill. He watched Prince exude more charisma than he'd ever seen from the man before. He watched Joseph become totally captivated by the man when he spoke. He knew only too well what was happening inside the other cardinal. Everything Prince said would somehow touch a nerve inside. By the end of the two hours, Joseph would want nothing more than to do whatever this Prince wanted. And there was nothing Louis dared do to prevent it—and he wasn't sure he wanted to.

It was getting late and the pub was about to close. The men were finishing up their final round of drinks when Prince finally got down to business. He leaned in close to Joseph and looked him dead in the eye.

"Joseph, my friend, I've known about you for a long time."

"How do you mean?" Joseph slurred his words.

"Well, let's just say that I find you very interesting. You know? Louis wouldn't be where he is today if it weren't for me. I put him in the secretary of state position. I could do you one better. I could make you pope!"

"And how could you do that?" He suddenly looked much soberer.

"Ah, that's where it gets tricky!" Prince leaned back in his chair. He folded his arms and placed his hand under his chin. "What are you willing to give for such power in this world, Joseph?"

Ah, here it came. He would spring the trap any moment. Louis felt half in awe watching it unfold. Prince was truly a master of manipulation.

"Provided you can deliver, I'd say just about anything. No more archives for me, right Louis?"

Louis rolled his eyes. Joseph was almost too easy a target. Prince must be thoroughly bored by the entire thing.

Prince spoke softly now. He looked intently into the eyes of the young cardinal. "Take my hand, Joseph. Let me show you what you could have." He reached out his hand.

Joseph hesitantly took the outstretched hand that clasped his. Like a trap. Louis shuddered.

Prince smiled triumphantly. "What do you see, my friend?"

Joseph's eyes glazed over as if his mind had left his body. "I see a man standing at a podium addressing a huge crowd of people. It's me. I'm standing on the papal balcony. I'm dressed as the pope, holding the pope's staff. Thousands of people are below, applauding as if I've done something miraculous. I'm waving and blowing kisses out to the mass of people."

Prince let go of his hand, and Joseph's eyes lost the vacant sheen. The place was now empty, except for the bartender and a few waitresses. Louis couldn't help smiling. It was all so neatly done.

"That was amazing! How did you do that? Who are you?" Joseph studied Prince.

"I am the man who can make you pope, Joseph. I already told you that."

"What do you want from me?" Joseph asked.

"I want *you*, Joseph. That's all. Just you."

"Well, if all you want is for me to work for you, then count me in. As long as I get to be pope, I don't care."

"Ah, but I didn't say I wanted your services, Joseph. I said I wanted *you*." The man raised his eyebrows and tilted his head.

"Yeah, whatever." Joseph dismissed him. "As long as I get to be pope."

"Good!" Prince stood and motioned for Joseph and Louis to do the same. "Let's take a walk. I'd like to show you something else, Joseph." He put his arm around Joseph and led him out the back door. "Louis has already seen this." He smirked at Louis. "Why don't you take care of our tab? We'll meet you out front."

CHAPTER 19

Oloron-Sainte-Marie

Anna and Father Vin sat in the backseat of the car as it drove along a small road. Anna could still taste the honey butter from this morning's breakfast. There was a small restaurant outside the hotel where they had stayed. Anna wanted to have croissants and espresso since she was in France. Father Vin had readily agreed. It was one of his favorites, as well.

Once again, the hotel that they had stayed in, the Minotel de Gramont, was a luxurious one. Once again, she had been listed under a fake name. And once again, she didn't get to cash in on the personal staff option. They had quickly taken showers, eaten breakfast, and gotten on the road.

The drive to Oloron-Sainte-Marie was a short one, filled with spectacular views of the Pyrenees Mountains. It was clear why this town was such a big tourist attraction.

The city was alive with vendors and small shops that lined the streets. There were a few chocolate shops that boasted they carried the world-famous Pryénéen chocolates, which happened to be made right there in Oloron-Sainte-Marie.

As they wound their way through the city, the cathedral came into view. The driver turned on the little road that led up the hill to the front entrance. Anna and Father Vin got out and told the driver that he would be called when they were ready to be picked up. He took a business card from the driver and stuck it in his billfold. The driver sped away as they headed up the stairs to the beautiful cathedral.

"I can understand why my grandfather wanted to surprise my grandmother with this," Anna said. "It's gorgeous."

"Yes it is," said Father Vin.

They opened the front doors and stepped inside. In the front of the great hall, a man was polishing a golden cross that stood to the left of the altar. A custodian of some sort, they assumed. Walking toward the man, Father Vin spoke. "Pardon. Do you speak English?"

"*Oui*," came the reply. "I do."

"Wonderful," Father Vin said beaming. "I am Father Vincent Marcella, from the Vatican." He showed him his credentials. "We are visiting your great city! Would it be all right if we looked around in this magnificent structure?"

"Oui," the man said, uninterested. "The schoolteacher and I, we two only are here at the moment. Make yourselves welcome. But please do not touch anything. I have spent the morning polishing and cleaning. I am about to go, but the doors. . .they stay open for the schoolchildren. Just let yourselves out."

As the custodian took his polishing tools and exited, Father Vin scanned the area for a staircase that led downstairs. Not seeing anything, he told Anna that they should split up and look for it. Anna agreed. They each went in separate directions, Anna to the left, Father Vin to the right.

As Anna made her way down the hall, she noticed a small room off to her left. She could hear voices, the sounds of children. She followed the noise until she was standing outside a door with a glass pane to look through.

She could see several rows of little desks occupied by children. At the front of the room, a very handsome young man, probably about her age, was pointing to a chalkboard where a bunch of words were written. The words didn't make a sentence. They were just random. Anna could hear the man say each word in French, then in English. Must be an English class.

He must not be a priest, since he wasn't wearing robes or a little white collar. He was dressed in a pullover shirt and khaki pants. She found herself staring at him.

Suddenly, the kids became aware of her standing outside the door. They started giggling and pointing. When she realized she was causing a disturbance, she quickly moved along. As she was leaving, she saw the man turn around from his chalkboard to see what the commotion was.

Father Vin cut across the sanctuary toward her. "Anna!" He waved his hand at her as he spoke in a whisper. "Come! Quick. I think I've found it."

Anna followed Father Vin to a big wooden door. He opened it and stepped inside, Anna right behind him.

They walked into what Anna could only assume was a confessional booth. Father Vin closed the door behind them and pulled back a curtain. There, along the back wall, was a staircase that led down.

"Old churches like this one," Father Vin explained, "usually have their basements under the priest's private chambers. When I couldn't find one there, I tried here. Go figure!"

There was a single bulb hanging from a string over the

entrance. Father Vin pulled on the little chain, and the stairwell came into light. "Here we go!" He took a deep breath and let it out again. "I'll go first," he said. "Who knows how long it's been since they've reinforced these old wooden steps."

Father Vin made his way down the rickety stairs with Anna trailing close behind. When she reached the bottom, she could make out the outline of a light switch in the dim light. Father Vin flipped the switch, and another single bulb hanging from the ceiling illuminated the small cavern. He motioned for Anna to join him.

"Okay. So now what?" Anna asked.

"So now we look," said Father Vin.

"Look for what?"

"Well, Thomas, in his letter, said we would have to study the stone wall. So, I guess that's what we do."

"Okay. You take that one," Anna pointed, "and I'll take this one."

They went to opposite walls and started to carefully study the sides. Neither one had spoken for nearly two minutes when Anna let out a big sigh.

"Vin, I have no idea what we are looking for."

"I know, dear. We just have to keep looking. Maybe something will jump out at us."

Anna pushed away a small cobweb. "I sure hope not."

They scrutinized every piece of stone they passed. Still nothing. Vin was about to start over when Anna suddenly shrieked.

"Anna, what is it?" he asked.

"Vin, come over here. I think I found something."

Father Vin rushed over to where Anna had her hands placed on a piece of stone that was at least a foot wide and eight inches tall.

"This stone looks like it's been removed recently," she said.

The mortar around the stone was a different color from the rest of the stones. It had more of a gray hue to it, whereas the rest of the wall had a worn-out, brown look about it.

"I think you're right." He took out a small pocket knife and began to test the area around the stone. The mortar crumbled as soon as the small blade was applied.

Anna held her breath. They had found it.

Father Vin began working on the stone. Inch by inch, the dried cement began to fall away like dust. Within a couple of minutes, the entire stone was loose. He placed the blade under the bottom to give it some leverage. Anna grabbed the stone and tried to pull it out.

It only moved an inch or so, but it was enough to get a better grip on it. She let go and grabbed the stone again. This time she was able to pull it out a good six inches. Father Vin put his pocket knife away and helped her pull it out the rest of the way.

The stone was pretty heavy, and when they tried to set it down, Anna lost her grip. The big piece of rock fell to the floor with a loud thud and shattered.

"I guess we won't be putting that back," Anna said.

"No, I guess not," Father Vin agreed. "I just hope no one else heard that."

He reached inside his pocket and pulled out a tiny flashlight. He shone it inside the dark hole left by the stone that they had just removed. Bending next to him, Anna saw the outline of a box pushed back inside the cavity. Anna reached her hands inside and felt the wood against her fingertips. Once she had a good grasp on it, she pulled. Out came a box, not unlike a shoe box, except this was much more elaborate.

The box was beautifully finished, a hand-carved dark mahogany. Etchings on the side looked like ancient Greek. Father Vin read the writing to her. "For the keeper of the Word of God."

"That would be me." Anna whispered.

Father Vin placed his hand on Anna's shoulder. "Yes. You are the rightful owner of this scroll. I hope this task brings you the same happiness it brought Thomas."

"Thank you, Vin. What say we open it?"

"You go ahead. I'm going to go wait upstairs for you." Father Vin turned around to leave.

"Vin, wait!" Anna said urgently.

"What is it, dear?" Father Vin spun back around.

"All these years. You've been protecting the protector of this box. Do you *really* not want to see what's in it?"

Father Vin stood there with a grin on his face. He folded his arms and let out a sigh. "Well, I must admit." He paused for a moment. "No. I *really* don't. It's not my job, Anna; it's yours."

"Vin," Anna pleaded, "stay here and open it with me. Please. For me. I don't want to do this by myself."

"Dear child," he huffed, "God blessed me for years with not having to see it. But I will, for you."

"Thank you, Vin."

Anna placed her hands on either side of the lid. She felt the smooth lacquer finish that had been applied to it. She could tell that the finish was relatively new. She figured her grandfather had done it to protect the box from the dampness of the dank basement. She placed her thumbs on the front of the lid, moved the latch holding it in place, and opened the box.

Jason Lang was standing at the chalkboard going through his lesson when he heard the kids start to giggle and make comments. As he turned to see what the commotion was, he caught a glimpse of a beautiful, young woman. And then she was gone.

Normally he wouldn't think anything of seeing someone pass by his class. He was a tourist attraction. The many people who came to Oloron-Sainte-Marie to visit would often stop by to peek in on one of his classes. He was the resident non-Catholic. Actually, he was a Baptist missionary. He had been here in Oloron-Sainte-Marie for almost two years now, teaching English to the children who lived in the town and the surrounding communities. But today's visitor struck an odd chord. First of all, it wasn't the normal time that tourists were usually out and about. Second, Father De Lorme was out of town for the week. He had been left in charge of the church. He didn't need anything suspicious going on during his watch.

He was just about finished with his lesson, anyway, so he let the kids go early. He waited until the last child was out of the church. Then he closed the door behind him and went off to find this mysterious visitor.

CHAPTER 20

Citôtel Roncevaux Hotel, Pau

Hale got out of bed and went to wash his face and brush his teeth. He came back into his room and reached for his phone. Last night he'd paid a visit to an old friend, Jean-Robert, who lived in the area and had the ways and means of finding out who owned the airplane that had been trailing them the day before. He was surprised Jean-Robert hadn't called him back yet—usually he was far more efficient about eliciting information.

When he picked it up and flipped it open, he noticed the display screen was blank. Strange. He didn't remember turning the phone off. He pushed the power button and nothing happened. The battery must have died on him during the night. He reached in his bag and found his spare battery. He disconnected the dead one and plugged in the charged one, and immediately the phone came alive.

He waited for the phone to go through its powering-up sequence. Once it showed the welcome sign on the display, he flipped it open again. The inside screen showed that he had five

117

missed calls and three messages. He felt his pulse quicken. He got a sick feeling in his stomach, the kind that told him he'd missed something important.

Quickly he punched in the voice mail number. He waited for the prompt and put his secret code in. He waited for the voice he knew he would hear.

"Hale, this is Jean-Robert. The plane you asked about just arrived. I will go and see what I can find out and call you afterward. Be sure to leave your phone on."

Hale pushed the button to erase the message and waited for the second one.

"Hello, Hale. It is me, Jean-Robert, again. I found out that your plane came from Venezuela. I do not know if that helps you or not. I will let you know as soon as I find out anything else. Good-bye."

The sick feeling in Hale's stomach got worse. This wasn't good. Not at all. He needed to get to Anna and Father Vin quickly. He knew where they were. It should only be about a forty-minute drive from the hotel. He just hoped he could get there before something bad happened. Again, he pushed the DELETE button and waited for the last message.

"Hale, my friend. Where are you? Why do you not answer your phone? I am afraid I have some bad news for you. I do not wish to leave it on this stupid machine. Call me the second you get this."

Hale broke out into a sweat. He was already off the bed rummaging through his bag, trying to find clothes with one hand while holding the phone with the other. There was no way this could be good. Not in a million years. He could feel it. He had been careless by letting his phone battery die. And now, Anna and Father Vin may be in danger. He had to move quickly.

He punched in Jean-Robert's number. Jean-Robert picked up on the second ring.

"This is Jean-Robert. How can I help you?"

"Jean-Robert, this is Hale. What's going on?" He was already putting his shoes on. He would be out the door in less than two minutes.

"Hale! Why you do not call me back? I wait and wait and wait. Finally, I go to bed. I say, 'He will call.' But you don't call. What is going on?"

"My battery on my phone died. I just realized it. I'm sorry." He grabbed his jacket and headed out the door. "What is this bad news you said you had?"

"Ah yes. The bad news. Well, I found out that your mysterious plane showed up, just as you predicted. It landed about two hours after you. That's when I called the first time."

"Yes, I heard the messages. Please. This may be important. Just skip to the news you didn't want to leave on the voice mail."

"Yes, well, like I said, I did some checking around. It seems that your friends from Venezuela are looking for a priest and a young girl. They asked a lot of questions. As soon as they got here, they had a car service waiting for them."

"How many of them are there?" He was outside and getting into the car.

"Two, as far as I know. I am told they went to a hotel, not the one you are staying at. They talked to the desk clerk and got a room for the night. I have a friend there. He is the concierge. He told me that the men were dealing out lots of cash for some information."

"Are they still at the hotel?" He was pulling out of the parking lot.

"No. This morning they left, not long after your priest and the young girl. That was about an hour and a half ago. I suggest you hurry."

"Thank you. Once again, I owe you tremendously." Hale hung up the phone and stepped on the gas. Father Vin and Anna had a big head start on him. He would have to get to Oloron-Sainte-Marie as quickly as he could. He only hoped that whoever it was following them was doing just that: only following. He flipped the phone open again and tried Father Vin's number. It went to his voice mail. He figured that if Father Vin and Anna were inside the church looking for the scroll, Vin probably had his phone off. He'd just have to get there in record time.

He reached inside his coat and flipped the strap on the holster. He pulled out the pistol and checked the magazine. Full. Good. He hoped he wouldn't have to use it. Placing the gun back inside the shoulder harness, he gripped the steering wheel and pushed the gas pedal down as far as it would go.

Oloron-Sainte-Marie

Jonathan and Larry sat in the rental car outside the cathedral. They had followed Anna and Father Vin from Pau. It had been hard trying to keep their distance on the narrow back roads. There hadn't been that much traffic. Twice they had to pull over just to put some distance, and a few cars, between them.

Larry sat in the passenger seat fidgeting with his 9mm. He didn't know exactly what Jonathan had in mind, but he was ready for anything. Jonathan did tell him that if he gave the word, Larry was to get out of the car shooting. There was no way they were to let the priest and the girl get away if they had the scroll.

Jonathan watched as the city slowly began to wake. More and

more people were out on the streets moving about, doing their daily business. He hoped that he could get this done without causing a scene. He was afraid, however, that wasn't going to be the case.

He had already talked to Wickham this morning and assured him that he was close to obtaining the scroll. He told him that he and Larry were, at that very moment, watching the priest and the girl go into an old, historic cathedral. He was sure that they were in there retrieving the scroll as they spoke. Wickham had just grunted and said to get it at any cost. If Jonathan had to guess, it sounded like Louis was trying to get rid of a hangover. He knew that the cardinal had spent the evening at Mad Jack's. He was a friend of one of the bartenders. The bartender had called him last night to let him know that Wickham was there, as per their agreement. He liked to keep tabs on the cardinal. One never knew when information like that would come in handy. Jonathan liked to keep his bases covered.

Jonathan was about to send Larry out for some coffee when the doors to the church burst open and twenty or so little children came running out. There was a man standing in the doorway, definitely not a priest. He was waving bye to all of the children as they left. Some kind of early morning class. He looked at his watch and saw that it was twenty minutes before the hour. Kind of a strange time for class to let out, he thought. Catholics always did things at weird times.

The man—who must be the teacher—waited until the last child had gone, looked both ways, as if to see if he was being watched, and then headed back inside. He couldn't have looked more suspicious. Something was going on in there. Jonathan placed his hand in his lap and grabbed the silenced pistol he had resting on his leg.

Larry saw Jonathan reach for his gun and sat up straight. "Are we going in?"

"Not yet. Let's wait and see what they come out with. I have a feeling this is about to be our lucky day."

CHAPTER 21

Oloron-Sainte-Marie

Anna moved the latch with her thumbs and opened the old wooden box. The hinges made a creaking noise as the lid raised. Father Vin stood over her shoulder, holding the small flashlight.

Inside the box were several scattered papers and small notebooks. Anna pulled them out, inspecting each one as she went. The papers were drawings of buildings, inside and out. Neither Anna, nor Father Vin, recognized any of them. The notebooks seemed to be journals of some sort. Many were written in foreign languages. Father Vin told Anna that the languages varied from Hebrew to ancient Greek. Those that were written in the foreign languages were tied, with a small piece of string, to another one that had been translated into English. Father Vin recognized the writing as Thomas's. He explained to Anna that her grandfather must have translated them, or more likely, had them translated.

There were several maps, ranging from topography maps to street maps, of Jerusalem, Cairo, southern Iraq, and the Persian

Gulf. If Anna was confused before, she had no idea what to think now.

One by one, she removed each document and placed them on the floor beside her. She lifted the last sheet of loose paper. It was a handwritten note from her grandfather.

To Whom It May Concern,

This is the scroll given to the disciple John by the angel of the Lord during his revelation of the second coming of Jesus Christ. It has been hidden for nearly two thousand years. By God's grace, provision, and leading, and because I, too, am one of John's descendants, I have been chosen to find it. Also enclosed are some notes that I have made concerning the contents of the scroll. If you are reading this, then I have to believe that God has led you here, for His will is perfect, and He is the author of all things. My prayer is that my granddaughter, Anna, is the one reading this. If you are, Anna, know this: I am very close to figuring out what the scroll means. Use my notes to help you. As I said before, you have a brilliant mind. You and your protector should be able to finish it. I have a feeling the end result will be one of the cataclysmic events. All of the rest of my notes are at the flat in London.

God be with you,
Thomas

Anna finished reading the letter and handed it to Father Vin. He took it and, even though Anna had read it out loud, read it again. He finished and laid it on top of the rest of the pile of papers and notebooks.

Anna reached her hand inside the box for the last time and

pulled out a bundle of red velvet cloth. It was about the size of a marble bag. She unraveled the cloth, revealing a tiny scroll about the length of an ink pen and about as round. Anna unraveled the scroll. The paper was a thick, almost leathery type of paper that Anna hadn't seen before. The most amazing thing was that it looked brand-new. Both she and Father Vin knew that couldn't be the case. If the story was true, this scroll was almost two thousand years old. And yet it looked as if it had just been made.

"This is amazing," Anna said.

"It's beautiful," Father Vin agreed.

Anna rubbed her hand over the scroll. "Feel it, Vin. It feels like leather." She handed the scroll over to him. Father Vin took it and again agreed.

He handed it back to her. As Anna held the outstretched scroll, Father Vin scanned his little flashlight over it. "My goodness! It's beautiful!" he repeated.

"What language is that, Vin?"

"That, my dear, is Greek."

"I don't read Greek, Vin," she said matter-of-factly.

"Good thing I do, huh?" Vin said smiling.

"Well then. . . ," she said.

Father Vin cleared his throat and said, "Oh right, yes. . .sorry." He moved his finger along the characters and read out loud.

What once was perfect, has now been broken.
At the point of no escape, the Father opened the way.
So shall He, at the point of entry.
The key is found in the temple.

They were both silent for what seemed like minutes. A hushed sense of the sacred fell over them. Anna felt small and scared.

She had to break the silence. "Well, that just about sums it up, doesn't it?" Her words were sharp with sarcasm, and she winced at the sound of them bouncing off the ancient stones.

"You'll figure it out." Father Vin patted her on the shoulder. "Like your grandfather said, he's left you all of his notes. And he said that he was close to deciphering it. You'll just have to do a little work."

"Vin, I'm going to need your help."

"I don't think that would be wise, Anna."

"Why not? You're supposed to be here to help me. Right?"

"I'm supposed to protect you. Not help you figure out some riddle sent by God two thousand years ago."

"Please, Vin. There's so much I don't even know about. Who's going to tell me all of the biblical stuff I need to know?"

"Anna, we can argue about all of this later. Right now we should pack all of this up and go before someone comes down here and wants to know what's going on."

"You're right. Let's get out of here."

Anna quickly rolled up the scroll, wrapped it back in the cloth, and placed it back in the box. She and Father Vin carefully stacked the papers and notebooks and placed them on top of the scroll. Once they had everything back inside, Anna closed the lid and latched it. She picked the box up and tucked it under her arm.

Anna let Father Vin go in front of her, and she flipped off the light switch. He was already a few steps in front of her on the rickety staircase. She kept her head down to see each step as she ascended. She didn't want to take the chance of stumbling in the dim light. When she had almost reached the top, she felt her head bump into something. It was Father Vin. He had stopped at the top of the staircase. She leaned around him to see what was the holdup.

At the top of the stairs stood a man with his arms crossed. He had a determined look on his face, and he definitely didn't appear to be happy that he'd found them here.

Anna stepped up one stair to be able to see the man better. Father Vin started to speak, but the man cut him off.

"Who are you people?" the man demanded. "And what are you doing here?"

CHAPTER 22

Just outside Oloron-Sainte-Marie

Hale maneuvered the little car along the winding roads as fast as it would go. That was one thing he absolutely missed about America: bigger cars and faster engines. He pushed down the accelerator and heard the tires squeal as he rounded a big curve. Almost there.

Despite the car's little engine and lack of horsepower, he had made good time. What normally was a forty-minute drive, he turned into just over twenty-five. He rounded the big bend and saw the sign that told him Oloron-Sainte-Marie was only a few kilometers ahead. He let off the gas and slowed down. The last thing he needed right now was to be stopped by the police. This close to town, you could almost guarantee the local constables would be out and about.

He knew where Anna and Father Vin were. He was sure that whoever was on that second plane was there also. He just didn't know who they were or what they looked like. The good news was, more than likely, they weren't expecting him.

Hale had been a Navy SEAL and knew how to "recon" an area

and not be seen. He figured that's exactly what he would have to do. He checked the pistol inside the shoulder holster again.

As he made his way into town, he saw the signs that would lead him up the side of the hill to the cathedral. He found a place to park and got out of the car. It was a good walk up the hill, but he couldn't risk driving the car up there. What if there wasn't a through road? Then he would have to turn around and come back down. That would look suspicious to anyone watching. He would blow his cover.

He couldn't really walk up the road, either. If someone stopped to talk to him, he could be distracted and lose valuable time. He decided on taking a path up the hillside. The small shrubs and trees would give him some cover. He just hoped that his counterparts hadn't thought of the same thing. He could stumble over them and walk right into a bad situation.

Quietly he made his way up the rocky terrain. When he got to the top of the hill, he could see the small parking area in front of the church. There weren't many cars, and the ones that were there were unoccupied, except one.

Two men sat in the front seat of the last car in the last row, nearly two hundred feet away from him. Hale didn't recognize either of them.

Quickly he weighed his options. Just by looking at the two adversaries, he knew he could take them out without even breaking a sweat. Unless they were armed, which they most certainly would be. That could cause an unwanted scene.

He could, however, make his way around to the other side of the church and look for a rear entrance. Obviously Anna and Father Vin were still inside. The problem with that was, what if, when he made his way around the building, Anna and Father Vin came out the front door? That would be bad. No, he decided, he would opt for taking out the two goons.

He crouched down as low as he could go and started to make his way over to the car. He could use the few cars in between to give him cover. He pulled the pistol out of the holster and made his move. He should be on top of them in just another minute. Two at the most.

The two men in the car suddenly opened their doors and stepped outside the car. Hale could see, from his angle, that they definitely were armed. They had their pistols out and their arms hanging at their sides. They both had their fingers on the triggers. Just as quickly as they got out of the car, they started walking toward the cathedral.

The front doors to the church were opening. Hale could see a young man, with his back to him. Behind him, Anna and Father Vin stood in the doorway.

"I asked you a question. Who are you? What are you doing here?" the man at the top of the stairs repeated himself.

Anna stared at the man she had seen in the classroom earlier. His eyes were ice blue, and he had a look of business on his face. She didn't know what to say. Was she supposed to tell this guy that she had just stopped by to pick up a box sent by God? No, that probably wouldn't go over so well. She honestly couldn't think of anything to say.

She was about to just give it a shot when Father Vin stepped in. He politely moved her out of the way and stepped to the top of the stairs so that he was standing eye to eye with the young man. He reached into his back pocket and produced the same identification card that Anna had seen him show the custodian.

"I'm Father Vincent Marcello," he said. "I am a special

investigator for the Holy Roman Church. I work directly for the pope." He handed the young man the ID. "This is Anna. She is one of my associates."

"Hey," Anna smiled and gave a short wave.

The man took the little card and studied it closely. "What's that?" He pointed to the box under Anna's arm. "Did you steal that? You can't just take anything you want around here. I don't care if you are from the Vatican."

"Look, my son, can you tell me who is the priest of this parish?"

"Father De Lorme," the man said matter-of-factly. "But he's not here. I'm in charge. And unless you two tell me who you are and why you're holding that box, I'm calling the cops."

This wasn't going all that well. Since Father Vin wasn't getting anywhere, she might as well try. She reached into her pocket and pulled out a small photograph. She had taken it from the plane. It was a picture of her grandfather standing with his arm around Father Vin. She held the photo out for the man to see and said, "I'm sorry. Can we start over? My name is Anna Riley. And you are?"

"Jason. Jason Lang," came the reply. "I teach English to the local children."

"Do you recognize this man?" She tapped her finger over the image of her grandfather.

"I'm asking the questions around here," Jason reminded her.

"Dude! Just tell me. Do you recognize him or not?"

He took the photograph and looked at it. "I may have seen him. Why?"

"That's my grandfather. His name was Thomas Riley."

"What do you mean 'was'?"

"Just what I said—'was.' He's dead."

"Anna," Father Vin tried to interrupt. "Maybe we shouldn't get into too much—"

"It's okay, Vin. I've got this," Anna said, holding up a hand. "What did you say your name was again?"

"Jason."

"Look, Jason, you may or may not believe this, but we are on a mission from. . .well. . .let's just say it's really, really, important. Okay? My grandfather left me this box here in your church. We have to get out of here and get to our plane. We have people waiting for us."

"What's in the box?" Jason asked again.

"I can't show you that," Anna said. "It's a matter of national security." She nodded, trying to sound convincing.

"Well, I'm not letting either one of you leave here until I see what's in the box."

He had to be kidding. She'd had this thing for all of five minutes, and already she was about to screw something up! She pursed her lips and said, "All right! You want to know what's in the box?"

"Anna!" Father Vin protested.

"Here!" Anna swung the box upward, hitting the schoolteacher squarely underneath his chin. She staggered with the impact, but he stumbled backward and fell.

"Quick, Vin, let's go!" Anna reached over and grabbed Father Vin by the arm and pulled.

"I can't believe you hit that man!" Vin said as he was being dragged down the hall at a dead run.

Anna saw the schoolteacher out of the corner of her eye cutting across the cathedral sanctuary. He was gaining on them fast. And with the route he was taking, it was going to be close as to who got to the front doors first. With a final hard tug on Vin's arm and a burst of the last bit of speed she could muster, Anna found the doors first. In one motion, she leaned out and pushed the arm of the door, swinging it open, and pulled Vin ahead of her and out onto the front steps. But just as she was turning to slam the door on their pursuer, she felt a hand around her wrist and was suddenly being pulled back inside, with Father Vin standing in the open doorway.

"Okay," said the schoolteacher, gasping for breath and rubbing his jaw with his other hand. "You two are going to tell me what's going on, or I'm calling the cops." He reached in his pocket and pulled out his cell phone.

Anna glanced at Father Vin, bent over on his hands and knees. He was breathing heavily.

"Anna! Get down!"

She flinched. The voice came from the parking lot outside the church. She saw Father Vin convulse. He moved his hand to his side. That's when Anna saw the red flowing through his fingers. He'd been shot.

CHAPTER 23

Oloron-Sainte-Marie Cathedral

Jonathan had fired two shots, swearing when the first missed. Someone from behind him shouted a warning to his targets. His breath hitched when he realized he'd been careless. The priest and the girl had someone watching from outside the church. No time to think about that right now. He fired again. The second found its mark. He watched the old priest jerk backward and fall to the floor.

As they continued to advance on the building, Jonathan saw Larry suddenly fall backward. The back of his skull hit the pavement with a loud thud! A single bullet hole shone dead center in his forehead. Two seconds later, Jonathan felt the ripping pain tear through his left thigh. He'd been hit. This guy was good. They had been zigzagging back and forth, with Larry covering the rear, and still they both managed to get shot. Larry was dead. Jonathan was badly hit.

He fell to the ground and scooted toward one of the parked cars. He could use it as cover. By now, the girl, he was sure, had gotten away. He'd failed once again. No matter. He found her once. He'd find her again. And this time, she wouldn't have the priest to look out for her. But right now, he needed to get away from whoever this shooter was and stay alive.

Hale moved as quickly as he could, still being cautious, to the side of the church. He noticed a door. He moved over to it and tried the knob. Locked. He stepped back and lunged forward with his leg extended. As he kicked the door, it gave way and splintered the doorjamb. He heard a scream from inside. He quickly pushed the door open and saw Anna standing behind a young man. Father Vin was lying on a bench seat, holding his side.

"Vin! Are you all right?" Hale called out.

"Hale! Is that you?" Anna quickly moved out from behind the young man and ran to the pilot.

Hale stood there as Anna wrapped her arms around him. She was crying and talking a hundred miles an hour. Navy SEAL training hadn't included what to do with a hysterical young woman.

"Hale, what are you doing here? Vin's been shot! What do we do!"

Hale gently extricated himself from her and rushed over to Father Vin. The old man's color was already draining. He looked for the bullet wound and found it, just below the rib cage. Probably punctured a lung. That kind of shot killed quickly. He had to get Father Vin to a hospital.

"Excuse me!" Jason interrupted. "Will one of you tell me what's going on? There's a man out there shooting at us."

Hale didn't bother looking at him. He tore off his shirt and pressed it against Father Vin's wound. "There were two shooters. One is dead; the other I think is severely injured. Who are you?"

"His name is Jason," Anna answered.

"Listen, Jason," said Hale. "I work for the Vatican. The men outside are trying to kill this young lady. I have to get this priest to a hospital. She needs to get to Pau. Can you take her?"

"Are you nuts? There are people out there shooting at us, man! I'm not going anywhere until the police get here."

"Hale, I'm going with you," Anna said, crying.

"No." Hale slammed his hand on the bench seat. "Anna, you're going back to the plane, where it's safe. Jason, I promise you, nothing's gonna happen to you. Not while I'm here. I need you to get her out of here. Right now. What she has in that box is life and death important. Are you a priest?"

Jason shook his head. "No. I am a Baptist missionary."

"Good," Hale continued, "then know that getting that box out of here right now is imperative. It's an order that I promise you came directly from God."

The young man hesitated. Hale could feel him weighing the words, struggling to decide. At last the tension left his face. "I believe you," he said. "What do you need me to do?"

Hale let go of the breath he was holding. Jason was a good kid. "Is there a back way out of here?"

"Yes," Jason said.

"Good. Take Anna out that way. I'll stay here and cover you. When you get out, get to the train. It runs directly into Pau. When you get there, take a cab. Anna can tell you where the hotel is—"

"Hale, I said I'm going with you!" Anna was still crying.

Hale walked over to Anna and placed his hands on her shoulders. He looked her directly in the eye. "Anna, everything is going to be okay. I promise. I've been doing this for a long time. I did it for your grandfather for twelve years. I know what I'm doing. Okay?"

Anna nodded and wiped her nose on her shirtsleeve.

"Okay," he continued. "I need you to calm down and compose yourself. Can you do that for me?"

Anna wiped her eyes and nodded.

"Okay. Good. You and Jason need to get out of here. It isn't safe. I don't know if those two guys out there have any backup, but we sure don't have any, so we need to get out of here quickly. Father Vin has lost a lot of blood. I need to get him to a hospital. I can't do that if I'm looking after you two. Jason will get you back to Pau. When you get there, go to the hotel. Be careful. Look for anything and everything. Grab your stuff and head to the plane. I'll call Miles and Marie as soon as I get out of here. They will be waiting. If I'm not there, Miles can fly the plane by himself. Go to London. You have a safe house there. Marie can tell you where it is and get you situated until Vin and I can come and get you."

He pulled Anna in and gave her a hug. He walked over to Father Vin. "Vin, where is it?"

"Left ankle." Father Vin's breathing was short and labored. "I never had a chance to get it out, Hale. I wasn't fast enough."

"It's okay, Father. We're going to get you fixed up. Just hang in there for me." Hale leaned over and lifted Father Vin's left pant leg. Strapped to his ankle was a holster. Hale unfastened the strap and pulled it off of Vin's leg. He handed it to Anna. "You said you know how to use one of these, right?"

Again Anna nodded.

"Good. Take it."

Anna took the gun. Still crying, she lifted her pant leg and strapped the gun to her ankle.

"Now get out of here."

Anna and Jason turned toward the back of the church to leave.

Hale quickly walked up behind Jason and grabbed his arm. Jason stopped.

Hale leaned in close and whispered, "I don't know what's in that box, Jason. I've never seen it. But I do know this. That old man over there"—he pointed to Father Vin—"has spent his life protecting it. Whatever's in there, it was given to the disciple John by God Himself. Anna is a descendant of John. That box has been in her family for two thousand years. You say you're a man of the cloth?"

"Well, I'm a missionary," Jason stuttered. "I'm a Christian."

"Good. Then I don't need to tell you how important it is for her to get to that plane with that box."

CHAPTER 24

Oloron-Sainte-Marie Cathedral

Hale waited until Anna and Jason moved to the back door. Signaling them to head out, he went out the front door looking for the assassin. As he opened the door, he heard the spit of three bullets hitting the doorjamb to his left. He dove into a sideways roll and came up firing. The black sedan, where he had seen the men in the first place, was fishtailing out of the parking lot. Hale took his aim at the rear tires. Again, he hit the target but missed the mark. All five of his shots hit the trunk of the car. The black sedan quickly rounded the corner and was gone.

Hale could hear the wail of the sirens. He figured he had two, maybe three, minutes before the police showed up. He needed to get Father Vin.

The old priest lay on his back, still holding his side. His clothes were soaked with blood, his color all but drained. He didn't look good. Hale tried to lift him up.

Father Vin groaned. "Put me back down!"

"Vin, I can't. We need to go. If you don't get out of here,

you're going to die."

Again Hale lifted the priest. He wrapped his arm around Father Vin's waist and draped Vin's arm around his neck and shoulder. They had only moved a few feet when Father Vin let go and fell to the floor.

"Leave me here."

"No." Hale gripped Vin's shoulders. "You get up and help me get you out of here, old man. I'm not leaving you. Now let's go!"

Father Vin sat in the middle of the floor. The sirens outside were getting louder. They would be here any second.

"Vin, I can't just leave you. What about Anna?" Hale felt a pain in his heart. First Thomas now Vin. He had spent the last twelve years of his life with these two men. He loved them dearly. Now, standing here, he knew this could only end one way. Even if he could get Father Vin to a hospital, the chances of him making it were slim to none.

"Anna will be just fine, Hale." Vin coughed. A small trickle of blood ran down his chin. His lungs were filling up with the liquid. "That boy, Jason." He coughed again. "He's the one. I'm sure of it." He winced as a sharp pain caught him.

"You mean. . ."

"Yes," said Vin. "He's the one to take my place."

Hale knelt down beside Father Vin. He leaned in and took him into his arms. He squeezed as hard as he could. He could feel the tears running down his cheeks. Father Vin lifted an arm and put it around Hale.

"Tell Miles and Marie that I love them. I will be looking down on them, and you, until we see each other again." His breath was coming in short gasps now. "Tell Anna. . ." He stopped as a coughing fit took control of him. "Tell her. . .I've never. . .been more proud. . .of. . .anyone. . .in my. . .life. Tell her. . .she can do this. . .without me."

Hale let go of Father Vin and just held his hand. The old priest laid his head back on the floor, still coughing. Hale buried his face in his hands and began to sob. He never looked as he heard the last ounce of breath wheeze from Father Vin's lips.

Hale was actually surprised that the cops hadn't already stormed in here. As he turned to leave, he saw in front of him a creature, both magnificently beautiful and frightening. He had never seen one before, but the way Father Vin had described them, he could swear that this was an angel.

"Hello, Hale. My name is Sammael." The angel bowed.

"Hello." Hale nodded.

"The reason I come to you is to bring you information."

"Information?" he asked.

"Father Vin is with Christ. Our Lord is most pleased with his service. There will be a great celebration tonight. Father Vincent will be the honored guest."

"I'll tell Anna. She will be happy to hear that." Hale whispered.

"Second, the Father has permitted me to tell you that this Jason is not an ordinary individual. Many years ago he was chosen to be a part of this task. He has been chosen to be with Anna. He is the new protector of the guardian. It is the Father's will. Go and tell Anna what has been spoken. She will need to hear this. The Father has allowed us this short time to speak. Once I have gone, things will return to normal. The law enforcement of this town are waiting at the doors. Go now. Hurry."

Hale turned and ran out the rear entrance of the church. He had to get back to his car. Hopefully he could get to the plane at the same time as Anna and Jason. He ran down the hill to where his car was. He started the engine and slammed it into gear. The tires spun dirt and gravel as he pulled out onto the road.

He reached into his pocket and pulled out his cell phone. He hit the speed dial, number two. The phone rang on the other line four times before someone picked up.

"Hello, this is Miles."

"Miles, this is Hale."

"Hey, Hale. What's up?"

"We have a problem. Several of them, actually."

"Why? What's going on—"

"Listen. I'll explain later. Right now, you need to get to the plane."

"Already there."

"Good. Anna should be getting to you in about an hour and a half. As soon as she gets there, get out of here. Go to London. Oh, and she has a friend. His name is Jason. I don't have any time to explain right now. All you need to know is he's cleared. Take him and Anna to the safe house. Stay with them until I get there."

"Hale, what's going on, man? Is this serious?"

"Vin is dead. They were ambushed. I was able to take out one of them."

"Why didn't you call us?"

"No time. I hit the other guy, but he got away. I don't think they'll be back in the near future, but they will be back. You need to get Anna and Jason out. I'll catch up with you later. I gotta go, man. Gotta call in. Get them out of here."

Hale pushed the END button and waited for the screen to clear. Next, he pushed the speed dial button, number three. There was a buzzing sound on the other end, a few clicks, and then a ring. After a few seconds, the line on the other end clicked, then a series of beeps. It was the prompt he was waiting for.

"This is Agent six, four, three, three, one, requesting secure line."

There were a few more clicks, another buzz, a dial tone, and then a series of rings. Finally, the call connected. He waited until he heard the voice on the other line answer.

"Hello?"

"Who is this?" Hale didn't recognize the voice.

"Who is this? You're calling a secure line here."

"This is Agent William Hale. This line is reserved for the pope. Again, I have to ask: Who is this?"

"I'm sorry, Agent Hale. The pope has taken ill. I have taken charge of all his business. You can speak with me. This is Secretary of State Cardinal Louis Wickham."

CHAPTER 25

Oloron-Sainte-Marie, Train Station

Jason relied on his familiarity with the city to make it to the train station unseen, taking back alleys and staying away from the main streets. He bought the tickets and kept Anna out of sight. Thankfully, the train was on time for once. They jumped on the last car and took a seat in the last row. As the train pulled out of the station, Jason breathed a sigh of relief. They hadn't been killed. Yet. And he still didn't know what was going on. All he knew was he was here, with Anna, and they were headed for a plane.

Anna hadn't said much of anything since they left the church. That was all right, Jason thought. He knew she was shaken. And he should be. By all things normal, he should be scared to death and running as far away as he could get. Yet for some reason he wasn't. Somehow he knew he needed to be here.

He nudged Anna's arm. "You okay?"

Anna turned slowly to face him, her face blank. "No." She buried her head in her hands rocking back and forth.

Jason didn't know what to do. He slowly reached his arm around her shoulder and squeezed. "It's going to be all right, Anna. We're safe now. Your friend back at the church said he would take care of everything."

Anna lifted her head. "What do you mean *we*? You're not involved in this."

Jason withdrew his arm. "I'd say I'm pretty involved! I'm here, aren't I?"

Anna took a deep breath and let it out again. "Look, I appreciate you helping me get out of there. I really do. But you have no idea what's going on here. Heck, I barely do! I've only been doing this for a couple of days, and already I've been chased halfway around the world and shot at! There's no way you can get involved in this."

Jason didn't have a response to what Anna had just told him. He only knew that, from now on, he was going to be a part of whatever all of this was. "I need to tell you something."

Anna wiped the tears from her eyes and looked at him.

"Your friend Hale told me who you are."

"What do you mean?"

"He told me you are a descendant of the disciple John. Now, that in and of itself is extraordinary. But he also told me a little bit about that box."

Anna's eyes got big. She pulled the box closer to her and held on tight.

Jason saw her reaction. He shifted in his seat to put some room between them. "I have no desire to take that box, or anything in it, away from you. You can trust me. What I wanted to tell you was this." He took a long breath and blew it out slowly. "A long time ago, I gave my life to Jesus Christ. When God gave me a new heart, it completely took me over. I've been made fun of, lost friends, had relationships dissolve—all because I've tried to be obedient to what He calls me to do. And a few years ago, through a lot of prayer and asking for God's leading, He led me here. For two years I've been sitting in that room teaching little French kids English, waiting for God to show me why. All I knew is that God had me here for some reason. And I've felt it, deep within me, that that reason is something big. And I know this sounds ridiculous, but I believe that this is the reason."

Anna let out a long string of air. Shaking her head, she stood up. "I—I can't handle this right now. I need to think." She walked to the front of the car and sat down in an empty seat. The box was tucked safely under her arm.

She couldn't think straight. Her head was pounding from a headache she'd gotten in the last ten minutes. Her stomach was doing flip-flops. She couldn't stop shaking. And the tears. Just when she thought she couldn't cry any more, they came billowing out again.

She sat there, going over it all from the beginning. None of this made sense. If God wanted her to do this, she needed answers. She had no idea where to go or what to do. She rested her elbows on her knees and covered her face with her hands. She let out a low whisper, "Please, God, tell me what to do."

"Anna."

Anna lifted her head and saw the boy sitting beside her. Everyone else on the train had disappeared. "Hello, boy," she said, scrubbing tears away with the palm of her hand.

The boy smiled. "Once again, He has sent me to talk to you. Your task must certainly be important. He's showing you a lot of attention."

"Could've fooled me," she said. "I haven't got a clue as to what's going on."

The boy looked at her intently. "You have to have faith. I promise you, He is with you every step you take."

"Yeah, you keep saying that, but right now I couldn't feel more lost."

"Anna, Father Vin has come home."

Poor Father Vin. She'd barely gotten to know him, but he'd become special to her so quickly. Her lifeline. It didn't seem right that he should be dead. The tears started up again.

The boy smiled compassionately, but a deep joy shone from his eyes. "Please don't cry. Vin is with our Lord. You should be happy for him. His service on this earth will be greatly rewarded."

"Well, that's just perfect! What am I supposed to do now? He was the only one around here who knew what was going on. I can't do this by myself!"

"You don't have to," the boy said. "Jason is here now. He is to take Father Marcella's place."

"*What?* Him? I don't even know him!"

"You didn't know Father Vin either," the boy reminded her.

Anna was on her feet now, pacing back and forth. "I don't care. At least Father Vin has been doing this for the last. . .however long!" She threw her arms up. "This guy doesn't have a clue. I mean, I've got more experience in it than him! That doesn't say much!"

The boy blocked her path, facing her. "He's been groomed for this assignment since he was thirteen. The Father put the two of you together for a reason. Trust your instincts, Anna. You know what Jason told you is the truth. You can feel it. So go. Go with him. Together you will figure it out."

Anna closed her eyes and pinched the bridge of her nose. When she opened them again, the boy was gone. Everyone was back on the train. Jason still sat in the backseat looking at her with compassion and sympathy.

She picked up the box and returned to her seat beside Jason. She wiped the tears away from her eyes again and shifted in her seat to look at him. "Okay. Let's get one thing straight. I'm in charge. What I say goes, or you go. Got it?"

Jason grinned. "Got it!"

CHAPTER 26

The Vatican

Cardinal Wickham hung up the phone. The press secretary had just given him the latest briefing. Once word got out that the pope was bedridden, the calls came like a flood. He gave the press secretary his statement, assuring them all that the pope was just suffering from a bout with the flu and should be up and about soon.

He could barely hide his excitement. With the pope being as sick as he'd become so unexpectedly, he should be running around showing nervous energy, trying to calm the rest of the Vatican. Instead, here he was sitting in the papal business office sipping a warm cappuccino. The next few days would bring lots of excitement. He deserved a little break from the activity.

The pope was gone. Well, not yet, but soon. He'd been careful. The doctors, just as he presumed, diagnosed the pope's condition as an abnormal strain of flu. This couldn't be going any better. As long as the doctors continued to treat him for this condition, everything would work out exactly as he'd planned.

He almost felt like putting the pope's robes on and parading around the hallways. After all, who would stop him? In a few days, he would be the most powerful man in all of Rome. Even more powerful than the pope. As long as everything went as planned, the new pope would be Joseph, and he had Joseph in the palm of his hand.

What would be the first thing he would do with all of his newfound power?

A jarring buzz interrupted his thoughts. First thing he'd do is hire an army of receptionists to handle the incessant phone calls. He flipped open his cell phone. "Yes?"

"We've got a problem."

Jonathan. Of course. Seemed the only thing he was capable of assassinating was a good mood. "What do you mean we've got a problem?"

"Well, one of my guys is dead, I've been shot, and the girl got away." Jonathan's statement showed no emotion. Just the facts.

"What do you mean, she got away?"

"Thanks for your concern about me and my guy."

"I don't care about you or your heathen employees. I hired you to do a job. Obviously, I made a mistake. Where is my scroll?"

"You're gonna get it!" Jonathan shouted back. "I've just had a setback. They had someone watching them. I made a mistake. I underestimated them. It won't happen again. You can be sure of it."

Wickham was breathing heavily now. His blood pressure was up, he was sure. "I'm growing tired of your excuses, Jonathan. Either get it done or I will be forced to conclude that your services are no longer required. Get me my scroll!"

He was still holding the phone out in front of him when he heard a strange beeping sound. He'd never heard it before. He didn't even say good-bye to Jonathan. He just hung up, slamming the earpiece shut on his cell phone. The beeping continued. He followed the sound. It was coming from the pope's private office—the small private room within the main office.

He turned the knob. Unlocked. He had only been in here on a couple of occasions. Typically, when he and the pope met, they would do their business out in the main office. This room was, for the most part, off-limits.

He walked to the desk and found the source of the beeping—a phone in a desk drawer. "Hello?"

"Who is this?" asked a male voice.

"Who is this? You're calling a secure line here."

"This is Agent William Hale. This line is reserved for the pope. Again, I have to ask: Who is this?"

He had often wondered about this. He knew that Thomas Riley and the agents had direct contact with Pope Paul. He just couldn't ever figure out how. Now he knew.

"Of course, Agent Hale." He smiled a big smile. Things were looking up after all. "The pope has taken ill. I have taken charge of all his business. You can speak with me. This is Secretary of State Cardinal Louis Wickham."

"I'm sorry, Cardinal Wickham," Hale said, "but what I have to say is for the pope's ears only."

Cardinal Wickham pulled the pope's big leather chair out from under the desk and sat down. "That's going to be a problem. It seems that Pope Paul has become suddenly ill. He has developed a rare case of the flu. The doctors are doing everything they can, but I'm afraid it doesn't look good."

Wickham paused and listened to the silence on the other end of the line. He knew why the agent was calling. Somehow he needed to befriend him, get the agent to trust him. This was his chance to get a personal link to Anna and the scroll.

"How bad is it?" Hale asked.

"Our official position is he'll be fine in a couple of days, but I'm afraid it may be worse than they originally thought."

"I see."

Wickham needed to get the agent to open up. This was going to be difficult. "Tell me, Agent Hale. Does this call have anything to do with a certain young lady? Perhaps someone you are in charge of looking after?"

The line went silent.

"It's okay, son. As I told you before, I am the pope's secretary of state. I know all of his business. You can talk to me about it. His Holiness immediately informed me of your situation when he took ill. He was afraid that, if something were to happen, no one would be able to look after you, if needed." Again the line was silent for a few seconds. He could almost hear the wheels turning inside the agent's head. "I really cannot help you, Agent Hale, unless you tell me what is going on."

Finally, the agent spoke. "I know who you are, Cardinal Wickham. I'm afraid I still cannot tell you what this call is regarding. If you would, though, please pass along a message for me. Tell the pope, when he recovers, my team and I will be code three for the next few days, perhaps weeks. We've had a situation, and we will be regrouping. I'll make contact again as soon as I can. Thank you."

The line went dead. Louis placed the receiver back in its cradle. He had no idea what code three was. He could assume, given the conversation with Jonathan. Obviously, Agent Hale and his team were going into hiding. This would be a perfect opportunity to do some planning. He had to speak to the pope.

He left the office and headed for the papal apartment. On the way, he pulled out his cell phone and called Jonathan. He didn't like making these kinds of calls where someone could overhear, but this was important. He needed to tell Jonathan about Agent Hale's call.

He was finishing his conversation as he approached the door to the pope's room. He closed the phone and nodded to the Swiss guard as he entered. The guard quickly acknowledged him. He was the second highest official in the hierarchy, after all. Next to the pope, he was probably the most known figure in all of Vatican City.

He walked over to where the pope lay and placed a hand on the sick man's shoulder. A doctor, two nurses, and the pope's personal assistant were all in the room. Wickham asked if they would all give him and the pope a minute of personal time. He said he needed to discuss a matter of extreme importance. Everyone nodded and stood to leave. The doctor explained that he would need to give the pontiff another round of antibiotics in a few minutes. Wickham assured him that he would be quick.

Wickham walked everyone to the door and closed it behind them. He turned the latch to the dead bolt lock. Pouring two cups of tea from the kettle on the bedside table, he reached inside his pocket and brought out the vial that contained the untraceable liquid. He unscrewed the top and let two drops fall into one of the mugs. He took a spoon and stirred the mixture. It was the third time in as many days. The poison, just as he was told, was doing its job. And the best part was that no one was the wiser. As far as anyone knew, Pope Paul VII had the flu.

He took a seat beside the bed and grabbed a hand towel that had been sitting next to the teakettle. He wiped the sweat from the pope's brow. Pope Paul VII slowly opened his eyes. A faint smile formed on his lips.

"Louis," he wheezed. "So good to see you. How is everything, my friend?"

"Everything is fine, Your Holiness." Wickham set the towel back on the table. "How are you feeling today?"

"I'm afraid, not too good." He coughed. "I've never felt like this with the flu."

"Yes, the doctor says it's a very rare strain. I'm sure you'll be back on your feet in a couple of days. Here, drink this. It will make you feel better." He handed him the mug of tea.

The pope took the hot mug and sipped it. "This is very good tea, Louis. Did you make it?"

"No." He chuckled. "I'm afraid I can't take credit for it. I think one of the nurses made it for you. I'll be sure and tell her how much you like it."

"Yes, do that. Very good tea, indeed. So, did you come just to visit? I'm sure that there is something important you could be doing. No use wasting your time sitting with a sick old man." He tried to laugh, which led to another coughing fit.

"Actually, Your Holiness, I did come here on business." He sat up in his seat and tried to look as innocent as he could. "I was in your office a little while ago. I needed to get some order form for something." He waved his hand, as if dismissing what he'd just said. "While I was in there, the gray phone in your desk rang." He waited for a reaction. Just as he thought, the pope immediately took interest.

Pope Paul VII sat up a little bit. He had a concerned look on his face. "I'm not sure what phone you're talking about, Louis. Gray phone?"

"Yes, you know. The one sitting on your desk. In your private study. It looks just like the one in your prayer room over there." Wickham pointed to the closed door across the way.

"Oh, that one." Pope Paul tried to act as if it were nothing.

"I went ahead and answered it since I was in there. I mean, you are obviously not in any kind of shape to be receiving calls. I thought it may be important. So I answered it."

"You did?"

"Anyway, an Agent Hale called to tell you that he and his team will be—what did he say?" He moved his hand in a circle, as if trying to recall. "Ah yes. Code three? I believe that's what it was. Yes. Code three."

"I see." Pope Paul VII now sat completely up in his bed. He had a concerned look on his face.

"Is something wrong?"

"Did he say anything else?"

"No. That was it. Just code three."

Wickham watched as the concerned look turned to one of fear. Obviously the pontiff was worried. And he should be. He tried hard to stifle his excitement. "Is there something you need to tell me about, Paul?"

Pope Paul VII slid back down in his bed. How could this have happened? How could Father Vin be so careless? Code three was bad. Really bad. Never in his term as pope had the guardian been code three. Actually, since the whole "code" system had been in place, no guardian had been code three.

Something was wrong. Code three meant that the protector, Father Vin in this case, was dead. It also meant that the guardian, Anna, was headed to a safe house. Hale, he knew, would see to it that Anna was safe and secure. As soon as she was, the pilot would then return to the Vatican and brief him. Hopefully Hale would get here soon and explain everything.

He knew that since the arrival of the scroll two thousand years ago, people had been trying to get their hands on it. Some got close. Some had even come close to seeing it. But no one had ever caused this much havoc in such a short amount of time. Lately it seemed that everywhere that scroll went, someone got hurt, ended up dead, or both. And now two of his closest friends, Thomas and Vin, were gone. Something was definitely wrong. Whoever was trying to get the scroll this time was serious. They knew too much about too many things. He wasn't naive. There had to be a leak.

Louis had asked him something. *Is there anything you need to tell me, Paul?* He studied the cardinal's face. Louis looked at him expectantly, like a child waiting for his mother to tell him it was okay to go outside and play. Did he know? Surely not. How could he? Then again, how could anyone? But someone *did* know. Someone close to him, no doubt. Better safe than sorry.

"No, Louis. Everything is fine. Just fine."

He watched as the cardinal's look of anticipation faded. Louis showed no sign of betrayal. That was good, though it didn't prove anything. He would still keep a tight lip on the situation.

Cardinal Wickham stood up and moved to his bedside. He patted him on the shoulder again and said, "Take care, my friend. If there is anything I can do for you, let me know. I'll be in my office."

"Louis, there is one thing."

"Yes?"

"Hand me my tea, please."

Wickham grabbed the mug from the bedside table and handed it to him. "Here, Your Holiness. I pray you feel better soon."

He thanked the cardinal and watched him walk out of the room. For the first time he could remember, Louis seemed annoyed with him. He needed to do something. But what? What could he do, lying here in this bed sick? He could only think of one thing. He reached for the cable that was draped over the side of his bed. He pushed the little red button and waited. Seconds later, the door opened up. A pretty, young nurse, the same one who had been at his bedside for the last two days, came in. She had a soothing smile and treated him like a normal patient. She was feisty, telling him to take his medicine—she didn't care if he *was* the pope, she was the nurse, and he was going to do what she said—even if he didn't want to! He definitely liked her.

"Yes, Your Holiness?" she asked.

"There is a key over there on my desk." He pointed. "It unlocks my door over there. Would you get it and unlock that door?"

"Certainly."

He directed her to the cell phone, and she brought it to him. After dismissing her, he punched in the number and waited for the other end to answer.

"Hello?"

"Hello, is this Hale?" He sat up again and tried to clear his throat.

"Yes. Who is this?"

"Hale, this is Pope Paul VII."

"Your Holiness, this is not a secure line."

"Yes, yes. I know. Listen. We need to keep this quick. I have become very sick. They say it is the flu. I'm not so sure. I may not have much time."

"Please, sir, don't say that. I'm sure you will be—"

"Listen carefully, please. Everything that has happened in the last couple of weeks—it cannot all be coincidental. Something is wrong. I suspect that someone here is helping whoever is trying to get the package. I don't know who it may be, but if someone here is involved in this, you and your whole team are in even more danger than before. Take the appropriate precautions."

"I will."

"Good. I'll call you if I learn anything else."

"Thank you, Your Holiness."

"No, thank you, Hale. Thank you for all you do. Get back here and brief me as soon as you can."

"I will."

He ended the call and reached for the nurse's button again. His head was pounding. His vision was blurring. He felt hot. He kicked the blanket off. He reached for his small leather-bound Bible and began fanning himself. He saw the door open, but the whole scene was blurry. He felt light-headed. He heard the nurse shout for the doctor and the rest of the staff just as everything went dark.

CHAPTER 27

Pau, France

Jonathan flipped on his turn signal and pulled the rental car off the main road. Dust and gravel were kicking up behind him. This little side road wasn't even on the map, and he'd almost missed it. Good thing he hadn't.

The bullet wound in his leg was seeping blood. He needed to get out of the car and get to the trunk. He always carried an emergency first-aid kit. It wasn't enough to treat a gunshot, but the kit did have some gauze, antibiotic cream, and pain medicine. It should hold him over until he could get it properly looked at.

He pulled the car to a stop, far enough off the main road that he was sure no one could see him. He slammed the door shut as he limped back to the trunk. The lid popped, and the dust that had settled on the surface from the little back road flew up into his nostrils. He sneezed.

The pain from the gunshot was killing him. He sifted through the bag until he found what he was looking for. He unscrewed the lid to the little bottle and popped three of the little blue pills into his mouth. He had no water, so he swallowed hard, forcing the little pills down. There was an old shirt in his bag as well. He unstrapped his knife and cut it into long strips. He took two of them and twisted one around the other, creating a kind of cloth rope. He propped his leg up on the bumper and tied the rope off a few inches above the bloody hole in his leg. Fortunately, the bullet missed any major artery. Had it not, he would have already bled out. He set his leg down, put the bag back, and returned to the driver's seat. He started the engine and put the car in gear.

The little back road was just wide enough for him to be able to make a U-turn. He stomped on the gas hard and watched the gravel shoot from the rear of the car. He slammed his fist on the dash just for good measure. He couldn't remember when he'd been this mad.

His cell phone was sitting on the seat beside him. He grabbed it, flipped it open, and punched in a number.

The voice was scratchy and deep. The German accent was deep and thick. "Hullo? What do you want?"

"Dieter, it's Jonathan."

"I know this. What do you want?"

"I need a favor."

"Imagine that."

"I've had an incident. I need a *cutter*. I'm in Pau, France."

"Go to the hospital."

"If I could go to the hospital, do you think I would be calling you?"

"Give me ten minutes. I will call you back."

He hated having to call him, but this was about staying alive. Surely Dieter would know that and not leave him hanging, even though there was no love lost between them.

At one time he and Dieter were partners. They were the most

feared hit man team in all of Europe. Their reputation even found its way across the Atlantic and into the West. They had made it a contest between themselves to see who could end up wanted on more charges in the most countries. Jonathan was in the lead by eight counts and two countries—it was the way it should be, no offense to Dieter. They had been the closest thing to best friends that hit men could ask for. They'd been inseparable. Until Prague.

It was a simple hit. Two shots from two different angles, scheduled to fire at the same time. Jonathan was on a rooftop on the south side of the street, while Dieter was in an apartment window on the west side. The target, a US diplomat, walked out of the embassy just as scheduled. Both men lined up their shots. Each had his watch synchronized to sound an alarm, a simple three beeps. On the third beep, they would pull the triggers. It was a routine that had been performed many times, each without incident.

Two bullet holes from two different angles was enough to stall even the best security detail. The mere fact that two shots were taken would confuse the security long enough for them to get out before it could be determined what direction the shots came from. That was the plan.

On the third beep, Jonathan squeezed his index finger. Nothing. He squeezed again. Still nothing. The gun was jammed. He looked through his scope to see a half dozen US Secret Service agents sweeping their arms, guns in hand, in circular motions throughout the street. The target was down, lying in a pool of crimson. Jonathan disassembled his rifle as quickly as he could and ran. He later found out that Dieter was captured. Somehow, after two days of interrogation, Dieter escaped. It was reported that six American agents were hospitalized with life-threatening injuries, while two more were found dead. Dieter wasn't someone you let your guard down with.

Jonathan never tried to contact Dieter after that. Word made its way back to him that Dieter held him responsible. Dieter thought he had sold him out. It took two years for the dust to settle. Jonathan finally tried talking to him. They met in a public place at a time of day when it would be crowded. Safety first. After two hours of cold coffee and stale bread, Jonathan finally convinced Dieter that he hadn't sold him out. Dieter accepted his explanation but felt it would be better if they just continued to work separately. Jonathan paid the check and left without even a good-bye. That was three years ago. They hadn't spoken until just now.

The cell phone started ringing. It was Dieter calling him back. He pushed the SEND button and said, "Yeah?"

"There is a Mr. Henri Rhette who can be found on Avenue Saint James. He has been called. He is expecting you. Tell me, Jonathan, for what reason did you call me?"

"Because unless I get this thing taken care of quickly, I'm gonna be taking a dirt nap. You're the only one I know who could find me a doctor in the middle of nowhere."

"You owe me."

"I know."

Like their last meeting, Jonathan didn't even say good-bye. He closed the phone and threw it back on the seat beside him. Pau was only a few more kilometers ahead. Hopefully this doctor wasn't some quack. Guess he'd soon find out.

He made one final call before he reached the city limits. This time it was to one of his people back in Rome. He explained the situation, told his guy what he needed, and hung up.

Now it was just a matter of time. Soon he would know the whereabouts of that pain-in-the-neck girl. Wickham's nagging voice crept up inside his mind. *Get me my scroll!* He really was starting to dislike that man. He'd figure out a way to deal with him later. Right now he had to stay focused. The pursuit of Anna Riley had almost cost him his life. The next time they met, he was determined it would cost hers.

Pau Airport, France

Jason made Anna wait to get off the train until he stepped outside and looked around. Once he was sure they were alone, he motioned for her to join him.

They hurried out of the terminal and up to the street, where they grabbed a cab back to the hotel. He looked around in the lobby for someone who looked like they didn't belong. Once he was satisfied, he and Anna jumped on the elevator and headed for her room.

Anna slipped the key into the lock and led the way in. Jason was impressed. It was probably the nicest room the hotel had to offer. At least they would be staying in some pretty swanky places if this was how Anna traveled. He walked around checking the place out while Anna quickly threw her things in her bag. Five minutes later, they were back downstairs and into another cab.

The drive to the airport was a short one. Jason could sense that Anna didn't feel like talking too much, so he kept the conversation to a minimum. There would be plenty of time for talking on the plane ride. The plane was impressive. He had never been on a Gulfstream jet before, but he had heard about them. Maybe this wouldn't be so bad after all.

As their cab pulled up on the tarmac of the airport, Anna saw Miles standing at the top of the stairs leading into the plane. Some local crew were milling around outside the aircraft, each one doing something different. A guy in a gray jumpsuit was holding a massive hose up to the wing. Someone else was under the plane inspecting the wheels, probably checking tire pressure and brakes. All in all, they looked like a bunch of ants moving vigorously about.

As they got out of the cab, Miles waved his arm at them, calling her and Jason aboard. The man with the hose flipped a switch and released the giant snake from the wing. He shouted something to Miles and did a mock salute. Anna and Jason nodded to him as they made their way up the stairs.

Miles met them halfway and grabbed Anna's bag. "Did you have any trouble?"

"Not once we got out of Oloron-Sainte-Marie," Anna answered in a sort of monotone. "Father Vin was shot."

Miles sighed heavily. "I know." He nudged her up the stairs. They would be leaving any minute now.

"Where's Hale?"

"He told us to get you out of here," Miles answered. "He said he'd catch up to us in London."

"No. No way." Anna shook her head. "This plane doesn't leave without him. We wait."

Marie came over and put a hand on her shoulder, a motherly look on her face. "Anna, dear, we have to go. It's for your own safety. Hale is the boss. He has given us explicit orders to go. We have to."

Anna blinked rapidly, her eyes wet with unshed tears. "Please, Marie, can't we wait for just a few minutes? I'm really scared. I want him here. Please?"

Marie's faced softened. She squeezed her shoulder and said, "I'll go talk to Miles. Maybe we can wait for a few minutes."

Anna thanked her.

Marie walked to the front of the plane and stuck her head in the cockpit. Jason watched, from behind as Marie talked to Miles. He saw Marie nod her head. Marie turned around and had a smile on her face. "Miles just got off the phone with Hale. He's right around the corner. We're waiting for him. He said he needed to talk to you."

Jason saw the look of relief on Anna's face. She needed everyone to be traveling together. He knew she needed to talk to Hale, too. She hadn't wanted to leave him behind. Especially after what just happened.

The left engine wound down. Marie stepped in front of them and moved to the forward door, where she lifted the hydraulic lever and let the stairs to the main cabin down. Seconds later, Hale appeared in the doorway. Anna flung her arms around his neck. He hugged her back and then let go. He stuck his head in the cockpit, said something to Miles, and then closed the cockpit door. "We're out of here," he said.

Anna showed Jason around the inside of the plane. She told him to make himself comfortable. He sat down in the big leather chair, the one Father Vin had sat in over the last couple of days. He didn't miss the forlorn expression on her face, but she didn't cry this time. She tossed her jacket onto the couch and plopped down beside it. She looked exhausted.

Jason leaned his head against the back of the seat. So here he was. Off to London. What next?

A funny scene from a Chevy Chase movie ran through his mind. *Look kids, Big Ben!* Unfortunately, this trip wouldn't be as humorous as the Griswolds' had been.

The plane's engines once again roared to life. Within seconds they were speeding down the runway. The Gulfstream's nose lifted, and the plane climbed into the sky.

CHAPTER 28

Rome

Joseph sat at the table waiting for Cardinal Wickham to arrive. As usual, he was early. He just couldn't stand being late.

He scanned the room for faces he recognized. Many people from the Vatican, priest and nonclergy alike, ate here frequently. It was a quiet little café located just down the street from St. Peter's Square. It had an outdoor patio, mostly used by tourists looking to have a nice view with their croissants and coffee.

Joseph hated the patio. Too many pigeons. The little rats with wings would trot around bobbing their heads, pecking on the ground for crumbs. Occasionally, one of the braver ones would flutter its wings and spring up and over the little railing, landing on a table or in the middle of someone's lunch plate.

Utterly repulsive. He simply refused to eat out there. At this very moment, he could see a woman shooing one off the railing next to her table. The rodent with wings squawked and flapped as it fell off the small railing.

Louis entered the room. Joseph stuck a hand up in the air and waved. Seconds later, Wickham took a seat at the table.

"Louis." Joseph nodded at the other cardinal.

"Joseph. Glad you could make it."

"You, too."

Wickham poured himself a cup of coffee from the carafe sitting in the middle of the table. He took two sugar cubes from a small plate and dropped them into the oversized mug. "I'm sort of pressed for time, so I'll keep this short and to the point."

Just then an attractive young woman appeared at the table. She had a bright white button-down shirt tucked inside a long black apron. She was wearing a long black skirt and black pumps with two-inch heels. "Hello, Louis," she said. "Good to see you today. Will you be having your usual?"

"Yes, thank you." Louis smiled at her. "He'll have the same." He pointed to Joseph without even looking at him. The young woman smiled, squeezed Louis's shoulder, winked at him, and left without another word.

"Didn't I see you with her down at Mad Jack's last week?" Joseph asked with a grin.

"No, you didn't."

"Whatever. Why are we here again?"

"Do you have someplace else to be?"

"Well, the archives are busy this time of day, Louis."

Cardinal Wickham frowned. "Tell me, Joseph. Do you *want* me to destroy your life? Do you *want* me to tell the world everything I know about you and your past? Or do you want to shut up, sit there, listen to what I have to say, and be the next pope?"

The smirk on Joseph's face faded. "You know I would love nothing more."

"Then I suggest you reexamine your attitude toward me— toward a lot of things, actually."

"And how are you going to make sure that I'm elected?"

"First of all, starting tomorrow you will be conducting daily Mass in St. Peter's Basilica."

"But what about the archives—"

"I thought you were here to listen," Wickham said with a disapproving look.

"My apologies."

"You have been transferred. I took the liberty to request that you and your whole office be moved to the papal apartment. They should be gathering your things"—he looked at his watch—"right about now."

"But I can't just move in—" Joseph held up his hands in surrender at Wickham's rolling eyes. "Sorry. Go ahead."

"His Holiness has been in office a long time. He is getting old. His health, however, has never been an issue. With that being the case, no one has even thought about who the next pope should be. Being the Vatican's secretary of state, I hold a lot of influence in matters such as that. And"—he sat back in his chair, folded his arms, and smiled—"I happen to have a lot of dirt on a lot of people. It will be easy for me to persuade the other cardinals to vote you in.

"Now the big problem will be public opinion. Nobody knows you. We are going to change that. That is why I have this."

Wickham stood up and pulled a piece of paper out of his pants pockets. He unfolded it and handed it to Joseph. Joseph read it carefully. He looked up at Louis and smiled.

"Pope Paul didn't write this. Did he?"

"No." Wickham smirked. "I did. But no one else knows that."

"No one will believe it. He and I hardly know each other."

"Past events can be fabricated, Joseph. You of all people should know that. I'll just take the liberty of spreading a few rumors of how you and Paul have long been friends. That he had you in the archives working on a top-secret study for him. I'll tell people that you and he would meet late at night to discuss your findings. By the time I'm done, people will demand that you be the front-runner for the papacy."

Joseph stared at Wickham skeptically. "There's still the issue of this letter." He held up the crinkled piece of paper. "Who's honestly going to believe His Holiness wrote this?"

"They will when they see his signature at the bottom. And besides, by this time tomorrow, he'll be so incoherent, no one will be able to question him to find out otherwise."

"And you can get him to sign it?" Joseph asked with anticipation.

"Joseph, my boy, I could get him to jump through a burning hoop wearing a tutu and combat boots if I told him it's for the good of the church."

"All of this has to do with *him*, doesn't it? He's the reason we're getting rid of Paul, right? I mean, when it comes down to it, *he* is the one who wants Paul gone, right?"

"Actually, I want that incessant windbag gone, but in the big picture, yes. But as far as we're concerned, it has to do with that scroll and all of the power we will obtain when we have it."

"He'll want it," Joseph said matter-of-factly.

"Of course he will. He has wanted it for two thousand years."

Joseph studied the other man. "You aren't planning to let him have it, are you?"

"It was given to the disciple John, supposedly by God Himself. Can you imagine the power that thing holds? I can. And it's here, now. Not some promise of some fairy tale that we may someday see if we're good, deny ourselves all of the riches of this world, live like paupers, and put every other human being's needs before ourselves. If *he* gets the scroll first, he wins. We can't let that happen. The Brotherhood *will* have that scroll."

"But what about *him*? What will he do to us?"

"He's not God, Joseph. What can he do? He's been trying to get his hands on the thing for two thousand years. Nothing. I've been at it for less than twenty years, and it's within my grasp. Now, who do you think is better at this, me or him?"

"We've pledged to serve him."

Wickham slammed his fist down hard on the table. "I serve no one but myself!"

A few people turned their heads to look at the commotion.

"Do you really think that we, with all of our technology, resources, and ability, can't outwit some college girl?" Wickham asked. "She has no idea what she has. We do. Even if she did know what she has, she doesn't know what it's for. When we have it, we will find out its secrets. And then we will have its power."

"He scares me, Louis. The other night, in the alley, he showed me things I could never have imagined. I could feel his power—power that he promised me if I serve him."

Wickham stood and pulled his billfold from his jacket. He grabbed some cash and threw it on the table. Throwing Joseph a disgusted look, he threatened, "If I find that scroll, you'd better fear *me*."

CHAPTER 29

Pau, France

Jonathan pulled the car up in front of the small brownstone. This was a semidecent neighborhood. Someone would surely notice a guy with a bloody tourniquet wrapped around his leg hobbling down the street. An older woman walking her dog passed by. She didn't even turn her head to see who was in the dust-covered sedan. Judging by the way she was dressed, he figured she was probably too snooty to acknowledge anyone unless they were wearing Gucci or Prada and sporting a Rolex. Even the little dog was wearing a neck scarf and a sun visor with little rhinestones.

Jonathan snorted and mumbled to himself, "Some people. . ." He waited for the pair to pass then opened the door. He swung his leg out onto the pavement and pushed himself up, using the steering wheel for leverage. He took off his jacket and wrapped it around his waist. It did a pretty good job of hiding the bum leg.

He took one last look around for any nosy neighbors who might be peeking out their windows. None. Good. He took a deep breath and started up the steps, wincing with every one.

By now the leg had gone numb. He had tied the tourniquet as tight as he could get it, and the circulation had been cut off. The pain was coming from his hip and back. With every step, a sharp, knifelike stab shot through him.

At the entryway, before he could push the little black doorbell, the front door swung open to reveal a short, balding man dressed in a white lab coat and wearing square bifocals. A stethoscope hung from his neck. He looked at Jonathan without speaking then shifted his gaze to the bleeding leg. He turned around and walked back inside, leaving the door open for Jonathan to follow him.

Jonathan followed the little man down a hallway and through a set of rooms, all of which looked like some kind of medieval torture chamber. Scalpels, knives, IV tubes, and things he didn't even want to ask about were scattered along the way. The maze ended in a room no bigger than an average bedroom at the end of the hall.

The doctor laid out a few tools and small vials of what looked like medicine along with some strips of gauze and a metal bucket. He gestured to a small cot.

Jonathan hobbled to it and sat down. He was starting to feel a little nervous about Dieter's recommendation. "So you must be Henri Rhette."

"Lucky for you," said the man. He turned to face Jonathan, holding a syringe filled with something. He started to push Jonathan's sleeve up and wipe his arm with a cotton swab.

"What, exactly, is that?" Jonathan asked.

"Just something to help with the pain, my friend."

Jonathan was starting to get a bad feeling about this, but at this point, he didn't have much choice.

The needle penetrated his skin, and a burning sensation ran up his arm. In seconds his head was swimming. He didn't know what the doctor had just given him, but he was pretty sure it wasn't a pain killer. Everything began to get blurry. The room was spinning. He felt like he was going to pass out. He could hear the little man start to laugh, even though the voice sounded like it was coming from far away. Something was definitely not right. Dieter had set him up.

Jonathan was a professional assassin. He should have known better than to let someone inject him with something without checking it out first. Now he was in trouble.

The little man began to tie him down with straps. He'd already gotten Jonathan's legs and now nearly had his arms. He had to think fast, which was nearly impossible with his head swimming like this. He tried to force his eyes open and look around. Where was his gun? In his bag, halfway across the room. That wasn't going to work. What else? There! On the table beside him was some kind of metal bar. It was about two feet in length and a quarter inch thick. He had no idea what it was. A torture device, more likely than not.

He only had a few more seconds. The little man was almost done with his left arm. He would be coming around the table for the right one any second now.

He tried to lift his free arm. It was so heavy. What had this guy given him? He gritted his teeth and willed every last ounce of strength he had. He watched with blurred vision as his hand fumbled around on the table, trying to grasp the steel bar. There! He had it. He took a deep breath and grunted as he swung his arm over his shoulder, trying to put all of the force he could into the blow.

The doctor, who had been finishing up tightening the strap on his left arm, saw the steel bar too late. He tried to lift his own arm up to cushion the blow to his head but never made it. There was a loud *thwack* as he blacked out and slumped heavily to the floor.

Jonathan's breathing became labored now. He felt like he was going to pass out. He couldn't. Not yet. He wasn't sure exactly how hard he hit the little man. Obviously enough to knock him out. But for all he knew, the little man was merely stunned. He needed to make sure the fat, little fellow wouldn't come around anytime soon.

It took him another three minutes just to untie himself from the straps. Dexterity wasn't exactly his strong suit right now. Whatever the doc gave him was pretty powerful.

With the last strap hanging loosely, he tried to stand up. That was a mistake. As soon as his feet hit the ground, the whole floor turned upside down on him. The brown, shag carpet came at him like a semitruck, smacking him in the forehead as he fell. He was now lying down, his eyes inches from the doctor's motionless body.

He placed his hands, palm down, on the carpet and took another deep breath. With all the strength he could muster, he pushed himself up onto his knees. He reached for the cot and slowly pulled himself up once again.

He took a second for his equilibrium to stabilize. Then using the cot as a crutch, he moved himself around to the other side of the room, where the counter with all of the medicine vials was. He picked each one up, reading the label, until he found what he was looking for. Adrenaline. He had done enough interrogations to know that no matter how doped up someone was, a good shot of adrenaline could bring them around to at least a semi-coherent state.

He found an unused syringe, still in the plastic wrapping, and opened it. He turned around and stole a glance at the unconscious Henri Rhette. Still not moving. Good. He stuck the needle in his arm and injected himself with the thick liquid.

By the time he pulled the needle out of his arm, he could already feel his senses coming around. He wasn't completely sober, but it was enough to do what he had to do.

He walked back around the cot to where the doctor lay. He grabbed him by his hair and dragged him up onto the cot. One by one, he fastened the straps, just as the man had tried to do to him. Only then did he check for a pulse. There was one, however very faint.

Now, to dress his own wounds. He found a hemostat and a scalpel. He doused his leg with alcohol and slammed his fist down hard on the counter as the pain of the disinfectant washed over his leg. He searched the counter for some morphine. He didn't see any. There was probably something else there that would help the pain, but he was no doctor himself. He didn't recognize any other labels. He'd just have to do it the hard way.

He sat down in a chair and propped his leg up on a little footstool that sat beside the cot. He took the scalpel and made a small incision just above the bullet hole in order to have enough room to maneuver the hemostat around.

With gritting teeth, he sucked in a deep breath and dug the hemostat into his leg. Instantly, more blood started flowing. The pain was almost enough to make him pass out. He blinked his eyes a couple of times and shook his head, trying to clear the cobwebs. He reached for some gauze and wiped away the blood.

The hemostat found the bullet. Luckily, it wasn't buried too deep. It seemed to have lodged itself just above the muscle. That was good. No permanent damage. He'd be really sore for a few weeks, but that was about the extent of it, barring an infection.

His hands shook as he maneuvered the tool around to get a grip on the tiny piece of shrapnel. Finally, he had it. Once again he gritted his teeth as he pulled the bullet out. He looked at it for a second, studying the size. It seemed like a small caliber. Probably a .38.

He threw the small bullet into the metal pan sitting beside him. Then he reached for the needle and thread. Now this was something he was familiar with. On more than one occasion he had given himself stitches. Being a professional hit man, he couldn't afford to go to the hospital frequently. They would accumulate too many records on him, and eventually he would be found. Given his job, he was always hiding out in some dank, dark, and usually dangerous place. Accidents such as cuts and scrapes were frequent. For that reason, he learned at a young age how to do a few necessary things, one of which was giving himself stitches.

It took him all of five minutes to sew up the gash. He cleaned and dressed the newly patched wound. Now he could turn his attention back to the so-called doctor.

Henri Rhette was about to wish he'd never opened his front door.

CHAPTER 30

The Vatican

Cardinal Joseph McCoy sat at his new desk in his new office in the papal apartment building. Wickham had worked fast—lunch, meeting, new office. No one questioned the move. No one ever questioned anything ordered or approved by Wickham. They merely went about their daily business as if nothing had changed.

Joseph had just finished straightening some loose papers on his desk when the door to his new office swung open.

"Joseph," Cardinal Wickham said, striding into the office, "what do you think?" Wickham swept his arms in a big arc around the room.

"I like it rather well. Thank you."

"My pleasure. It seems that your moving in here has caused quite a buzz."

"I don't know about that. But I have, however, heard numerous quips about some letter the pope gave you to circulate around to the senior cardinals." He smiled.

"The delightful part is that no one has even seen the letter yet.

There is only rumor of the letter. And everybody already assumes that Paul wrote it. I didn't even have to tell them. Which, by the way, is perfect, because when I tell them the pope did, indeed, write it, they'll just take it as fact. There won't be any question. My word is gold around here. You know that."

"So when will you unveil the letter?"

"I actually have a meeting with the senior staff in about two hours. I will stop off to see Paul, have him sign it, then go to my meeting, where I will show them the letter. After that, we wait."

"For what?"

Even to Joseph, Wickham's smile seemed particularly nasty. "For the obvious."

"You mean. . ."

"It shouldn't be more than a couple more days. He's very sick. And the doctors haven't got a clue as to what's going on. They still think it's the flu. Poor man. If only he'd listened to me ten years ago when I told him the medical staff here wasn't what they should be, he wouldn't be in this predicament."

Joseph sat quietly for a moment. It was really happening. Louis was actually going to kill the most beloved religious figure in all the world. And then he, Cardinal Joseph McCoy, would become the next pope. He was filled with a mix of emotions—excited, nervous, and scared all at the same time. He sat back in his chair, folded his hands, and rested them under his chin. He looked up at Louis, who was standing on the other side of his desk, arms folded, wearing a menacing-looking grin. This was it. No turning back. "Well then," he said, "I guess you'd better be going to see the pope."

Pope Paul VII was sound asleep when Wickham entered his room. There were a few doctors and nurses milling about but doing nothing really. They were only there in case the pontiff woke up and decided he needed something.

He asked them if he could be alone with the patient for a few minutes to discuss church business. The medical staff filed out of the room, one by one.

When the door closed, Wickham reached into his pocket and brought out the small cylinder that carried the killer liquid. He unscrewed the lid and put a few drops of the agent into the already hanging IV drip. It was the fourth method this week. He was being smart by changing it up. A cup of tea here, a spiked IV there. No one would be able to pinpoint one definite source of the poison were they ever to discover it at all. Once he finished, he placed the cylinder back inside his pocket. He waited a few seconds then gently nudged the arm of the sleeping pope.

"Paul," he said. The pope's eyes fluttered. "Paul, it's me, Louis. Do you feel like waking up for a few minutes? There are a few things I need to discuss with you. Very important."

Pope Paul VII's eyes opened fully now. Without moving his head, he scanned the room to see what was going on. He noticed that no one, other than he and Wickham, were in the room. He licked his dry, cracked lips and mumbled, "Water."

Wickham took the pitcher of water and two paper cups from the bedside table and poured. He figured he could use one as well. He reached his hand behind the old man's neck and helped him into a sitting position, then handed him the cup of water.

"Thank you," the raspy voice replied.

"My pleasure."

"I'm so tired, Louis."

"I know. You need to rest."

"This flu. . .I've always been in good health. Perhaps it is something else that is wrong."

"While I'm certainly no doctor, I think everything will be fine. Just do what they tell you, and you'll be up and about in no time."

Pope Paul covered his mouth and began to cough. His breaths were coming in short gasps. "What was it you needed? Church business, did you say?"

Wickham nodded his head and leaned over to the side to grab his briefcase. He reached inside and pulled out a stack of papers. "I just need your signature on some end-of-month statements and a couple of requisition forms. It should only take a couple of seconds."

Pope Paul VII began coughing again and nodded his head. He motioned with his hand for Wickham to hand him the papers. "Could you hand me my glasses over there?" He pointed to an end table.

Wickham turned around in his chair and saw the glasses sitting on top of the wooden table. He looked to see where the pope was focusing his attention. The barely lucid man seemed to be staring into outer space. He stood up and walked behind his chair, swiftly palmed the reading glasses, and stuck them in his pocket. Then, moving a few magazines and loose papers aside, he said, "I'm afraid I don't see your glasses. Maybe one of the nurses put them away so that they don't get broken. Why don't I just put your hand on the line that you need to sign, and you can write. Surely you don't need them for just that. Do you?" He tried to sound as polite and caring as he could.

"I suppose not."

Wickham tried not to laugh. If this were any easier, he might get bored.

He put the ink pen in the pope's hand and grabbed the old man's frail wrist to move it to the bottom of the first page. "There you go. Now just sign right here."

With a shaky hand, the pope scratched out his signature. Wickham removed the top sheet and repeated the process. The first four documents actually were requisition forms for one thing or another. The fifth and final one was the letter. And Pope Paul, by his own admission of not being able to read anything without his glasses, didn't even bat an eye when Wickham stuck it in front of him. He just waited for the cardinal to move his hand until it was in the proper position. Then he signed his name.

CHAPTER 31

Somewhere over Western Europe

The engines of the G-5 roared as the private plane passed over northern France at forty-five thousand feet. Hale had informed everyone they should be touching down in London in just under an hour.

Anna and Jason sat beside each other in the big leather chairs that took up most of the forward cabin. Anna couldn't think of any reason to delay the conversation she knew Jason was itching to have with her. "So, what do you think of all of this?"

"Honestly"—he shrugged his shoulders and lifted his hands, palms up—"I really don't know what to think. I really don't know that much about what's going on. I figured you'd tell me when you were ready."

"Well, now's as good a time as any, I suppose. Let me ask you something."

"Yeah?"

"Ever seen an angel?"

"An angel? Sure. I've seen pictures, paintings. . . Ooh! There was that really cool one in that movie. . .ah, what was it called?" He snapped his fingers trying to remember.

Anna reached for his hand and stopped his fingers from clicking. "No, Jason. I mean a real angel. In person. In the flesh— or whatever they are."

He looked at her quizzically. "You're serious?"

"As a heart attack."

"Then, no. Well, maybe. Once when I was a kid, but I'm not sure. May've been just a weird. . .I don't know."

"Well, I have," she said. Then more to herself, "A couple times, actually."

"Okay," he finally said. "So what's going on?"

Anna took a deep breath and began recounting the story. Fifteen minutes later she had arrived at the present.

Jason didn't speak for a moment. When he did, it was in a restrained tone. "That's the most amazing thing I've ever heard."

"So you believe me?"

"Crazy as that probably makes me, yes. When Hale said it had been given to your family by God Himself, I didn't think he actually meant *by God Himself.* Do you know what this means?"

"Well, I'm not stupid. Yes, I know it's an important scroll."

"That's not what I mean," he said, catching her hand in his own. "Ever heard of Moses' staff? Or maybe the holy spear? The holy grail? The ark of the covenant? Any of that stuff?"

She shrugged. "Sure. Your point?" She felt she should be irritated with him, but all she could feel was that it was a very nice thing to have someone hold her hand.

"My point is this. All of those things I mentioned were given to men by God."

"Okay. . ."

"Okay. Ever heard of going to see an exhibition at a museum

for any of those things?"

"Well, no. I guess I haven't."

"That's because no one has ever found them! As far as anyone knows, they'll never be found. You have the only known artifact in existence that God gave to a human being. That's why you're being shot at! That's why someone's trying to kill you!"

"So I guess it's worth a lot of money, huh?"

"A lot of money—it's priceless!"

"I never thought of it that way. I guess it is. But that's not why someone's trying to kill me."

"What? What do you mean?"

"Well, I don't think that's the *only* reason someone's trying to kill me. I don't think it's about money. I haven't told you everything."

"What do you mean? There's more?"

"Kind of."

"Okay. Let's hear it."

"There's a riddle on the scroll."

Jason chuckled. "A riddle?"

"Yes."

"Anna, do you speak Greek?"

"No. Why?"

"So then, how do you know there's a riddle on the scroll? It would've been written in Greek, or at least Hebrew."

"Ever think my Grandpa could've had it translated, Sherlock?"

"Sorry. So this riddle. . .what does it say?"

"Well, that's just it," Anna said. "It's really weird. I don't even know if you'd call it a riddle. It's just three individual statements. I don't know what to make of them. Neither did Vin."

Jason folded his arms and said, "Humph. Do you want to show it to me? Or am I not allowed to look at it?"

Anna made a very serious face. "Oh no. Didn't anyone tell you?

I'm the only one who can look at it. The rules say that if anyone else looks at it other than me, they'll turn into a pile of ashes!"

Jason was confused. "Didn't you just say that Father Vin looked at it with you?" Before he could even finish, Anna had a grin on her face from ear to ear. He smirked, raised his hand, and said, "Gullible, party of one!"

"Yes, you can look at it," she said. "All I know is that it has to do with religious, biblical stuff. Obviously! I mean look where it came from. And that's precisely the problem. I didn't go to church much when I was a kid, or since I've been an adult, for that matter. So I'm pretty much in the dark about the whole thing."

"Wow. I'm sorry."

She slid her hand free. Pitying Jason wasn't nearly as nice as excited Jason. She didn't need pity just because she'd rarely set foot in church. "Why are you sorry?"

He looked at her freed hand with an expression of regret. "You've lived your whole life without knowing what it's like to know the God of the universe. It's something I deeply cherish, and I'm sorry you haven't had that chance."

What did a girl say to that—"Thanks"? "I'm okay. Just need to figure out this riddle."

"Well then, it's a good thing I came along when I did."

"Why's that? You're a schoolteacher. How's that going to help?'

"I'm a Baptist missionary who happens to teach little French kids English," he corrected her. "And I happen to know a little bit about the Bible."

Anna bit her lip and said, "I'm sorry, Jason. I didn't mean to sound condescending. To be honest with you, I guess I don't really know that much about you, do I? I mean, the only thing I really know is that some angel told me you were supposed to be here. He said you're taking Father Vin's place."

"Two things. First, I didn't know him, but I'm pretty sure I'll never be able to take Father Vin's place. Second, no, I don't guess you do know anything about me. Ever since we've met, we haven't really talked about me. So ask away. I'll tell you anything you want to know."

"Okay. Who are you? Where are you from? How'd you get to France? Where'd you get that little scar above your right eye. . . ?"

"Goodness, woman!" He laughed and held up his hands in surrender. "Do I need to write this down, or can we take them one at a time?"

"Sorry." She chuckled. "You may answer at your own leisure. I yield the floor to the distinguished gentleman from. . ."

"Atlanta, Georgia."

"Yes!" She gave him a mock salute. "Atlanta, Georgia."

"Thank you, madame." He nodded, insinuating a bow. "Well, you know my name, Jason Lang, and that I'm from Atlanta. I'm twenty-four years old. I like long walks on the beach. My favorite color is red. I'm a Capricorn—"

"Okay," she interrupted, "I'm taking back the floor."

"You can't do that!" Jason protested.

"Yes I can," Anna argued. "It's my plane!"

"Well, if it's going to be like that," he said, "then I'm taking my toys and going home!"

Anna smiled. She decided she liked this Baptist missionary who taught English to little French kids. "You make me laugh, Jason Lang. I like that."

"Glad I could be of service, Miss Anna," he said in his best John Wayne voice.

Anna took his hand again. It really was so much better that way. "Today has been a very difficult day for me," she said. "I've been shot at, chased all over a city I'd never been to before today, and worst of all, I lost Father Vin. Five hours ago I thought I was

186

going to just break down and lose it. I have no idea what's going on here. I don't know why I'm even involved in this. I just know I have to be. Does that sound stupid, or what?"

Jason squeezed her hand. "It doesn't sound stupid. As a matter of fact, it's the bravest thing I've ever heard of. I can't imagine going through what you've been through in the last three days. And I know you miss him, but Father Vin is in a much better place. I know that sounds like a stupid cliché, but it's true."

"The angel told me the same thing, so you're off the hook. If an angel says it, it can't be a cliché, right?"

"You're gonna have to tell me more about this angel thing."

"Stick around," she said. "He seems to be showing himself to quite a few people, I've heard. You'll probably see him, too. Now, all kidding aside, I do want to hear your story. You have the floor again."

Jason nodded his head in acceptance and continued. "Like I said, I'm from Atlanta. Marietta, actually. Just north of Atlanta. My mother is a Sunday school teacher at the church I grew up in. My father owns an insurance company. We were the typical middle-American family. I have two older brothers, Jeremy and Joshua, who considered me their human guinea pig. And thus the scar. They talked me into jumping out of a tree when I was six to try out this pair of wings they made. Swore up and down that the wings would work. Needless to say—remember, gullible party of one here—they didn't. I fell twelve feet onto our concrete sidewalk. This little beauty here"—he pointed to the scar—"is just one of many. Like I said, I was the guinea pig."

Anna winced. "Ouch! Did they get in trouble?"

Jason laughed. "Not as much as I did for believing them. Anyway, I gave you the brief version of how I became a missionary. There's a lot of training, book studying, and hands-on work that went along with it. And that's pretty much my life story. Any more questions?"

Anna thought for a second then asked, "Who was your last girlfriend? And why didn't it work out?"

"Julie Buckley. And because I wasn't concerned with driving a Jaguar or living in Buckhead—that's a very wealthy suburb of Atlanta."

"Okay then," Anna said. "I guess that about covers it!"

Jason looked at her quizzically. "So what about you? Who is Anna Riley?"

Anna spent the next fifteen minutes telling Jason about her childhood and growing up in Nashville. She told him about her parents and her grandparents, what she knew of them. She told him about the schools she went to, who her friends were, what she did for fun, and of course, her last boyfriend, who was basically an idiot. She finished by recapping the last few days, which she'd already told him about. Just as she was finishing, Hale's voice came over the intercom to announce that they were about to land in London.

Anna and Jason made sure their seat belts were secure and radioed to the cockpit that they were ready for landing. Hale replied, telling them it should be a smooth descent. They would be on the ground in just a few minutes.

"So what now?" Anna asked, turning her attention back to Jason.

"Well, I guess we should probably get settled in at the safe house. Don't you think?"

"Hey," she said, "you're the bodyguard. You tell me."

"Okay then," he answered, "we'll get settled in at the safe house and then take a look at that scroll. There's something else I forgot to tell you about my childhood."

"Oh yeah? What's that?"

"I've always been pretty good with riddles."

CHAPTER 32

St. Peter's Basilica, the Vatican

The giant sitting in the next to the last pew in the sanctuary wore a huge trench coat and a large-brimmed hat pulled down over his eyes to hide his body and face. He was massive by anyone's standards. Several people, all tourists, were milling around inside the basilica. A couple of them even tried to move closer to him to get a better look, but to no avail. Each time someone would enter his row, he would shift his weight. Just the slightest movement of the giant seemed to unnerve everyone. They would turn back around and move to a different pew. That is, all except one man wearing a custom-tailored three-piece, charcoal, pinstriped suit. He walked through the main entrance and moved directly toward the giant. At the end of the row, he paused, turned, and faced the altar as if he intended to genuflect.

"Ha!" he said, then sat down at the opposite end of the pew from the giant. He never turned to acknowledge him but instead sat picking at his long fingernails and whistling an obnoxiously loud tune.

A few people showed their displeasure with him by turning and frowning at him, giving him a "Shh!" or "Humph!" He squinted his beady little eyes and hissed at each one of them.

The two sat together in the same pew, neither one saying anything for about five minutes. By then the room had mostly cleared out, and there were no people within earshot of the two. Finally, the giant spoke first.

"I hear you're going by 'Prince' these days. Presumptuous, don't you think?"

"My, what a large word, Michael." Prince sneered. "*Pre-sump-tu-ous.* Did you finally enroll in a vocabulary enrichment course? Usually, all you can manage is 'Fear not.' I'm impressed."

"What are you doing here?" Michael asked coldly.

"I could ask you the same question," the other replied. "Shouldn't you be out waging some silly battle or something?"

The giant angel mumbled, more to himself, "Father, just say the word. . ."

"I'm sorry. What was that?" Prince raised his eyebrows and craned his neck toward the giant.

Now Michael pushed back the brim of his hat, showing his emerald green eyes. They were burning with fire. "I said"—he pointed a finger at him—"when He gives me the go-ahead, you'd better hope you can move faster than me!" His voice was now booming, echoing throughout the enormous chapel.

Prince chuckled and brushed a piece of lint off his lapel. "Michael, you and I both know that even if His theory on this whole shebang"—he waved his hand in a circle above his head—"is correct, you are going to be the last one He sends after me. We all know what the fairy tale says. His high and mighty Son gets all the glory. Remember?"

"Thanks be to God!" Michael raised his hands in praise.

"So what *are* you doing here anyway?"

"Not that it's any of your business, Lucifer, but I have a new assignment."

"Really?" He drew the word out in a long breath. "And what would that be?"

"It's classified."

"Well, we can all just about guess that it has to do with me and that scroll. Let me save you the trouble. Go back and tell your *Daddy* that I *will* have it. And when I do, I win. I may not know what exactly is on that scroll, but I have a good idea what it's for. And as long as I have it. . . Well then, I guess you're just going to be waiting around a lot. Huh?"

"Lucifer, I swear if I could—"

"Uh, uh, uh! Don't swear! He doesn't like that." He made an "Oops!" look with his face. "That's what got me into trouble. Remember? Ha, ha, ha!"

In the time it takes a lightning bolt to streak across the sky, Michael shot across the pew and had Lucifer by the throat. "You listen to me, you sick piece of garbage!" he said through clenched teeth. "Your days are numbered. You will never have that scroll. I have pledged to the Father that you shall never lay your hands on it. Do you understand me?"

Michael squeezed harder now, cutting off Lucifer's airway. He wanted to end this right now. And he could. Lucifer was nothing more than an angel, just like him. Though God did give him authority over the flesh of this earth, he was still an angel. And Michael could destroy him.

But he knew his place. If he were to do such a thing, he would be no better than Lucifer. He let go of the fallen angel, but not before he gave him a swift, hard right cross to the face.

Lucifer never batted an eye. He ran his fingers through his hair and straightened his suit coat and tie that Michael had disturbed. "Temper, temper. You sure you don't want to come over to my side? I could use a warrior like you. You know, between the two of us, we could really wreak some havoc down here!"

Michael had regained his composure. He stared down his sworn enemy and said matter-of-factly, "Thanks, but not interested."

Lucifer shrugged his shoulders and said, "Oh well. Too bad. We could've been great together."

Michael just stared at him.

Lucifer stood up and stepped out of the pew. He buttoned his coat and said, "As riveting as this conversation is, I've got an important meeting to attend. Besides, this place gives me the creeps." He laughed and shivered mockingly. He was halfway to the door when Michael called to him. He turned back around to face the great archangel, who was now standing an inch away from him. Michael towered over him by a good eight inches. "Yes," he said. "What can I do for you?"

"Nothing," Michael replied. "I just wanted to correct you."

"Oh? How's that?"

"On that day, the day when you will fail and be destroyed, it will be the Son who slays you. But you forgot what it says in the twentieth chapter of Revelation—and I quote: 'I saw an angel coming down from heaven, holding in his hand the key to the bottomless pit and a great chain.'" Michael's face lit up with a big smile. He turned around and started walking away from Lucifer. Halfway down the aisle, he turned back and taunted, just loud enough for Lucifer to hear, "I'll give you one guess who that's talking about!"

CHAPTER 33

The Vatican

Six armed Swiss guards stood watch at the front entrance of the papal audience hall, located just south of St. Peter's Basilica. They had been informed of nothing except that their presence was wanted and that no one, except for the people whose names were on the list they each had a copy of, were allowed to enter. It was, they were told, a matter of Vatican national security.

Cardinal Wickham was the last to arrive. Naturally. He never arrived first at a meeting that he called. He liked to make a grand entrance. Flamboyancy was far more interesting than decorum.

With quick steps, he walked across the Piazza del Santo Uffizio toward the hall. He didn't even acknowledge the guards as he sidestepped his way past them and in through the front entrance. Neither did the guards acknowledge him. Wickham was the most well-known persona in the entire Vatican, next to the pontiff. The guards were well aware who had called this meeting of the senior cardinals. And each of them at some point in time had had the displeasure of being chastised by him for one thing or another. His arrogance and temper were also well known.

Wickham found the other cardinals all sitting down waiting for him, the room filled with the quiet buzz of conversation. He made his way to the front. "Ahem."

Everyone quickly quieted and focused on the secretary of state. Wickham knew that while many of them were annoyed that they had been summoned to attend, interrupting whatever business they already were engaged in, none of them would have missed this meeting for the world. His rumors had been flying like a migration of birds. They'd come to learn about the mysterious letter. And he was not about to disappoint them.

"I'm sure you've heard about a certain letter today," he began. "I will get to that in a moment."

Heads turned and murmurs quickly scattered throughout the rows of seats. Every last one of them was pathetically predictable.

"Gentlemen, please. . ." He waited for the men to quiet down again. "Thank you. Now if I may continue, I will keep this brief.

"We all know the physical condition of our supreme leader. To put it plainly, the pontiff is not well."

Again the crowd became vocal.

Wickham held his hands up, palms outward, to silence the men. "I, as well as a few of you, have made daily visits to the pope's chambers. He is incoherent, has trouble focusing, and sleeps nearly all day. It saddens me to see such a great man suffer like this."

"What are the doctors saying?" The voice came from one of the back rows.

"They say they are doing everything they can. We all know that the pontiff's medical staff is top rate. However, barring a miracle, it's time we face reality: our beloved pope may not make it through. We have to be prepared to act fast if that course of events should happen."

This time the murmuring broke out into a full ruckus. Some began to stand and turn around to face other colleagues. Others started raising their hands to the heavens, saying short prayers. Still others just sat and let the information they had just heard sink in.

Wickham allowed the small outburst this time. One could hardly speak openly about the death of the pope and not let the natural reaction of such comments take its course. When he felt that he had let enough time pass, he stepped back in front of the small lectern and spoke again. "Which brings me to the letter."

The room fell silent as quickly as it had erupted. Everyone retook their seats and stared quietly ahead.

"Gentlemen, let me explain." He pushed the lectern aside and walked to the edge of the stage. He took a big breath, as if he were resigning to an idea he wasn't in agreement with, then stepped down from the stage and leaned against it. Silence rattled throughout the auditorium.

"A couple of days ago, His Holiness called me into his office. We spoke about how he was feeling, and then he gave me this." He reached inside his overcoat pocket and produced the now famous letter. Every eye was glued to it.

"Our beloved," he continued, "told me it could be the most important letter he's ever written in his entire life. He said the fate of the church could be determined by how we—that is, all of us—react to it. Given his condition, he insisted that I take it. Though it gives me no joy to see him decline so quickly, I'm glad he had the foresight to plan ahead for this eventuality." Wickham hoped he looked mournful enough. "What I am about to tell you, gentlemen, is extremely top secret. If I find out that any of you let word of this slip, it will be grounds for immediate excommunication from the faith. Is that understood?"

The men, most with their eyes wide and mouths open, nodded in unison.

"Good. Then we can continue. It seems that our beloved pope has been busy these last years. Apparently he has come across a document that was written by Jesus Himself." Once again the murmurs started up, but he continued, talking over the buzz. "And also apparently this document is very controversial. It's controversial because it's incomplete. Only half of the page was found. Now, I haven't been informed of what exactly the document says. I only know that what is on it, thus far, could destroy the church as we know it if it got into the wrong hands. It could be exploited to do great damage to our faith. The pope believes that the rest of the document will clarify the first half, not destroying our faith, but making it indisputable. And he believes he knows where it is." Wickham returned to stand behind the lectern on the stage.

"For the last three years, His Holiness has had someone working on this project for him. He has become a great friend to Pope Paul and is an extraordinary man. Most of you would know him in passing. His name is Joseph McCoy. Don't bother to look around. I've excused him from this meeting for obvious reasons. Do not bother to ask him what it is he is researching for the pontiff. He has taken a vow of secrecy. He will only talk about it with the Holy Father." Wickham held up the letter. "And that is what the first part of this letter is about. The next part even I found hard to accept. But, as my duty to the Holy See, as well as to our pontiff, I will reveal the rest of the letter. I think it would be better if I read it in his own words rather than paraphrase."

In a clear voice, Wickham read the words that would open the door for his dearest dreams to come true.

*. . .and so my brethren, it is with a heavy heart that I ask
you to consider my request. I, probably better than anyone,
understand that what I ask of you is unheard of. However,
having read the first part of my letter, you can surely see the
importance of my request. The entire fate of the church could
depend on this. There is only one man who knows every detail
of this document and what it represents to the church, other
than me. The importance of what he knows and what he has
seen could save our faith.*

*Therefore, brothers, I humbly ask that in the event of my
untimely death, you would appoint as my successor Cardinal
Joseph McCoy."*

May God be with you in your decision.

Pope Paul VII

Wickham set the letter down on the lectern and waited for the
turmoil he knew was coming.

"That's outrageous!" someone yelled.

"Who does he think he is?" cried someone else.

They really were all so very predictable.

The room became chaotic. Everyone was up, out of his seat,
and weighing in on the situation. Wickham was in awe of his own
performance. He was bursting on the inside. He felt like he had
just won the lottery. It was a performance worthy of an Oscar. It
took him a full five minutes to call the meeting back to order.

The members of Wickham's secret brotherhood sat there
holding their tongues. They knew never to question Wickham.
Especially in public. They glanced at one another, silently speaking
their thoughts. Wickham would have some explaining to do at
their next meeting. They tried to hide their anxiousness and look
as surprised at the news as the rest of the clergy.

"Gentlemen! Please!" Wickham yelled. "Take your seats. This is not a circus. We are not children. Let's act accordingly."

Finally, the room was restored. "Thank you. Now, I know how all of you feel. I felt the same way when I first read the letter. That is why I waited until this evening to tell you all about it. I wanted to spend some time in prayer and think about what Pope Paul had written." He paced in front of them, taking on a professorial air. "Yes, it is an absurd request. We all know that. But look who it came from. Pope Paul is one of the most beloved popes in the history of the office. He is a great man. Each of you would gladly lay down your life for him. Am I correct? Consider that fact as you debate what it is he is asking. Do you honestly think that Pope Paul VII would make a request like this if he didn't think the life of the church depended on it? If that man, lying on his death bed, thinks that our way of life depends on Joseph McCoy being the next pope, then how can I disagree? I will go on record right now by saying that if anything should happen to him, I will do everything in my power to see to it that Joseph McCoy is elected the next pontiff. And I would hope and expect that you all would do the same. That is all, gentlemen. Dismissed."

Everyone in the room remained silent as they filtered out through the side exits. Wickham sat and watched as they each left. There was definitely a heavy scent about the place. He may as well have dropped a bomb on the Sistine Chapel. The effect wouldn't have been any less surprising.

Wickham was about to leave, thinking he was the last one in the building, when he noticed a shadow sitting in the back. The man stood up and began clapping his hands, giving a standing ovation. "Bravo! Bravo! Louis, I couldn't have said it any better myself. I do believe you had them eating out of the palm of your hand."

Wickham recognized the voice and felt beads of sweat on the back of his neck. "What are you doing here?" he asked shakily. "How did you get in?"

"Louis, do I really have to explain that to you again?" He walked to the front of the room. "I'm the Prince of Darkness. I can go anywhere I want. This is my world. Remember? Where's my scroll?"

"I'm working on it."

"Well, you see, Louis, I have a new problem now. Do you know what it is? Of course you don't. You're only a stupid human. A glorified monkey. I'm sorry. I should know better than to give your race the benefit of the doubt. I'll just tell you. I just had a nice little meeting of my own. Totally unscheduled, of course. Nonetheless, it was necessary."

He put his arm around Wickham's shoulder as if they were old buddies. Wickham wanted to vomit.

Prince's fingers dug into Wickham's arm. "You see, one of my faithful servants informed me that someone very important from my world stopped by today. His name is Michael. Ever heard of him?" He let his eyes get narrow and said, "I cannot afford for you to blow this, Louis."

"I'll get the scroll. Don't worry."

"Oh, you know what, Louis. I really don't doubt that. I'm sure you will. What I want to make sure of is that you know who it belongs to when you do find it. You *do* know who it belongs to, don't you? Or will I have to remind you?" He turned and walked away without looking back.

CHAPTER 34

London, the Safe House

The driver dropped Anna and Jason off in front of a two-story, two-bedroom flat on a street called Tufton Court, just west of the House of Parliament. It was a quiet street. A few children were still outside playing. Several couples walked hand in hand, probably out for an evening stroll.

Jason was the first to speak as the driver retrieved their bags out of the trunk. "Not bad, huh?"

Anna nodded in approval. "Yeah. It looks like my grandpa had pretty good taste. Wish I'd known about this place before. I might've spent some time here."

"Well, I guess it's yours now," said Jason. "You can spend as much time here as you want. Let's go inside. You got the keys?"

Again Anna nodded her head. "Hale gave them to me when we left the airport. You'd be surprised what all is in that little safe on that plane."

"I'm sure. Speaking of Hale, where is everybody? Aren't he and the others staying here with us?"

"No. He said they never stay with us. They have their own place a few blocks away. Don't worry. He said that he has eyes on us at all times. Apparently I have a ten-person team assigned to me here in London. It's one of the few cities where I have that privilege. I guess my grandpa stayed here quite a bit. They're probably watching us right now."

As they walked into the foyer, Jason let out a low whistle at the same time Anna murmured, "Wow!"

A beautiful crystal chandelier towered over them, glistening with shards of light reflecting off the vaulted marble archway. The foyer had hardwood floors that gave way to hand-cut tile, as the entryway ended with a two-step drop into what looked like a formal living room covered in lush cream carpet. A bookcase took up one wall with a rolling ladder that went back and forth the entire length of the shelves. A dark red leather chair sat along the other wall, while a matching sofa rested comfortably in the middle of the room. There was a fireplace, complete with a black, wrought-iron grate and poker set tipped with gold handles. Above the fireplace hung a painting that Anna recognized.

"How about that?" She pointed at the painting. "I own a Van Gogh."

After thoroughly checking out the downstairs, they headed upstairs to see what surprises awaited them there. They found two bedrooms, both master suites. Each was decorated differently, but both were equally fit to house royalty. Each had a master bath, complete with whirlpool tub and separate shower, dual vanities, and heated towel racks. And each had beautiful french doors that led out onto a balcony. The views from both balconies were extraordinary. From the east bedroom, you could see the Thames River, the Westminster Abbey Museum, the House of Parliament, and the famous Big Ben. The west bedroom overlooked Victoria

Street. In the near distance you could see the beautiful St. James's Park. A little farther west, and farther off in the distance, stood Buckingham Palace.

After their tour of the flat, Anna and Jason both agreed that there were probably some nicer places they could be stuck in, but it would be hard to find one.

Anna grabbed her bags from Jason and threw them on the bed in the east bedroom and said, "Okay. You can have the Queen and Prince Charles. I'm taking Big Ben."

"Fine by me," Jason said. "I just want to take a hot shower and let my muscles relax."

"Yeah, that sounds great," Anna said. "I think I'll take one, too. Why don't we meet downstairs in, like, fifteen minutes. I'll show you the scroll."

"That sounds good," Jason said. He stood there with his lips drawn and his brows furrowed, as if he was trying to remember something.

"What's wrong?" Anna asked.

"Well, I just realized something. In all the chaos that we've been through today, I just left."

"What do you mean?"

"I mean, I just followed you out of the church in Pau and left. I don't have anything. No clothes, no toothbrush, no razor, no anything. Just this." He pointed to the clothes he was wearing.

"This place looks like it's pretty well lived in. Maybe there are some of Vin's or my grandpa's clothes in one of the closets. Let's look."

They found a couple of pairs of sweatpants and a few long-sleeved T-shirts. Jason said that he could wear them for the night, but tomorrow they were going to have to go shopping.

"No problem," she said. "I just happen to know about some

202

really nice places here."

"How's that?" Jason asked. "I thought you'd never been here before."

"Any woman with half a sense of fashion knows about shopping in London."

"Okay," he said, smirking. "I'm sorry. I shall never again question your authority on matters of clothing."

"Good. Then I don't want to hear any arguing when I pick out some cool outfits for you tomorrow."

"What's wrong with the way I'm dressed?" He crossed his arms as if offended, but a tiny wink gave him away.

"Nothing. . .as long as you don't mind looking like a schoolteacher."

"I am a schoolteacher."

"Yes, but you also look like one—which is the problem."

"How is that a problem?"

"Well, I thought missionary schoolteachers were supposed to be adventurous."

"We are."

"Well, Indiana Jones, you don't look that adventurous with your black dress pants, red button-down Gap shirt, and Steve Madden loafers." She motioned with her hand to the clothes he currently had on, and then she folded her arms and waited for a reply.

"I'm going to go take a shower now," he said, laughing. "I'll see you in fifteen." He backed out of the hallway and into the bedroom he was going to be sleeping in. Still staring at Anna, he nodded with a smart-aleck grin and said, "Buh-bye!"

Anna laughed as she heard the *click* of Jason's door when it shut. She walked into her own bedroom and shut the door. She opened her bag and got a fresh change of clothes. She was going to need to go shopping for herself pretty soon. She was almost out of clean things to wear. Good thing she noticed a washing machine and dryer downstairs. Maybe she could throw a load of clothes in tomorrow before she and Jason went shopping.

She opened the bag that held the scroll and pulled out the box. She lifted the lid and stared down into its contents. Yep. Still there. She left it open as she headed for the shower. She hoped Jason really was good at riddles. Guess she would soon find out.

She was just turning on the water in her shower when she heard the faint ringing of the satellite phone in her purse. She hurried out of the bathroom, grabbed it, and pushed the SEND button.

"Hello?" she said.

"Hey, Anna. It's Hale. Just making sure you and Jason got settled in."

"Yeah. We're good. I was just getting ready to get cleaned up. We're going to spend the evening trying to figure out what's going on with this whole thing. Jason's in the shower right now."

"How are you two getting along?"

"I like him, Hale. He's very sweet. I mean, how many people do you know that would risk their life, like he did, for someone they don't even know?"

"He's been chosen for this, Anna. Just like you have been."

"Yeah, I guess so. It's just hard to comprehend. You know?"

"It'll get easier. God will give you a peace about all of this. Soon it will be like you've been doing this for years."

"It already feels like it."

Hale laughed. "Don't worry, Anna. This will all calm down. It's not always like this."

"Well, just as long as I know you've got my back, I think I can handle it."

"Don't worry, we do. Your team is already in place. They've had you since we left the airport. They're pretty sure no one's following you. You should be safe, but don't be careless. As you well know, things can change pretty quickly around here."

"Yeah, I know."

"All right. You two have a good evening. I'll see you in the morning. I will be bringing the team leader over to meet you. He wants to brief you on how they will be working."

"That sounds fine, Hale. Just not too early. I think I want to sleep in. I'm pretty exhausted."

"I know, kiddo. How's about eleven?"

"That'll be good. It'll give us time to get up and eat a good breakfast. We're going to have a busy day tomorrow."

"Oh yeah? What's on the agenda?"

"Shopping, dude! Shopping!"

"Great town for it."

"Yeah, I know. Besides, Jason doesn't have anything but the clothes on his back."

"Did you check the closets? I think there's some stuff in there. That reminds me. How do you like the place?"

"Are you kidding me? It's amazing! Did you know there's a Van Gogh hanging over the fireplace?"

"Your grandpa bought it a few years ago. He said it reminded him of you. Said Van Gogh was your favorite artist."

Anna was genuinely surprised. "How did he know that?"

"He knew a lot of things about you, Anna. He loved you more than you'll ever know."

Anna let the statement hang there for a minute. Once again, she felt cheated out of a life she never knew she had. "Thank you, Hale. Thank you for everything today."

"Just doing my job. I'll see you tomorrow. Okay?"

Anna hung up the phone, tossed it on the bed, and headed for the shower. This had been the longest day of her life. And as the thick streams of hot water pounded on her shoulders, she felt the tension of the day start to wash away. She wrapped her arms around herself and leaned against the wall. She began to slide down the side of the wall as she thought about everything that had happened today. Her emotions got the better of her, once again, and she let the tears come. She tasted the salt from the tears as the hot water washed them down her face. She cried for a few minutes before she finally stood back up. She placed her hands against the wall and hung her head under the spray to let the hot water massage her neck.

She couldn't remember ever praying by herself. But right now, for the first time, she was about to. She lifted her head up out of the stream of the shower head and closed her eyes.

She told God that she was scared. She told Him that she was willing to take this task that He'd given her. She promised to try to do the best she could with it. And all she asked was that He give her a peace about it. Give her a confidence that she could do it.

As she reached to turn off the water, she felt a heavy, slow wind sweep through the shower. Except it wasn't cold. It was very warm. And it swirled around her for several seconds. Then, just as suddenly as it came, it was gone. And so was the anxiety. And so was the fear. Anna felt as if a huge weight had been lifted off her shoulders.

She thought about Father Vin and smiled. She was genuinely happy that he was no longer stuck here on this earth. And she knew, beyond any shadow of a doubt, that she was the rightful keeper of the scroll. She was filled with a burning desire to solve its mystery. She had been given exactly what she'd asked for.

In a split second, God had answered her prayer. She was a

little freaked out at what had just happened, but she had to admit, it was what she asked for. She just didn't expect something to literally sweep through and take all of her anxiety away. "Wow," she said, looking around the room. "That was pretty cool!"

CHAPTER 35

Paris, France

The evening had settled nicely in the city of romance. Couples strolled the avenues and parks. The lights of the Eiffel Tower could be seen in the distance. The temperature was pleasant for this time of year. And the assassin named Jonathan sat watching it all, nursing his vodka tonic.

Never one to drink regularly—given his job, he needed to stay sharp—he sat in the smoky bar trying to kill the incessant pain that throbbed in his wounded leg. He had found a few painkillers at the doctor's house in Pau, but they had lasted him only a few hours. And he couldn't just walk into a drugstore and pick some up without a prescription. So this was the next best thing. Vodka. Cheap vodka at that.

He had left the doctor's house as quickly as he could, taking care not to be noticed. He called his contact and had the plane waiting for him. He hurried to the airport and climbed aboard the private jet. Without knowing exactly where the girl was headed, he decided to get to the nearest major city he could. Paris.

He did this for three reasons. One, he was vaguely familiar with the city. Two, it was a good place to be—more or less centrally located in Europe—once he found out where the girl had gone. That is, unless she took off halfway around the world.

And three, Remy lived here. He'd have a place to crash. And in the morning, he could get to someone he trusted to take a better look at his leg. As for Dr. Henri Rhette, well, he wouldn't be seeing any more patients. Ever. He would have to remember to give Dieter a call and thank him for the reference. That would probably be an interesting call.

It was getting late, and Jonathan decided to pay for his drink and leave. He threw a few dollars on the bar counter and nodded to the bartender. The bartender didn't even ask if Jonathan wanted any change as he walked over and pocketed the bills.

He stood and walked out the front door and across the street to a pay phone. His cell phone battery was about dead, and he needed to save it. He was expecting an important call at any minute. He stepped inside, pulled the glass door shut, retrieved a few coins from his pocket, threw them in the slot, and punched in a number. The phone rang four times before anyone answered.

"Hello?"

"Remy, it's Jonathan."

"Hey, good-looking. What are you doing?"

"I'm in town and need a place to crash. Can you put me up for the night?"

The female voice on the other end of the line drew in a long breath then let it out. "I suppose so. You're not on the run or anything, are you?"

"No. Just a little banged up. I'm going to need to see someone tomorrow. Your brother still in business?"

"Yes, but it'll cost you."

"How much? I don't have a lot on me right now."

"How bad is it?"

"Not bad. I stitched it up myself. I just want to make sure no infection is going to set in. I'm in the middle of something big, and I need to be operational."

"Okay. Probably a couple hundred."

"That I can do. See you in about twenty minutes."

"You need a ride?"

"No. I'll take a cab."

"Okay."

The line went dead. Jonathan stepped out of the phone booth and hailed the first cab that came by.

He thought about the woman he was going to see. Remy. She was someone he hadn't been in contact with in more than two years. Like him, she was also a professional. A very good one. But with a different style. She was a gorgeous, fiery redhead with a temper that would rival that of Genghis Khan. She was one of the best. Jonathan had worked with her on several assignments.

When they worked together, it was always a prominent male target. Remy would play the role of the seductress, drawing her prey into the lion's den. With her looks and charm, she usually had the target eating out of the palm of her hand and promising her the world within two to three days. That would set up the shot. Jonathan would use her to get the target into place. It was always a good thing, because it put him in total control of where the hit would take place. And they had pulled off countless assassinations.

He hadn't seen or heard from Remy in a while. Last he heard, she was getting out of the business. Too many nightmares. She had enough money to last her a lifetime, and she just wanted to settle down on a tropical beach somewhere. He was actually surprised when she answered the phone. He figured she would've been long gone by now.

At the warehouse-looking apartment, he waited for the driver to pull away before he walked over to the big, garagelike door. A small camera mounted in the corner of the doorway hummed as it moved to point directly at him. It stayed there for a few seconds before he heard the buzzing of the lock. He pulled the lever on the door and slid it open, but not before reaching inside his jacket and pulling out his 9mm and chambering a round. After the good Dr. Rhette, better to be safe than sorry.

He stepped inside and pulled the heavy door shut. He heard the *click* as the lock slid back in place. A single bulb hung from a wire in the ceiling, illuminating a long, narrow hallway. He followed it until he came to a solid steel door. As he was about to push the black buzzer that was mounted on the wall, the door opened. Remy stood there, a .357 Magnum pointed directly at his head.

"Nice to see you too, Remy."

"Let's have it," she said. She stood with her free arm extended, palm up, and wiggling her fingers.

"Have what?"

"The 9 mill. Habits are hard to break, Jonathan. And you have a bad one of standing on one's doorstep holding one behind your back."

"That's a lot of 'ones.'" He laughed.

She didn't. "Now, unless your arm has been grotesquely disfigured in the last two years and is permanently stuck that way, I suggest you take it from behind your back, slowly, and hand me the piece."

Jonathan smiled a big, toothy smile. "Remy, that's why I love you. You always know just how to talk to a guy." Slowly he pulled his arm out from behind his back and let the 9mm dangle from his trigger finger. He extended his arm and handed her the gun.

"Thank you," she said, palming the weapon. "Come on in." She turned and walked inside, leaving Jonathan to follow. "So what brings you to my neck of the woods?"

"Actually," he said, "I was kind of surprised you even answered the phone. I thought you were headed to Tahiti or something."

"I am. Next month."

"Why the wait?"

"Had to tie up a few loose ends."

"For two years? Come on. You can tell me. You were waiting for me to come back and run away with you. Tell the truth." He gave her a sly grin.

"Jonathan, if you and I were the last two people on this earth, one of us would kill the other. And it would probably be me. Killing you. Now, why are you here?"

Jonathan walked over and sat down on the sofa. He propped his leg up on the coffee table and pointed at it. "I just had to give myself a bullet-ectomy. I sewed it up myself, but I need your brother to look at it and make sure everything's all right. I think it'll be fine, but I want to make sure."

"And why did you have to remove a bullet from your own leg? Getting sloppy?"

"Something like that. And I wasn't supposed to be doing it myself. Dieter set me up with a cutter that apparently didn't like me."

Remy gave a throaty laugh. "I think it's Dieter who doesn't like you."

"Yeah. I figured that out about five minutes after I was there. The doctor tried to kill me."

"Compliments of Dieter, of course."

"Of course."

"So what are you into?"

"Can't talk about it. But I might have some work for you later down the road. If you're up to it."

"Who's the mark?"

"My current boss. Has a thing for good-looking ladies such as yourself. And personally, I don't like him very much. He pays well. That's about it."

"Sorry. I'm retired."

"Yeah, I figured you'd say that. Anyway, where's your brother? He coming over tonight?"

"Nope. Said he didn't care if you bled out right here in my living room." She watched as Jonathan rolled his eyes. "But I told him I had a buyer for this place and I didn't want to have to get the carpets recleaned. So he'll be here first thing in the morning."

"Thanks, Remy. Really. I owe you."

"You want to pay me back? After tomorrow, don't ever try to find me. I'm gone. For good this time."

"Fair enough. Thanks."

"Don't mention it." She walked down the hall and opened the door to a closet. She pulled out two pillows and a blanket, carried them back to where Jonathan sat, and threw them at him. "Good night. You're sleeping out here."

She turned around, walked back down the hall, walked into her bedroom, and closed the door. Jonathan heard her slide the dead bolt into place.

He gave a long sigh and fidgeted around with the pillows. He swatted and punched at them until he had them just right. He pulled the blanket up over his head. It wasn't that late, but he was exhausted. He figured he'd just go ahead and go to sleep. That's when he felt the vibrating inside his pocket.

"Hello?" he said, flipping the phone open and pushing the SEND button.

"She's in London."

"Thank you. I'll be there tomorrow." He hung up the phone, smiled, and pulled the covers back up over his head.

London. Now there was a town he hadn't been to in a while.

CHAPTER 36

London, the Safe House

Anna got out of the shower with a renewed vigor. She couldn't explain what happened to her a few minutes ago, but she knew she wasn't crazy either. Her whole outlook had changed. She had a confidence about what she was doing here. She knew she would just have to take it one step at a time, and eventually, she and Jason would figure out what her grandpa had spent his life trying to achieve. She was actually excited about it.

She got dressed, pulled her hair back in a ponytail, brushed her teeth, and hurried downstairs. She found Jason sitting at the desk in the study. He had a pair of black sweatpants and a long-sleeved T-shirt on and was sipping something from a huge coffee mug.

"Whatcha got there?" she asked.

"Only some of the finest hot chocolate I think I've ever tasted."

"Oh yeah? And where did you find that?"

"In the pantry. Would you like some?"

"I would, thank you."

Jason leaned back in his chair and pointed toward the kitchen.

"It's in there. Third shelf down on the left," he said with a playful smile.

"Gee, thanks!" Anna rolled her eyes and started for the kitchen.

Jason stopped her before she took two steps. "Just kidding! Here." He reached to his left and produced another mug, which he had hidden behind a picture frame. "I heard you coming down the stairs. I made you one."

"Thank you," she said sweetly. "You're a scholar and a gentleman." She took the mug from Jason and gave it a taste. "Wow! You weren't kidding! This is great. What kind is it?"

"Actually, it's kind of my own recipe."

"You have a recipe for cocoa?"

"Yep. My mom's. I just happened to find all of the stuff I needed in there to make it."

"Yeah? Like what?"

"Like cocoa powder, milk, and my secret ingredient, freshly ground cinnamon."

"Cinnamon. No kidding." It was more a statement than a question.

"Yup. Cinnamon."

"Well, tell your mom I said thanks."

"I will, the next time I see her." He set down his cup and picked up a small notebook that was sitting in front of him. He waved it at Anna and said, "Do you know what this is?"

"No. I've never seen it before. What is it?"

"I have no idea. I was hoping you would know."

"Well, what's in it?"

"Just some sketches. Come here. Take a look."

Anna walked around the desk to where Jason was sitting and leaned in over his shoulder. "So what is it? Where did you find it?"

"I don't know what it is, for sure. And I found it in this drawer."

He pointed to one of three drawers lining the side of the desk. "It was the only thing in any of them. I kind of did some snooping. Hope you don't mind."

"No, that's okay. I don't mind. I mean, we are supposed to be doing this together, I guess. So what do you think it is?"

Jason turned the sketch around, then around again, trying to get it to make sense. "It's weird. It's like it's some kind of pool."

"Pool? Like a swimming pool?"

"No. I think it's some kind of underground pool. Here, look." He pointed to the shading around what looked like a drawing of a long skinny pool of water. "See how this is all shaded? It's almost like it's a rock wall or something. And here, look at these." He flipped back through some of the earlier pages in the notebook, showing drawings of tunnels. "See? On every page they all have the same starting point. Here." He pointed to a crude drawing of a building. "Then each one follows the same shaft, until here." He marked the spot with his index finger. Each tunnel drawing started out exactly alike until it reached the point where his finger rested. "Then, if we look past this point, they all go in different directions. But at the end of the map, so to speak, each one just ends like this." He pointed to a big question mark that was at the bottom of the page, where the drawing of the tunnel ended. "Then, if we flip through the notebook to the last page that has writing on it, we find this drawing of the pool."

"That is weird," Anna said, studying the notebook. She flipped through the pages then handed the notebook back to Jason. "So, what do you think it means. Is it important?"

"You tell me. I barely know what's going on around here. Remember?"

"Well, obviously my grandpa was trying to find this pool. And we know that he was trying to hide this notebook. So it must be important. I guess we're going to have to figure it out. Anything else in the desk?"

"Nope. I looked in every drawer. That's it. Just the notebook."

"And you said it was in that drawer?"

"Well, not exactly in it."

"What do you mean?"

"Well, I was sitting here at the desk rubbing my eye, and my contact fell out. I got down on the floor to look, and I noticed that up underneath here," he said, getting down under the desk, "there's a seam along the panel." He pointed.

Anna ran her fingers along the hairline crevice.

"When I pushed on the panel—"

"What? You just thought, 'Hey, I'll push this and see what happens?'" she quipped. "You're just a regular Hardy boy, aren't you?"

"Funny," he said. "Anyway, I pushed the panel, and it clicked." He demonstrated. "And there you go."

Anna felt inside the small cubby, just big enough for a small book. "So it was hidden?"

"It appears that way."

"Well, that's good." Anna began pacing back and forth, the wheels in her brain churning. "That means it's important. Otherwise, he wouldn't have hidden it. We have to find out where that building is and why my grandpa was trying to find that pool." She walked over and grabbed Jason by the hand to pull him out of the chair. "Come on," she said. "Let's go look at the scroll."

Anna and Jason sat in the middle of the floor in the living room directly across from one another. The box and all its contents were strewn about the floor around them. There were loose papers, some with ancient Hebrew and Greek written on them, scattered all over. There were a few journals, some written by Thomas Riley, others written by guardians in the past, stacked off to the side. Several drawings of maps, various buildings, rivers, and artifacts were piled up, off to the other side. And Anna had placed the scroll directly between them. They were all set.

Jason marveled at the size of the tiny scroll, no bigger than Anna's hand, as she unrolled it and placed it in front of him. A feeling of reverence came over him. At that moment, he felt he was the most privileged person on the planet. He knelt, folded his hands, and began to pray out loud, thanking God for this awesome privilege.

"I'm sorry." He wiped his eyes and sat back upright. "It's just that. . .well, it's. . ."

"Don't apologize, Jason. I think it was cool. I kind of had that same feeling when Vin and I saw it earlier."

"It's just that, God gave this thing to John. I mean, I've read about this scroll in the Bible a hundred times. And now here it sits, right in front of me! This thing is an actual artifact from scripture!"

"But we can't show anyone."

"I know. Still, I can't help but think what this would do for the world."

"Or what it would do *to* the world."

"Yeah. It could cause a lot of commotion."

"Did you look at it, Jason?"

"What do you mean? Yeah, I looked at it. It's right there!" He pointed to the scroll lying open on the floor.

"No, I mean, did you *look* at it?"

"Oh, I guess not." He leaned in to look at the writing that was printed on it. It looked as though it had been written five minutes ago. It showed no signs of its age. "This is incredible," he said. "This thing should be weathered, faded, wrinkled—anything but look brand-new!"

"I know. It's pretty amazing. So what do we do now?"

Jason read the translation that Anna handed him of the scroll. He tried to absorb the words as he read. And he spoke them out loud.

What once was perfect, has now been broken.
At the point of no escape, the Father opened the way.
So shall He, at the point of entry.
The key is found in the temple.

He read them again and again, speaking the words out loud each time he read through it. Finally, he looked up at Anna. "Well, I'm absolutely confused. How about you?"

Anna threw her arms up in the air. "I thought you were good at riddles. What do we do now?"

Jason smiled and said, "I am. But this is a tough one. I mean, it's two thousand years old and no one has cracked it yet. You honestly think we're going to get it right off the bat?"

"I guess you're right." Anna sighed. "I just don't want everything that happened today to be in vain."

"Don't worry. It won't. I promise. You said your grandfather told you that he had figured some stuff out. Right?"

"Well, he said he had all of his notes and things. He said I could figure out the rest."

"Then we will." He stood up and stretched his arms up over his head. "I think we should call it a night. Sleep on it. Sometimes it helps me to think about something overnight. We can start fresh tomorrow—after we go shopping and get me something to wear."

Anna straightened up the mess they had made and then stood up. She told Jason she was going to go to the kitchen and get a glass of milk. Jason agreed and said he'd like one, too. He got the glasses while Anna retrieved the milk from the refrigerator. She poured them each a glass then put the milk away.

Jason laughed at Anna when she pulled her glass away from her mouth. She had a milk-mustache. She obviously knew what he was laughing at, because she took the sleeve of her shirt and wiped it across her face.

"Is that better, Mr. Milk-Mustache Police?" she said playfully.

"I don't know. I kind of liked it. It looked good on you."

Anna walked over to him and wound her arms around his neck. Then she let go, and without a word, she turned around and headed upstairs.

Jason sat in the kitchen for a few more seconds. He didn't know what to think about what had just happened. He knew that Anna was a sweet girl. But she couldn't have any interest in him. They'd just met. No, he decided. It was just a friendly hug. But if something else was a possibility, he certainly wouldn't object. Because when he saw her this morning for the first time, he thought he'd seen the woman of his dreams. And now it was his job to keep her alive.

CHAPTER 37

London, the Safe House

The morning broke early for this time of year. Anna lay on her back and squinted as the laser beams of sunlight shot through tiny spaces between the slats in the blinds. She pulled the covers up over her head and groaned. It couldn't be morning already. She had just closed her eyes.

A light rap on her door told her that she wasn't the only one who was up at such an awful hour of the day. She peeked her head above the covers and whined, "Gooooo awaaaaay!"

The muffled voice on the other end of the door chuckled then said, "Okay. But you're going to miss out on my famous eggs and bacon. If you thought the cocoa was good, well. . ."

Anna sat up a little bit. She stretched and yawned, replying as she let out the big gulp of air, "Scrambled, limp bacon, and wheat toast."

Again Jason laughed at the response. "This isn't the Waffle House! How about over-medium, slightly burned, and croissants?"

Now it was Anna's turn to laugh. "Like I said, that sounds great!"

"Good," Jason said. "See you downstairs in twenty."

"Thirty!" she yelled through the door.

"Twenty! We have a very busy day today. Get up and get moving. Now you've got nineteen!"

She thought he was gone, but then he knocked on her door one more time. "Yeah?"

"Put something nice on," he said through the closed door. "We're going to the Israeli embassy."

She was dressed and headed downstairs eight minutes later.

The smell of food hit her nostrils as she opened her bedroom door. Her stomach instantly started growling. She didn't realize until just now how hungry she was.

She found Jason sitting at the table, already enjoying his breakfast.

"Want some?" he said, finishing off a croissant.

"Looks like you're getting enough for both of us." She laughed.

He finally managed to swallow the mouthful of food and said, "I'm getting ready to go back for seconds, so you'd better hurry up before I *do* eat it all."

She immediately jumped over a chair, ran for the counter, grabbed a plate, and started piling heaps of food on it. "No way, José! I'm starving!"

Anna had barely finished swallowing her first bite when she brought up the conversation they had started on opposite sides of her bedroom door. "So what's going on? Why the Israeli embassy? Did you find something?"

Jason smiled and tapped the top of his head with his index finger. "I'm psychic. Something tells me we need to go there today." He drew his eyes tight, pursed his lips, and raised an eyebrow.

223

"What do you think of that?"

Anna folded her arms and looked sideways at him and said, "I think you need psychiatric help. That's what I think!" She smiled.

"No really, all kidding aside, I was leafing through one of the journals last night. I took it up to bed with me. I figured it would give me something to read. Put me to sleep. Well, that didn't work. The next thing I knew, it was two hours later, I was wide awake, and I was starting to get to know your grandpa a little bit. He was a very smart man, you know. Just the way he wrote in that journal tells me that he was way ahead of his time with his thinking. There were a few times he mentioned you in there."

"Really? What did he say?"

"Just that he'd been following your life, seeing that you were taken care of, looking out for you. That kind of thing. He was very proud of you."

"I'd like to read that. Would you show me later?"

"Of course. I'd be happy to. So anyway, the reason why we're going to the Israeli embassy is because your grandpa, Thomas, had a meeting today. And I think we should go in his stead."

"And why would we do that?"

Jason stood and walked over to Anna's seat and set the journal down in front of her. It was opened to a specific page. The date read three weeks ago. She read the words staring back at her.

Today wasn't completely a bust. I have eliminated all but two. These were the only two that I even considered to begin with. Even so, I did need to check out the others. Wouldn't want to be lazy in my efforts. These last two, however, have me puzzled. I don't know why.

I feel confident about my meeting with Benjamin. I'll be meeting with him on the eleventh. He says that the embassy is

the safest place to meet. I hope he's right. We can't afford another
episode like the one we had the other day. That was close. Maybe
now we can put this business of the temple to rest.

It was signed with a slash, then "Thomas," scribbled in cursive. Beside his name there was a star of David etched on the paper.

"Today's the eleventh," she said.

"I know. We have to go in his place."

"And how do you suppose we do that?"

"Easy. We go and ask for Benjamin. Then you tell him you're Anna. I'm sure your grandfather has told him about you."

"And what if he hasn't?"

"Well then, we'd better come up with something brilliant. Huh?"

"How do you know it's the Israeli embassy?"

"I Googled it. A Benjamin Shoenfield is the minister of public relations there."

"I hope you're right."

"Me, too."

CHAPTER 38

Paris

Jonathan awoke to the sound of muffled voices down the hall. He forced his eyes open and squinted as the sunlight streaming through the living room window, attacking him like a giant tidal wave. He checked his watch. Eleven thirty. Wow! He hadn't planned on sleeping this late. He guessed his body shut down because of the gunshot wound.

He stretched his arms out and pushed himself up on the couch. He was instantly sorry. A pain shot through his leg that felt worse than the initial bullet. He gasped for breath and tried not to pass out. It felt as if his heart had relocated to his thigh. He was sure that if he looked hard enough, he would see his leg pulsating.

He sat there for a minute trying to breathe through the pain. Once it subsided a little, he realized his leg wasn't the only thing hurting. His back and neck were stiff. He would have to remember to thank Remy for the comfortable accommodations.

He was about to try to sit up some more when he heard footsteps behind him. He craned his neck over his shoulder to see

Remy walking down the hall, followed by a skinny, little, weaselly-looking fellow. He was carrying a black bag. He wore horn-rimmed glasses and a tweed jacket. His hair, which looked as if it had been saturated with vegetable oil, was stringy and parted to one side. And Jonathan was extremely glad to see him.

Remy walked behind the couch and patted Jonathan on the head. She looked down and said, "Jonathan, you remember my brother, Edmond."

Jonathan nodded his head. "Edmond, good to see you."

Edmond stood in front of him with folded arms and a smug look on his face. "It looks like once again you've gotten yourself into something you shouldn't have. And who has to come to the rescue? Me, that's who." He sat down on the coffee table next to the couch. "Now, I personally couldn't care less if you just up and died right here. My sister, however"—he rolled his eyes and gestured to Remy—"still has a thing for you, I guess. So let's have a look. Shall we?"

Jonathan didn't bother to answer. He knew Edmond's distaste for him. Like so many other people, Edmond was someone Jonathan had apparently wronged. The problem was Jonathan didn't know how or why. He only knew that Edmond, for some reason or other, truly didn't like him.

Edmond reached his arm out and pulled the blanket away from Jonathan's leg. He stared at the bandaged limb. "Well, let's have it then. Take that stuff off." He pointed his index finger at the leg.

"I appreciate this, Edmond," Jonathan said, unwrapping the gauze. "I know you're only doing this for your sister."

"I'm doing this for the money. Let's be real here. Speaking of, where is it?"

"How much?"

"Five."

"Hand me my jacket there." Jonathan pointed to his coat hanging over the arm of the recliner next to the couch. Edmond reached over and grabbed it by the collar and handed it back to him. Jonathan reached inside the breast pocket and pulled out his billfold. He withdrew five crisp one-hundred dollar bills and handed them to Edmond.

Edmond laughed, waving the bills in front of him. "Funny," he said. "What? You're some kind of comedian now? Five *thousand*, you imbecile. I'm not some hack doctor you can just go crawling to. I get *paid* for my services." He threw the bills back at Jonathan and stood up, looking at Remy. "I'm leaving. When he has the money, call me back." He didn't wait for a reply. He grabbed his bag and was out the door in a matter of seconds.

"Remy." Jonathan waited for her to chase after her brother. She just stood there looking at him. "Remy!" he said again.

"Jonathan, I do not control my brother. You know how he is. And he hates you. I'm sorry, but there's nothing I can do. Do you have five grand?"

"If I had five grand on me, do you think I would've let him go?"

"Well, can you get it?"

"I can't get anything! I'm laid up here on your couch. I can barely sit up! My leg is killing me."

"I could go get it for you if you tell me where."

"You think I just have a duffel bag of cash lying around Paris in case I need it?"

"I'm not an idiot, Jonathan. I *know* you have a duffel bag lying somewhere around Paris in case of something just like this. The problem is, you know there's more than five grand in there, and you think I'll just take it and leave you to die."

Jonathan said nothing.

"Looks like you're going to have to trust me."

He said nothing.

"Jonathan, I doubt there is enough money in there to lose any sleep over. I have more than enough. I promise you, I won't take your precious cash. I just want you out of here so I can get on with my retirement."

"There's a lot of cash in there, Remy. And you said it yourself. Old habits are hard to break. You never were one to turn down money."

Now Remy said nothing.

"Suppose I do decide to trust you. What would I have as collateral?"

"How about your life? If you don't get that money, you could die."

"It would be painful, but I'd get out of here and find help somewhere else. How about yours?"

"You mean my life? As collateral? You've got to be kidding." She let out a chuckle.

"It wasn't meant to be funny."

Remy raised her eyebrows at that statement. "Do you mean professionally or personally?"

"Well, we both know that you still make my heart flutter every time I see you. So, if you want, I'll come with you and we can retire together. Or, if you still don't want anything to do with me anymore and you steal my money, I'll just come after you and kill you."

"How you gonna find me?"

"You're going to tell me where you're headed."

"And why would I do that?"

Now Jonathan smiled. "Two reasons. One, you're still in love with me."

Remy rolled her eyes and pursed her lips.

"Two, you really want to know how much money is in that bag. I can see it. And we both know the only way you're going to find out is if you tell me where you're going. Besides, it would only be a courtesy. We both know that if I put a couple of man-hours into it, I could find you in about two weeks."

"You're pretty sure of yourself."

"I'm the best. Period. We both know that."

"Dieter might disagree."

"Dieter isn't going to be disagreeing with anything after I get out of here."

"Well, you're right. I am curious about the money." She smiled. "But you're wrong about the other thing. I don't still love you. That was a long time ago. But all right, you win. I'll tell you where I'm headed. I'll go get your money. And after you get out of here, you can go check and see if I did rip you off. After that, we'll just have to play it by ear."

Jonathan smiled and nodded his head. He was about to lose over six million dollars, but how much fun it would be trying to find it again. "Okay. I have a safe-deposit box in the CIC Banque Transatlantique. Here's the key." He took the little key off a small key ring that was in his pocket and handed it to her. "Now will you go tell your brother to come back in here? I know he's still waiting outside."

"How do you know that?"

"Because I can see him right there." He pointed to the security monitoring screen across the room. Edmond was standing out on the sidewalk, leaning against the big garage door. Jonathan knew the little man wouldn't leave until he was sure of whether he would get the money he asked for. And Edmond knew he would get it. He was the only "doctor" of his kind in all of Paris.

"Okay," she said. She walked over to the monitor and pushed a

230

button that buzzed for a second. "Edmond, come inside."

Jonathan watched the greasy-haired man grab his bag and step through the big garage door. Less than fifteen seconds later, he was back inside the apartment.

"So you have my money?" He stared at Jonathan.

"It'll be here by the time you're done." Jonathan looked to Remy who had just come back from her bedroom. She had a bag draped over her arm and was putting on her coat. "Just remember what I said."

She walked over and whispered something in his ear. As she pulled away, she winked at him. "And the beaches are white sand. You know how I love white sand."

Jonathan said nothing. He just watched as she let herself out the door.

Edmond took his time coming back to the coffee table. He removed his jacket, took off his shoes, and went to the kitchen. Jonathan could hear him opening cupboards and moving things around. He laid his head back against the armrest and closed his eyes. His leg was killing him. It was burning. And it itched. He knew that Edmond was about to tell him something he didn't want to hear. The leg was infected.

Edmond finally returned to the living room, carrying a coffee cup, a bowl full of some kind of liquid, and a roll of paper towels. He set them down on the coffee table then sat down beside them. "Now," he said, "I have my coffee and other necessities. Let's have a look at that leg."

He waited until Jonathan had removed the bandages. He reached inside his bag and pulled out some latex gloves. He put them on and leaned in to look at the leg. He gently touched the area around the bullet hole. Jonathan sat upright and screamed.

"Easy there, killer," Edmond said. "Here." He handed him a

leather strap. "Bite down on this. I have to poke around here for a second. It's going to hurt."

Jonathan took the strap from him and bit down on it. If it weren't for the fact that the little weasel was helping him, he would've killed him right there.

Edmond continued to poke and prod around the wound. Little pockets of white fluid started to ooze out around the hole. He grabbed some clean gauze and wiped it away. "I'm afraid this isn't good. You dressed the wound fine. You just didn't clean it that well. It's infected. You'll probably lose it."

"What?" Jonathan spit the leather strap out of his mouth. "You'd better be kidding, you little psycho!"

"Relax." Edmond waved his hand. "I am kidding. You're going to be fine. In about a week."

"I don't have a week."

"Yes, and I'm sure my sister doesn't want you staying here for a week. However, that is not up to you and me, is it? The bottom line is, it's infected. You need antibiotics. And a lot of rest. You're not going anywhere for at least a week. That is, unless you really *do* want to lose that leg. Now lie back and let me fix this mess."

Jonathan leaned back and closed his eyes. Wickham was going to lay an egg when he heard this. He would just have to deal with it. He certainly wasn't going to lose a leg over that girl or some scroll.

The pain over the next twenty minutes could only be described as sick, demented torture. The little weasel was enjoying this.

Edmond finished redressing the wound and said, "There. That should do it." He stood up and walked toward the door. "I'll be right back." He opened the front door and disappeared.

Edmond hadn't been gone ten seconds when Jonathan's phone rang. Remy. He flipped it open with a grimace.

"Six million dollars, Jonathan? Are you kidding me?"

"Hello, Remy. I'm going to be fine. Thanks for asking."

"Well, I must tell you. I was expecting a good bit of cash, but this? This is ridiculous. Why do you have six million in a safe-deposit box?"

"For a rainy day."

"What? Is this like your entire life's work here?"

"It's a pretty good chunk of it. Want to help me spend it? On your little white-sandy beach?"

"What did Edmond say?"

"He said I'm your new roommate. At least for another week."

"That's a shame."

"Why's that?"

"'Cause I'm not coming back."

"I'll find you."

"For six million, I'll risk it."

"Your choice. I'm going to kill your brother."

"He's only my half brother, and go ahead. I've never really liked him anyway."

"Good-bye, Remy. I'll be seeing you soon."

"Well, if you do find me, as least give me a heads-up. Who knows? I may have changed my mind about us by then."

"We'll see."

Jonathan pushed the END button on the phone and threw it across the room. It hit the wall and shattered.

The front door opened and Edmond came back in carrying a set of crutches. He walked over to the couch and set them down. "There," he said. "I'll throw those in for free. At least you'll be able to go to the bathroom on your own."

Jonathan stared at him with an icy glare. "Do me a favor."

"What's that?"

233

"In your sister's bedroom there's a painting on the wall. Behind it there's a safe. The door's open, I'm sure. Inside there is a little black satchel. Bring it to me, please."

"I'm hardly going to go rummaging around in my sister's private things."

"It's not your sister's. It's mine. And she put it there last night for me, for safe keeping."

Edmond let out a long sigh and disappeared into the bedroom. He came back carrying the bag. He tossed it over to Jonathan.

Jonathan reached inside the bag and felt the cold steel of his 9mm. He could tell by the weight that it was still loaded. "Your sister has your money. She's going to be joining you soon. You can ask her for it when you see her."

He pulled the gun out of the bag and shot Edmond five times in the chest and once in the forehead.

CHAPTER 39

The Vatican

Cardinal Wickham slammed the phone down. Really hard this time. His patience was at an end. He had been trying to get Jonathan on the phone all morning. Each time he got the same result, a fast busy signal. He was starting to think Jonathan was avoiding him.

He went to his kitchen where a fresh pot of coffee was percolating. The aroma of the French roast wafted throughout the apartment. It would be his fifth pot of coffee in seven hours. He'd been up since three o'clock this morning, unable to sleep. Each time he would doze off, visions of the scroll would occupy his mind. He was having horrible nightmares now. Some were recurring.

In this one, he was standing on the edge of a cliff, the scroll hovering above him just out of reach. Each time he would stretch out for it, he would lose his balance and fall over the side. On the way down to the bottom, he would see Jonathan standing in a crevice of the cliff, laughing as he fell. When he looked down, there was nothing but a gaping black hole. At the far bottom of the hole was Thomas Riley, waiting for him with a sword, pointed upward, waiting to impale him as he reached the bottom.

He poured another cup and sipped it slowly, savoring the bitter taste. He was exhausted. It looked like he would be running on caffeine all day.

To make matters worse, the pope was still sick, still hanging in there like a hair in a grilled cheese sandwich. That also infuriated him. The person he bought the drug from said it would take only a few days. A week tops. They were fast approaching the week mark. Maybe he could up the dose and hurry it along. He decided he would go see the pontiff this morning. See how he was doing.

What worried him the most was Lucifer's news. Michael, the archangel, was here, walking the earth. He knew his Bible, even if he didn't live and abide by it. And as far as he knew, Michael didn't make a habit of interfering with humanity. That meant problems. He needed to find that scroll. Fast.

If he were truthful, he wanted it for himself. That was always the objective. Now, however, he was scared. He thought back to the conversation he recently had with Joseph when he told Joseph that he didn't fear anyone or anything. He was starting to admit now that was a lie. He was afraid.

As a child, he had always heard stories of the devil and his legions. He guessed he even believed them. But seeing them face-to-face, feeling Lucifer's anger firsthand—that was something altogether different. He feared the fallen angel. And since Lucifer promised him power beyond all that he had ever seen, he decided that he would take him up on his offer. He would give the scroll to him.

Wickham had asked several times what was on it. Lucifer told him when he found it, he would see for himself. He asked what the reason was for wanting to possess it. Lucifer told him that when he had the scroll in his possession, he had won. Game over.

Wickham knew that he had turned his back on God a long time ago. He was too caught up in what this world had to offer. He liked this world. He knew that the only way to preserve what he had was to serve Lucifer. Lucifer promised him eternal life here on earth. He told him that he didn't have to be afraid of dying. He would make him immortal. And he would give him a great kingdom here on earth. People would bow to him. They would revere him, not as a pope, but as a king. All he had to do was get the scroll.

After a quick shower, he felt a measure of renewed vigor. He knew he was close. Jonathan would be calling in any minute now, telling him the scroll was within his grasp. He would call Joseph and see what the buzz around the Vatican was this morning. It was going to be a good day. And that was confirmed with the ringing of his telephone.

He walked over to his desk and lifted the receiver. "Good morning. This is Cardinal Wickham. How can I help you?"

The voice on the other end of the line was shaky. The woman tried to get the words out but choked between sobs. "Cardinal Wickham. . .you need to come over here. His Holiness is dying. We don't know how much longer he'll be with us."

Wickham grinned. He tried to muster up a soothing, peaceful voice. "I'll be there as soon as I can. Don't fret. Tell the pontiff that I'm coming. He needs to be given his last rites. I'll hurry."

He hung up the phone, grinning from ear to ear. If he didn't think he'd draw the attention of the Swiss guards, he would've shouted to the top of his voice. It was, indeed, going to be a good day.

CHAPTER 40

London, the Safe House

Dishes were scattered about the kitchen, the aroma of coffee and bacon filled the air, and two empty plates sat in the middle of the table. Anna and Jason had just finished stuffing themselves with breakfast.

Anna was halfway to the sink with a stack of breakfast dishes when the doorbell rang. She stopped midstride and looked back. Jason raised his eyebrows. They weren't expecting company. That's when Anna remembered her conversation with Hale. She quickly dumped the dishes into the sink and made a beeline for the door.

"It's okay. It's Hale. He's bringing the head security guy over this morning."

Jason jumped out of his chair, knocking it over behind him, and ran into the living room. "Wait!"

The bell rang again.

"What? I told you: it's just Hale."

Jason squatted next to her. He lifted her pants leg up to see the revolver strapped to her ankle. He unfastened the strap and took the gun and handed it to her. "Now we can see who it is."

Oh man. She'd been assuming that it was Hale. And it probably was. But she couldn't afford to be that trusting, especially with the scroll and all of the notes and papers lying all over the place. Anyone could easily walk in and grab them up. "I'm sorry, Jason. I wasn't thinking. I'm still not used to all this cloak-and-dagger stuff."

The bell rang for the third time.

Jason brushed past Anna, moving her behind him with his arm, and crept to the door. He bent his head and peered through the peephole. He finally let out the breath that he'd been holding. "It's Hale." He unlocked the dead bolt, slid the chain back, and opened the door.

Behind a worried-looking Hale stood an extremely big man dressed in a suit—an expensive one, it looked like. He held a very large, shiny black pistol, his thumb on the hammer and his index finger brushing the trigger.

Hale stepped through the doorway. The man with the gun followed. "I was about to have Christopher here call the team and rush the house."

"Just being cautious," Jason explained.

"Good. Glad to hear it. Guys, this is Christopher Wallace. He is the head of your London security detail."

The man returned his gun to the holster inside his jacket, stuck out his hand, and greeted them both. Both Jason's and Anna's hands disappeared inside the man's grip. "Your grandfather and I were very close. He talked a lot about you, Anna."

"Yeah, seems like everyone but me knew that," she said sorrowfully.

"I'm sorry to hear about. . .you know. . ."

"It's okay, Mr. Wallace. Thank you for your concern."

Hale gently took Anna by the elbow. "Chris, please excuse us for a moment. I need to talk to Jason and Anna alone if you don't mind."

"Not at all." Christopher nodded his head and waved a hand in the air.

Hale led Anna and Jason into the kitchen. "I just wanted to make sure that everything is all right."

"Everything's fine, Hale. Is something going on?" Anna had a worried look.

"No. Everything's fine." Hale saw the coffeepot sitting on the counter. He could smell the fresh brew. "Mind if I have a cup?"

"Go ahead," Anna said. "So what's Mr. Wallace's deal?"

Hale took a mug from the cabinet and poured himself a cup of coffee. He didn't bother to sweeten it or add cream. He just tipped it straight up and drank. "Now that's good coffee." He had a smile from ear to ear.

"Thank you," Jason said. "I have been known to make a good pot of coffee every now and again."

"Mr. Wallace," Hale continued, as if he hadn't even stopped to have the coffee discussion, "is strictly a hired gun. No pun intended. But that's what he is. Just a hired gun. He knows nothing of the scroll. Therefore, he knows nothing of anyone chasing you around. He especially knows nothing of what happened in Pau. He only knows that your grandfather was working on some kind of archaeological thing for the Vatican. He knows that Thomas had an 'accident,' but I've decided—and you can override me if you want—not to tell him anything else. But I think it's the right call. He and his team are really good. They will shadow you everywhere you go. You will not see them. They will be on the lookout for anything or anyone that seems out of place. If they think you are in danger, they will send someone in, probably a woman, to make contact with you. They will then take you out of wherever you are and get you to safety. Any questions?"

Anna and Jason looked at each other then back at Hale. Neither of them said anything. They just nodded in agreement.

"Okay then," Hale said. "Let's go."

They walked back into the living room and found Christopher Wallace sitting on the sofa.

"So," Hale began, "now that everyone's met, let's let Christopher go ahead and explain everything." Everyone nodded, and Christopher leaned forward on the sofa.

"Your grandfather hired my firm about fifteen years ago." He looked at Anna. "We were fairly new then. Actually, it's quite amusing. We hadn't been up and running for more than a month when your grandfather hired us. Since then, he has been our only client."

"Business not as good as you thought?" Anna asked.

"No, young lady, quite the opposite. We decided early on in our endeavor not to take on an enormous clientele. Your grandfather made it easy for us. He paid us six times our normal asking price. His only stipulation was that he be our only client. We agreed, of course, given the offer of money. Since then we have been working for him."

"And did you travel with him?" This time it was Jason with the question.

"No, sir. We were only on duty when he came to London, which wasn't that often. He would come and stay for a month or just a few days. It didn't matter to us. As long as he was here, we were there, watching him."

"Sounds like a pretty good deal," Anna said.

"The best I ever had." Christopher smiled. "And Thomas was the nicest man I've ever had the pleasure of working for."

"Well," Anna said, "I don't see any reason to change anything. Do you Hale?"

Hale shook his head. "None at all. As long as you are okay with it."

"Suits me fine," Anna replied. "How about you, Jason?"

"Makes me feel safer."

"Good. Then we're all set." Anna looked around waiting to see what was next.

Christopher pulled out a manila folder. He opened it and pulled several loose sheets of paper from it and handed them to her. They were pictures of five men and one woman. Each was dressed in a military uniform decorated with ribbons and medals. "This is your team, Anna."

Anna took the papers and looked at them one by one. She passed each one along to Jason. They both scanned over the pictures and the bios written at the bottom of each page.

"Do you need to know our schedule?" Anna asked.

"No, ma'am. You may come and go as you please. As long as you're in London, we will be within fifty yards of you at all times. You'll never know we're even there. I just wanted you to have these in case, by some ridiculous foul-up on our part, you happen to notice any one of these people following you. But I can assure you, you won't."

"How will you know when we're here in London?" Anna asked. "I mean, do we let you know that we're coming, or what?"

"Hale will always let me know, since he's the pilot. He's always the first to know that you're coming here." He reached inside his billfold and offered Anna a business card. "If for some reason you aren't with Hale, you can reach me by any of those numbers. The one at the top is my cell. I have it on me at all times." He stood up to leave.

Anna, Jason, and Hale all stood with him. Anna stuck out her hand and said, "Thank you, Mr. Wallace. I hope I never get to see you in action." She gave a little laugh. "Seriously though, just knowing you're out there makes me feel safer."

Wallace shook Anna's hand. "My pleasure. And please, call me Chris." He shook Jason's hand as well and then moved toward the front door. Hale accompanied him and let him out. Once Wallace had left, Hale turned back to Anna and Jason.

"So, what do you think?"

Anna and Jason looked at each other then back at Hale. Anna shrugged her shoulders and said, "I like him."

"Me, too," said Jason.

"Great!" Hale said. "Then I'll be on my way. You two kids stay safe, and I'll see ya soon. Call me if you need anything."

"Where are you going to be?" Anna asked.

"Well, normally I would be going back home. Thomas never liked us hanging around. He said that we all had lives to live, and he wanted us to 'get living them,' as he liked to say. Under the circumstances, I need to get back to the Vatican. I need to debrief the pope. He's expecting me. I'll fly out this afternoon. Miles and Marie will stay here in case something comes up. I can be back in two and a half hours if I need to. If it's an emergency and you need to get out quickly, Wallace has a plane. Push your panic button, and he'll be at your side in less than thirty seconds. He'll let us know immediately that you've left. We'll come to where you are and pick you up. Okay?"

"Okay."

"I'll call in and keep track of you."

"I would like that," Anna said.

"Me, too," Jason agreed.

"Don't worry, guys. Chris Wallace and his team are some of the best soldiers this world has ever seen. I feel supremely confident leaving you alone, knowing he's on your tail."

"Then so do I," Anna said. "Go to Rome. Tell the pope we said hi."

"Thanks, Anna. I will. You two got any immediate plans?"

Jason nodded his head. "Yeah. I found something in one of Thomas's journals. He had a meeting with some guy named Benjamin today at the Israeli embassy. Do you know him?"

Hale shook his head. "Honestly, guys, yesterday was a weird thing. I've never done anything other than fly the plane. We were hired, of course, because we all have military backgrounds. But we've never been involved in anything like what happened yesterday. And I can honestly say that I'm glad. That scared the living daylights out of me. I didn't realize it until this morning, after I'd had time to reflect on it." He looked embarrassed as he chuckled. "That was the first time I've seen any kind of combat in about twenty years."

"Well, I think you were brilliant." Anna smiled at him. "You saved my life."

Hale stood, solemn-faced. "Thank you," he finally said. "I have to go now. Remember, anything goes wrong, push the little black button. Wallace will be right there."

Anna walked over and gave Hale a hug and a kiss on the cheek. Jason stuck out his arm and shook Hale's hand. They watched his car pull away from the curb before walking back inside and shutting the door.

"So what do you think?" Jason asked. "You got your own little panic button and everything."

Anna looked at him with a grin. "Well, I'm kind of a big deal, you know."

Jason laughed and gave her a friendly nudge in the shoulder.

"Well, Ms. Big Deal, what next?"

Anna crinkled her nose and tapped her chin. "Well, we both need something nice to wear to the embassy. I say we go shopping."

CHAPTER 41

Paris

Jonathan knew the risks of using a landline, but he didn't have much of a choice, since he threw his cell phone against the wall and he couldn't really get around all that unnoticed. He needed help.

He pushed himself up on the crutches that Edmond had given him and stumbled his way over to the other side of the room. An antique-style phone, complete with rotary dial and separate ear- and mouthpieces, hung on the wall. Remy always was one for antiques. He would've preferred a normal, present-day cordless unit. Whatever. A phone was a phone.

He lifted the earpiece and pinched his crutches between his armpits. With his free hand, he dialed the number from memory. The line was picked up after the first ring.

"This is Waukeem," the deep Jamaican voice said.

"Waukeem, this is Jonathan."

"Oh hey, boss. How you doin', mon? I thought you were coming to London, mon."

"Change of plans. I need you and three others to come to Paris. Bring a laundry basket." Jonathan knew his man would know what he was talking about. When he hired him, as with all of his employees, he discussed certain talks of code with them. This particular one meant that there was a dead body and a mess to go with it. He needed a cleanup crew.

"Sure thing, mon. I be there in four hours. With basket. Anything else?"

"Yeah. Bring me a new phone. Mine got broken. What's the girl doing?"

There was a pause on the other end of the line. Finally, Waukeem spoke. "That's the thing, mon. I tell Frankie yesterday to tell you. We don't know."

"What do you mean you don't know?" Jonathan could feel his temperature start to rise.

"We haven't been able to find her, mon. All we know, she is in London. We are working on it. Been at it since we get here early this morning."

"Well, tell Frankie to light a fire under his rear end. I want to know where she is by tonight. Got it?"

"Got it, mon."

"Leave Frankie and Joey there to track her down. You, Hank, and Nicholas get here as fast as you can. I'll call you back at"—he looked at his watch—"five o'clock this afternoon. You should be here, in Paris, by then."

"Got it, mon. See you then."

Jonathan hung up the phone. He looked around and checked out his surroundings. Nothing here he could do except maybe watch some TV. He had a dead body that was sure to start smelling up the place in the near future. As much as it may hurt, he needed to get out of there. He wasn't about to sit around and wait for the foul stench of death to attack him. Besides, he wanted to go to the bank. He needed to see for himself that Remy did, indeed, clean him out. He lifted the phone again, dialed the operator, and asked to be connected to a cab company. His French was broken at best, but he was able to get his point across. The dispatcher told him that a cab would be waiting for him within the next ten minutes.

He shuffled himself to the end of the hall. There was a thermostat mounted just before the bedroom door. It was set on seventy-two. He turned the knob counterclockwise and watched as the little arrow on the outside ring settled on forty. It was going to be cold enough to snow when he got back, but at least he wouldn't be smelling dead Edmond.

He hobbled his way into the bedroom. At one time, he had left a couple of suits here. He wondered if Remy still had them. He checked the closet and found what he was looking for. As quickly as he could, he got out of his clothes and changed into the suit. It was a very painful experience, but he was going to need to look important.

He finished dressing and checked a few drawers, the medicine cabinet in the bathroom, and finally a jewelry box sitting on the bedside table, before he found a spare set of house keys. He maneuvered his way back down the hall and out the door. He was starting to get the hang of the crutches, but the sides of his body, just above the rib cage, were starting to get sore. He knew a couple of bruises were soon to come.

Down the dimly lit hallway and out through the garage door he went. He crossed the street and made his way around the corner. There, parked along the curb, was an old yellow Peugeot with a little white light mounted on the hood. He hobbled over to the car and jumped inside. He told the driver where he needed to go. The driver never said a word, just pulled the gearshift down and punched the gas.

At the bank, Jonathan asked a young female clerk for the bank manager. The young lady returned a minute later, trailed by an older man with silver hair. He wore a three-piece suit, complete with a pocket watch. His spectacles rode low on his cherry-red nose. He had a paper-thin mustache and beady little eyes.

"Can I help you, monsieur?" he asked without interest.

Jonathan didn't have his key. Remy did. And he picked this particular bank after months of checking it out. They weren't quick to allow someone without a key to open a safe-deposit box, so this was going to take some creativity on his part. "Yes, you can," Jonathan said tartly. "First of all, when I come in here, I don't expect to have to ask a subordinate to see the bank manager. You should have greeted me yourself." Jonathan watched as the little man stared at him, nonplussed. "Weren't you told I was on my way?" He waited impatiently for an answer.

"I–I'm sorry, monsieur! I had no idea—"

"Enough!" Jonathan let his voice rise enough to attract the attention of bystanders. He leaned his crutches forward until he was towering over the man. "Perhaps I will just take my sixteen billion dollars in assets elsewhere!" He spun around and headed for the door, murmuring and cursing to himself.

At the mere mention of the word *billion*, panic struck the heart of the little bank manager. He quickly raced after Jonathan, who was covering a rather large amount of space in a short time, given the crutches. The manager waved his hand. "Monsieur, monsieur, wait! Wait!" Gasping for breath, he reached out to stop Jonathan from leaving. "Monsieur, please wait. I am terribly sorry for the mix-up. I can assure you, it won't happen again. I will fire my secretary immediately for not making me aware of your arrival."

Jonathan looked at the man with a disgusted look on his face. He could read the name that was engraved on the man's gold tie clip. "Listen to me, François. When I come to a place of business to do business, I expect a little more attention and hospitality from my associates. Do I make myself clear?"

The man nodded vehemently. "Yes, monsieur. I do apologize. I can assure you it will not happen again. Now what can I do for you?"

It took everything he had not to laugh out loud, but Jonathan kept his composure and carried on with his charade. "A little while ago, I sent my sister in here to retrieve something from my private box. A redhead. Very attractive. Surely you noticed her."

"Yes, monsieur. I believe I know the woman you speak of. I led her to the quiet room myself."

"Good. Then you know what I am here for."

The man's eyes widened, and he slowly shook his head.

Once again, Jonathan feigned his disgust. "Good grief, man! What on earth do they pay you for around here!"

"I am sorry, monsieur. Perhaps you can refresh my memory." The little man gave a pleading look.

"The box, man. The box! I need to see it."

"Absolutely, monsieur! If you will give me your key and follow me, I will be delighted to take you to it."

Jonathan rolled his eyes and looked as if he were completely going to lose it. "I don't have the key, you twit! I just told you. My sister has it! Don't you have a spare?"

"Monsieur, surely you know that we cannot allow anyone to enter the room without a key." Little beads of sweat were now forming on the man's brow.

Jonathan let out a big sigh. "Of course I know that, you idiot! Do you think I would keep important documents and the like here if I didn't?"

The man was now sweating profusely. He pulled a handkerchief from his waistcoat and mopped his brow.

Jonathan knew he had him now. He moved in for the kill. "Listen to me, you imbecile. In exactly ten seconds I'm walking out that door. When I leave, I will be making a phone call. I'm sure the man who will be here to replace you in an hour will be more than happy to let me into *my* private box." He put the emphasis on *my* to show his annoyance. And it worked.

"That won't be necessary, monsieur. Please wait here one moment." The little man quickly walked back down the corridor and stepped into the office he had originally came out of. Ten seconds later, he reemerged with a gigantic key ring and almost ran back to where Jonathan stood. "If you'll follow me. . ." He extended his arm out to show the way then started walking.

Jonathan now let a controlled smile appear on his face. This was the most fun he'd had in a year. He followed the little man down the hall and into a secure room. Inside the room there were little cubicles, each having its own door with a dead bolt on the inside. The little man walked over to one of the larger boxes and pulled the key ring from his pocket.

"I believe this is the box you were referring to, monsieur." He tapped a finger on the face of the box.

"It is. Thank you." Jonathan kept his serious demeanor.

The man unlocked the main lock with the giant key ring then took a single key out from his pants pocket. He inserted it into the other lock and turned it. There was a *click* as the tumblers gave way. He pulled down on the lever, and a hiss of air escaped as the seal gave way. The door to the safe opened and inside sat the large box. He pulled it out, walked into a private cubicle, and set it down on the table. "Just let me know when you are finished, monsieur. I will be happy to put it back for you. Let me know if I can get anything for you. Would you care for an espresso, latte, or a tea?"

"That will be all. Thank you," Jonathan said. He waited until the man left and then locked the dead bolt on the door. He lifted the lid on the box and held his breath. Could Remy really have taken all of his money? Surely she would know that he would come for her.

He pulled up the lid and was surprised. There were two bundles of cash and a note from Remy. He picked it up and read.

Dear Jonathan,

I do hope that you will forgive me, although I assume you won't. Anyway, I left you some cash. I wouldn't want you to be totally broke. Here's twenty thousand dollars. Don't spend it all in one place! I know you said you would come after me, and I hope you do. I have to admit, after seeing you last night, I do still have a thing for you. Let's just say I took your money to make sure you would come after me. I only hope that you will find it in your heart to remember what we had together. I guess that's the only thing that will keep me alive!

See ya soon,
Remy

He folded the paper and stuck it in his pocket. Now he had a dilemma. On one hand, he'd lost nearly six million dollars. Contrary to what Remy thought, it wasn't his life's earnings. He had at least ten other safe-deposit boxes in other cities with as much, or more, cash in them. But it was the principle of the thing. Could he just let someone walk away with his cash?

On the other hand, he did still have a thing for her. It would be fun chasing her down. And who knew? Maybe she was being honest in her letter. Maybe she still did have a thing for him, too.

He would find her, but not until he dealt with this scroll business. He was sure she wouldn't really be where she had said. He'd known that all along. No matter. He would find her. And for her sake, she'd better hope she still had a thing for him.

CHAPTER 42

The Vatican

Wickham strolled through the courtyards and the people on his way to the papal apartment. He wore a smart smile on his face—not too jovial, but reassuring and polite. Soon he would be the one everybody relied on to get them through the crisis of a recently deceased pope. He needed to appear strong. But inside he was as happy as a schoolchild enjoying his first day of summer vacation.

He nodded as he passed a young couple, probably on their way to the Sistine Chapel. He could see the brochure in the young man's hand. They smiled, holding hands, and brushed past him as if he wasn't even there. That would soon change. He would have one of the most recognizable faces in the world. The death of the pope was going to be a spectacle. And he would be in the center of it.

He took his time walking, contrary to what he'd told the young lady on the phone he would do. He couldn't care less about giving the old man his last rites. He slowly made his way through the maze of the buildings until he finally arrived at the apartment. He nodded to the Swiss guard standing outside the door, turned the knob, and let himself in.

The room smelled of death. It lingered throughout, reminding him of a nursing home. He'd been to enough of them to know. Early on in his career as a priest, it was his duty, as with all young priests, to visit the elderly. He could recall the smell just by thinking about it. And now here it was again, stinging his nostrils.

Paul lay in his bed like a statue. The color had already drained out of him so that his face resembled that of a wax figure at some museum. His eyes were closed, and a sheet was tucked under his chin. Wickham touched his forehead. It was cool.

No one had said anything yet. There were at least ten people in the room, counting medical staff, and clergy.

"He's gone, Cardinal Wickham," a young nurse sobbed. She tried to control her tears, but they just streamed down her face.

No one acknowledged that she had even said anything. Everyone stood there with their heads down, eyes at the floor. He assumed they were all saying some kind of prayer for the old man. He knew now was the time to take charge. Any faltering, and it could cause him problems later. He needed to assert himself quickly. The only thing he could think of, spur of the moment, was to ask a simple question. "Who gave the last rites?"

The voice he heard was not the one he expected. Actually, he hadn't even seen him when he had walked in. But from behind him, he heard the unmistakable voice of Cardinal Joseph McCoy. "I did."

He turned to see the cardinal stepping out from behind a doctor. Joseph walked over and put his hand on Wickham's shoulder. "Louis, I wasn't sure if you would make it in time."

"No, that's fine, Joseph. I'm glad you did." He was still trying to figure out what in the world Joseph was doing here in the first place. As if reading his mind, the younger cardinal filled him in.

"One of the nurses alerted me. She had heard that Paul and I were very close." He raised an eyebrow. "I rushed in here to find him barely able to breathe. I just finished giving the last rites when you walked in."

Wickham readied a suitably somber expression and addressed the rest of the room. "Let's all remember Paul in our prayers, as well as the church around the world who will mourn his loss. I'll need to prepare a statement for the press. Don't discuss his passing until after we've released that official statement. There is much to do." He started for the door. "Joseph, would you come with me? I could use your help."

Cardinal McCoy fell into step right behind Wickham. Outside, the chill of the cool February air stung their faces. Joseph pulled his jacket up over his collar. He reached out and grabbed Wickham by the shoulder. "Louis, I'm nervous about this."

Wickham looked around to make sure no one was within earshot of them. "What's to be nervous about? It's done. He's gone."

"What if there's an autopsy? What are they going to find?"

"Nothing."

"What do you mean, nothing?"

"Just what I said, Joseph, nothing. There's not going to be an autopsy. There's never been an autopsy on a pope. And we're not about to start now."

CHAPTER 43

London

Anna kept trying to spot one of her guards. She figured that they were as good as they said, because she'd been trying for the last two hours and still hadn't even caught a glimpse of one. She had spent a good hour studying the faces in the photographs. It almost made her wonder if they were really there. Finally, while stopping for coffee at a café in Piccadilly Circus, a lady in a waitress outfit set a small piece of paper in front of her. She unfolded the note and stared at the five little words written in very neat handwriting:

Don't worry, we're here, Anna!

She showed the note to Jason who laughed heartily at her reddened face.

They finished their coffees and headed back out into the craziness that was London shopping. Every street was lined with store after store carrying clothing from designer one-of-a-kinds to straight-off-the-rack-we-got-ten-more-just-like-it-in-the-back. Shops with elaborate window scenes donned every corner. A person could easily find anything here, from beach sandals to formal evening wear.

Suddenly, Jason stopped at the corner of the street.

Anna backtracked to rejoin him. "What's up?"

"Pay phone. Over there." He pointed to the other side of the street, opposite the way Anna had started.

"What for? Use your cell."

"Pay phone's untraceable. Never know who's listening. And we need to find out when we can go to the embassy."

"So you're just going to call? And say what? 'Hi. This is Jason. We want to come over and see some guy named Benjamin. Can you tell him we're coming?'"

"Ha, ha! Smart aleck." He headed for the phone, Anna trotting after him. "No, but we need to know hours of operation. And. . ."

"And what?"

"And I don't know. We'll see what comes up."

"Well, I guess it's better than nothing."

They crossed the street, and Jason stepped inside the tiny phone booth. Anna waited outside. There was barely enough room for Jason to get in.

He dialed a number, nodded a few times, said something, and then hung up. He extricated himself from the booth. "Guess we need some formal clothes. I need a suit, and you need a dress, or a gown, or whatever you call it." He shrugged.

"A gown? What are you talking about? To go to the Israeli embassy? Man, are they strict!"

"I thought you women loved getting dressed up."

"For a formal ball, maybe. Not just to go see some guy at a foreign embassy."

"Well, that's exactly where we're going. To a formal ball."

Anna just looked at him blankly.

"It seems," he continued, "the embassy is closed today. Tonight is some annual ball that they have. It is, from what I understood, quite a big deal. Invitation only. That's what the lady said."

"And how do you suppose we get into this ball?"

"My guess is, if your grandpa was planning to go to the embassy today, he must have been on the guest list. We just need to hope that whoever's working the door doesn't know what he looks like."

"Well then, we'd better hurry."

They passed in front of a men's shop that had a mannequin standing in the window wearing a charcoal-gray suit. The suit was shiny and looked expensive. It was a four-button and was accented by a crisp white shirt and a deep red tie. The sign in the window said: CERTAIN MERCHANDISE 60 PERCENT OFF.

Anna snagged Jason by the elbow and led him inside. "I think that would look awesome on you." She pointed to the window. Jason said nothing. He just looked back as Anna dragged him inside the store.

A little bell hanging above the door chimed as they stepped inside. A man in a suit similar to the one in the window stepped out from behind the counter. He was tall and skinny. He had a pointy nose that had little rectangular glasses trying to fall off the end of it. He pushed them up with the tip of his fingers and tilted his head back to see who had come to visit him in his little boutique.

"Good day. How may I help you?"

"How ya doin'?" Anna greeted the little man. "My friend here needs a new suit."

"Ah, Yanks, I see!" The man moved forward and stuck out his hand. "My name is Chester Winfield, the Third." He rolled his *r* when he said *Third*. "I don't get many Americans in here, even though it does seem that the lot of you love to shop here in Piccadilly Circus. No, I guess the little shop and rather bland sign out front don't usually appeal to the tourists." He had turned around and started walking back to his station. He evidently realized he was rambling on when he turned back around. "Oh! I'm sorry! Do forgive my rudeness. Now, where were we? Ah, right! Your man here needs a suit of clothes. Right! Let's see, then. Shall we?"

The old man extended his arm in front of him. They followed him toward the rear of the store where Chester Winfield III busied himself getting a tape measure and a piece of chalk.

"Step up here, please." He motioned Jason onto a wooden block sitting in front of a set of three mirrors. The two outside ones angled in to give the onlooker an almost 360-degree view.

Anna, meanwhile, sifted through some different fabrics and looked at already tailored suits. She folded a few pieces of the fabric over her arm, grabbed two suit coats, and walked back to where the men were. The old man was jabbering away. Jason looked as though he was being held captive. His arms were stretched out to his sides, and his head was facing straight ahead. His feet were together and his legs were ramrod straight.

"Excuse me," Anna said.

The shopkeeper stopped dead in his tracks. He was bent at the waist, stretching a tape measure along the outside of Jason's leg. He tilted his head upward to face Anna. His rectangular spectacles were barely hanging on. Anna suppressed a laugh and moved a hand to cover her smirk.

"Yes, young lady. I am here at your service." He outstretched his arm, a servantlike gesture, and watched as the pieces of fabric and the tape measure fell to the floor.

"I'm sorry, Mr. Winfield." Anna giggled. "I didn't mean to interrupt you.

"Nonsense! I'll have none of that." He made a stern face. "You, my dear, are a customer. And I provide a service. Therefore, you and your friend here are the most important things in my life right now. What is it you need?"

Was this guy for real? She had heard that the English were unbelievably friendly, but this guy was over the top. Regardless, he was delightful. "I saw a suit in the window. It was very handsome. Is it available? And how much is it?"

The man placed his finger on his chin and looked as if he were trying to recall the exact suit, despite there being only one in the window. Jason still perched, stiff as a board, on the box. He shifted, catching Winfield's attention. "You may step down now, sir. I believe we have exactly what you need." Then to Anna, "I love that suit. And there's only two of them left." The corners of his mouth softened and his brow crinkled. "Actually, come to think of it, there were only two made. Yes, I'm sure of it! Only two."

This time Anna couldn't help herself. She let out a hearty laugh.

"Now then," said Mr. Winfield. He moved over to the side wall and slid back a panel that revealed the front window. The mannequin wearing the suit had its back to them. He leaned in and retrieved it. He stepped back out and placed it in the center of the room. He looked over to Jason. "How tall are you?"

Jason looked at him incredulously. The man had just measured him head to toe. "I don't know," he said. "Six foot, six foot one?"

"Yes," the man smiled. "Very tall, young man. Right! That suit will never do."

"What?" Anna asked, disappointed. "What do you mean?"

Winfield waved her off. "Oh, not this one, dear." He pointed to the mannequin. "The other one. The one I was going to have this lad try on. This one"—he pointed at the charcoal-gray jacket—"is magnificent! It will look spectacular on you."

Anna and Jason watched as the old man went to work, undressing the mannequin. In no time, he had the suit off and folded neatly over his arm. He ushered Jason back onto the box in the rear of the room and handed him the jacket.

"Try this on," he said.

It was a little short in the sleeves, but otherwise, it fit great.

"Now the pants." Winfield tossed them up to Jason, who stood there looking blank. "The pants, lad, try them on."

Anna giggled. "Don't mind me. I'll turn around."

Winfield turned around and looked startled to see her standing there. "Oh right! I forgot. In here, lad." He opened a door behind him revealing a changing room. "Good gracious! A man deserves some privacy, doesn't he?"

Jason tried the pants on while Anna and Mr. Winfield discussed the price of the suit. He told her that business had been good this month and he was feeling very generous. He told her that the suit would normally sell for around 600 pounds. It wasn't one of the items that the sign in the window suggested was 60 percent off. He then told her that he was, however, having more fun with them than he'd had all day. He told them that Americans fascinated him. He told her he would let them have the suit for 280 pounds.

"And don't tell your boyfriend that I gave you such a good deal," he said in a whisper. "You can take the extra money and go get something nice for yourself."

Anna looked a little embarrassed. "Um, he's not really my boyfriend."

Winfield looked appalled. "Nonsense! I've seen young couples come in here for thirty years, young lady. If that boy in there isn't head over heels for you, then I quit!"

Anna smiled. "Maybe you're right."

Winfield was about to respond when Jason came back out. He had the pants on, along with the jacket. He stepped back up onto the box and waited for the little man to start making his marks and pinning the cuffs. It took all of two minutes for Winfield to finish.

"There," he said. "You may go and change, young man. I will have your suit ready for you in about an hour. Give or take ten minutes. I do have tea coming along in about fifteen minutes."

Jason stepped off the box and back into the changing room. Anna went to the front, waited for Winfield to write up a sales receipt, and then paid him. She thought about what Winfield had said. She remembered what she was thinking when she peeked her head into Jason's classroom a couple of days ago and saw him for the first time. She had thought that he was one of the nicest-looking guys she'd seen in a long time. And if she were anywhere else doing anything else, she would have made a point to at least talk to him and find out if he was an idiot or not.

Jason came out of the dressing room and met them at the counter. Anna had already picked out a shirt and tie to match the suit, the same ones they had seen in the window. She handed them to Jason and thanked Mr. Winfield. She assured him that he was the most interesting person she'd met in her entire time in England. He shook Jason's hand and then nodded to Anna with a smirk, leaning in and whispering in her ear, "Head over heels, I tell you. Don't you forget it!"

Anna gave him a slight nod and moved toward the door. Jason thanked the man and hurried to catch Anna. As they left the store, Jason was fumbling with the bags, trying to get them situated the way he wanted to carry them.

"You all right there?" she asked, giving him a hard time.

"Yeah, I guess. What'd he say to you back there?"

"Oh nothing. Let's go find me a nice dress while we wait on your pants."

They started walking down the street. Jason was holding the bags in his hand that was between them. Anna stepped around to the other side.

"You afraid I'm going to knock you in the back of the legs or something?" he asked jokingly.

"No," she said. "I just couldn't do this from over there."

She reached down and took his hand in hers. They interlocked their fingers and walked on. Jason looked over at her, and his smile met hers. They walked down the street holding hands as if they had been together like that for years.

CHAPTER 44

Paris

Jonathan sat in Remy's apartment, staring at the coffee table and what was left of the money she'd stolen. Normally he wouldn't listen to medical advice, but this time was different. Just the short trip to the bank and back had left him feeling as if he'd run a marathon. Every square inch of his body ached, and he was exhausted. He could lie back and probably fall asleep in seconds. But he wouldn't.

He had to get Edmond's lifeless body out of the middle of the floor and into the kitchen. Remy had a chest freezer in the back of the room. He spent the next fifteen minutes cleaning it out. He threw out cartons of ice cream, frozen dinners, and all sorts of meats like they were yesterday's newspaper.

He set his crutches aside and pulled a chair over to the giant box. He sat down so he could take the pressure off his legs. He bent over and rolled Edmond so that he was on his stomach. He grabbed him by the shirt collar and heaved his dead weight up until the front half of his body was inside the freezer. From there he just flipped his legs over, watched the crumpled body fall the rest of the way in, and then closed the lid. Now he wouldn't have to smell the foul odor while waiting for Waukeem and his team to get there. He fumbled into the bathroom and grabbed some towels. Then he looked around under the sink for some cleaning supplies. Finding what he needed, he hobbled his way back into the other room to finish cleaning up the blood.

If he was exhausted before, he was borderline comatose now. His heart pounded. His breathing was labored, and sweat poured from his brow. He wanted to lie down. Take a quick nap. But he couldn't. Not yet. He still had one more thing to do. Another phone call. This one he was already regretting. He didn't have the energy to argue with Wickham. Nevertheless, that's exactly what he was about to do.

"Hello, this is Cardinal Wickham."

"Louis, it's me. We need to talk." He waited for the eruption he was sure was soon to come.

"I can't really talk right now," Wickham said pleasantly. "Why don't I call you back in about twenty minutes or so?"

Jonathan pulled the phone away and looked at it quizzically. "That's not possible. My phone is dead. I'm calling from another number. Tell me when I can call you back."

"Give me five minutes."

"All right. I'll call you in five minutes."

Jonathan hung up the phone and leaned back on his crutches. Now that was weird. Never in the history of his talking to that odious man had he heard a tone like the one he had just witnessed. What was going on? Either something was very, very wrong, or something was very, very good. He hoped it was the latter.

Five minutes later, he redialed. "We need to talk," he said again when Wickham answered.

"So talk."

"I've got a problem."

"And what kind of problem would that be?"

"I've been benched."

"What do you mean, *benched*?"

"You know. Benched. Taken out of the game. Put on the sidelines. Out of commission."

There was silence for a moment. Then a big sigh. Finally, Wickham spoke. His tone changed. It went from polite to disappointed.

"Jonathan, why do you always have to ruin the perfect day? Did I do something to you in an earlier life? Is this some kind of elaborate scheme to get me back for some wrong I've done you? What is it? Revenge? Tell me. Because right now, this moment that I'm trying to enjoy is the pinnacle of my life's work so far. And you are ruining it."

"I'm sorry. There's nothing I can do. I'll be out of pocket for at least a few days. A week at most."

"Do you know what I'm doing right now?"

"Probably seething. Foaming at the mouth. But I can't change it. That's the way it is."

"No Jonathan, I'm not seething. Nor am I foaming at the mouth. Actually, I'm celebrating. It seems our beloved pope has passed away."

Jonathan had never been a spiritual man. He never cared for going to church. Whenever he would find himself in a conversation about faith or religion, he would just shrug it off. The fact that the most famous and powerful religious figure in the world was dead wouldn't normally mean anything to him. But this was different.

In the span of two seconds, his entire view of Cardinal Louis Wickham changed. He wasn't just dealing with a determined employer. He was dealing with a lunatic. Wickham had killed the pope.

"How'd he die?"

"He's been sick."

"I see."

"Do you?"

"What do you mean?"

"You know what I mean, Jonathan. Tell me about your problem."

"I told you already. I'm down for at least a week."

"Why? What happened?"

"Well, let's just say I had to get a second opinion on a medical issue."

"Get a third one if you have to. I want my scroll."

"And you'll get it," Jonathan snapped. "Just not for another week."

There was silence on the line for several seconds. Finally, Jonathan heard Wickham cursing under his breath.

"Here's the thing," Jonathan said matter-of-factly, "I'm gone for a week. You don't like it, find someone else to get your stupid scroll. Otherwise, pay me my money, like a good boss, and deal with it!"

Jonathan heard the labored breathing on the other end of the line. "You have a week," Wickham spat. The line went dead.

Jonathan hung up the phone and made his way back to the couch. He sat down and leaned his head back, closing his eyes. He was over it. He hated everything about that stupid little scroll. He didn't care what it was for, what it did, or who it benefited. He hated Wickham. The man was a sleazy, rude weasel. And he hated being bested by an amateur. That's what the girl was—an amateur. And so far, it was a million to nothing in the girl's favor.

He would take the week to get better. Then he'd take care of this scroll business once and for all. He didn't care who he had to beat up, run over, or flat-out kill to get it done. Then he would tell Wickham to shove it. He smiled to himself. That part was going to be fun.

One other thing, too. He was done. No more. This was going to be his last job. He was tired. He was getting old. And he was rich. And after he found Remy. . .well, he decided to play that one by ear.

The Vatican

Wickham hung up the phone and shook his head. Jonathan had once again ruined his day. Couldn't he have just one victory without someone or something getting in the way?

He pulled the collar of his jacket up over his face and walked back out into the cold. He crossed the courtyard and stepped back into his building. Fumbling for his keys, he undid the lock and moved inside. A voice startled him, and he dropped his keys on the floor.

"Bravo, Louis! Bravo!" the voice said.

Wickham turned around slowly to face his visitor. "What are you doing here?"

"You know, Louis, I think I've tolerated your insubordination long enough. I guess you've forgotten who your master is." Lucifer moved close to Wickham and stuck out his hand, palm down. "Kiss my hand, Louis. Show me you still serve me."

Wickham began to tremble as he bent at the waist and took hold of Lucifer's hand. Lucifer quickly pulled it away from him and slapped him hard across the face.

Lucifer grabbed Wickham by his hair and screamed, "You kneel when you pay homage to me, you stupid monkey!"

Without saying a word, Wickham quickly knelt to one knee and kissed Lucifer's hand.

Lucifer smiled and stepped back. "Little trained monkeys. That's all you are. You know that? Your whole species. Little trained monkeys. I still, to this day, do not understand why He even bothered with you. I mean, weren't we good enough for Him? Didn't we love Him? Isn't that what He created us for? And me!" He threw his arms up in the air. "Do you know that I was the most beautiful one of all?" He started pacing around in a circle. "I was the angel of worship. My entire body was one giant musical instrument. Every word I spoke came out like a concerto that even your Mozart would envy. He loved me. I was the angel of light. I was spectacular."

He paused again, stopped walking, and bent over so that he was right in front of Wickham's face. Then he began screaming again. "And I knew it! I was the most spectacular thing He'd ever created! Nothing could even come close to what I was!" He paused and lowered his voice again. "And that was the problem. I knew it. And I liked it. And if I was so spectacular, why couldn't I be like Him? Well, you know what, Louis? I am spectacular. And I may not have the power He has, but I've got the means to stop His cute little fairy tale." He stopped and snapped his fingers with a disappointed look on his face. "Oh wait. That's right. I don't. Because"—and now he started screaming again—"you haven't gotten me my scroll!"

Louis stared blankly at him. "You'll have your scroll before next week."

"Well, I certainly hope so," Lucifer said. "For your sake." He stepped over to Wickham's desk and sat down at his chair. "Now, on to other business. I do have to say, you have rather impressed me on the other matter. I mean, to actually *murder* the pope? Incredible! For a while there, I thought you were going to screw that up, too."

"I'm going to be busy this week. It'll be like a circus around here," Wickham muttered.

"Yes it will. I will leave you to your business. But I'm telling you, Louis. After you see to it that Joseph gets elected, I'd better get that scroll. For two thousand years I've searched for it. And your predecessors failed me. I promised them the same things I've promised you. They couldn't get the job done. And now they are paying for it. Don't make me show you how they are spending their eternities. It's not pretty."

"What's on the scroll?" Wickham asked.

"I don't know," said Lucifer. "But I do know what it does."

"What's it do?" Wickham asked

"It keeps me from owning this world free and clear. And that means it keeps you from having all the power I promised you."

"I'll get the scroll."

"Like I said, let's hope you do. For your sake."

CHAPTER 45

The Vatican

I need to see Cardinal Wickham." Hale stared at the receptionist. She looked at him as if he were speaking Japanese. He was getting impatient. The woman hadn't said one word to him since he'd been standing there. She just held the receiver of the phone she was holding to her ear. She was nodding her head up and down, as if the person on the other end could hear her nodding. Again she held up a finger, letting Hale know he was going to have to wait until she was finished.

He had barely gotten the plane in the air when the news came over the radio. Pope Paul was dead. At first he couldn't believe it. Hale truly loved the man. He wasn't just a spiritual teacher for him, he was like a father. Hale had never known his father, and Paul had treated him like a son.

He spent most of the long flight crying and recalling memories of Paul and himself. Some were nothing more than simple conversations they had shared. Others were more significant. One in particular came to him, the day he became a Christian. Paul had been the one who led him to make that decision. It was, Hale thought, the best day of his life.

His last conversation with Paul, over the phone, let him know that there were enemies of the Vatican within its own walls. Paul's death couldn't have been due to some flu. It had to be something more involved than that. And he had a feeling that a certain nosy cardinal was to blame.

The woman at the desk finally hung up the phone and stared at him with an uninterested look.

Hale repeated himself for the third time. "I need to see Cardinal Wickham."

"I'm afraid he's busy right now. Is there something I can help you with?"

Hale sighed in frustration. He didn't like being rude with people, but he saw no other choice. "Listen, lady. I understand that the cardinal is busy. I know he's dealing with everything that's going on today."

"We lost our spiritual father today, sir. I think you could be a little more sympathetic."

That was it. Hale had reached his limit. "What's your name, miss?"

"Claire. Claire Costello."

"Well, Claire, here's the deal. I'm going to ask you again to get Cardinal Wickham for me. After that, I'm going to go find him myself. When I do, I'm going to let him know how you let one of his special agents, with level-nine clearance, I might add, sit out here when he needed to give the cardinal a highly classified message."

The woman looked at him blankly. "I don't know of any special agents with level-nine clearance, nor do I have any idea what it means."

"Well, you're looking at one right now. And he's not enjoying this little jousting session with you. Now, where's the cardinal?"

The woman moved her arm across the desk and lifted the phone. She never took her eyes off Hale. She pushed a button and spoke. "Cardinal Wickham, I have a Special Agent Hale here to see you. . . . Uh-huh. . . . Okay. I'll tell him." She hung up the phone and smiled. "The cardinal will see you now."

Hale gave the woman a smart smile and said, "Thank you."

Miss Costello motioned with her hand to the office door that stood behind her. "He's in there."

Hale was already halfway around the desk. He knew where the cardinal's office was. He'd walked past it a dozen times or more in the past.

Cardinal Wickham was sitting behind his desk, his feet resting on an open drawer. He had his hands folded neatly in front of him, and he seemed to be suppressing a smile. He never changed his position as he studied Hale.

"Hello, Agent Hale. I understand you needed to see me?"

"What happened to him?"

Wickham's expression was thoughtful. "Well, he was sick. You knew that. Everyone knew that."

Hale grabbed a chair and thunked it backward in front of the desk. Straddling it, he rested his arms over the back. "Let me tell you what I know."

Wickham raised his brow and waved his hand in front of Hale, as if to say, "Go ahead."

Hale fixed Wickham with a piercing glare. "I know what didn't happen to him."

Wickham looked genuinely surprised. "What do you mean?"

"I mean," Hale said, "that he didn't die from some flu."

"I see." The cardinal stood up and walked from behind his

desk. "And what makes you think that?"

"I also know that since Paul's untimely death, you're in charge around here."

Wickham had now moved to within inches of Hale. He leaned over and said, "That's how our government is structured around here. What are you insinuating?"

"I also know that Paul thought he had an enemy around here."

Wickham was now almost nose to nose with Hale. His beady little eyes were bloodshot. His lips moved into a thin line as he pointed a finger in Hale's face. "I suggest you either quit talking in circles and tell me what you came here for, or get out." He jabbed a finger back at the door.

Hale stood up. He was a good six inches taller than the cardinal. "I came here to tell you I've got nothing to say to you." He turned around and headed for the door but called back over his shoulder, "Except that I'm going to find out what really happened. And when I do, you'd better hope you didn't have anything to do with it."

Hale touched the doorknob.

"Tell me about the girl," Wickham said from behind him.

That was it. Now he was positive. Paul, unless he was drugged and couldn't control his faculties, would never mention Anna or the scroll to anyone. He turned to face Wickham. "Excuse me?"

"The girl. Paul mentioned something about her just before he passed."

"I don't know what you're talking about."

Wickham tried to look innocent. "Neither do I, Agent Hale. Paul was barely able to squeak it out. He said, 'Ask Hale about the girl.' I just assumed that was what you came here about."

Hale returned that innocent look with one of his own. "Like I said, I don't know what you're talking about, Cardinal."

"If someone's in trouble and you're keeping it a secret, I'll have your badge! You will be looking for employment elsewhere, sir!"

Hale walked out the door without another word.

CHAPTER 46

London

It was getting late in the afternoon when Anna and Jason finished up their shopping trip. They had visited several boutiques before Anna found exactly what she wanted. She had initially chosen a beautiful deep red gown with a high collar and long sleeves, but Jason noticed that wearing something so bold would draw attention to them—and that wasn't what they wanted. So she found another, equally beautiful black dress. It was simple, but when Anna stepped out of the dressing room to show him, he declared that, whether they wanted the attention or not, it was going to be hard to avoid when she looked so beautiful.

Anna couldn't remember the last time she'd blushed that hard.

After asking the cab driver to drop them off a few blocks from the safe house, they watched over their shoulders as they walked the few blocks back to the old brownstone. It didn't seem that anyone was taking special notice of them.

They hadn't been inside more than a few minutes when they heard a knock on the door.

Carefully, Jason moved to the foyer and peeked out of the peephole. There was nobody there. He undid the locks and opened the door an inch. The chain was still engaged, and the door was reinforced steel. If anyone tried to force their way in, the chain would easily stop them.

He looked out and didn't see anything. Anna was behind him whispering, "Who is it?" He didn't bother to answer but just waved his hand at her as if to say, "Shh. . ."

He was about to close the door again when he noticed a note lying on the doorjamb. He picked it up and closed the door. He turned back to Anna and held it up. It was a note addressed to him.

"Well, what is it?" she asked.

He rolled his eyes at her. "What am I? A psychic?"

He opened it and read it aloud.

Jason,

We were very impressed with your attention today. Keep it up, but don't worry. We're still watching. We won't contact you again unless it's an emergency.

P.S. Anna, we loved the red dress, too. But Jason was right— too much attention!

The security team

"Well," Anna said, "looks like you're just a regular James Bond!"

Jason laughed. "Just trying to keep us alive."

"I know. You did good."

She walked over, reached up, and moved the hair out of his eyes. Then she leaned up on her toes and kissed his cheek. "I mean it, you know. I never once felt unsafe today."

"Thanks." He smiled.

She pulled back, feeling suddenly shy. "I guess now we need to figure out how to get in to that embassy."

They started in the office where Thomas kept his notes. Jason went through drawers as Anna sifted through notebooks and loose papers, looking for any information about an embassy ball. Nothing.

They moved from room to room, looking everywhere they could think of. Finally, after leaving Jason to rifle through her grandfather's study, she went back to the kitchen where she noticed a small stack of unopened mail sitting on the far counter. She thumbed through the first few pieces and stopped. An envelope with the Israeli embassy letterhead stared back at her. She tore open the end and pulled out the contents. She breathed a sigh of relief and ran back to the study.

"Hey, I found it!" She waved it in the air like a baton.

"I see that. What does it say?"

She opened it up and read it. "It says here that the Prime Minister's Ball," she said it with a swanky slur, "starts precisely at eight and goes until midnight." She turned it over and looked at both sides. "It doesn't say how many guests the invitation is good for."

"Well, let just hope it's a 'bring a date' invite," Jason said.

Anna raised her eyebrows, pursed her lips, and said cheekily, "Oh, so now you're my date?"

"No," Jason said matter-of-factly, "you're *my* date."

"Oh really?"

Jason grabbed the invitation out of her hand. He held it up and ran his finger under two words. "Yes, really. Unless you can convince them you're Thomas Riley." He chuckled and pointed to the box sitting on the table. "And in that dress, I don't think that's humanly possible."

Anna threw her hands up in the air. "Well, sir," she said,

"would you like to have a beautiful young lady accompany you to your function this evening?" She tilted her head and batted her eyes.

Jason smiled and bowed. "I would be delighted, miss."

Rows of horse-drawn carriages and limousines lined Old Court Place. People wearing their finest attire stood along the street, waiting to get into the Israeli embassy. The annual Prime Minister's Ball was in full swing.

Jason handed the woman at the reception area his invitation. Anna held her breath. The woman glanced at the invitation, looked back at Jason with a curious stare, and handed it back to him. She then picked up a piece of paper with a list of names on it. She ran her finger down the list until she found the name she was looking for. She took her pen and marked a check by the name Thomas Riley. She smiled and said, "Enjoy your evening, sir."

Jason nodded and led Anna by the arm into the main reception room. "So far so good," he whispered.

They were about to sit at the first empty table when they noticed names printed on little white cards that sat at the head of each place setting. Along the far wall, by a beautiful stone fireplace, they found two that said Thomas Riley and Guest.

It was Jason's idea to sit and study the crowd for a while. If this Benjamin was also looking for Thomas, they might be able to spot him. Their table was mostly empty, and very few people were talking to one another. Aside from a few speeches, it was a remarkably dull affair. Anna felt disappointed—a ball at the embassy had sounded so glamorous.

As they were finishing their salads, a woman at their table knocked over a glass of wine. Jason offered to go get a waiter and ask for some napkins. He disappeared around the corner he'd seen the wait staff come from.

Anna decided it was a good time to visit the ladies' room. She'd seen several women leaving through a side door and then returning some minutes later. She figured that's where it would be. She got up from the table and headed that way.

As she reached the door, she felt someone take her elbow from behind. It was a tight grip and not very friendly. She was about to look behind her when she felt the cold steel of the barrel of a gun in her back. The man quickly pulled her from the doorway and shoved her down a secluded hall. He spoke only once. It was a command not to turn around or scream, or he would shoot her right where she stood.

She complied with the man's order and walked down the hall, tears brimming in her eyes. She had only left Jason for a minute. Now she was being kidnapped. She wondered if her security would come to her rescue. Probably not. They'd be waiting outside the building to make sure she came out safely. That wouldn't do her much good if her captors brought her out dead.

The man led her down a hallway that ended with a beautifully carved wooden door. The man pressed her against it. He held her still and fumbled with some keys. She heard the tumblers of the lock give way, and then the door opened.

He pushed her inside and closed the door behind them. She couldn't see anything but shadows. The only light coming in was that from the street outside. She heard the dead bolt being slid back into the door.

"Please, sir, this is a mistake—" she tried to say.

"Do not speak until I tell you to. Unless I like what you have to say, this will be a very short evening for you."

Anna's hands trembled. She felt like she was going to pass out.

She took a deep breath and tried to think. Jason would immediately come looking for her when he got back and didn't see her. Maybe she could buy some time until he found her. Stupid thought. How was Jason going to find her in some room on the other side of the building? The embassy wasn't a small place. It could take hours. By that time she could be dead. No, she decided, she was going to have to get herself out of this one.

She took a deep breath and stomped her foot in anger. "Do you know who I am?"

"No, I don't. And that's why we are here. Who are you and how did you get here?"

"My name is An—" She stopped. "Never mind what my name is. Who are you?"

"I am the one with the gun, so I am the one to ask questions. That's sensible, is it not?"

"What are you going to do, shoot me? Right here? Someone will hear. I have people who are going to be wondering where I am back at the ball. They're probably looking for me right now."

"Yes," the man said calmly. "I will shoot you if you don't tell me who you are and how your friend came into possession of a dead man's invitation."

It took a few seconds for Anna to put it together. But as she stood there staring at the man holding the gun, it dawned on her that she had found the man she was looking for. Or at least she hoped.

She said a quick silent prayer and hoped that what she was about to do was right. If not, she might just end up dead anyway.

"My name is Anna Riley. Thomas Riley was my grandfather. We came here looking for a man that my grandfather was supposed to meet. So if you're him, please put the gun away and let me go get my friend. I'm sure he's tearing this place apart trying to find me. And if you are who I think you are, then you don't want any attention drawn to us."

The man moved to the center of the room and placed the gun against Anna's temple.

When Jason returned to the table, Anna was gone. He touched one of their tablemates on the shoulder. "Excuse me. The woman I was with—did you see where she went?"

"She's probably off to the *loo*, boy. I know she's stunning, young man, but you shouldn't be so possessive. We ladies don't like that."

"I'm sorry," Jason said. "It's not like that. I just need to find her. It's an emergency."

The woman looked uninterested and pointed to the doorway across the hall. "The women's washroom is over there." Then she turned and went back to her conversation, picking up in midsentence, as if she hadn't been interrupted at all.

Jason hurried across the room and out into the hallway. He saw a sign for the ladies' room. He hurried to the entrance and listened. He could hear several voices inside. None of them sounded like Anna. They all had some kind of foreign accent. He waited a few seconds. One by one, women came out of the entryway.

Finally, when he was almost sure no one else was in there, he stepped in front of the entryway. "Psst! Anna, are you in there?"

There was no reply.

"Anna," he said a little louder this time, "It's me, Jason. Are you in there?"

A woman came around the corner and almost walked right into him. "I was the only one left in there, lad," she said with an Irish accent. "I do believe your Anna is somewhere else. Have you lost her, dear?"

"Um, yes ma'am," Jason said. "Sorry."

The older lady raised her eyebrow at him and put her hand on his shoulder. "I'm available, you know. In case you can't find her." She winked and smiled at him.

"Thank you," Jason said wearily, "I'll keep that in mind." He brushed the lady's hand from his shoulder and walked back down the hall. Where could she have gone? Suddenly he felt sick. What if someone grabbed her while he wasn't looking? He cursed himself for not being more careful. He had to hurry. She could be in serious trouble.

He'd just have to try every door until he found her. Three hallways and countless doors later, still no luck. Surely, any minute now, some security guard would come and haul him away for trespassing or something.

As he turned to go down the fourth hall, an older man wearing an expensive silk suit stopped him. "I say, lad, what's got you running about the place like you own it?"

Jason stammered for a second then said, "I. . .I'm looking for someone."

The man's face brightened. "Ah, the young lady you were with? Stunning, I tell you! She's absolutely stunning!"

Before he could think better of it, Jason grabbed the man by his lapels and pushed him up against the wall. "What do you know about her! Did you do something with her?"

The man turned white. "Good gracious! I've done nothing with her! I was just complimenting—"

Jason let go of the man and held his hands up in surrender. "Sir, I am so sorry. Please forgive me. It's just that she may be in trouble. I have to find her. Sorry!" He turned away and started down the fourth hall again.

"Lad! Wait!"

Jason didn't have time to be talking. He ignored the man and kept trying doors.

"I say, I was talking to you."

Jason stopped and whirled around on the man. "I said I'm sorry. That's all I can do right now. I'm very busy. Please let me be. I'll make it up to you later. I promise."

The man snorted. "Yes, boy, I know! That's what I'm trying to tell you. I saw her not five minutes ago."

"Where?"

The man swatted Jason's hands away. "Please stop grabbing at me. You're wrinkling my new suit!"

Jason let go. "I'm so sorry, sir. Please, where did you see her?"

The man took a breath and pointed his finger. "Over there."

He pointed to a narrow hallway that seemed to lead on and on. Jason couldn't see the end of it. It wasn't lit. "Down there?"

"Yes, lad. She was walking arm in arm with another gentleman. They looked like they were in a hurry. Are you sure she didn't just run off and leave you? It happens to the best of us." He chuckled.

"Thank you!" He ran for the hallway. The man called out something about how he could pay him back by letting him have a dance with Anna when he found her. Somehow, Jason didn't think Anna would have much time for dancing this evening, if she even survived.

At the end of the hall was a heavily carved door. He heard the faint murmur of voices, one female. Taking a deep breath, he cracked open the door.

He found himself staring into the barrel of a gun.

CHAPTER 47

The Vatican

Cardinal Wickham walked down an unimportant street in an anonymous part of town toward a nearly unnoticeable phone booth.

To place a call that would end a man's life.

A long time ago, Jonathan had given him the number of one of his colleagues. Wickham had never needed to use the number until now. With Jonathan out of pocket for the week, he had no choice. He needed a job done.

At the pay phone, he got a voice message that left directions to a fax machine. Jonathan had already told him what to expect, so he came prepared to write down the number.

Around the corner was an Internet café. Inside, he slipped his money into the bill collector and sent an electronic fax to the number he'd been given on the phone. Then he waited.

The call came just minutes after he sent the fax. A computerized voice with instructions. He left the café and hailed a cab, and ten minutes later he was in front of an old, run-down pub. The music was loud, the room smoky. The bartender looked to be a hundred years old. There were only three people in the place besides himself. He went to the back of the bar just as he'd been told to do. He sat down, waited five minutes, and then went to the restroom as instructed.

He went to the last stall, closed the door, and against his better judgment, sat down. From here, he didn't know what was to happen. He guessed he'd find out. If not, then he would just leave and call it a loss.

Another five minutes. He stood to leave.

"Sit back down."

He couldn't see anyone. He hadn't heard anyone come in. He sat back down. When he did, he noticed something he hadn't before. Up in the corner of the room, behind him, there was a small camera with an even smaller speaker mounted under it. It was pointed directly down at him.

"You have my number," the voice said. "So obviously you need some help."

"I do."

"Do you know who I am?"

"No. I only know of you from a friend. His name's Jonathan."

"And how is our friend Jonathan?"

"He's obviously not doing so well, or I wouldn't be talking to you."

There was a slight laugh. "Do you have the information for me?"

"I do."

"Behind the toilet there is a loose piece of tile. Open it. Inside there is a drawer. Put the information in there. And the money. You did bring the money with you?"

"Yes, I did."

"Good."

Wickham stood up and stooped down behind the toilet. He found the tile and removed it. He placed the folder inside the drawer and then replaced the tile. When he finished, he sat back down. Several minutes passed before he heard the voice again.

"This man," said the voice, "is no ordinary man."

"No," said Wickham, "he's not. He's very highly trained and very dangerous. He works for me. And now he's become a problem."

There was a pause. Then the voice. "I didn't know that the Vatican was in the habit of snuffing people out, Cardinal."

This was bad. This person knew who he was. He had to get out of here. He stood to leave.

"Sit back down, Cardinal Wickham," the voice said sternly.

There was a *click*. Wickham tried the door. It wouldn't budge.

"I said sit back down, Cardinal. The door is locked. I can control it from here."

Wickham sat back down.

"Don't worry, Padre, your secret's safe with me. I'm only in it for the money. I don't care who wants who dead. If someone paid me enough, I'd probably kill you. So don't worry. This is business."

Wickham sat back down and steadied his breathing. He guessed he'd have to trust this person.

"Now," said the voice, "tell me more about this man."

Wickham's voice was shaky. "His name is Hale. He's a pilot."

The Israeli Embassy, London

Without saying a word, the man holding the gun motioned for Jason to come inside.

Jason slowly walked into the room. There was Anna. She ran and put her arms around him.

"It's all right," she said. "This is Benjamin."

Jason stared over Anna's shoulder at the man holding the gun. He felt an overwhelming sense of relief, yet at the same time, he felt like he had failed the woman in his arms.

"Anna," he said, "I'm so sorry. I shouldn't have left you."

Anna shook her head vehemently. "No, Jason, I'm sorry. I shouldn't have gone off without you."

"What were you doing, anyway?" he asked.

"I was just going to the ladies' room."

He grabbed her hand and said, "It's all right. We're safe."

"For now," Benjamin interrupted.

Jason gestured to the gun still in Benjamin's hand. "Could have fooled us."

"I am sorry. But I had to find out who she was."

Jason frowned at Anna. "How did he know it was you? You told me Father Vin destroyed all your real identification."

Anna and Benjamin grinned at each other and then back at Jason. "Facebook," they said in unison.

"Enough chatting now," said Benjamin. "It's time to leave. Between the three of us, I think we've caused quite a stir this evening. Come with me."

Before either of them could say anything, Benjamin had slipped out of the door and started down the hallway. Jason and Anna followed him to a stairway. At the bottom, they were met by a giant steel door that had a keypad mounted on the wall to the left. Benjamin punched the keypad several times until it beeped and a red light on the pad turned to green. There was a soft *click*, and when Benjamin turned the knob, the door gave way.

Hurrying outside, Jason saw they were in an alley, and a car was parked about fifty feet away.

"That is my car." Benjamin pointed at the vehicle. "We hurry."

Twenty minutes later, they stopped in front of an old church. Inside, the wooden floors creaked under their feet. In the dim light, Jason took Anna's hand as they followed Benjamin all the way to the front of the sanctuary to sit in the first pew.

"Will you tell us why my grandfather planned to meet with you?" Anna glanced at Jason. He could read the hope in her eyes.

Benjamin frowned. "I do not actually know."

"But you've got to," Anna pleaded. "I mean, he was supposed to meet you. His journal said that you would help him put the mystery of the temple to rest."

"Yes, dear, I promised him I would get him into the temple. But for what, I do not know. He only told me that it was a matter of life and death. Beyond that, I am as lost as you."

Now Jason leaned forward. "Wait a minute. You mean you were going to get him into the temple at Jerusalem?"

"Yes."

Jason was astounded. "How? I mean, he couldn't get in there. Unless he was a Muslim."

"This I know," Benjamin said softly. "But I have friends. They are friends who are formerly of the Muslim faith. They have converted to Christianity. They were going to help me."

"Wait a minute," Anna said. "Aren't you Jewish?"

"I am what you would call a messianic Jew. I believe that the Christ child was the Messiah. I am a Christian."

"I thought the temple was a Jewish thing," said Anna.

Jason squeezed her hand. "During the crusades, the Muslims took over Jerusalem. They built a mosque on the site of the former Jewish temple. Since then, that site has been the centerpiece for war, terrorism, and any other kind of disagreement between Jews and Muslims. It is considered, by some, the holiest place on earth."

"And my grandfather thought that he could find the answer to the riddle there."

Benjamin nodded.

"Did he explain to you what he was working on?" Anna asked.

"No. I never wanted to know. He only told me that it was a riddle. I believed that he was doing God's work. I offered to help him. He just said that he needed to get inside."

"And how could you get him in?" Jason asked.

"I am a member of the Mossad," Benjamin said. "It is like your CIA. Through my contacts, I was able to arrange a chance for him to get inside and do some snooping around."

"And when was that supposed to happen?" Anna asked.

"Next week," Benjamin answered.

Anna held up her hand. "Still confused here. What good is getting into the mosque if the temple has been destroyed?"

Benjamin let out a sigh. "Underneath the mosque, there is a maze of tunnels and caverns. There are everything from tombs to secret tunnels leading out of the city. Your grandfather believed he could find a room under there called the Holy of Holies. Are you familiar with it?"

Anna shook her head. "What is it?"

Benjamin's eyes glowed as he continued. "In the time of Jesus, there was a great curtain that separated the Holy of Holies from the rest of the temple. Only the high priests were allowed to enter. It was said that the presence of God dwelled there. When Jesus was crucified, the curtain was miraculously torn from top to bottom, without human hand, signifying that man had the right to know God personally. Of course, the Jewish leaders still tried to keep everyone out. They refused to believe that Jesus was who he said he was and held on to the Mosaic law, the covenant of the Old Testament. Because it was such a secret place, your grandfather thought that what he was in search of could be found in that room."

"But wouldn't it have been destroyed?" Anna asked.

"Perhaps. But he was willing to risk his life to find out."

"Risk his life?" Anna was confused. "What do you mean?"

Deep sorrow showed on Benjamin's face. "For centuries, no Jew or Christian has been allowed there. To be caught would mean certain death."

"Wow," Anna said. "That's pretty heavy."

There was silence in the room for a while. Anna sat with her elbows on her knees, her chin resting in her hands. Benjamin had leaned back, looking at the ceiling.

Anna finally stood up. She looked at Benjamin. "Can you get us in?"

Benjamin half laughed. "You? Are you serious?"

"That's crazy. We can't go in there," Jason agreed.

"Why not?"

"You'll be killed, for one thing," Benjamin said. "It would have taken almost a miracle to sneak Thomas inside that place. It would be absolutely impossible to get you—a woman—inside."

"Anna, listen," Jason interrupted. "If we were caught, we would be killed. No trial. No jury. Just shot. Probably in the back of the head. Do you understand that?"

She looked at Benjamin. "You said you were a member of the Mossad, right?"

"Yes."

"And they're like our CIA?"

"Well, I think we are a little more efficient in some matters, but yes. Sort of." He smiled.

"Well, I've got news for you. If it meant continuing a mission sanctioned by God Himself, my CIA would get me in that building."

"Anna, be reasonable!" Jason ran frustrated fingers through his hair.

"My grandfather thought that the answer to the riddle was in there. He was willing to risk his life for it. And now it's my job."

Jason cupped her face with his hands and brushed her bangs back. "And it's my job to protect you."

"Then do it," she said softly. "I made a promise that I would continue my grandfather's work. I promised Vin. And more important than that, I promised God." She looked him in the eyes. "I'm going in that temple, with or without his help. Are you coming with me?"

After a moment, Jason stepped back, shaking his head. "Okay." Then he pointed a finger at her. "But you do what I say once we're inside. Deal?"

Anna just rolled her eyes at him. Then she looked back at Benjamin. He had a sour look on his face, as if he'd been insulted. "So what about it, Mr. Mossad? Are you going to get us in, or what?"

Benjamin stood up. He walked over to Anna and leaned in. He had an awful scowl on his face. "Let me tell you something, young lady. Neither I nor the Mossad has *ever* been bested by your CIA. Don't you forget it." Then he smiled and softened his tone. "I'll see you at the King David Hotel in Jerusalem in five days."

CHAPTER 48

Hale pressed the button on the radio and asked for clearance to land. The reply came back in seconds. He was instructed to land on the north runway. He touched down and engaged reverse thrusters. Within seconds the small aircraft was taxiing toward the hangar.

It was late. He hadn't been able to get out of Rome as early as he had wanted. By the time he'd gotten to the airport, there was a big delay, holding up every aircraft. Apparently there was a fuel spill. It took almost four hours to clean up the mess and make it safe to resume all flights.

He had called Marie and Miles from the air. He told them all that had happened that day. They said that they had already heard about the pope's death and had the same suspicions as his. He told them to meet him at the hangar for a debriefing. They moaned about how late it would be by the time he got back. But in the end, he still outranked them. They said they would be there waiting. And they were.

As he pulled in front of the hangar, he saw Miles swing the massive door outward. Marie stood inside, waiting for the plane to come to a stop.

The nose of the jet swung wide as Hale made the turn. He gave the engines a little push, and the jet rolled inside. He shut down the engines and heard the soft whine as they cycled to a stop. Outside he could hear the loud thud of the hangar door being closed once again.

He did his postflight checks quickly then moved to the rear to open the door for Miles and Marie. What he saw nearly knocked him over.

Standing in front of him, holding a Smith & Wesson 9mm, was a beautiful redhead. Her hair was long and hung over her shoulders. She was wearing all black. Her shoes were steel-toed combat boots. Her pants were loose like fatigues. And her shirt was some kind of athletic zip-up. The gun had a silencer attached to it. It was pointed directly at his head.

"Hello, Hale," she said calmly.

"Who are you?" he asked. "And how did you get on this plane?"

"You know," she said, "I would love to tell you all about that. But Miles and Marie are waiting. Don't you think you should open the door and let them in?"

"You have no idea what you're doing," Hale said tersely. "Give me the gun, and I promise you won't get hurt."

The redhead laughed heartily. She moved the gun a fraction of an inch and pulled the trigger. The gun spit, and a flash flew out of the silencer.

The burning was immediate. Hale's hand flew to his ear. He felt blood washing over his hand. She had expertly shot his earlobe off.

"I've been doing this as long as you have, I can assure you," she said. "Maybe even longer. Now open the door."

Hale did as he was told. He moved to the side and pulled the lever and popped the door. As he did, he felt a sharp pain in the back of his head. Then he felt his eyes roll back up into his head. His vision went blank as he lost consciousness.

When he woke, he was bound and tied, lying on the couch. He strained to focus his eyes. Everything was still blurry. And his head felt like a semitruck had rolled over it. He had no idea how long he'd been out. He shook his head and tried to clear the cobwebs.

As his vision began to focus, he noticed that Marie was sitting on the floor, bound and gagged. She was also unconscious. He felt a rocking motion and realized they were in the air. Someone was flying the plane. Miles? He wasn't anywhere in the rear cabin with him and Marie. He must be piloting the plane. And what about the redhead. Where was she?

Almost as if reading his mind, she appeared from the bathroom. "Well," she said, "I see we're getting up from our little nap. Did you sleep well, honey?" She smiled a sly grin.

"So, would it do me any good to ask who you're working for?" Hale asked.

"Well, let's just say I work for the same people you do."

"I work for the pope," Hale spat. "Filth like you wouldn't even be allowed in his presence."

"Ooh. . .testy now, aren't we?" She chuckled and squatted to put the muzzle of the gun against his forehead. She reached down, grabbed him by his bound wrists, and pulled him up into a sitting position. "There. That's better. Now you can look straight at me when I kill you."

"Is Miles flying the plane?"

"I told him to fly or I'd kill all three of you right then."

"Where are we going?"

"Rome. I wanted to kill you there, but I knew your friends"— she pointed behind her at Marie—"would be a pain in my rear. So I just decided to hitch a ride and take care of all three of you at once. Pretty smart, huh?"

"I'm going to watch you die when I kill you," Hale said matter-of-factly.

She made a sympathetic face. "Oh honey, that's so sweet. You think you're going to kill me." Then she started laughing. "Like I told you before, I've been doing this a long time." She stood back up. "Wickham wants his plane back and you dead. I want my money. Actually, I can't believe I even took this job. It just so happened that I was in the neighborhood when he called. And, well, I couldn't turn down the shot at a pro like you, now could I?"

They felt the nose of the plane dip forward. Then a sharp left turn. They were starting their descent.

"Well, looks like we're almost there," she said. "I have enjoyed our conversation, Mr. Hale. I'm sorry it can't continue. I'm only supposed to get the plane back to Rome. Once we land, my job's complete."

She reached into a drawer and pulled out a roll of gaff tape. She pulled a piece long enough to tape over his mouth and cut it. She put the tape over his mouth and pushed him back down into a lying position.

Five minutes later they were back on solid ground. She was in the cockpit with Miles, holding the gun to his head. Hale heard her tell him to taxi to the far end of the runway to another private hangar. In a few moments, the plane came to a stop. The woman forced Miles back into the rear cabin with him and Marie. She leveled the gun and shot him twice in the head.

Hale tried to scream and shake his way loose of his bindings but had no luck. He was tied up tighter than a banjo string. He felt the tears rolling down his cheeks as he watched Miles's lifeless body slump to the floor. He could only be thankful that Marie was still unconscious. At least she didn't have to see it.

Next, she moved the gun to Marie. She repeated the process quickly and without mercy. Finally, she turned back around to Hale. She undid the tape from his mouth.

He didn't scream or even talk. He knew. He knew he was going to die. In his last final minutes, he prayed that God would watch over Anna and Jason. And then he rejoiced, knowing that he was about to be with Christ.

"Are you ready?" she asked.

He didn't answer.

"Suit yourself. Oh, and just because I don't want you to think I'm totally unsociable, I will answer your question from before. You asked me who I am. My name's Remy." She pulled the gun up and fired two shots directly into his forehead.

CHAPTER 49

London, the Safe House

Anna scooped up a stack of papers and let them flutter to the floor. "We have piles of notes, loose pages, maps. And not one clue as to what my grandpa was looking for."

She and Jason had been sitting in the middle of the floor with all of Thomas's journals and notebooks around them for the better part of two hours.

"It's late." Jason restacked the scattered pieces of paper. "Let's get some rest. We can start again tomorrow."

Anna let out a big sigh. "I guess you're right." She tossed the notebook she was holding onto a pile of ten other ones. "It's just that my grandpa spent his whole life leading up to this point. And we only have five days to figure it out before we meet Benjamin."

"At least we know we're looking for a key."

"To what?" She threw her arms in the air. "That's exactly what I'm talking about. Grandpa knew. Or at least he thought he knew. We don't know squat!"

"We'll figure it out," Jason said. "I promise."

"We have to. I won't let all of his work be in vain."

"It won't." He stood up and reached his hand out for her. She took it, and he helped pull her up. "Go to bed. You look rough." He smiled.

"Gee, thanks. You really know how to make a girl feel good." She turned to go upstairs to her room.

"Anna."

She stopped and looked back over her shoulder. "Yeah?"

Jason walked over to her and brushed her hair out of her eyes, smiling at her. He loved the way her hair always fell down into her eyes. He loved watching her stick out her bottom lip and try to blow it out of the way. He guessed she didn't even know she did it. And then there was the way she crinkled her nose, as she was doing now. She really was the most beautiful woman he'd ever seen.

He swallowed the lump that was in his throat and said again, "Anna."

She smiled. "Yes?"

"I just wanted to say good night. Sleep well."

She giggled a little and nodded. "You, too."

He cleared his throat. "Um, okay. See you tomorrow." He turned around to walk to the kitchen. Suddenly, his mouth was as dry as the desert sand. He needed a drink of water.

He found a glass and turned the faucet on. He held it under the water and noticed that his hands were shaking. "Come on, you gotta be kidding me," he mumbled to himself. "She's just a girl."

"Oh, so I'm just a girl?"

With the water running and him clanking around in the cupboards for a glass, he hadn't heard her behind him. He turned, and there she was, arms crossed and looking perturbed.

"That's what you said—just some girl."

He stood there with his mouth open, but nothing came

out. He had been talking to himself. He hadn't meant anything derogatory by it. And besides, what was she doing here? Didn't she go upstairs to bed?

"I mean, first you tell me I look like crap. Then you say I'm just some girl." She stood there waiting for a reply. "I mean, I guess I thought—"

She never finished what she was saying. Jason set the glass of water in the sink and reached out and took her hand. He tugged her close to him. "Would you just hush!" He brushed her hair away from her face again and tilted her head back. Then he kissed her.

The kiss was soft. And the warmth of her lips gave him goose bumps. He pulled away and looked her in the eyes. "There! Now if that doesn't tell you how I feel about you, nothing will."

She stared blankly back at him for a moment. Then a smile creased her lips.

"Now, go to bed, young lady!" He laughed and pointed his finger at her.

She giggled and turned around to leave. She started back up the stairs to her room. Halfway up, she looked back over her shoulder. "Good night, Jason Lang," she said.

"Good night, Anna Riley," he said softly.

Any chance of sleep was out of the question. Yes, he was exhausted physically. But now his mind was racing a million miles a second.

He couldn't believe what he'd just done. He played it over and over again in his mind. Each time it ended the same way. She kissed him back. She didn't just let him kiss her.

She kissed him back.

Obviously, he wasn't going to sleep anytime soon, so he refilled his glass of water and went back into Thomas's study. He would try to relax his mind and see what he could figure out.

301

The room was exactly as he and Anna left it. A total mess. He picked up a set of topographical maps of the Middle East. Each showed the same location but a different time period, from 600 BC to the present. What was so interesting about this location that Thomas had wanted to study its topography throughout history?

Jason rubbed his eyes. He was officially beat. The excitement of the kiss with Anna had finally subsided. He figured he'd go to bed.

He was standing up to go upstairs to his room when something started nagging at his mind. Something about the maps. He couldn't quite figure out what it was. He decided to sleep on it. Maybe it would come.

He climbed into bed and hoped that he could finish his prayer time before he fell asleep. He was praying and thanking God for His perfect love when it hit him. *Perfect love.* He sat up in his bed. Quickly, he finished his prayer and ran back downstairs. He needed to take another look at the scroll.

He pulled out the box to open it and gently removed the scroll. He read it once. Then he read it again. He grabbed the maps and studied them one by one. Then he scanned row through row of bookshelves until he found the special edition study Bible he was looking for. He flipped it open to the back where the maps were.

He walked back over to the maps that were lying out on the floor. He compared them to the ones he was looking at in the Bible. This was it. It had to be.

He fell to his knees at the weight of his discovery. Was it possible? He had always believed that the Bible was the actual word of God. He believed that it revealed the will of God to man, and that the content and testimonies contained in it were absolute facts. If so, then it was time to put that belief into practice.

He flipped to the first page and began reading the book of Genesis.

CHAPTER 50

Rome, Just Outside the City

It was almost midnight when the meeting came to order. Wickham sat at the head of the table as usual. The rest of the brothers sat around him. The room was quiet for the first time since they had arrived. Wickham rapped his knuckles on the hardwood to signal that the meeting was officially beginning.

No one had really said anything yet, but Wickham knew they must be wondering what was going on. It wasn't that they were called out of their warm beds for a meeting. He did that to them all the time. The question was, who was the stranger standing behind him, leaning against the wall?

Wickham cleared his throat. "Brothers, welcome. We will keep this brief. First, I want you all to know that the scroll is moments away from being in our possession." He held up his hands to quiet the murmuring. "Second, there is the matter of Conclave." Again, he had to quiet the men. "Now, we all know that Joseph has been thrust into the spotlight."

This time the eruption was more significant. Some stood up,

waving their hands, speaking indignantly. Others pounded their fists on the table, demanding an explanation. Since their meeting in the papal audience hall, none of the brothers had spoken to Wickham. And he left a lot to be discussed. Now, away from the rest of the Vatican, they let their questions fly. It was Ibrahim who finally rose to the top of the noise to be heard.

"How dare you make a decision like that without consulting us first!" Ibrahim's face was red. "We are all well aware that you orchestrated that letter. You likely wrote it yourself. But to suggest Joseph? Have you lost your mind? There is no way he will be the next pope. Even I am much more qualified."

Again the room became a ruckus. Wickham expected it. He hadn't explained himself since he made the announcement, but he needed to do so now. He grabbed a wooden statue sitting on a pedestal and slammed it on the table, creating a thunderous boom that reverberated through the room.

"Now, gentlemen," he said, placing the statue back on the pedestal, "if we may continue?"

Everyone took their seats. Menacing stares roved around the table as all the brothers looked at one another.

"Yes, I did fabricate the letter. Yes, Joseph was my idea. And yes, I did consider all of you for the job. But to put it quite plainly, none of you would be even a possible choice for the papacy. You would be laughed out of the room by everyone voting. You all have a lot of baggage."

"And this buffoon is a better choice?" Ibrahim motioned over to Joseph. "You think *he* can get elected? He's been buried in the archives for the last three years. No one even knew who he was until that letter."

"That's exactly the point. We can make him into a great man. By the time we all work our magic, Joseph will be the most beloved cardinal in the whole Vatican. There's no way he won't get elected."

The meeting became total chaos. Finally, the man who had been standing behind Wickham stepped forward. Everyone had forgotten he was even there until he spoke.

"Excuse me, gentlemen." He barely spoke loud enough to be heard, but his voice pierced the noise like a dagger. The room fell to a dead silence.

The man smiled and walked around the table, touching each brother on the shoulder as he passed. One by one, they all sat down and stared blankly at him. When he got around the table, he brushed Wickham out of the way and took his seat.

"You are wondering who I am. Why I am here. I'm surprised, really. For a long time each and every one of you has served me. Some of you have done well. Some of you haven't. Nevertheless, you know who I am."

And they did. Instantly. One by one, they nodded. A mixture of fear and sadness etched on their faces. A mood of shame and self-pity hung in the air.

"It was my decision to make Joseph the next pope. I need him."

Again everyone nodded.

"And I expect you to do whatever it takes to get him elected. Is that understood?"

Again everyone nodded.

"Good. I promise you will all be rewarded. Soon I will have total control over everything you see around you. Not just Rome or the Vatican, but the world. Contrary to what that fairy tale says, I can and will rule this world forever. And as soon as I have that scroll, you will see. And when I have what I want, I will make you all great kings of great nations. You will rule over this earth. And you will live forever. And you will bow to me and worship me." He stood and moved his chair into the center of the room. Then he sat back down. "And you will start tonight. Come here, each of you, and bow before me."

CHAPTER 51

Jerusalem, 5 Days Later

The flight into Jerusalem had been stressful. They had tried to get hold of Hale and the rest of the flight crew, but there was no answer. Hale's phone just went to voice mail. They even made contact with the security team and talked to Christopher Wallace. He hadn't heard from Hale or the rest of the crew since their meeting earlier this week. He said he would look into it. But for now, they needed to be careful and just stay in London.

Unfortunately, that wasn't an option. They had to go to Jerusalem. Christopher told them that under the circumstances, he would break protocol and arrange for agents to meet them in Israel. Anna and Jason thanked him and told him that they would be staying at the King David Hotel. He booked their flights to make sure an agent got on board with them while he and the others took a later charter with all their equipment on board. And he promised he would do all he could to find out where Hale and the rest of the crew was.

The last five days had been something Jason couldn't even describe. With not much else to do and the assurance of the security team, he and Anna spent most of their time sightseeing and talking. And not even about the scroll. They talked about their families and where they grew up and the things they liked to do. They argued over pizza versus cheeseburgers. They tried to decide which was better, Rocky Road or Turtle Tracks. Anna told Jason that living in Nashville, it seemed there was nothing to do, but whenever guests came, she was quickly reminded of how much there actually was to do—the Frist Museum, the Country Music Hall of Fame, Printer's Alley, the Parthenon. He'd never been to any of them, but he saw them through her eyes.

In the end, what happened was more important than anything else. Jason lost his heart. He knew he was falling in love. Anna had basically felt the same way and, as much, told him. They talked about it and decided that even though their relationship was fairly new and founded under extreme duress, they knew what they were feeling for each other was real. Jason had prayed about it every night since the first kiss, and God pretty much confirmed it in his heart that she was "the one." He just hoped they lived long enough to see it grow. The way things had gone since he met her, it could be a coin flip.

Now Jason got out of bed and walked across the expansive hotel suite to knock on Anna's bedroom door. "Anna, you up?" He heard a faint moan come from the other side. "Hey. . .slacker! Get up. We've got things to do today." He smiled, waiting for the smart comment he was sure was coming.

The door swung open, nearly knocking Jason on his backside. Anna stood there, fully dressed, with her toothbrush hanging out of her mouth.

She turned around and walked into the bathroom. She rinsed

the toothpaste out of her mouth and turned back to Jason. "I was trying to say come in."

"Sounded like a moan to me. I thought you were still sleeping."

"That's what you get for assuming."

Jason let out a big yawn and ran his hands through his hair. He scratched the stubble on his chin and looked at her as if he were totally uninterested in anything she just said. "I just came over here to tell you that Benjamin called. Said to meet him tonight at eleven o'clock."

"Wow! That gives us all day," she said.

"Yep. We can sleep in this morning." He turned around and went back through the dividing door. He looked back over his shoulder as he was pushing the door shut. "I'm going back to sleep. See you in about three hours."

She grabbed him before he could escape the room. "I'm up. I'm dressed," she hissed. "You want to tell me again that I could have slept in?"

He dropped a kiss on her nose. "You're really not a morning person. You know that?"

"I am too a morning person."

"Really? You think so?"

She started laughing. "Well. . .I love breakfast." She pushed him away again.

"Me, too. How about eggs?"

"We have some?"

"No, but I bet we could find a nice little restaurant."

"Sounds good." She leaned up and gave him a peck on the cheek. "Get a shower and get ready. I'll go call the lobby and ask them where we should go."

"Okay, I'll only need fifteen minutes. I'll be right out." He walked into his bathroom and shut the door. He could hear her placing the phone call: "Ah, yes, sir. I was wondering where we could get a nice breakfast this morning. We like eggs."

Twenty minutes later they were downstairs at the hotel's breakfast buffet, which the concierge insisted was the best in Jerusalem. Halfway through their meal, they both agreed that the concierge had been right.

They had a fairly secluded table in the back of the room, with one other table within earshot of them. Just three young children and two emotionally drained parents, none of whom had any interest in eavesdropping. That was good, because Anna had something she needed to talk about.

Ever since their first real kiss five nights ago, Jason had been very quiet. She didn't know what to make of it. It was as if he had something he needed to tell her but couldn't. She had played the last few days over and over in her mind, trying to figure out what it could be. The only thing she could figure was that maybe he had a girlfriend he wasn't telling her about. She quickly dismissed the thought every time it crept up into her mind. Surely he would have said something. And so she just let it go. But something was going on. He wouldn't even talk about the scroll with her. Every time she brought it up, he just said he was thinking about it. But he would always reassure her that they would figure it out. "Don't worry, Anna," he would say. "It will come to us. Just wait. You'll see." Well, she was getting tired of waiting. They were supposed to meet Benjamin in a few hours, and they had no idea what they were doing.

On the bright side of things, their relationship, if you could call it that, was taking off tremendously, aside from the nagging thought of his possible girlfriend. The last five days had been mind-numbing. She and Jason had taken walks all over the city. They had visited Albert Hall and the Museum of Natural History. They had tried out countless cafés and restaurants. They had even taken in a show. Jason had surprised her with tickets to *Les Misérables*. It was very romantic.

She felt strangely safe with him. The whole time they were bouncing around London, she never once felt the urge to look over her shoulder or wonder what was around the next corner. It was as if she knew by some weird sense that she was safe as long as Jason was around.

It also didn't hurt that he was one of the handsomest guys she'd ever seen. But it was his heart that really captivated her. He was so genuine and transparent, talking about this passion for God that he had deep within himself. A passion for being a servant to other people.

He told her that not a day went by without him thinking about what his life would be like if he were not following Christ. That should have sent up red flags. To this point in her life, she would have done anything to avoid the "Bible thumpers." But Jason was different. He wasn't like other religious people she had met. He told her not to judge all Christians by the actions of a few. He said that too many people made Christianity about cleaning up your life and getting the outside stuff fixed. And they completely missed that it was about letting God change the inside. He didn't just talk about it; he lived it. And for some reason—one that she couldn't explain—that was one of the most attractive things about him.

Breakfast was over, and they sat drinking their coffee. Anna took his hand. She hesitated, but Jason just smiled at her. She might as well get it over with. She had to find out what was bugging him once and for all.

"I'm going to ask you a question that I've asked you several times this week. Only this time, I want an answer. If we are going to do this—I mean us"—she waved her hand back and forth between them—"then I need to know that you're not keeping something from me."

"Anna, I—"

"No," she held up her hand, "listen to me. Let me finish."

He nodded.

"This week has been something else. I mean, I really have some strong feelings for you. But I will not be manipulated or lied to. Do you understand me?"

Again he nodded. Strange—he didn't look like he was hiding anything. At least nothing bad. But there was a secret light to his eyes. He was keeping something from her. That couldn't continue. "My last boyfriend lied to me. I can't deal with that again. I don't have the patience to deal with immature little men who can't get their heads out of their. . ."

"Anna."

She looked at him, a little perturbed at being cut off.

"You want to know why I've been so quiet this week. And why I've been keeping to myself at times."

"Yes. You don't have a girlfriend or something like that, do you?"

He burst out laughing.

"What?" she asked, annoyed.

"Are you serious?" He continued to laugh. "You think that I have a girlfriend?"

"Well. . . ?"

He stopped laughing and held her hand up to his lips and kissed it gently. "No, Anna. I do not have a girlfriend. At least not one that you don't know about."

"What does that mean?"

He smiled. "You, silly. I mean you. You are the only woman in my life at this point and time. Scout's honor." He held up two fingers.

"Then why have you been so quiet and reserved for the last few days?"

"'Cause I've been trying to figure out what all of this is about. And until last night, I couldn't be sure. But now I'm fairly positive I know what the riddle on the scroll means."

Anna's face lit up. "You've figured it out?"

"I think so."

"So tell me."

"Not here. Let's take a walk. Or go back up to the room."

"Let's go for a walk. We'll find someplace quiet."

They made their way outside and walked down King David Street.

"Can you give me a hint?" she asked.

Jason leaned in and whispered in her ear, "Are you familiar with Moses' staff?"

She pulled away and looked at him quizzically but nodded yes.

He leaned back in and whispered, "Do you know where it is? Or rather, where it's supposed to be?"

Again she looked at him, but this time shook her head.

He leaned back in and smiled. He knew this would get her blood going. "Ever hear of the ark of the covenant?"

CHAPTER 52

The Vatican

Cardinal Wickham was in his study reading a book and smoking his pipe when the phone rang.

"Hello?"

"It's me. I'm back in the game."

So the rat had come crawling back. Wickham had wondered if he'd ever hear from Jonathan again. "I can't talk right now. I'll call you back in fifteen minutes." He looked at the caller ID. Blocked. "Give me the number." He grabbed a pen and jotted it down. "Okay. Fifteen minutes."

Twenty minutes later, dressed in blue jeans, sweatshirt, and ball cap, he was dropped off by cab in front of a small café. Once seated at his usual table, he ordered the four-cheese omelet and punched in the numbers on his phone.

"You're late. Why can't you just say thirty minutes if that's what you intend?"

"Oh, calm down, Jonathan. What's fifteen more minutes?"

"It's a lot when you need to catch a flight."

"Where are you going?"

"Jerusalem."

"Jerusalem? Why?"

"'Cause that's where that girl and your scroll are."

"Really? And how did you find that out?"

"What do you think you pay me for, Wickham?"

"I was beginning to wonder that myself."

"Very funny. Listen. I've had her tailed for the last week. I was told she hopped on a flight to Jerusalem last night. A commercial flight."

"Yes, so?"

"So I was wondering why she would fly commercial and not her little G-5?"

Wickham paused for a minute. Should he tell Jonathan about Hale and the girl assassin? No, probably not. He would wait and see how it played out. "I have no idea," he finally said. "Where in Jerusalem?"

"I don't know yet, but I have people working on it. I have a couple of Palestinian friends who owe me big favors. I'll put them on it. If they can't find her, no one can."

"Just get me what I'm paying you for."

"If everything goes right, you'll have it by this evening."

Wickham didn't even say good-bye as he hung up the phone.

The waitress brought him his breakfast, along with his Bloody Mary. A broad smile creased his face as he took his first bite. Good. Very cheesy. Just like he liked it. And the Bloody Mary. . .ah yes. Just enough spice.

He set down his fork down and reached for his phone again. He punched in the numbers and listened to it ring.

"Cardinal Wickham's office. May I help you?"

"It's me."

"Oh, hello, sir. What can I do for you?"

"I'm going out of town on an emergency. Cardinal Joseph McCoy is in charge until I get back. Understood?"

"Yes, sir."

"Good. And as far as anyone else is concerned, you don't know where I am or when I'll be back. I'm simply out of the office. Call the head of the Swiss Guard and tell him I need a pilot. Someone who is qualified to fly a Gulfstream 5. Have him meet me at the airport at three o'clock, sharp."

"Yes, sir. Anything else?"

"No, that will be all."

"Okay then. Have a nice flight."

Again, he hung up the phone without saying good-bye.

He picked up his fork and started eating again. Yes, yes, indeed, very cheesy. Just the way he liked it.

Jerusalem

"The ark of the covenant! Are you serious?" Anna stopped in her tracks. They were standing just outside the hotel. "Forget going for a walk. Let's go back to the suite so we can talk."

They didn't say much on the way back to the hotel. At the suite, Anna closed the door. Then she reopened it, hung the Do Not Disturb sign, and shut it again with a *click*.

"Jason, what are you talking about? Do you mean that my grandfather was looking for the ark of the covenant?"

"Not exactly."

"Then what?"

Jason pulled the chair out from the little desk that sat along the wall and sat down. Anna plopped down on the sofa.

"Okay. This is gonna sound really outrageous, but trust me. I think I've figured it out."

Anna sat there with raised eyebrows.

"Okay. Your grandfather has all these maps of temples and churches, right?" He watched Anna's head bob up and down. "Well, we know that he dismissed all but two: the temple here and, from the looks of the maps, the Vatican." Anna was still nodding in agreement. "Okay. Now back to the riddle. 'The key is found in the temple.' I think your grandfather knew what the key was. And if he's right, then this is really big, Anna. I mean *really* big. The ark. See—and when I finish explaining, this will all make sense—the ark was kept in the temple. Inside the ark there were some things—the most famous were the stone tablets with the Ten Commandments inscribed on them. But what we're looking for is Moses' staff."

"Why would we need Moses'—"

"I'm getting to that."

"Sorry."

"Okay. So here's the deal. Throughout the Bible, there were narrow escapes and miraculous getaways. The most famous of these is probably the parting of the Red Sea. Just like the second part of the scroll says, God opened the way. There was another time later when Joshua needed to cross the Jordan. The Israelites didn't know what to do. Joshua commanded the priests who were carrying the ark to go stand in the water. When their feet touched the river, it opened up, just like the Red Sea, and they all passed over the Jordan, completely dry. Some people believe that because Moses' staff was in there, it had the same effect on the river that it did on the sea. We need Moses' staff, which is supposedly still in the ark. Like the scroll says, it will open the way. I think it's the key. And it's in the temple."

Anna sat there, jaw open, staring at him. She finally let out a *"Whew!"* She ran her fingers through her hair. "Jason, I don't know a lot about this Bible stuff, but didn't I hear somewhere that the temple was destroyed, with everything in it?"

"Yes. You did, but here's the thing. When the Babylonians destroyed Jerusalem, the ark became a thing of legend. No one knows what happened to it. Some believe it was taken back into heaven by God. Some people believe it's buried somewhere in the Middle East. The Ethiopian Orthodox Church actually claims it has possession of it. They say it's hidden in a 'treasury' that only their high priest can visit. Most people think that's a pretty bunk theory. Here's what I think. And apparently your grandfather thought it, too." He hopped up from the desk and settled next to Anna on the sofa. "I think that at some point, after the Babylonians destroyed Jerusalem, the ark was brought back here and is inside the mosque. The other theory is that it's in the Vatican. There's our two temples your grandfather wrote about. Now, I adamantly disagree with the thought that it's in the Vatican."

"Why?"

"Because, think about it. If the Vatican had anything like that, something that could lend that much credibility to the Roman Catholic Church, don't you think it would've been made public? Not to mention, your grandfather was in with the pope, just as you are. Well, I mean—you know. . ."

"Yeah, you're probably right. But why do we need Moses' staff?"

"I'm getting to that." He stood up and started pacing. "See, this is where it gets a little far-fetched. It was the first thing the scroll said that was the real mystery. 'What once was perfect has now been broken.' I mean, what the heck does that mean?" He stopped with his arms outstretched, as if waiting for an answer. "Then I started to study the maps your grandfather left us. You remember all the maps of the Middle East?"

"Yeah," Anna said, unsure. "I think so."

"At first I thought your grandfather subscribed to the theory of the ark being buried in the Middle East. But I had to dismiss that when I realized that's what he was looking in the temples for. So here I was, staring at these maps. I looked them over. Then I looked them over again. Then I saw it."

"What?" Anna was on the edge of the sofa. Her eyes were wide with anticipation. "What? Saw what?"

"The rivers."

"The rivers?" She sat back again, frowning.

"Each one of the maps had different rivers marked on them. But they were all the same map of the same region."

"So what does that have to do with anything?"

"It has everything to do with everything." He stopped pacing and sat back down. "Okay. It's like this." He shifted and pulled one leg up under him so he was face-to-face with her. "I didn't think much of it because of the names of the rivers. But the more I studied them the more it made sense to me. Those rivers had different names long, long ago. All except one, the Euphrates. It still has the same name."

Anna stared blankly at him. "So?"

"I did some studying on my own. Many people believe that their names were the Pishon, the Gihon, and the Hiddekel—all very important rivers named in the Bible."

He grabbed his Bible off the desk, opened it to the book of Genesis, and handed it to her. As she read the section he pointed out, her eyes became wide. Her finger traced the words as she read them. She looked up at him with disbelief. He nodded a "yes" to her. She read it again. She opened her mouth, but nothing came out.

"I know," he said. "Pretty cool, huh?"

"I don't believe it."

"Believe it. This is what your grandfather was looking for. This is what the riddle on the scroll is about. 'What once was perfect, has now been broken.' The only thing that has been perfect in this world, since God created it, was our relationship with him. It was perfect. Then we screwed it up. Adam and Eve ate the forbidden fruit. The relationship was broken when Adam and Eve sinned against God." He opened the Bible and pointed to the page. "And that's the only place where it was ever perfect."

Anna looked at him, still in disbelief. "The Garden of Eden."

CHAPTER 53

Outside Rome

Wickham finished his breakfast and hailed another cab. He told the driver to take him to his house in the country. The place was a mess. He had rented it out for a social event last night, and the cleaning crew hadn't been by yet today.

He pushed his way through the foyer and into the living room, moving chairs and end tables out of the way. Dirty wine glasses and paper plates were everywhere. Some still had the remnants of food on them. The whole place stank of bite-sized sausages and merlot.

He walked upstairs to his private study, protected by a dead bolt lock and a keyless number pad. He undid the locks and went inside to his desk to retrieve another key. He crossed the room to a wall where a Picasso hung and removed it, revealing a safe also protected by a two-lock security system.

He entered his code and turned the key. There was a grinding sound as the metal from the dead bolts retreated. He turned the lever of the handle, and the door swung open.

A small leather briefcase sat on the shelf inside. He took it out and relocked the safe. After setting the case on his desk, he opened it and grabbed the small .38 caliber handgun concealed inside.

He'd bought the gun on the black market several years ago. The serial numbers had been filed off, and the whole firing mechanism had been replaced twice. When he bought it, he was told that the gun was a ghost. He'd only hoped that was correct.

He pulled the clip and checked the ammo. Still full, minus two rounds. The only two he'd ever fired. That night he'd first used the gun was one he would never forget. It was the reason he bought the gun. A young, vibrant college exchange student from Russia named Alexi.

Needless to say, she would never talk to the media and tell them about the wild weekend they spent together in Monte Carlo. That's what she'd threatened to do unless he gave her a half million dollars and bought her a nice apartment in the city. He would've been ruined.

What he did that night was what led him to find people like Jonathan. He'd spent the next month looking over his shoulder, living in fear. He vowed never again to get his own hands dirty with something like that. He liked the power of wielding life over death. He just didn't want to do it himself. It was enough simply knowing he ordered it. So he spent the next month in back alleys and seedy places asking questions about people who could "get things done." He was actually amused at how easy it was to find such people.

But now things had changed. If Jonathan screwed up again, Wickham would be dead. The risk was too great to rely on someone so inept. He had no choice but to get his own hands dirty. If everything worked out the way he envisioned it, not only would he have the scroll in his possession by tonight, but there would also be no more loose ends.

CHAPTER 54

Ben Gurion Airport, Jerusalem

Wickham's plane touched down and pulled to the private terminal. He stepped off the aircraft and immediately into a car that was waiting for him.

The car took him to his hotel, where he quietly made his way to his room. He stretched out on the bed and massaged his temples—something he liked to do after a flight.

After a fifteen-minute rest, he opened his bag and took out his phone.

Jonathan answered on the fourth ring. "Hello?"

"Where are you?"

"In Jerusalem. I told you that."

"I mean specifically."

"In an old CIA safe house. What does it matter?"

"It doesn't, I suppose."

"Well, did you call me just to ask where I was, or did you need something? I'm kind of busy right now."

"I called for a progress report," he said agitated. "I *do* pay you,

you know. I think I'm entitled to know what's going on."

"Where are you, Wickham?" Jonathan asked with hesitation.

"What? What does that have to do with anything?"

"Nothing," Jonathan said. "She's staying at the King David Hotel. We are watching her."

He almost lost his breath. The King David Hotel. She was here. In the same building. "If you know where she is, then why haven't you taken her yet?"

"Four or five guys snatching a young American girl off the street would gather some attention, don't you think? Why don't you let me do my job and get off my back!"

He was too excited to let Jonathan's tone upset him. The girl was right under his nose. This might be easier than he thought. "Yes, Jonathan. You know what—never mind. Just do your job and get me that scroll. Oh, and I need you to send me a photo of her."

"What's going on, Louis?" he demanded.

"What—oh, nothing. It's just very busy around here. You know. I'm a little distracted right now."

"*You* called *me*."

He cleared his throat. "I need to go. Do your job and get me what I'm paying you for. Send me that photo. You can send it to my PDA. You have that number, yes?"

"Yeah, I have it," Jonathan said. "I'll send it."

Wickham hung up the phone and tried to contain the excitement that was coursing through his veins.

Jonathan heard the abrupt *click* through his earpiece. Wickham had hung up on him again. One of these days, he was going to have to teach a certain cardinal some manners.

His team was up and moving around the house, getting ready to leave. He had two men watching the King David, ready to call the minute the girl left the building. Everything was in place, and the plan was a good one.

And yet he had that awful sinking feeling in his gut—the one that told him he'd better have eyes in the back of his head or he might not have a head anymore. He'd only had that feeling four other times in his life. Three of them, it saved his life. The last one he ignored. And it got him a bullet in his leg and almost cost him his life, not to mention the six million Remy stole. He tasted the bile in his throat as he remembered the cathedral at Oloron-Sainte-Marie.

"Listen up, everyone!" he shouted. Everyone stopped in their tracks and focused on him. "I don't know what's going on, but something's not right. Keep your eyes open and your ears on full alert. When Frick and Frack call back here with an update, we'll move. But, and I'll only say this once, you do nothing without my explicit permission. Is that understood?"

The men nodded.

"All right. Then mount up and be ready to move."

He reached inside his briefcase and retrieved a photo of the girl he'd taken. He opened his laptop, scanned the picture, and sent it to Wickham.

The laptop chimed and alerted him that his mail had been sent. The bile in his throat returned. Something definitely wasn't right. That sinking feeling was getting stronger.

The King David Hotel

"Jason, what are we going to do?" Anna paced back and forth across the living room of the suite. "I mean, I'm sure that people have been looking for that place for thousands of years. Even before Jesus. And now we, a Baptist missionary and college student, are going to just miraculously discover it?"

"Yes."

"Jason"—she blew out a breath in exasperation—"this is crazy. We can't do this."

Jason smiled. "Aren't you the same person who, just five days ago, sat next to a special agent of the Israeli government and threatened him? That doesn't sound like someone who thinks she can't do something."

"Yeah, but that's different. We're talking about the Garden of Eden."

"Anna, think about it. You have in your possession the most significant Christian relic in the history of Christianity. Its sole purpose is to show the possessor of such relic—that's you—how to get there! We can do it."

She let out a long breath and sat down on the sofa. Jason could see the worry on her face. He walked behind the sofa and massaged her shoulders. "We can do this. We can. Your grandfather thought so. So did Vin. And so do I."

The tension lessened from her neck and shoulders. "Okay. We can do this. Now what?"

Jason leaned down and put his cheek against hers. "Now we go to a cosmetics store."

"What?"

He straightened and sat on the back of the sofa. "We're supposed to meet Benjamin in twelve hours. Neither one of us looks Arabic. So I was thinking we should try to find something that will change our complexion. And we need to get you a haircut."

"What's wrong with my hair?"

"Well, it's long," he said, stating the obvious.

"Yeah? So?"

"So, only women have long hair here. Not guys. And if you're going to get into that mosque tonight, you need to look like a guy."

CHAPTER 55

The King David Hotel, Jerusalem

Anna and Jason stopped at the front desk and asked the concierge where they might find some shopping. He told them that the neighborhood of West Jerusalem was a very popular area of town for just that.

They found a little boutique where they purchased a dark makeup base, some scissors, and some hair coloring. Hungry, they grabbed lunch at a sidewalk café.

They hadn't been sitting there for very long when a young lady passed by their table, dropping a small folded note onto their table. She didn't stop or turn to look at either one of them. The note was simply dropped, inconspicuously, right in front of Anna.

Anna almost called after the woman, but she remembered the note that was given to her before in the same manner at a café like this one. After reading the note, she grabbed Jason's hand. "We need to go. Now!"

Jason didn't bother to ask why or what was going on. He

quickly retrieved a twenty shekel note, threw it on the table and hurried after her.

"Anna, what's going on?" he asked, falling in behind her. "What did that note say?"

Pulling him by the arm, she used her free hand to open the door to a cab sitting on the corner. She jumped in the backseat and dragged him in with her. The door shut and the cab sped off. She turned to him, eyes wide, and handed him the note.

Anna,

Don't make a big scene. As soon as you finish reading this note, get up from the table. There is a cab waiting for you across the street. It is yellow and has a black stripe down the side. Get into it, and it will take you to someplace safe. We'll be waiting there for you. We will explain when you get there. Do it now.

Christopher Wallace

Jason immediately sat up straight. "Anna," his words were sharp and hushed, "what are you thinking? You don't even know who these people are. This could be a trap! These people could be trying to kill you."

"No, it's okay. The lady who dropped the note. . .she was the same person who gave us the note at that café before."

"Are you sure?" His question was almost desperate. "I don't like this. How am I supposed to protect you—us—if you just take off like that without—"

"It's all right, Jason. I'm positive. I never forget a face. It was her."

He relaxed a bit. "Okay. If you say so, but I still don't like it. Do you have your"—he pointed at her ankle—"you know."

She shook her head. "How could I? We flew commercial, remember?"

The cab made a sharp turn into an alley and then immediately into a garage. Two men appeared out of nowhere and shut the big door behind them, casting the room into almost complete darkness. The locks in the doors snapped as the two men made their way from the garage door to either side of the cab. They opened the doors simultaneously and reached inside.

Gently but firmly they grabbed Anna and Jason and pulled them out of the car.

"Where are you taking us?" Jason demanded. "You let her go! Now!" He tried to twist away from the man, but it was no use. This guy was very big and very strong. And the way he had Jason locked in his grip, there was little to no chance of him getting away.

"It's all right, sir. We're here to help. This is all just precaution."

The other one chimed in. "Miss Anna, we're sorry for all the confusion. We're almost there."

The men led them from the garage through a doorway that led to a steep set of stairs. They climbed all the way to the top and through the door that awaited them. The men let go. One of them moved to the windows and pulled all the curtains. The other secured the door they just came through. When they were finished, they stood at attention. Seconds later a door that stood against the opposite wall opened and the woman who had given them the note appeared.

"Hello, Anna. Jason." She nodded at them. "Sorry for all the cloak-'n'-dagger!" Her accent was cockney and very thick.

"What's going on?" Jason demanded again.

The woman smiled and held her hand up. "It's all right, love. Nothing to worry about. Well, not anymore. I didn't see them all the way here. Not that good, they ain't!"

"What in the world are you talking about?" Anna spoke for the first time since arriving.

"Well, deary, it seems you've acquired an admirer," the woman said.

"What do you mean?" Anna asked.

"I mean you got a tail, love." She smiled a quirky smile.

Anna stared blankly at her.

"Someone's been following you," she said, as if she were explaining it to a little child. "And they don't look friendly."

CHAPTER 56

West Jerusalem

The two men watched Anna and Jason get up from the table abruptly and head for a cab. Before they could even get away from their own table, which was directly across the street at another café, Anna and Jason were gone.

They were standing in the middle of the street looking both ways when a man asked one of them for a light. He had a cigarette dangling from his mouth and a sly grin on his face. As the lighter was being offered, he reached out and stuck the barrel of a gun under the man's arm.

"Both of you come with me," he said casually. "And don't make any sudden moves or I'll pull the trigger. And my friends watching us will shoot *you*"—he nodded to the other man"—right between those pretty blue eyes."

The men glanced at each other and complied. Apparently they had the good sense not to want to die quite yet.

Christopher Wallace had been a little leery of sending a team with Anna to Jerusalem. But now, seeing what was taking place here, he was glad that he did. And he was glad that he came himself. His years of service to Thomas, Anna's grandfather, wouldn't allow him to abandon Anna, especially after hearing from an informant what happened to Hale. He glared at the back of the two buffoons he'd intercepted as he nudged them forward and into a deserted alley. He then motioned them into an abandoned building and closed the door behind them.

"Sit down, both of you."

The men just looked at him.

"Gentlemen, I'm not in the habit of repeating myself. That's rule number one. If I have to again, I'll shoot one of you. Then the other one can tell me what I need to know. Now, sit down."

Both men sat in the middle of the floor.

"What do you want—"

Christopher stopped him in midsentence. "Rule number two: you don't talk unless asked a question. Otherwise, I shoot one of you and the other one tells me what I want to know." He looked quizzically at them. "Do you see a pattern developing here?"

Both men nodded.

"Okay. First, introductions. Names, both of you."

"Frick."

"Frack."

Christopher rolled his eyes. "Oh, that's brilliant. Fine. Who wants to tell me why you are following a pretty young American girl around?"

Neither of the men answered.

"Rule number three: if I ask a question and neither one of you answers, I'll shoot one of you and ask the other one—which in effect is breaking rule number one, 'cause I already told you I don't like repeating myself." He pulled the hammer back on his gun and took aim at the man sitting to his left.

"Stop! Wait!" Frick pleaded with desperation.

Christopher lowered his gun.

"We were just supposed to follow her. That's it."

Christopher raised his pistol and fired. He hit Frick square in the shoulder. The man screamed. Frack started shouting.

"He told you, you lunatic! We are just supposed to follow her. That's it!"

Christopher turned his attention over to Frack. "Yes, but that's not what I asked, is it? I asked you *why* you were following her. Not *if* you were following her."

He raised his pistol and shot Frick again in the other shoulder. Again the scream filled the room. "Now why are you two following the American and her friend?"

Frick was in shock. His eyes rolled back in his head, which was bobbing back and forth. He looked as if he would pass out at any given second. Frack sat there motionless, staring down his adversary.

"We were paid to follow her," he finally said.

"By whom?"

Nobody answered.

Christopher shot Frick above the left knee. This time the scream was slightly weaker. He was losing a lot of blood and was only semiconscious.

"I can't tell you," Frack answered in a pitiful whine.

"You'd better," Christopher said. "Your friend here doesn't look like he's in much shape to do any talking. That leaves you. And it's going to be quite difficult for you to tell me anything when I get done with him and start on you."

"He'll kill us if I tell you!" Frack shouted.

"I will kill you if you don't."

"Then go ahead," Frack said, defeated. "We're dead either way."

"Last chance," Christopher offered.

There was no reply.

Christopher was many things. A murderer wasn't one of them. He had killed in the line of duty, sure. But to take a man's life purely out of choice—he couldn't do it. He'd put these two clowns out of commission for a long time. There was a hospital just around the corner, and he could make sure they would get the medical attention they needed. One thing he'd learned: a man who thought he was already dead would not divulge any secrets. It was pointless to interrogate these men any further.

At the same time, he couldn't afford either of these men communicating with their boss. That meant he had to inflict more pain and damage to them. He hated the thought of it, but Anna's life could be in danger. And it might be the only way of keeping her safe. He would have to make sure that neither of these two men would be able to talk or write for a good long time. That meant breaking fingers and jawbones.

He pursed his lips and walked over to the one who'd been telling him everything.

"You're right," he said, "you're both dead men. Only I'm not the one who's going to kill you. I'll leave that to your boss."

He turned the gun around in his hand so that he was holding it by the barrel and raised it over his head. He swung down, knocking the man in the back of the head, rendering him unconscious. He pulled out his phone and pushed the speed dial.

"I need a car here, quick. Got to get these two to a hospital."

CHAPTER 57

West Jerusalem

The room was dimly lit, and that was good because Anna felt a headache coming on.

"Who are they?" she asked.

"Don't know," the woman answered. "Christopher is interrogating them as we speak. That's why we didn't see them following you."

"He's here? Christopher?"

"Yes."

"But I thought—I mean I knew he was sending a team, but I didn't know he was coming himself."

The woman smiled. "We all loved your grandfather, Anna. There's not much any one of us wouldn't have done for him. And right now that means taking proper care of you. So yes, Christopher's here. And it's a good thing too, love. He's the one who spotted your tail."

"Could be the same people that followed us in that other plane," Anna thought out loud.

"Could be." The woman stuck out her hand. "My name's Patrice."

Anna shook the woman's hand. "This is Jason."

Jason stood and greeted the woman. "Thank you, and I'm sorry. I should've seen the tail. I wasn't looking hard enough."

Patrice smiled and said in her thick cockney accent, "It's okay, love. I've been doing this a long time, and even I wasn't sure. It was Christopher, it was. He's the best I've ever seen."

"So what happens now?" Jason asked.

"Now we get you two out of here and figure out what's going on with those two bozos that were following you. We'll probably take you back to England for the time being."

Anna was already shaking her head. "No. No way. We have something we have to do in"—she checked her watch—"less than six hours. We're not going back to England. Have any of you heard from Hale?"

Patrice looked away.

"Patrice, please. What have you heard?"

She lifted her head to meet Anna's gaze. There was a sad look on her face. She just shook her head and said, "I'm sorry, love."

Anna didn't say anything. She sat back down with a blank look on her face. She could feel the tears welling up inside her.

Jason put his hand on her shoulder and looked at Patrice. "What happened?"

Patrice sighed. "All I know is that they found all three of them in a very bad part of town. They were all shot, and it was made to look like some kind of drug deal gone bad."

"That's ridiculous!" Jason said. "Aren't the authorities doing anything about it? Aren't they trying to find out what really happened?"

"I guess not," Patrice said.

Anna finally stood and moved toward the door. "Take us back to the hotel."

"We're supposed to wait on Christopher," Patrice objected.

"I said take us back to the hotel," Anna snapped.

Jason moved to where she was and placed his hands on her shoulders and said almost in a whisper, "Anna, we should wait on Christopher. Come sit back down. Please."

Anna slumped to the floor and began crying. Jason knelt down with her and held her in his arms.

"How many more, Jason? How many more have to die because of me?"

"Anna," he lifted her chin, "it's not because of you. No one has died because of you. These are sick, evil people, whoever it is doing this. They couldn't care less about you or anyone connected with you. You know what they want. And it's not you."

She didn't say anything.

"Look," he said as he helped her back to her feet, "we're very close. We need to meet Benjamin tonight. Soon all of this will be over. And then you can do whatever you've dreamed of. You're rich. Remember?"

She half smiled.

"Come on. Let's go sit down and wait on Christopher to get back. He'll tell us what he knows, and we can get on with this. Look at the bright side. He's here and has caught some of them. Maybe he can tell us who they are and how to avoid them. Or even better, maybe how to beat them. For good."

King David Hotel, Jerusalem

Wickham sat in a small chair in the lobby with his back to the front door. He held the newspaper in front of him and pretended to read. He'd been pretending for nearly two hours. He was beginning to feel self-conscious. He had been up and walked around the lobby and into the gift shop several times already. Hopefully no one had taken notice, or if they did, would think he was just a tired old man trying to waste the day away.

He was about to give up for a while when a young couple walked in. He probably would've ignored them altogether if it hadn't been for the grainy photograph that he held in front of the paper. From the back, the woman didn't look like her at all. But when she turned to say something to the young man she was with, he knew he'd found his prize.

Casually he folded his paper and stood up. He needed to hurry. The couple was already a good twenty steps ahead of him. If he was going to make their elevator, he needed to move it.

He got there just as the doors were starting to close. He stuck his hand out, and the sensor immediately withdrew the doors back into the folds of the wall. He stepped on and moved to the back wall, looking only at the floor.

It was deadly quiet for the eight-floor ride. The elevator jolted to a stop. The doors opened, and the couple got off. Wickham followed, this time purposefully staying a good distance back. Still, the two young people didn't talk. Someone might even think they didn't know each other if it weren't for the fact that they were holding hands.

Now that presented an interesting situation. Apparently Anna's companion was more than just a friend. This could be a problem, or it could be a solution. He just had to figure out which.

They stopped in front of their door and used the key card to let themselves in. As their door opened, he turned his head away from them and passed them by. He was almost at the end of the hall, so he went a few more steps and pulled out his own card. He stuck it in the slot in front of him. Of course it didn't work, but by the time he tried it two more times—like anyone who has stayed in a room that many floors up and doesn't want to go back down to the lobby—Anna and Jason were inside their room and he was in the clear.

He turned around and headed back for the elevators. Now he knew what room they were in. He didn't know what good that information was to him, but it seemed like something he needed to know at the time. He got back on the elevator and pushed 3.

When he got back to his own room, a thought came to him. Could he pull it off? Of course he could. He was one of the most powerful men in the world. He sat down on the bed and flipped open his cell phone. He punched in the hotel number plus the room number.

"Hello?" the voice on the other end of the phone said. It was the girl.

"Anna, you don't know me, but please, don't hang up. My name is Cardinal Louis Wickham."

There was an uncomfortable pause.

"I—I need to speak to you. It's about Hale."

"How did you know where I am?" she asked hesitantly.

"Anna, please let me explain. Hale came to me. He needed my help. There are some bad people in the Vatican. I'm sure you've already heard. Our beloved pope is dead."

"Yes, I've heard. What about Hale?"

Wickham could hear in the background the young man talking now. He was asking her who it was and telling her to hang up the phone. Wickham could sense that she was considering doing what the young man had suggested.

"Anna, please listen to me. Don't hang up. You are in great

danger. There are men in Jerusalem who are trying to kill you. Apparently you have something they want. I was trying to help him—Hale that is."

"I'm going to go now," Anna said.

He had to think fast. What was he to do? He couldn't let this opportunity slip out of his hands.

"Anna, I know all about the scroll." He blurted it out before he even had a chance to think what the ramifications would be. There was silence on the other end. But she was still there. Finally, she spoke.

"Go on."

He let out the breath he'd been holding. "Anna, I'm the secretary of state of the Vatican. I was Pope Paul's closest confidant. There are some who think he was murdered for the information he held about the scroll. Unfortunately, there won't be an autopsy. We'll never know. The bottom line is, Paul knew he was dying. He trusted me. He told me everything he knew. Hale called me to set up a meeting. He never showed. I'm sure by now you've heard what happened and what the police are saying. It's all nonsense, Anna. He and his team were good people. I want to help you. Nothing else."

Again he held his breath. Had he said too much?

"How can you help?"

This time the young man with her was adamant. He could hear him telling her again to hang up the phone now. There seemed to be a discussion going on between them. It was very muffled. It sounded like she was covering the mouthpiece. Then there was a *click*. He thought that she had hung up on him at first. Then he heard an ambient noise. He was now on speakerphone. And this time it was the young man who was addressing him.

"Look," he said, "I don't know who you are or how you got in touch with us, but let's get one thing straight. You are not on the list of people we trust. Is that clear? Don't call back here again."

"Jason!" It was Anna. "Hang on a second. Let's hear what he has to say."

"Anna—"

"Jason! Please, just listen."

Wickham began to feel light-headed. He'd been holding his breath again. He let it out with a *whoosh*. "Anna, we need to get you someplace safe."

"I am safe."

"You need to get out of Jerusalem."

"I have a security detail here. I'm safe."

Well, there was something he wasn't aware of. That could pose a problem. He'd deal with that later. Right now this wasn't working. She was too stubborn. He needed to convince her to let him help her. It was too perfect. She had to. He thought as quickly as he could.

"Hale, your pilot, was one of the most skilled, trained men I've ever known. They got to him. And his team, Anna. This is not a joke."

Again there was silence on the other line.

"When are you leaving Jerusalem?"

"Hopefully tonight. If everything goes right."

"What are you doing there?"

"I can't tell you."

"Anna, please. You have to trust me. Just tell me what you are doing in Jerusalem. I can help you."

Again silence. He could picture the two of them looking at each other, trying to decide whether or not to tell him.

"We're going to the—"

"Anna!" It was the young man again.

341

Again, there was a *click*. He was off speakerphone now. He could hear the muffled sounds of arguing again. He needed to end this. It was only going to get worse. Besides, he'd already gotten the info he needed.

"Anna. . .Anna." He tried to get her back on the line.

Click. Speakerphone again.

"What?"

"I'm leaving the Vatican right now." A lie, of course. He was just a few floors below. "I'll pick you up in your plane at the airport."

A pause. Then, "You have my plane?"

"Yes. I told you. Hale came here for a meeting with me. He never showed, but the plane is here. I will take a couple of Swiss guards with me and a pilot I trust. We'll be there waiting for you."

Click. Off speakerphone. Again there was the muffled conversation. *Click*. Back on. It was the young man this time. "I'm sorry, whoever you are. Don't bother. We won't be there."

Click. The line went dead.

Wickham slammed the phone back into its cradle. That stupid girl and her boyfriend were going to die. He would see to it. He needed a new plan. His mind began racing with ideas. Finally, he settled on the best one he could think of. He would force her to the airport, if necessary, and make his move when he could. But she did say she had a security team with her. That posed a problem.

He picked up his phone again and hit the speed dial. Jonathan answered on the first ring.

"Hello?"

"It's Wickham. I have some information for you. I know where she is going to be."

CHAPTER 58

Jerusalem

Ben Gurion Airport's private terminal, hangar number five, at midnight. That's what Wickham said.

Jonathan's mind raced trying to make sense of the phone conversation he just had. How in the world did Wickham know that? More importantly, *why* did Wickham know that? And what in the world was going on around here? This was all fouled up. Wickham had just told him where the girl was, precisely. And now he was to make sure she was at the airport by midnight by any means necessary. Oh, and there was the other brilliant piece of information. She had security. No kidding! Who the heck did Wickham think put him out of commission for the past week! The man was an idiot! He couldn't stand him anymore. His resolve to finish this—and Wickham—was growing stronger by the second.

"Listen up!" He turned to face the men. "We know where she is. She has a security team with her. They're probably good. I'd like to tell you that they aren't that good, but we can all see the condition my leg is in. So here's what we're gonna do."

He spent the next fifteen minutes explaining the plan. Twenty minutes later they were loading their gear into the trucks.

They were headed down the road toward the hotel when Waukeem closed his phone and turned around to face Jonathan who sat in the back.

"Frick and Frack in the hospital, mon. They pretty bad, mon. Broken fingers, and they both have they jawbones wired shut. The only way you gonna get any info out of them, mon, is if they can write with they toes, mon."

Jonathan let out a sigh. "Perfect."

He sat thinking for a minute. Neither of the two men would be able to tell him anything, but he would still be able to read their eyes. He decided he needed to see them first.

"Waukeem, take us to the hospital."

"But what about de girl, mon?"

Jonathan thought about this for a minute. He couldn't take a chance of losing her if she left the hotel. And they needed to get into place to be able to spot her security and take them out.

"Radio the other car and tell them to pull over."

Waukeem did as he was told, and the two vehicles pulled over to the side of the road. Jonathan told Waukeem to take the other truck to the hotel, just as they had discussed. He would go to the hospital and visit Frick and Frack. The men shifted some gear that Waukeem would need to get set up from one truck to the other. Jonathan took a driver and one other person with him as backup and headed to the hospital. Both trucks pulled back onto the road and went their separate ways.

Ten minutes later Jonathan walked into the emergency room. Like any ER, it was busy. A woman was there holding an ice pack on her forehead. A young man was sitting there with torn jeans, a deep cut just below his knee. And about fifty others were tending to other minor injuries or doubled over in pain. The staff behind the desk looked both extremely busy and disinterested.

He used that to his advantage. He walked right through the lobby and straight through the double doors that had a sign hanging over them, both in Hebrew and English, that said: AUTHORIZED PERSONNEL ONLY. No one even gave him a second glance.

Down the hall he found a linen closet with some scrubs in it. He put them on over his clothes and headed down to the nurse's station. After a little charm and some schmoozing, he was given the information he needed.

The elevator at the end of the hall took him to the fourth floor. He stepped out, walked down the hall, took the first left, and stood in front of the room. He had a thought and stopped for a second. He had just passed a supply closet.

He quickly backtracked and tried the door. Locked. He looked around to see if anyone was looking and pulled out a little leather case from his shirt pocket. He checked again. All clear.

He picked the lock with precision and was inside in seconds. He closed the door and felt against the wall for a switch. The room was instantly filled with light. There, over in the corner, was what he was in search of.

He opened the door a crack and checked the hall again. The coast was still clear. He let himself out and relocked the door.

On his way back a doctor and a nurse turned the corner and headed right for him. They seemed to be deep in conversation. He put his head down and walked right past them. They never gave him a second look. This was working out perfectly.

He checked over his shoulder one last time. The doctor and nurse were out of sight. He found the room and walked inside, locking the door behind him.

Both men were lying in bed unconscious. The beds were beside each other with enough room for someone to walk in between. He leaned over the one called Frick and patted his face. Nothing. He turned around and did the same to the one called Frack.

Frack slowly opened his eyes. They were glossy, and his pupils were dilated. He was drugged heavily, but it only took a couple of seconds for him to recognize the man who stood before him. The glossy look in his eyes was instantly replaced with fear. A bead of sweat formed on his forehead and trickled down his face.

Without any dialogue, Jonathan's questions were answered. They had talked.

He didn't bother to make conversation with the man. He just went about his task. He reached inside his scrubs and pulled out the empty syringes. He took the plastic tips off each of them and turned to face each man's I.V. drip. He disconnected the solution from each one and pulled back the plungers of the syringes, filling them with nothing but air. He carefully inserted the needles into the lines. He could see a look of panic in Frack's eyes. His head began to twist back and forth, and a desperate moan escaped his wired-shut lips.

Jonathan turned his head to face the man. "Be still."

Frack stopped and looked at Jonathan, pleading with his eyes.

"Remember what I told you when you came to work for me?" Jonathan asked him.

A tear slipped from Frack's eye and down his cheek.

"I told you that I can understand mistakes. I can even accept failure, on occasion. But I would never tolerate a traitor. You knew that and still you talked. So you don't have anyone but yourself to blame for this."

Frack shook his head vehemently, tears now streaming down his face. Jonathan paid him no attention as he turned away, placed his thumbs on the plungers, and pushed.

Almost in unison, both Frick and Frack arched their backs as their bodies went rigid with the embolisms.

Jonathan let himself out the same way he came in. Right through the front door. And as he made his way throughout the hospital, not one person paid him any attention.

CHAPTER 59

Jerusalem, the King David Hotel

Anna woke up from her nap and found Jason reading in his room. She walked in, leaned down, and kissed him on the nose. He looked up from his Bible and smiled.

"Wow! What's that for?" He smiled.

"Nothing. Just felt like it," she said.

"Well, I'll take one of those whenever you feel like it again."

She giggled and leaned in and kissed him on the lips this time. They both laughed, and Jason stood up.

"I guess we'd better get ready to go meet Benjamin," he said.

"I have scissors and hair dye waiting in my bathroom."

Jason tossed his Bible on the bed and followed her from the room.

Anna stood in front of the mirror in the bathroom, Jason behind her looking over her shoulder.

"Are you sure you can do this?" he asked.

"Let's do it." She handed him the scissors and stared straight ahead.

Jason grabbed the back of her shoulder length hair and twisted it into a kind of ponytail. "Here goes." It took several rough hacks before the mass of hair fell to the floor.

Anna let out a squeak.

"Sorry," Jason said.

Anna pursed her lips and said, "No, it's okay. I just haven't had my hair this short since I was a little girl."

"Well, I think you look even more beautiful," he said.

"Thank you, Jason, but you don't have to try and make me feel better about this. This was all my idea. Remember?"

"I wasn't. You *are* beautiful."

Anna smiled as another giant lock of hair fell.

Five minutes later they stood there admiring the ragged new haircut.

"It's. . .not bad," Anna said, wincing. "Kinda like a European-freakish thing."

Jason laughed. "Now for the dye."

Anna let out a big sigh and stuck her head under the sink while Jason read the instructions. They were simple enough: just wash and rinse.

Anna toweled her head as Jason put on the protective gloves. He massaged the solution into her scalp thoroughly. Two minutes later, she rinsed her head under the sink. When she stood up, she had short, choppy, coal-black hair.

Next on the list was a bottle of instant tanner.

Anna's skin complexion was naturally dark anyway, but Jason was extremely fair skinned. The tanning solution said that it would instantly give the appearance of rich, olive-toned skin. And that was what they both needed if they were going to pass for a couple of Arabs.

The effect was immediate—just as the bottle promised—and convincing.

Next was the wardrobe and makeup. They couldn't very well just walk in wearing Nikes and jeans from The Buckle. They had found a Muslim clothing store nearby and bought the needed attire.

A half hour later, with a little makeup, the right clothes, and the instant tanner, Jason and Anna both looked ready to visit the mosque.

Jason sat on the edge of the bed watching Anna as she finished packing her backpack. The scroll was neatly tucked inside one of the pockets. She looked like a young Muslim boy. It made him chuckle. But still he was bothered.

"Anna, about this Cardinal Wickham, I just don't know. . . ."

"Yeah, I know."

"I don't trust him," Jason said flatly.

"Well, he's got our plane. What should we do?"

"I don't know. I'm thinking about it."

Anna sighed. "Bottom line, we need the plane."

"Then I guess we'll just have to take it back," Jason said.

She nodded and grabbed her backpack. "We'd better go if we're going to make it on time. It's 10:30. We'll worry about Wickham later."

The Wailing Wall

Benjamin sat on a bench across from the wall, watching the people place their little notes inside the cracks. Prayers. It was a custom here at the wall. Young and old, native and foreigner, all alike, seemed to stand in awe of the great biblical structure.

It was a quarter past the hour, and he'd seen no sign of his friends. He was starting to get worried. What if he'd been turned in? What if someone got to those kids before he had a chance to get them inside. What if he was sitting here, a marked man, waiting for the bullet to penetrate his brain at one thousand feet per second?

He shook it off. No, nothing happened to them. He was just being paranoid. They would be here any minute now. He just needed to be watchful. They would be in disguise. He would have to look for the sign.

Several more minutes passed and still no sign of them. They were a half hour late. He was sure something was wrong. He stood to leave. And that's when he noticed two young Arabs strolling through the courtyard. He sat back down and resumed his act of reading the pamphlet he'd picked up from one of the tourist booths nearby.

The two Arabs strolled silently through the courtyard with their arms folded and heads down. They walked to the end of the wall, directly across from where Benjamin sat.

He watched as the shorter one pulled something from his robe. It was a picture. Then, just as Benjamin had instructed, the young Arab took the picture and tore it in two. He placed one half inside a small crack in the wall. The other he kissed and placed back inside his robe. That was the sign. His friends had made it. And with pretty good disguises, too, he might add. He didn't recognize them at all. Of course, they wouldn't have recognized him either. He had also changed his appearance.

He stood from his bench and walked to them. They both had their backs to him, staring at the great wall. He casually stepped up to them and touched them on the shoulder as he passed. No words were spoken. The two immediately turned and followed him as if they were being led by a leash.

They walked a few blocks to an old building. Benjamin took

out a ring of keys and unlocked the door. They followed him inside and down a set of stairs. They were in some kind of basement. It was dark, so Benjamin took out a small penlight to illuminate their way.

At the other end of the basement stood a stack of boxes. He set the small light down and moved them aside to reveal another locked gate. Again he pulled out his ring of keys and went to work. The gate swung open with a creaking sound, letting them know that it had not been opened for quite some time.

"Glad to see you made it," Benjamin said in a hushed tone. "I can honestly say I didn't recognize you. You both look splendid."

"Ditto," said Anna. "Sorry we were late. The hair took a little longer than I thought."

"No matter," Benjamin said. "You're both here, and to the best of my knowledge, no one followed you."

"That's another reason we were late," Jason added. "We tried to be extra careful and not be seen."

"Good job, lad."

Benjamin smiled and gave him a pat on the shoulder. He reached inside his jacket pocket and pulled out a shiny pistol. He handed it to Jason. "Here, take this. I hope and pray you don't have to use it. But if you get in a tight spot, it might save your life." He pulled out another smaller pistol, safely strapped into a holster, and handed it to Anna. "This is an ankle holster. You just strap it on like—"

Anna took the gun. "Thanks. It's just like mine." She pulled up her robe and strapped the holster to her leg.

Benjamin let out a long sigh. He nodded. "Anna, just so you know, I loved your grandfather. He was like a brother to me. We had a good relationship. I never asked him exactly what he was working on. And I won't ask you either. But I will say that I know, whatever it is you're doing, is the work of the Lord. And for that, may He bless your efforts immensely."

Jason and Anna both thanked him.

"Now," Benjamin continued, "this gate leads to a tunnel. It runs parallel to the wall. About 150 feet that way"—he pointed—"you will find another gate. It's called 'Warren's Gate.' It is sealed off. It lies directly beneath what we believe was the Holy of Holies." He handed them a small package. "This is a small amount of C-4 explosive. It is shape charged. Place it over the four corners of the sealed door. Take the small metal rods and place them inside the clay like this." He used his finger to simulate a rod and poked it into his hand. "Once you've placed it, come back here and use the detonator to blow it. It will make some noise, yes, but at this hour, no one should be down here. It will go unnoticed."

Anna and Jason stood there, mouths gaping in disbelief.

"You mean you want me to blow up the tunnel?" Anna said.

"Not the tunnel, dear, the gate. And don't worry. I promise you, it will go unnoticed."

"And how is that?" Jason asked, still not believing what this crazy old man was suggesting.

"Because I am going to cause a distraction at the exact moment that you push that button," Benjamin said with a sorrowful expression.

"Benjamin, what are you going to do?" Anna asked hesitantly.

"It doesn't matter. All that matters is that you get inside and find what it is you're looking for. Then get out. As quickly as you can. Once the ruckus settles down outside, security will be diverted back to the mosque. They will immediately think they are under attack by the Jewish nation. You will have ten, maybe fifteen minutes after that. Here." He handed them a stopwatch. "I have synchronized this with my own. At exactly a quarter till—to the second—I will set off my diversion. You must, and I stress *must*, push that button at exactly the same time. Do you understand me?"

"I'll do it," Jason said. "I won't be late."

Benjamin chuckled. "Don't be early either."

"I won't."

"Is ten minutes going to be enough time?" Anna asked worriedly.

"It's all you'll have, dear," Benjamin said. "I can tell you this. I have colleagues that have been in there. Don't ask me how or why. I don't know. But I have spoken with them, and they tell me that it is a small place. A room about the size of a normal bedroom. There's not a lot of area to search."

Anna stretched up on her toes and gave Benjamin a kiss on the cheek. "Thank you," she said, "for everything."

Benjamin blushed a little and said, "Don't thank me, dear. I'm only doing what God would have me do."

Jason and Anna turned to enter the tunnel.

"Wait! I almost forgot!" Benjamin had a horror-stricken look. "Good grief! What was I thinking?"

"What? What is it?" Anna and Jason asked together.

"Here, take these."

He pulled a ziplock bag from his pocket. Inside were two canisters about the size of a hairspray bottle and glow sticks. Each canister had a mouthpiece attached to it.

"These are air tanks. You stick them in your mouth and turn the knob, here at the top, like this." He turned one of them on quickly and then shut it off again.

Anna and Jason stared blankly at him.

Benjamin continued. "I nearly forgot to tell you. The northern end of the wall contains a channel that fed water into the Temple Mount. It was believed to have been stopped when Herod did his 'remodel.' This, however, is not the case. I have also learned that directly behind the Holy of Holies there is a cavelike tunnel that leads down into an underground stream. I won't lie to you. As far as anyone knows, it is completely underground. There is no open air above it for the entire length of the Western Gate. But it does finally end. It eventually dumps you out in the Stroutioun Pool at the northern exit, where you will find yourselves on the Via Dolorosa. It will be dark, and you will be swimming downstream. The current will be moving fast. These canisters have enough air in them to last you an hour each. That's it. After that you'd better hope you can hold your breath."

"Why on earth would we have to swim?" Jason asked dumbfounded.

"Because when they realize the gate's been blown down here—and they will eventually realize it—there will be at least fifty guards down here waiting for whoever it was to come back. Meanwhile, there probably will be more than fifty working their way down from the top of the mosque, trying to flush you out. You have no choice. It's the only way you can escape with your life."

"I was on the swim team in school," Anna said nonchalantly. "I can do it."

"Good, good. Glad to hear it!" Jason said. "'Cause I was worried you might be claustrophobic!" He threw his hands up in the air. "Are you kidding me? We're supposed to swim in the dark into some pool to get out of there?"

"Precisely," Benjamin said.

Anna smiled and put her arm around Jason. "You told me you asked God for something big. Well, I'd say this is it. Remember those drawings my grandfather had with the tunnels and the stream that led to a pool? This answers that question."

He took a deep breath and nodded. "Yeah, I'd say so. Okay, let's do it."

Benjamin took both of their hands and asked if he could pray for them. They both agreed and bowed their heads.

As soon as the prayer was said, Benjamin left and Anna and Jason headed down the tunnel, all keeping a close eye on their stopwatches.

They had twelve minutes.

CHAPTER 60

Jerusalem, outside the Dome of the Rock

Their disguises were good. Jonathan had to give them that. They looked exactly like two young Muslim men. He'd almost missed them, actually. It was the girl who gave them away.

Jonathan had been around plenty of Muslims in his life. He'd interacted with them on several occasions. Even had sat at the same table and shared a meal or two with several of them. And in all his experiences with them, he never saw one walking that gracefully in his life. All the Muslim men he'd ever seen walked with a purpose, a strong cadence to their steps. And that was the tell.

This young, short Muslim he was watching just kind of sauntered down the street. Like a lady. Not to mention the fact that "his" backside was swaying back and forth. That was not a man's walk. And it definitely wasn't a Muslim man's walk.

He watched from the vehicle as the girl and her boyfriend, or whatever he was, followed another strangely dressed individual. This one was dressed as a rabbi, in full regalia, carrying a large duffel bag.

357

He had a bead on all four of the security team. They were spread out in two-hundred-yard perimeters. He had watched them move when Anna and her friend left the hotel. They were good. Not obvious, but not hard to find if you knew what you were looking for. Maybe they weren't as good as he'd thought. Boy, wouldn't that be nice. Regardless, he wasn't taking any chances. He waited until Anna and her friends moved from the wall and went into an abandoned building. It was time to take out the security.

He left Waukeem stationed at the building and told him to let him know if anything happened. He was fairly sure nothing would. Whatever they were doing inside that building, they were probably going to be in there for a while. If everything went smoothly, he would take out the security and then go in after them.

He checked out his ammo and his "toys" and patted Waukeem on the shoulder.

"I'll be back in less than ten minutes," he said. "If they move, give me two clicks on the radio.

"Will do, mon," Waukeem said with a nod. "Happy hunting."

Jonathan smiled and crept away as quiet as a church mouse.

Jerusalem, outside the Wailing Wall

Benjamin made his way back up through the building and out the back door. He was sure they hadn't been followed in. He wanted to make sure he wasn't seen coming out. This back alley exit emptied directly behind a dumpster. Unless you knew the building, you wouldn't even know about it.

He checked his watch. He had seven minutes. More than enough time. He just needed to get into place. The trigger needed to be within a hundred meters in order to transmit.

He had called in some big favors for this one. For thirty years he'd served his country flawlessly. He had the ear of the prime minister, as well as numerous other powerful people throughout the state of Israel. And it was many of them who had set up this covert operation. Of course, he'd not been fully honest with them. As far as they knew, he was orchestrating one of the most brilliant "snatch-and-grabs" in the Mossad's history. As far as any of his contacts knew, he was working with a black-ops CIA team to take into possession a ruthless terrorist responsible for the deaths of over a thousand Israelis. What the powers-that-be didn't know is that the infamous terrorist Shaliek Arsowie Mohamed had been in custody for six days now. And it hadn't been as hard as anyone thought it would be. The Muslim killer had a weakness for American women. Funny, Benjamin thought. If Shaliek had been successful in his grandiose schemes, every American woman would be dead.

What Benjamin looked at now was no terrorist. It was, in fact, a row of six cars parked one in front of the other along the side of a street, rigged with explosives, and set to go off at the push of a button. A button that Benjamin held loosely in his left hand. The cars were all lined up against the curb along Bab Alsilsileh Street. He checked his watch. Three minutes. He crouched behind another car a safe distance away from the line of rigged cars. He bowed his head and said a little prayer for Anna and Jason. If everything went right, very little damage would occur. The charges were shape charges developed by the US Navy. The best in the world. Unless someone was standing within ten meters of the cars, the only thing that person would feel would be immense heat and the concussion of the explosion. It may knock them down, but that was it. No death and dismemberment.

One thing would happen though, he was sure. An explosion

this close to the wall, and at this hour of night, would definitely be seen as an attack on the mosque. Tonight was a special night for the Muslims in Jerusalem. The Imam had called a special prayer session in honor of the Hamas leader's birthday. The mosque would be full for the next three hours. The moment the explosion was heard, there would be chaos. Every Muslim inside that mosque would come running out, probably armed and taking aim at the first threat they saw. It would hopefully, buy Anna and Jason the time they needed to get inside. And hopefully, more importantly, mask the sound of the explosion Anna and Jason were about to set off themselves.

His watch began to beep short bursts of tone. Twenty seconds. Fifteen. Ten. He raised the cap over the button. Five. He shielded his eyes and crouched down as low as he could get. Three. He placed his thumb over the button. One.

Jerusalem, the Wailing Wall

Patrice sat on the bench two hundred yards away from her nearest team member. Standard procedure. She could hear the static over her earpiece from her radio. There were some clouds out tonight, and it was affecting the reception of the satellite radios. She had been trying to convince Christopher for six months now to go back to the normal radios. They didn't have the same range that the satellite radios had, but at least they didn't glitch and cut out anytime a big cloud passed over. Christopher, being a huge proponent of technology, wanted to give them more of a chance.

The radios weren't the only thing bothering her tonight. Call it women's intuition or whatever you want, but something didn't feel right. Something bad was about to happen. And most of the time that feeling paid off.

Breaking protocol, she stood from the bench and decided to walk around a bit. Check out the area. She still had her radio on. What could it hurt? She would still be within her area of watch.

Nothing was happening at her end of the street. Anna, Jason, and the old man had gone completely to the other end of the neighborhood and into an abandoned building. So she decided to head that way. She knew that Christopher would probably grump at her, but oh well. She had that *feeling*. And this was the only thing that would make her feel halfway better.

She hadn't gone far when she heard a bizarre sound shoot through her earpiece. She stopped dead in her tracks. What was that? It wasn't normal, that she was sure of.

They were on complete radio silence, the only exception being an emergency. Still, she thought about calling for a radio check. She contemplated it for a few seconds, waiting to hear the sound again. She didn't, so she dismissed it and continued on another twenty yards or so.

There it was again. She stopped. Now she was concerned. The same sound twice in three minutes. And it wasn't normal. She decided not to break radio silence just yet. Instead, she thought about the stage plot for their positions. Ramon would be closest to her. She headed that way.

He wasn't there.

Now she wasn't just concerned. She was worried. While she was one of the most skilled people on Christopher's team, she wasn't one who necessarily always followed the rules. Christopher would get on her case about it all the time. The fact that she was better than anyone else on the team gained her some leeway. Ramon, on the other hand, was mister rules-and-regulations. There's no way he'd leave his post unless he had a direct order from Christopher or received a code red on the radio. And he wasn't here. That was it. Time to break radio silence.

She reached at her waist to press the radio. She stopped. There it was again. That sound. It was just a quick squeal. She'd heard it before. And not just the two previous times in the last ten minutes. She reached for the button. She stopped. She felt the blood drain from her face. She knew where she'd heard that sound before. It was the sound of the transmitter cord being ripped out of the radio.

She found cover and drew her weapon. Her entire body tensed, fully alert. She swept the area around her.

Nothing.

She crouched behind a parked car and keyed her radio. "Command, this is Bravo One. Check in. Over."

Nothing.

"Bravo Two, this is One. Check in. Over."

Nothing.

"Three, check in."

Nothing.

She pinched the bridge of her nose. This was bad. No one was checking in. She knew they were dead. How, she didn't know. She only knew that it was true. Otherwise, someone would have found her or contacted her by now. When one of the team broke radio silence, it was understood that no matter what the circumstance was, you always checked in. That was the rule.

She moved from behind the parked car to check out the other posts and confirm her suspicions.

Twenty feet away she spotted a dumpster tucked back in an alley. Something stuck out from the other side. She hugged the wall and moved in, all the while sweeping her weapon from side to side and up and down.

Ramon was slumped over, soaked with blood. His throat had been cut from ear to ear.

Quickly she made her way back out the alley and headed toward the Dome of the Rock. That's where Christopher was supposed to be.

She hadn't gone very far when she saw a brilliant flash light up the night sky no more than a hundred yards in front of her.

Immediately, she heard people screaming. Seconds later she was thrown backward as the concussion from the bomb threw her against the brick wall.

CHAPTER 61

Jerusalem, the Abandoned Building

Five. . .four. . .three. . .two. . . Jason pushed the button as he and Anna shielded themselves behind the door opening. They felt the ground tremble and heard the explosion. Dust and heat flew at them from the cavern behind the door.

They flipped on their flashlights and hurried into the dark passageway. The gate had blown, exactly as Benjamin said it would. There was an opening large enough for a single adult to crawl through.

Jason readied his pistol and poked his head through the opening, sure that he was about to be fired upon.

Nothing. He could make out the outline of a small room with a hallway that led upward in the back. It was the hallway that Benjamin told them would lead them to the Holy of Holies.

Jason and Anna quickly stepped into a room that was really nothing more than a cellar. The walls were rock and the floor was dirt. A few boxes were strewn about, making it look more like a storage closet than anything else. They pushed a few of them out of their way and slipped into the hallway.

As they crept up the winding path, they could hear muffled voices coming from above, along with the sound of many feet running. Obviously, Benjamin's distraction was working. It sounded like total chaos above.

Less than twenty meters up the hallway, they were met with another door. This is where it would get tricky. Benjamin had told them that this door led to the main underground tunnel network. Not even Benjamin knew what would be waiting for them on the other side of the door. The only thing he did know was how to get to the Holy of Holies from here. If they ran into any worshippers—or worse, guards—they would have to decide for themselves how to proceed.

Jason tried the door, he and Anna both poised with their pistols outstretched. The knob turned easily, and the door opened a crack. He could see a dimly lit open area, not very big, that looked a lot like the cellar they had just come from. This one, however, had a set of stairs at one end and two other tunnels on either side of the stairs. He could see two people standing with their backs to him just a few feet away. Both held AK-47 rifles.

Jason silently closed the door and whispered to Anna, "Two guys, both armed with automatic rifles—backs to us. Here's what we're going to do." He finished telling Anna his plan and then opened the door again.

This time it was Anna who took the lead. She stumbled out of the door, holding her side and coughing as if she were injured. She was doubled over with her head down. She was motioning to the two guards to come to her, as if she needed help.

They reacted in shock. They didn't expect someone to come in from behind them. As far as they had known, the only thing down there was some storage cellar and no entrance into it, except from their end. And they hadn't seen anyone come down those stairs since the explosion just a few minutes ago.

As Anna looked like a fellow Arab in her disguise, they quickly took the five or so steps over to her as she continued to cough and convulse. They let their assault rifles drop to their side, hanging from the shoulder strap. As they did, she straightened up just as Jason flung open the door and knocked one of them over the head with his 9mm. The man instantly fell to the floor, limp. The other was fumbling with his robe, trying to get a hold of his own weapon. Since he was already caught off guard, it was easy for Anna to step around him and knock him in the back of the head as well. Both men now lay unconscious on the floor.

"Quick," Jason said, "let's get these guys out of the way."

They each grabbed a man and dragged him through the door that they had come through. Anna retrieved a small roll of duct tape from the backpack she had concealed under her robe and quickly taped the men's hands, feet, and mouths. The only way these guys were going to get any help was if someone found them. She hoped someone would find them—eventually. While she didn't want them hindering what she and Jason were trying to do, she certainly didn't want the men to come to any harm. Someone would find them. She was sure of it.

Back in the tunnel network, the noise above was getting more intense. It had only been three minutes since they entered the room below them. They needed to find the Holy of Holies fast. Another group of armed guards could come down here any second. What then? Would they be forced to shoot someone? Anna pushed that thought out of her mind.

"Come on," she said. "Benjamin said it's down this hall." She grabbed Jason's hand and they entered the tunnel.

The tunnel wound down and around a good twenty or so

meters. The last few or so, they were met with a set of seven steps made of marble. They were lined with what looked like solid gold. And inside the solid gold lining there were rubies and diamonds. At the bottom of the steps stood a great curtain, which looked like it was made of a very thick wool. It stood every bit of twelve feet in the air and was hung by bronze curtain rings. And last but most exciting to Anna and Jason, it was torn from top to bottom and was parted down the middle.

Jason couldn't breathe. He had heard about this his whole life. He had read about it in the Bible. Heard preachers talk about it. Had seen it—or at least a Hollywood representation of it—in movies. And now here he was standing in front of the curtain that was torn when Jesus expelled his last breath, signifying that no longer would man have to come to God through another man. From that point on, Jesus was the bridge between man and God. The new covenant.

It seemed like hours. But after only a few seconds of staring in awe, Jason felt his arm being pulled by Anna.

"Jason, come on! We don't have much time!"

"I—I know. It's just that. . ."

"I know, Jason. It's real! It's incredible, isn't it?"

"Yes, Anna, it is," he said in awe.

Anna pushed aside the curtain as she and Jason stepped into a small room. It was exactly as Benjamin described. Nothing more than what looked to be about the size of a small bedroom. There were a few carvings on the walls. Words mostly. And they looked to be in Hebrew. This floor also was marble tile with jewels in the center.

A golden box with four handles protruding from it sat on the ground. It looked to be about three feet tall, three feet wide, and roughly five feet long. It was covered in dust, but that didn't obscure the intricate carvings that lined its top and sides. The lid held jewels that were as big as a man's fist. The sides were draped in silk cloths and beads, and drawings of an altar were expertly carved into it. Even someone with little knowledge of the Bible would know this box.

Jason began to weep. He fell to his knees and whispered, "My God, my King, I am not worthy."

Anna didn't know what was happening to her. She couldn't see for the tears that flooded her eyes. She trembled with fear. But it wasn't the kind of fear that one would normally associate with being scared. It was more of a respectful fear. She felt her knees give out, and the next thing she knew, she was lying prostrate on the floor next to Jason.

Three feet from the ark of the covenant.

CHAPTER 62

Jerusalem, outside the Wailing Wall

Patrice dusted herself off and checked that she didn't have any major injuries. A scraped knee, a few singed hairs, a knot on the back of her head—which, by the way, felt like an egg and was throbbing to beat the band—and a couple of bruised ribs. Nothing serious.

Someone had killed Ramon, and God only knew who else. She found her radio and keyed the mike. "Bravo One to command. Come in, over."

Nothing.

With her weapon drawn, Patrice continued down the street to where Christopher was supposed to be. She knew that she had only a few seconds to do this. Right now, whether her team was dead or not didn't matter. Anna and Jason were in danger. She needed to find them and get them out of here. But where in the heck were they? Christopher was the only one who would know that, because he was the one watching them. She and the rest of the team were simply posted around the area to watch for suspicious activity. Guess they'd get an A plus on that one.

She found Christopher lying facedown behind a couple of trash cans. He had some newspaper over his body. He looked like a homeless man who was trying to keep warm.

When she turned him over, she saw that he had been shot three times. Twice in the chest and once in the hand. He must've had his gun shot out of his hand.

She was about to leave when she felt a small squeeze on her arm. He was alive. She rolled him onto his back to give him CPR.

She was pushing on his chest, trying to pump his heart, when she heard the gurgling sound come from his mouth. He was trying to tell her something.

She leaned down and put her ear to his lips. "What, Chris? What is it? Who did this to you? To us?"

His words were strained and came in short gasps. "Listen. . .to me. . . . Find them. . . . Anna. . ."

"Yes! Yes! Where are they?"

"Mossad. . .old man. . .helping them. . ."

"What? You're not making any sense!" She patted his cheeks. "Stay with me Christopher! You hear me?" She beat on his chest. "This mission is not over! You open your eyes and debrief me right now. That's an order!"

His eyes fluttered open a little bit and a smile creased his lips. He coughed a little blood out of his mouth and pulled her back down.

"They. . .are with. . .a Mossad agent. . . . I saw them. . .go into. . .that building." He pointed to the abandoned building down the street at the end of the block.

"Are they safe?"

"No." He coughed. "Find. . .them. . . . Must get back. . .to London."

"Come on, Christopher! Stay with me," she yelled as he coughed up some more blood.

"Mossad...is okay....Trying to help...only one guy...friend of Thomas...Riley...have seen him...before."

"What about Anna and Jason? How do I find them?"

"Don't...know....Find Mossad guy."He coughed some more. This time a lot of blood came up. "Hurry...leave me...mission not over—"

And with that, a small bubbly breath escaped his lips. Christopher Wallace was dead.

Patrice held his head in her hands for another moment. She closed his eyes and said good-bye. She checked her weapon and stood up. She needed to find this Mossad guy. She went exactly where Christopher told her to go. The abandoned building.

Jerusalem, the Holy of Holies

Anna felt as if it had been hours since she and Jason had been lying on the ground, though it was only a minute or two. She stood up first, wiping the tears from her eyes. She touched Jason on the shoulder, and he stood up with her.

"Anna, do you realize that we are staring at the literal place where God's presence dwelt with his people! This was *the* most sacred thing in all of Israel."

She was about to say something when she heard another voice. They both were startled. The voice came from all around them, but there was no one there.

"Welcome, Anna, Jason."

And then they saw him. Or it. They weren't sure.

A little white light appeared before them, hovering at eye level.

371

Then the light began to grow in intensity and size until the entire room was flooded with blinding white. Just as quickly as it came, it disappeared, leaving a giant with wings holding a mighty sword and wearing a breastplate. He was clothed in a purple robe, and his eyes were greener and more brilliant than the finest emerald. The sword he carried was at least eight feet long and had a serrated blade that was stained with what they could only assume was blood. The breastplate was dinged and scratched and looked as if it had seen much battle. His head was bald except for one lock of white hair in a braid that trailed all the way to the floor. The braid was held in place, at the tip, by a blood-stained razorlike blade, as if the creature used his hair as a weapon.

"I am Michael."

"Uh. . .you mean Michael? As in *the* Michael?" Jason stammered, still shocked at seeing the giant.

"The archangel. Yes."

Jason found his voice. "What are you doing here?"

Michael almost smiled but not quite. "You two have caused quite a stir around here. Do you realize that God's people haven't seen the mercy seat for centuries?"

"You mean the ark?" Jason asked.

"Yes," Michael answered. "You are standing in one of the holiest places on your earth. What you call the ark, we call the mercy seat, because it used to be the earthly throne of the presence of Yahweh."

"What do you mean 'used to'?" Anna asked.

Now Michael smiled fully. "Since God became flesh, His spirit lives within those whom Christ has saved. He has no more need of an earthly throne."

Anna had a worried look on her face. "Michael, I don't mean to be rude, but we really have to hurry. There could be men with guns coming in here any second."

Michael nodded. "What you seek is not here."

"What do you mean?" Anna asked. "It has to be! This is where my grandfather's research leads. The ark. It's right here!"

"All I can tell you is, the key you seek is not the ark. And it is definitely not here."

The air seemed to leave the room. Anna and Jason again felt as if they had failed.

Michael moved out from in front of the ark of the covenant. "You may stay here and worship for a few more minutes if you like, but remember that which you worship does not dwell in this box, beautiful as it may be. So pay no homage to it. Worship Him who sits on the throne of heaven. The Father has given us these few minutes to speak. Once I leave you, I will once again be engaged in battle. This place, believe it or not, is one of the fiercest battlegrounds we angels fight upon. When I am gone, only several seconds of your time will have passed. You needn't waste precious time looking around. You must get out. I believe your friend, the old man, told you of a way?"

"Yes," Anna answered. "An underground stream that we can swim through and escape."

"That is the way you need to leave," Michael said. "I will hold off any attacks from my side of the world against you. Trust me, you will be fine. Just remember to pray. Only God can deliver you from the dangers you face."

CHAPTER 63

Jerusalem, the Wailing Wall

Benjamin watched the giant fireball engulf the night sky. Seconds later the heat of the explosion concussed against him. His part of the mission was successful. He only hoped that Anna and Jason had been as successful.

He knew that what lay ahead for the two youngsters was a very difficult task. The chance of getting what they came for and escaping unharmed was slim. He knelt behind the cluster of shrubs and prayed for them.

The cold steel of the silenced pistol poked him in the back of the neck. Then there was a hand placed on his shoulder. A big beefy hand. The voice that accompanied the hand was stern.

"Okay, mon. Get up slowly and put your hands behind your back."

He placed his hands behind his back and stood up slowly.

He had just gotten to his feet when the big man suddenly went limp like a rag doll. He fell to the ground and lay there, unmoving. A trickle of blood seeped out from underneath the man's head.

Benjamin looked up and saw an attractive young female approaching him. She had a silenced Smith & Wesson .45 in her hand. It was still outstretched from her arm and pointed at him.

"Who are you and what are you doing here?" she demanded.

Benjamin had to decide quickly. This woman obviously had just spared his life. But why? Who was she? And how did she just happen to come upon his situation just then?

And then he remembered. Anna and Jason had a team of specialized security with them here in Jerusalem.

"My name is Benjamin. I believe we are on the same team, my dear."

"Uh, uh," she said, waving her gun at him. "Keep those hands where I can see them, love." She moved closer. "Now tell me who you are and what you're doing holding a detonation device in your hand. And you'd better make it good or I'm going to split your skull open. Understood?"

Benjamin realized he was actually in little danger. It would only take him convincing this woman who he was and what he was doing here to diffuse the situation. But this didn't need to be done out in the open with hundreds of people rushing around in chaos from the blast. He knew they both needed to get someplace safe. The large Jamaican man who lay dead at his feet definitely had friends.

"Follow me," he said to the woman. And then he took off at a brisk pace away from the wall.

One block west. Two blocks north. Down a little alley and into the door of a building that looked condemned. Patrice dropped her guard as she entered the doorway just enough for him to get the upper hand on her. Within a matter of seconds, she was the one on the ground having her own weapon pointed at her.

"Now, young lady," Benjamin said with a smile, "as I said before, I believe you and I are on the same team." He released the grip on the gun, flipped it around in his hand, and handed it back to her. As she took it, he reached his hand down to help her up. "You are unhurt?"

She smirked. "Other than my ego, I think I'm fine."

He stuck his hand out to her. "My name's Benjamin. I am a Mossad agent, a former friend of Thomas Riley, and a current associate of his granddaughter, Anna. I am the one who helped them into the mosque."

Patrice told him who she was and how her whole team had been eliminated.

"Well, we're safe in here. I assure you," Benjamin said after she finished.

"Maybe, but Anna and Jason aren't. Whoever did this to my team is good—no, better than good. 'Cause my team was the best, and they're all dead. And if they think we're all dead, there's nothing to stop them from going after Anna and Jason except us. Where are they now? Anna and Jason?"

"I would imagine, by now, they are swimming through the underground stream."

"Underground stream?"

"Yes. That is how they were to escape. There is a stream, or river, that flows under the mosque. It has been there since the first temple was built. It empties out a few blocks away from the wall."

"We have to go." Patrice grabbed his arm. "If those people know about that underground river, they'll be waiting for them on the other side."

Jerusalem, the Holy of Holies

As quickly as Michael had appeared, he was gone. Anna and Jason wasted no time leaving the sacred room. They could already hear the heavy footsteps above them getting louder. It would only be a matter of minutes, if not seconds, before they would be discovered.

They found the spiraling pathway that supposedly led down to the underground stream. With flashlights in hand, they hurried down the dirt path, ducking jagged rocks that lined the walls.

Less than fifteen meters later, the path abruptly ended in what looked like a giant puddle. Surprisingly, the water was crystal clear. They could see straight to the bottom if they shone their lights into it. It was roughly five meters in diameter and looked to be about eight or ten meters deep.

Anna secured her backpack with the front straps while Jason reached into his to retrieve the breathing devices and the glow sticks they had been given. He handed Anna one set and then secured his pack again. The footsteps became louder. They had already used up precious time removing the robes they were wearing. The used garments now lay in a pile on the dirt. They both wore neoprene running pants and close-fitting T-shirts they'd bought at a sporting goods store in London, intending to work out as much as they could. The workouts hadn't happened, but it seemed good clothing to wear under their disguises. And now they'd get their workout after all—swimming for their lives.

The footsteps echoed down through the tunnel. They had to go. Anna was about to jump in head first when Jason grabbed her by the arm.

"Wait!" he said.

"Jason, they're coming!"

He took her hand. His words came in a tumbled rush. "God, please watch over us and keep us safe. In Jesus' name, amen."

"Amen," Anna said. "Now let's go!"

She jumped in head first and felt the surprisingly warm water soak through her clothes. Jason followed. The men's footsteps could be heard coming down the path. They each twisted the little valve on their breathing tanks and put them in their mouths. They gave each other a thumbs-up signal, cracked the glow sticks, and dove down toward the bottom of the pool.

The first bullet ripped through the water just centimeters from Anna's head. Within seconds the guards stood above them showering bullets into the small pool. They dove deeper, and the water below turned murky and dark.

CHAPTER 64

The Via Dolorosa

Anna and Jason pushed their way through the crowds that had gathered to see what was going on at the Dome of the Rock. Reporters stared into their cameras giving what details they knew to the rest of the world. No one paid any attention to the fact that there were two young Americans standing in the middle of the street soaking wet.

The swim through the stream was an easy one. Most of the way the path was clear and wide enough for them to swim side by side. Only twice did they have to go single file, and then only briefly.

There were several cabs waiting across the street. They ran to the first one they came to and jumped in.

"Airport, please," Anna directed the driver.

The man pulled the gear shift on the steering column and punched the gas. "It will be fifty dollars, US."

"What?" Jason said. "Are you kidding? It's only like ten minutes from here."

Anna saw the man through the rearview mirror shrug his

shoulders and curl his mouth. "Bombs go off, people need to get away quickly, I don't ask questions. Fifty dollars, US. You are American, yes?"

"Fine." She reached into her backpack and grabbed two twenties and a ten out of her zipped pocket and fed them through the slot in the glass that separated them from the driver.

She stared down into the backpack and at the scroll. It amazed her that something so small could cause all of this trouble. She felt a twinge of anxiety as she ran her fingers along the steel casing that she had purchased to house it. She didn't know how much more of this she could take.

Jonathan turned the corner just in time to see one of his men waving to him from the passenger window of an SUV. The big Suburban's tires squealed as it made a U-turn out of the parking space and pulled up beside him. The rear door flung open just long enough for him to jump in.

"That's them, in the cab up ahead," his driver said.

"Don't lose them," Jonathan ordered. "And don't bother staying back. As soon as we get out of this traffic, I want to take them out."

"What? Right here in the city?" one of the men asked.

"Yes. Every cop and emergency vehicle in the whole town is heading for the Wailing Wall. No one will even bat an eye at us. At least not for a while."

"What do you want me to do?" the driver asked.

"Just wait till we get a little farther up ahead." He pulled the pistol out of his waistband and checked the clip again. Still full.

After a few more minutes, the traffic seemed to be dispersing. The road took a winding turn and then opened up into a kind of multilane freeway. A sign for the airport appeared, and the cab flashed a signal to change lanes.

"She's headed for the airport," said Jonathan. "We have to stop them before they reach it."

"No problem," the driver said. Without another word, he yanked hard on the steering wheel and the Suburban flew across the lanes, cutting off three other vehicles.

"Now!" Jonathan said. "Get me up beside them."

The big SUV roared as the driver punched the gas. The needle on the speedometer swept across the dash as they inched closer to the cab. Just when it looked like they were going to ram the little car from behind, the driver of the Suburban yanked the wheel again. The SUV shot out and around to the side of the cab. Jonathan rolled down his window and stuck out his arm.

Jason had his head against the window with his eyes closed and Anna was lost in thought when the cab driver spoke up.

"Do you two have someone chasing you, perhaps?"

Jason immediately came alive. "Why?" he asked, turning around to look behind them.

"Because," the cab driver explained, "there is a rather big vehicle weaving in and out of traffic. It seems to be following us."

Anna and Jason were both staring out the back window now. And both of them knew that this wasn't good.

"How far from the airport are we?" Anna asked.

"Less than five minutes," the driver answered.

"Step on it!" they both said in unison.

Jason kept an eye on the truck behind them while Anna fidgeted around in her backpack. He could hear the rustling beside him. He turned around for a quick second, only to see Anna pulling out one of the handguns Benjamin had given them.

"Is that a gun?" The cab driver had angled his mirror to see into the backseat. "You can't have a gun in here. It says right here on the sign." He pointed to a little sticker on the dashboard.

Jason still had his head turned around watching the Suburban as it closed in on them. Without any warning, the SUV was right behind them and then it wasn't. Anna started to say something to the driver when Jason grabbed her from the back of the head and pushed her down to the floor. "Get down!"

Jonathan watched the mirror on the passenger side door of the cab explode. Just then his driver jerked the wheel again. The gun flew out of his hand and onto the floor as the truck veered onto the side of the road to miss rear-ending another car, whose driver decided to slam on his brakes, in their lane. The cab instantly shot ahead of them.

"Get back on the road!" He felt for his gun under the seat. "Am I the only one here who's packing? Did I not buy nice firearms for all of you?" The men in the truck looked at him with bewilderment. "That was a rhetorical question! What are you waiting for? Shoot!"

All four windows on the Suburban went down as each of them stuck their arms out the window and began firing at the cab ahead of them.

"What did you two get me into? Get out of my cab!" the cabbie said, slamming on his brakes.

Jason banged on the back of the driver's seat. "No! Drive faster. If you stop, they'll kill us and you."

The driver saw the gun pointed at him and punched the gas as the Suburban swerved off the road to avoid hitting another car.

That allowed them to get ahead.

Anna crept back onto the seat and rolled down her window.

Jason grabbed her arm. "You're not shooting at them in the middle of the highway!"

"They don't know I have a gun. If I shoot back, we can gain some distance from them."

"Or it could just make them mad. Have you lost your mind?"

The rear window exploded and shattered all over the backseat. "Okay! Shoot back!"

Anna turned around in the seat and leveled her arm. She took a deep breath and squeezed the trigger.

The front windshield of the Suburban cracked like a spider's web as three bullets hit it. The driver's visibility disappeared. He slammed on the brakes and skidded to a stop on the side of the road. "They're shooting back!"

"No kidding, Einstein!" Jonathan spat. "What are you doing? Get after them!"

"I can't see anything!"

Jonathan crawled over the seat, reached across the man sitting beside him, opened the door, pushed the man out, then leaned back and kicked the front windshield until the glass flew out of it's frame and onto the side of the road. "Now let's go!"

The Suburban's tires kicked up gravel as they spun back onto the road. The cab was almost out of sight now.

"It worked!" Anna shrieked, as the Suburban skidded to a stop behind them.

The cab was now a few hundred yards ahead of the Suburban,

which had pulled off the side of the road. The cab driver hadn't said a word since the first gunshot. He seemed in shock. The airport was just ahead, and the signs for the private terminal were already coming into view.

"There!" Anna said. "We need to go to the private terminal."

The cab changed lanes and sped onto the off-ramp. The terminal was just ahead. They passed a sign for the parking lot just as the driver slammed on his brakes.

"No more!" he yelled. "You get out!"

They were less than a hundred yards from the runway. Anna could see her plane sitting there ready to take off. They just had to get through the little security building and out onto the tarmac. "Come on, Jason. We can make it."

"We'd better hurry!" Jason said, as he saw the headlights coming at them.

They jumped out of the cab, barely getting out before the driver punched the gas and sped off. They ran as fast as they could toward the security building. They could hear screeching tires behind them. They entered the building just as the Suburban stopped at the front doors, screeching to a halt.

They hurried down the hallway, trying not to draw attention, and exited the building. They could see the plane at the front of the runway, engines running, and the stairs down. A man in a windbreaker and ball cap was standing at the top of the stairs waving frantically at them. Knowing their attackers were moments behind them, they took off running toward him.

Jonathan exited the building just in time to see Anna and Jason running for the plane. Something wasn't right. He stopped for just a second. Wickham was standing at the top of the stairs, waving at them like a beacon. What the heck was Wickham doing on Anna and Jason's plane? He pulled his gun and started running after them. He took aim and tried to pull the trigger but couldn't. His arm went slack.

His leg collapsed beneath him. He couldn't breathe.

And what was this pain shooting through his chest?

He fell to the pavement, blood pouring out of his arm, his leg, and his chest. Shot.

This was it. Not how he expected it. He always thought of dying at his home on the beach. The sun would be setting, there would be a lazy breeze, it would be warm—oh yeah, and he would be really old.

He'd been shot from behind. But how? Double-crossed by his own men?

Blood. Pain. His breaths came in short gasps. He tried to lift his head. All he could see was Anna and Jason looking back at him. They both looked confused. What was going on?

He turned his head to look behind him. His vision was getting blurry. No air. Who was that? It looked like an old man. And he had a woman beside him. They were both holding guns, drawn on him, their barrels trailing with thin wisps of smoke.

He hated them in that moment. Hated all of them. He coughed, a coppery liquid filling his mouth. It dribbled from his lips. The woman approached him. How he wished he had the strength to kill her.

She studied him closely for a moment. Anger mixed with pity darkened her face. She bent down and whispered in his ear. "I take no pleasure in killing you, but my job is to protect that boy and girl. I do, however, feel sorry for you, love. You think you're in pain right now. But if you think that hurt, it's nothing compared to what you're about to face."

CHAPTER 65

Jerusalem, the Airport

Out of the corner of her eye, Anna saw the man chasing after her and Jason as they were running for the plane. She was about to scream and dive for cover when he fell to the ground. Out of the shadows she saw Benjamin and Patrice running up to the body.

Within seconds she was back down on the tarmac running to them with Jason close behind. "Benjamin! Patrice! Oh, thank God! You saved our lives."

Benjamin put his arm around her and shook Jason's hand. "We followed you. It's a long story. Let's just say that God's timing is perfect. Two seconds later and you both may have been dead."

Anna stepped back, looking at the dead assassin. She had completely forgotten about the plane until she noticed the man closing in on her.

"Anna," the man shouted.

Drawing the other's attention, they turned to face Cardinal Wickham, who had his arm outstretched. He pulled the trigger of the small revolver in his hand.

The gun exploded. Benjamin dropped to the ground. Anna screamed and lunged for him. The cardinal grabbed her shoulder and placed the barrel of the gun tightly against her head.

"Anna, just stay calm," Patrice shouted, as she moved toward them. "Nothing's going to happen to you. Just stay calm."

"All I want is the scroll," Wickham shouted, wrestling Anna back to the plane. "Give it to me and you can all go about your way."

Patrice aimed her gun at him. "Let her go, or I'll shoot you in the head."

Wickham laughed. "You do and you're dead a second later." He pointed with his head at the two guards. "Just give it to me," he said in Anna's ear. "We can end all of this right now."

"You're going to have to kill me first," Anna snapped.

"Don't tempt me."

"Anna, you stay put." It was Benjamin. He had gotten to his feet holding his arm. It was bleeding, but other than that, he appeared unhurt.

Three men dressed in black and sporting automatic weapons sprinted out of the terminal building. They were less than a hundred yards away.

Anna knew that in a few more seconds she would be inside the plane. After that she would be this man's prisoner. She couldn't allow that to happen. Not after all she'd been through. She shouted to Patrice, "Shoot him!"

"What?" Jason said. "Are you nuts?"

"Patrice! You told me you can hit a moving target the size of a baseball card. Shoot him! Now!"

"Let her go, mister!" Patrice ordered. "This is the last time I'll tell you."

Wickham backed himself and Anna up the stairs. "I told you,

give me the scroll and she can go free."

Shots rang out from the tarmac. Jonathan's men were gaining and shooting at everybody. Benjamin and Jason dove behind a small Cessna a few feet away. Benjamin pulled his pistol and returned fire. Jonathan's men scattered behind some barrels and crates that lay off to the side of one of the hangars and kept shooting back. The two Swiss guards shot at Benjamin, Jason, and Jonathan's men.

"Shoot him! Now!" Anna screamed.

Patrice pointed the gun at Wickham's head, frowned, moved a few inches to the right, and pulled the trigger.

Wickham's left shoulder exploded as he was thrown backward from the blast. Holding on to the only thing he could, he fell backward into the plane. Anna dove the minute she felt Wickham release his grip on her, but something restrained her. The backpack. She twisted her arms and fell free from it. She tumbled down the short stairway and onto the hard blacktop of the runway.

Wickham fell backward into the plane, her backpack in his hand.

Patrice ran to her, firing shots into the doorway of the plane. She grabbed Anna by her shirt and hauled her away. She hit one of the guards, while the other one dove into the cabin. The plane was already moving, turning in a circle to line up for the runway. The stairs started to retract as the pilot gunned the engines. Within seconds the powerful G-5 was speeding down the runway.

Patrice dragged Anna safely behind the door of the hangar they were next to. "Are you okay? Were you hit?"

Anna shook her head and tried to speak, but no words came.

"Anna!" Patrice snapped. "Are you hit? Are you okay?"

Anna still didn't answer. She lay there on the floor of the hangar crying. Patrice quickly checked her over and found no injuries. "Anna, you're fine. You're not injured. What's wrong?"

"My backpack. . . . He has it. . . . The scroll was in there." She pointed as the G-5 lifted off into the night sky. There was no way to stop it now.

She had failed. Failed her grandfather, failed all her ancestors, down to the apostle John. And most of all, she had failed God.

She had lost the scroll.

CHAPTER 66

The Vatican

The G-5 touched down at the private airstrip and pulled into the hangar. A Vatican limo waited there for the plane's passenger to disembark. The plane pulled in, circled around, and came to rest. Wickham exited the plane and jumped inside the limo. Without a word, the stretch Mercedes pulled out of the hangar and left the airport.

His shoulder was killing him. Luckily, the bullet had passed through. Both he and one of the Swiss guards had been shot. The other was a trained medic and took the task of patching them up. Thankfully, one of the plane's state-of-the-art facilities was a first-aid cabinet, complete with sutures, sterilization tools, and bandages. It also had prescription painkillers. He reached inside his pocket and retrieved two of them. He popped them in his mouth and downed them with a shot of scotch from the limo's stash.

The funny thing was, he didn't care about the pain. He didn't care about being shot. As a matter of fact, this was the happiest day of his life. He had finally managed to possess the one thing that had consumed him for years. He had the scroll.

The limo pulled inside the security gates of the Vatican and dropped him off. As soon as he walked inside, he was met by his secretary, who seeing his arm in a sling, bandaged and bloodstained, immediately began firing questions at him. He ignored her and walked into his office and locked the door. He pushed the intercom button on his desk and, before she could get a word in, told her that he wasn't to be disturbed.

He sat down at his desk and opened his briefcase. He spent a few moments just looking at the scroll. When he was on the plane, he hadn't examined it. He'd been in too much pain and had been too tired to do anything but rest. And he hadn't wanted those idiots with him asking any questions.

He picked it up and held it in his hands. It was small and weighed nearly nothing. He placed it back on the desk and unraveled it. He assumed it would've been written in Hebrew or Greek, languages that he was fluent in. And it was. Beautiful Greek.

But the words made no sense. Cryptic. Mysterious. Meaningless.

He pushed the button on his intercom. "Get me Joseph McCoy!" He picked up a paperweight from his desk and threw it against the wall.

The speaker on his desk buzzed. "Cardinal McCoy will be here in five minutes, sir."

Ten minutes later the door to his office opened, and in walked the young cardinal. He sat down at Wickham's desk. "You wanted to see me?"

Wickham pushed the scroll across the desk and asked, "What do you make of this?"

Joseph looked at the leathery paper for a minute and finally said, "It's Greek."

"I know that, you idiot!"

"It looks like a riddle."

"I know that, Joseph. I can read Greek."

"That's the scroll?"

Wickham muttered a curse. "What's happened since I left?"

"The cardinals are grumbling about the letter. None of them are happy about Paul suggesting his successor. But I think that they are going to do it."

"What makes you think that?"

"I don't know. I just do. We all know that you have great influence over everybody. And our brothers in the order have agreed that they can make sure the others will fall in line."

"And how can they be sure of that?"

"Because they know that you would have them killed if they don't."

A thin smile creased Wickham's lips. "Good. I'm glad we are all on the same page."

Joseph looked back down at the paper on the desk. "So now we have it. What do we do with it?"

"Well, obviously, we have to find someone to decipher it."

"I thought that once we had it we would obtain this great power," Joseph said mockingly. "I don't feel any different."

"You know, I used to think you were an idiot. Now I know it! Power is information. How can we have the power if we don't have the information? The information is in the answer to the riddle!" He shoved back from his desk. "So why don't you do something useful and go find us someone who likes riddles!"

Joseph let out a sigh. "Fine. I'll find somebody. But Conclave is supposed to start in the morning. We may have to wait until after."

Wickham's face reddened. "I will not wait! Do it now! Find me someone!"

Joseph stepped closer to Wickham, his face mutinous. "I'll do it after Conclave. Everybody around here is on pins and needles until the next pope is elected. Conclave starts in the morning. You are in charge of leading that, or have you forgotten? That thing"—he pointed to the scroll—"has eluded the Brotherhood since before you or I were even born. One more day isn't going to kill you. Besides, if you've taken care of everything like you say you have, by noon tomorrow, I'll be the next pope. And you'll have the Vatican's full resources at your disposal."

CHAPTER 67

London, the Safe House

Anna sat alone on the couch downstairs, her head in her hands. She'd been crying since they'd gotten home two hours earlier. It was nearly daylight, but she couldn't sleep.

The trip across the airfield had been a short one. They'd managed to get to the other side of the runway unnoticed. Benjamin, true to his word, led them to the end of the fence line, where a section of the fifteen-foot electric privacy fence had been cut. Wrapping his coat around his hands, he held the cut piece of fence back until everyone was through safely. From there they sneaked their way back to the main terminal where Patrice called her own chartered flight crew. They said they could be ready in thirty minutes. Fearing that they would be recognized at the private terminal, Benjamin made a second phone call and got special allowance to have her plane depart from the main terminal. The plane was waiting for them forty minutes later. They boarded and took off without any more delay. A few hours in the air and a short cab ride brought them back to the flat in London. Jason, Patrice, and Benjamin had all gone to bed as soon as they had gotten home. Anna couldn't sleep, so she let Patrice have her room. Benjamin was in the study, sleeping on a pull-out sofa, and Jason was in his own room. Anna made herself some hot tea and flopped down on the couch. She hadn't moved since then.

For two thousand years her family had been entrusted by God with a secret. And now, in less than two weeks, she'd lost it. Jason had told her not to worry. The scroll was just a riddle. If they could figure it out, then the scroll itself wouldn't matter. That only made her feel a little better until she reminded herself that they had no idea how to solve the riddle. The key obviously wasn't where they thought it would be. They were at square one.

She wiped her eyes. She put her tea mug down on the coffee table and took a deep breath. No one could fix this but her. She had to stop acting like a three-year-old and pull herself together.

She had her grandfather's notes. She had his maps. She knew what the scroll said. And she may not be the world's most knowledgeable person on matters of the Bible, but Jason knew a lot. Her grandfather had been working on this for two years. Cardinal Wickham had only had the scroll for one day. She could do this. She could still figure it out.

Beams of light poked their way through the wooden shutters. The sun was already breaking the horizon. Jason had gotten enough sleep. She needed help.

She marched to the top of the stairs and banged on his door. "Get up! We've got work to do."

From the other side of the door a weak voice spoke back. "Anna, go back to bed. The sun's not even up."

"Yes it is. I watched it come up myself, because I haven't been to bed. And if I'm not too tired, then you're not too tired. Remember, I make the rules. Get up! I'll meet you downstairs in ten minutes."

The muffled voice groaned. "Don't I even get a shower?"

"Sure," Anna said. "Just make it quick. You now have nine minutes!"

She walked back downstairs and found Benjamin in the kitchen. He was making coffee.

"I didn't know you were up," Anna said.

"I wasn't until a few minutes ago, when a crazy woman began shouting upstairs."

"Yeah, sorry about that." She moved over to the coffeepot. "Here, let me do this for you." She took the coffee beans from him.

"Thank you," he said, and sat down at the breakfast nook.

She pulled two bowls out of the cabinet and a couple boxes of cereal. She set them on the table and got the milk from the refrigerator. "Thank you, Benjamin. For everything."

Benjamin smiled. "Anna, I am an old man. I've lived a good life. The only thing I regret is that I took so long to surrender to Christ. Half of my life was wasted. The only thing I want to do is whatever I can to help you. I know that my role in God's plan was to help you and your grandfather. I don't know what that scroll is or what it says. But I know that it was given to John by God. And I would gladly give my life for its purpose. So you don't have to thank me. It is I who thank you."

"You can stay here as long as you need. Just make yourself at home. Okay?"

"As much as I would love to stay and see what will happen next, I do still work for Mossad. They will want to know where I am and what I know about the bomb at the Wailing Wall. I will be leaving shortly after breakfast."

Jason came into the kitchen fully dressed, hair wet, and a toothbrush in his mouth. Patrice followed right behind him.

"Morning!" Anna said. "And right on time."

Jason went to the sink and rinsed his mouth. "Still got thirty seconds." He pointed to his watch. He gave Anna a snide grin and set his toothbrush on a napkin. "So, you cooking, or what?"

"Yep," she said, and tossed him a box of cereal. "Here you go. Freshly made."

"Gee, thanks. I fix you eggs, bacon, toast, the whole works. And what do I get? Cold cereal."

"You'll thank me for this the first time you ever eat my cooking," she said, returning the snide grin as their hero gunslinger walked into the kitchen. "Patrice, make yourself at home."

"Thanks, Anna, I'll just have some coffee. And maybe the other half of your grapefruit if you're not eating it."

"Sure. Here you go." Anna handed her the other half. "Spoons are in the second drawer on your left."

When they'd all sat down at the table together, Anna spread her hands flat on the tabletop. "Okay. So what do we do now?"

Jason swallowed a bite. "Well, I think we need to figure out where the key is."

CHAPTER 68

The Vatican

This was a momentous day. A new pope was being elected. The Vatican was bustling with reporters from around the world. The city and the rest of the world all were standing by for the sign: white smoke coming from the Sistine Chapel's chimney. Black smoke would only mean an undecided vote.

All 117 eligible-to-vote cardinals were gathered together at St. Peter's Basilica for a midmorning meeting and prayer session. They had already held their celebration of the Eucharist earlier that morning. It was a ten o'clock. Soon all voting cardinals would be sequestered inside the Sistine Chapel, where they would stay until a new pope was decided on.

Cardinal Louis Wickham stood at the front of the group and called them to order. "Gentlemen, this morning we are called to a great burden. As many of you know, I was very close to Paul. His time as our pope was cut too short. I hope you've all been in prayer about this. I'm confident that we will come to a quick decision." He stuck his arm out in a welcoming gesture. "Cardinal McCoy?

Lead us in prayer, if you would, please."

The cameras flashed and rolled tape as Cardinal Joseph McCoy lead them in prayer. This was a very odd thing. Pre-Conclave goings on were rarely, if ever, made public. And this was going to be one of the most watched papal elections since the invention of the television. To have access to the proceedings taking place at this moment was one of the most coveted journalistic privileges in the world.

Immediately after the prayer, the men formed a line and followed Cardinal Wickham into the Sistine Chapel. Two Swiss guards closed the door behind the last to enter and took up sentry posts. No one would disturb the cardinals for as long as it took to elect the new pope.

Inside the mood was already nasty. Arguments roiled through the divided room. Wickham stood on one side of the room surrounded by the Brotherhood. He wasn't about to let this get out of hand. He had a scroll to decipher. He moved a chair out into the center of the room and stood on it. He cupped his hands around his mouth and shouted, "That's enough! All of you, shut up!"

The room fell silent. All eyes were on him. Just the way he liked it. He made eye contact with everybody. "We all know how this works. Those people out there are expecting to see some smoke very shortly. They expect a preliminary vote, as is custom. I say we shock them. Give them smoke, but give them white smoke!" The room erupted again. This time he merely held up his hands and the room returned to order.

"Our church is in desperate times. The world is looking to us for clarity. How can we give them the perception of clarity if we can't decide on our own internal matters in a timely way? You all know what Paul's wishes were. He made that very clear. We believe that, as pope, Paul's words were infallible. I say let those words dictate how we vote."

One of the senior cardinals pushed his way to the front of the crowd. "Wickham, you are a vile, corrupt man. I will not stand by and watch you manipulate this system for your own benefit!" The room erupted again.

Wickham raised his hands and shouted above the noise again. He looked directly at the French cardinal who challenged him. "Jean-Francis, whatever you think of me doesn't matter. What does matter is this." He held the falsified letter up over his head. "In his own, infallible words, our beloved pope gave us the direction we are to take. Now, you can stand there and argue your point, but I suggest that if you question the pope's role in this organization, then I say you are not fit to even be in this room!"

The room stood quiet. Finally, with the shaking of his head, Cardinal Jean-Francis said, "Then let it be on your head." Then he turned and walked away. The other cardinals stood stone-faced, looking at Wickham.

He stepped down from his chair and said, "I hereby call this session of Conclave to order. We will take our first vote in ten minutes."

London, the Safe House

Benjamin shook Jason's hand and kissed Anna's cheek, wished them well, and said good-bye. Patrice walked him outside to his cab.

Inside Anna and Jason sat in the study, poring over Thomas's notes and maps. They had been there since breakfast, and neither one had come up with anything.

Anna massaged her temples and said, "My eyes are burning. Everything is starting to blur."

Jason looked up from the map he was holding. "That's what happens when you don't sleep, Anna. You need to go rest."

"I can't. This is my fault. I'm the one who lost the scroll."

"And you can't do anything about it when you're exhausted. Now go lie down. I'll keep looking at this stuff. If I find anything, I'll come get you."

Anna nodded and stood up. Jason hated to see her looking so fatigued. "I'll be upstairs. You come and get me the moment you find anything. That's an order, mister." She bent down and gave him a quick kiss and left.

Jason wasn't working on much sleep, but at least he did get some. He was determined not to let Anna blame herself for losing the scroll. He would stay up for the next week if he had to, in order to decipher the riddle.

He'd prayed last night before he went to bed, asking God to give him wisdom beyond his years. A sense of peace had flooded him, a sure knowledge that possessing the scroll was not as important as solving its riddle.

He surveyed the books and maps and sticky notes adorning every wall. Thomas had been thorough. He was absolutely sure that they were looking for the Garden of Eden. The question was, what was the key? And did finding out that information give the exact location? Because if he was right, they definitely were going to need more than a general idea. According to all of his studying and what he'd concluded, the Garden of Eden was at the bottom of a very big body of water: the Persian Gulf.

He closed the journal and rubbed his eyes. He'd been reading for the better part of four hours. He couldn't remember what he read twenty minutes ago, let alone two hours ago. He went to the kitchen to get a glass of water. Patrice was sitting at the small table, reading the morning paper. "Anything about us in there?"

Patrice looked up and said, "Not us, specifically, but the whole front page of the international section is about the explosion at the wall."

"What are they saying?"

"They think it was some radical Israeli group trying to goad the Muslims. One article suggested that the Muslims did it to themselves so that they could have reason to start a conflict with the Jews."

"When are they ever going to get it?" He shook his head.

"Who?"

"Everyone. I mean, granted, we were responsible for this particular explosion. But things are so bad right now that every little thing sets someone off. We could have set firecrackers off at the wall and the result probably would've been the same."

Patrice sighed. "Yeah, you're probably right, love. I guess we'll just have to wait for the new Jerusalem to see the end of that little tiff. Unfortunately for them, one side thinks Jesus was just a prophet, and the other side called him a heretic. The whole lot of them is going to be surprised someday!"

"That's it!" Jason clapped his hands.

"What's it?" Patrice asked.

Jason closed the ten-foot distance between them in three strides. He had a huge smile on his face. He grabbed Patrice on both sides of her face and planted a giant kiss on her forehead. "I have to go wake her up!" He ran out of the kitchen. "We have to leave. Right now!"

Patrice hurried after him. "What are you talking about?"

Jason took the steps two at a time. "The key! I know what it is! And more importantly, I know where to find it!"

CHAPTER 69

The Vatican

Getting elected pope was no easy thing. It required a two-thirds vote. And if after the thirty-fourth vote, no new pontiff was elected, then the cardinals had the option of choosing to take a 51 percent overall majority. This was a provision that Pope John Paul II put in place to end difficult elections. Because there were only to be seven votes per day, the whole process could take several days. And on many occasions, it had.

The crowds stood outside the Sistine Chapel, waiting for the smoke that was sure to come any minute now. Conclave had been in session for nearly thirty minutes. As was custom, there would be a preliminary vote. In most cases, cardinals would vote for themselves, or if they already held strong allegiances, they would vote for their candidate. Usually it was nothing other than a formality—a chance to get everyone used to the system that they would be adhering to for the rest of their sequestration. Still, it would be the first sign of a vote. And once the initial one was out of the way, people would wait on pins and needles until the announcement was made. Until they saw the white smoke.

Ten minutes later, the crowds gasped. The reporters scrambled to get into place. The people who were gathered began to sing. They began hugging one another, cheering, as all eyes turned toward the roof of the Sistine Chapel and the white smoke that poured from its chimney. A new pope had been elected.

Inside the chapel, Cardinal Joseph McCoy was being ordained as a bishop. The pope-elect could not take office until he was first a bishop. The cardinal dean stepped forward and asked, "Do you accept your canonical election as supreme pontiff?"

"I do," Joseph replied.

"And what name will you go by?" the cardinal dean asked.

He'd thought about this over the last couple of days. Pope John II was the first pope to take a name other than his birth name. He did this because of his conversion to Christianity. His birth name, Mercury, was not befitting a supreme pontiff, given its relation to the pagan Roman god. Between John II and Sergius IV, only a few popes took different names. But after Sergius IV, every elected pope had taken a different name, save two. And it had been over five hundred years since one had broken that tradition. He looked at the cardinal dean and said, "I shall be known as Joseph I."

The master of pontifical liturgy was summoned into the hall to record the acceptance and the new name of the pope.

Immediately following, Pope Joseph I was led to the Room of Tears, where every new pope came to clothe himself in the papal robes. He chose his robes and put them on. Next he donned the gold corded pectoral cross and red embroidered stole. Finally, he placed the white zucchetto, the skull cap, on his head. There was only one thing left to do.

He stepped out of the Room of Tears and followed the senior cardinal deacon to the main balcony of the basilica's main facade.

The senior cardinal deacon opened the french doors, stepped out onto the balcony, and said, "*Annuntio vobis gaudium magnum:*

"*Habemus Papam!*

"*Eminentissimum ac Reverendissimum Dominum,*

"*Dominum Joseph, Sanctæ Romanæ Ecclesiæ Cardinalem McCoy, qui sibi nomen imposuit Pope Joseph I.*"

The crowds erupted as their new pope walked out onto the balcony. He spent at least five minutes listening to the applause, occasionally raising his arms and waving to the masses. Finally, he motioned for the crowds to be quiet. He was about to give his first papal blessing. He stepped up to the small microphone and uttered the words that every pope says as their first papal blessing, "*Urbi et Orbi.*" To the city and to the world.

Again the crowds erupted. The people began to sing and dance all around the balcony. The news reporters relayed the news to the world. The cameras focused on the crowds and the celebration that was taking place. Church bells all throughout the city of Rome chimed in one giant symphony of noise.

The rest of the cardinals were dismissed after the vote was confirmed and Joseph accepted his election. Many of the cardinals stayed behind, hoping to get some of the spotlight either by being seen with the new pope or by giving an exclusive to one of the many news reporters.

Wickham, however, was far too busy to waste his time placating reporters, the public, or any other buffoon who wanted to be involved in that circus. He stepped into his office and sat down at his desk. He slid open the top drawer, pulled out a flask, and took a huge gulp of the twelve-year-old single malt. He put it back inside the drawer and stood up.

Across from his desk he opened the armoire and removed the false back. He turned the knob three times and heard the *click* as the last tumbler rolled into place. He pulled the scroll out and sat back down at the desk. His whole body tingled with excitement. It would still be a few hours before Joseph would finally be left alone. But when that happened, he would be waiting for him in his private chambers. At that point, Joseph would merely need to pick up the phone, and the scroll and its secrets would be decoded in no time.

He opened the drawer again, took another pull from the flask, setting the scroll beside it. He unbuttoned his collar, kicked his feet onto his desk, tilted his head back, closed his eyes, and fell asleep.

He had barely drifted off when he could feel the warmth of breath on his cheek. He half opened his eyes to see the man towering over him, bent down only a half inch from his face.

"Wake up, little monkey," the voice sang.

Wickham fully opened his eyes and sat up. "Hello, my lord. I didn't see you come in."

"It's a talent of mine, Louis. If I wanted you to see me, you would have. Anyway, where's my scroll? I hear you have it."

"It's safe."

Lucifer's face grew red. "Did I ask you if it was safe? No! I asked you where it is!"

After their last meeting Wickham was terrified. His hands began to shake. "It's. . .it's right here, my lord." He opened the drawer. "But. . .but. . .I don't understand it."

Lucifer grabbed the scroll out of his hand. "What do you mean you don't understand it, Wickham? Are you an idiot? Did you finally become the monkey that you really are?"

"No. . .I. . .I mean I can understand it; I just can't *decipher* it.

406

It's some kind of riddle."

Lucifer unrolled the scroll and held it in his hand. A thin grin creased his lips. "He who has ears, let him hear."

"So you know what it means?"

"Yes, Louis, I do."

Wickham's face brightened. "Then we win! We know what it means! Tell me! Tell me! What does it mean?"

Lucifer rolled the scroll up and put it in his pocket. He smiled, patted Wickham on the shoulder, and said, "It doesn't matter."

Wickham looked confused. "What do you mean, it doesn't matter? You said that if I got you that scroll, then we win. That I would be given power unlike anything seen on this earth."

"Don't worry, Louis, you're going to get everything you deserve."

Wickham looked blankly at Lucifer. "I did everything you asked. I gave my life to looking for this stupid thing. You know that. I promised you I would get it. And I did. You told me that I would be a king. That I would rule over millions!"

Lucifer's eyes grew fiery red. He walked over and grabbed Wickham by the throat. His long fingernails dug into Wickham's flesh. When he spoke his voice was twisted and pure evil. "This is my world. I rule over it. I do what I want when I want. You are nothing to me. You served a purpose. You were a means to an end. And now I have that end. I told you you'd get what you deserve, and so you will. You will be paid exactly what the going rate for betraying your Creator is." He continued to squeeze Wickham's throat. With the other hand, he reached into one of his pockets and pulled out a small velvet bag. He opened it with his thumb and forefinger.

Wickham's vision was blurring. His brain was losing oxygen and he was getting weak. He could feel his life ending. Somewhere from deep inside his soul, a tiny voice cried out in sorrow and pain, showing him the vile, corrupt man he'd become. He'd sold his soul for a lie. He wanted to cry out to God for forgiveness but couldn't. Whether it was pride, guilt, or the fact that God had hardened his heart as he had Pharaoh's, he just couldn't.

"Look at me, Louis. . ." Lucifer toyed with him, dangling the velvet bag in front of him. "Here's your payment." He turned the bag over and smiled. A single tear ran down Wickham's face, as he watched the bag empty itself.

As the last of its contents hit the floor, Lucifer placed his free hand over Wickham's heart and dug his fingernails into his chest. Wickham would have screamed if he could have. The talons sank deeper.

Lucifer pulled Wickham close to whisper directly into his ear. "And now that you've been paid, I'll take what you owe me. Your life." Without another word, Lucifer crushed Cardinal Louis Wickham's larynx. He ripped open his chest and tore out his heart and walked out of the office.

Wickham's dead body lay in a heap on the floor. Beside him was an empty velvet bag and thirty pieces of silver.

CHAPTER 70

London, the Safe House

Jason ran to the top of the stairs and into his room. He grabbed his Bible off the nightstand and flipped it open. He thumbed through the pages until he found what he was looking for: the book of Revelation. He perused the text until he found the verse that mattered. This had to be it, what Thomas had spent his life trying to find. And all this time, it was right in front of them. Jesus had always said, "He who has ears, let him hear!" Understanding Jesus wasn't about your physical ears. It was about spiritual discernment. Jason realized that the same held true for the scroll. But in this case, it was more a metaphor than a parable.

He threw some clothes in his bag, grabbed his Bible, put it in the front pocket, and zipped it up. He woke Anna up and told her to be ready to leave in the next half hour. He then ran downstairs into the study and gathered a few maps, Thomas's journal, and the notebook that he'd been taking notes in. In his haste, he accidentally knocked over a porcelain lamp on one of the small tables. It fell to the floor and shattered. Jason moved to clean it up. When he stooped down, he noticed that inside the lamp was hidden a roll of papers rubber-banded together, along with a small electronic device. He picked up the papers and pushed the power button on the device. The small screen came to life. Jason laughed out loud and lifted his face upward. "Thank you."

Anna walked into the study. She was rubbing her eyes and looked like she was still asleep. "Okay, I'm up. What's going on?"

He held up the bundle of papers. "I figured it out!"

Anna was awake instantly. "What! You did? Well, tell me!"

"I will. On the way. Get dressed. We're leaving."

"And where are we going?"

"Where's who going?" Patrice stuck her head in the room.

"Me and Anna," Jason answered. "We're going to the airport."

"Not without me." Patrice left the room to gather her belongings.

"Hey!" Anna shouted. "Someone tell me what's going on!"

But Jason was too hurried to reply. There was time to explain, but not now. He grinned. He looked forward to telling her everything.

The plane was in the air thirty minutes later. Anna appeared ready to burst. "Explain. Now."

Yeah, it was time. He took out his Bible. "You know what a parable is?"

"Yeah, I guess."

"You mean like Jesus' parables?" Patrice asked.

"Exactly!" Jason said. "He who has ears, let him hear!"

Anna slumped. "I'm confused."

"Anna, when Jesus taught, he used stories that would convey His message to the people. He told His disciples that the god of this age, Satan, had blinded unbelievers from seeing the truth. Therefore, if anyone was going to understand Jesus' message, the Father would draw them and they would need to seek it. It wouldn't just be obvious to them."

"Okay," she said, shrugging her shoulders, "I still don't get it."

"Jesus said, 'He who has ears, let him hear.' That meant that anyone whom God was drawing to Him could hear His voice and receive His message. They just had to look deeper. That's what I did, Anna. I looked deeper. And I found it!" He slapped his leg. "The scroll, it's Jesus' words, too. Remember?"

"Yeah, I guess so. . ."

"Anna, there is no 'key.' There is no 'temple.'"

Anna looked at him as if he were an idiot. "What are you talking about? The scroll said in black and white that the key is found in the temple. There is a key, Jason. And we don't have it, nor do we know where the temple is."

Jason's face softened a little. "Don't get mad at me when I tell you this. I don't mean it condescendingly."

Anna looked on with anticipation.

"Technically, there is a key and a temple. Just not what you think. And I have it. Actually, millions of people have the key. Unfortunately, you don't. Not yet. But you can. And when you have the key, you'll know where the temple is."

Anna looked sourly at him. "I don't know what you are talking about. But I really have to tell you, you're making me awfully mad. Would you stop talking in riddles and just say it straight out?"

"Anna," he said softly, "the key is salvation. It's Jesus."

Anna leaned back in her chair. Her breath came in little pants, and her face was sickly pale.

"Anna," Jason said worriedly, "what's wrong? Are you all right?"

"I. . .it feels like someone has punched me in the stomach."

Jason grabbed her wrist. "Your pulse is racing. Are you feeling sick?"

She shook her head. "No." She gasped for air.

"I'm sorry. I didn't mean to upset you."

She gripped his hand. "You didn't. I mean. . .you did. But I'm okay. I believe you. I know it's true, but I feel so. . .strange." She started fidgeting with her seat belt. "I need to use the lavatory."

The latch flopped open and her belt fell to the sides of the chair. She staggered to the back of the plane where the restroom was. Jason and Patrice just watched as she left the cabin.

"You think she knows what you meant?" Patrice asked.

"Judging by the expression on her face," he said, "I'd say she knows exactly what I meant."

"I felt the same way when I was called, you know," Patrice said matter-of-factly.

"Me, too," Jason nodded.

The door to the cockpit opened up and the copilot stepped into the cabin. "Just received a news wire you might be interested in," he said. "Seems a new pope has been elected."

"Fascinating," Patrice said.

"There's more," the copilot said. "Cardinal Louis Wickham was found dead just a little while ago. The entire Vatican is under lockdown."

Jason's eyes grew wide. "That's the man from the airport yesterday! He's dead? What about the scroll?"

The copilot shook his head. "I only have a contact inside. He didn't mention anything about a scroll. But he did say that Wickham's death was very brutal. His larynx was crushed and his heart was ripped out."

Jason's stomach lurched. "Who do they think killed him?"

"They don't know. No one saw anyone coming or going. His secretary was right outside the door. She saw him go in and didn't see anyone come out. She only found him because the new pope was trying to get him on the phone. When she buzzed him, there was no answer. She went inside the office to get him, and there he was."

"That doesn't make any sense," Patrice said.

"Here's the weird thing," the copilot said. "My contact says they found an empty bag and thirty pieces of silver next to the body."

Jason stood up. The hair on the back of his neck was tingling. Horror slid in icy drops down his spine. "Quick! Go tell the pilot he needs to hurry! We have to get there as fast as we can!"

Patrice stood up. "Jason, what's wrong?"

Jason turned to her. "Just tell him to go faster. We have to get—"

"Why?" Patrice interrupted him. "What's going on?"

Jason looked at her with desperation. "Please, Patrice, tell the pilot to floor it. I'm pretty sure we're not the only ones who know where we're going."

CHAPTER 71

The Vatican

Pope Joseph I sat at his desk in the papal apartment. His things would be brought over in the next few days. But for now, the office was empty, save the desk, a few chairs, and a couch.

Word of Wickham's death surprised him. He never liked the man, but at the same time, he wasn't sure he felt safe having a cold-blooded murderer running around. He shouldn't have to worry though. Next to the president of the United States of America, he was the most protected man on the planet. That reminded him: he needed to call the president. Wish him well.

He hadn't heard the door open or anyone announce themselves coming in, so the footsteps he heard behind him caused his heart to skip. He swung his chair around to face his guest. "Oh, it's you."

"Hello, Joseph."

"You shouldn't be here. In case you haven't heard, Wickham is dead. Murdered. Brutally, from what I'm told. The whole place is under lockdown."

"Yes, I heard. And to be honest with you, it wasn't that brutal.

I barely touched him." He smiled a sneaky grin.

Joseph felt suddenly faint. "You. . .you did that?"

Lucifer placed his hand on Joseph's shoulder. "Joseph, do you know who I am?"

Joseph nodded slowly.

"Then you know that I make the rules. I do what I want. This is my world, Joseph. It was given to me. Louis was a worker bee. You, Joseph, you are a prince! You will be my son. I will be your father. I will give you all of my authority. You will do great things in my name. The people of this world will worship me through you."

"How," Joseph asked. "Why?"

Lucifer pulled the scroll out of his pocket. "Because I have this."

"Yes, Wickham showed it to me, but it's just a riddle."

"I'm very good at riddles, my son."

"What does it mean?"

"It reveals the location of a very special place. And how to get there."

"Where?"

"To the place where your original parents first broke His heart. Awww, isn't that sweet?"

"The Garden of Eden?"

"Yes. I suspect that He decided that if one of His little monkeys could figure out how to get back there, He'd let them back in. And then that little carpenter boy would be free to come back here and finish what He started."

"Is that really how it was supposed to go?" Joseph asked, glued to Lucifer's words.

"It doesn't matter. It won't happen now."

"What about the girl?"

"I'll make sure that they don't get there."

"What if they do?"

Lucifer slammed his fist on the desk. "They won't! And as soon as I stop them, this world will be mine forever. I will be the god that these people pray to!"

Joseph lowered his eyes and said, "Father, I don't mean to question you, but how can you be sure?"

Joseph could see Lucifer liked the sound of that word, *Father*. He would have to use it often. Anything to keep this dangerous being happy.

Lucifer smiled. "If none of you monkeys ever find this place, I will rule this world forever."

CHAPTER 72

Al-Basrah International Airport, Iraq

Anna stood beside Jason in the hangar, waiting on their ride. She'd spent the last half hour of the flight alone. After coming out of the restroom, she'd taken a seat in the back of the plane. Jason and Patrice had kindly left her alone.

The camouflage-painted Jeep pulled into the hangar. Its driver got out and handed Jason the keys. "Your ride." His English was broken but understandable.

"Thank you," Jason said. He threw his backpack into the back of the Jeep. Anna did the same.

Patrice was standing at the rear of the plane, taking the remainder of the bags from the pilot as he handed them down from the baggage compartment. She walked over to Jason and said, "I need to talk to you. Alone."

"Sure. Let's talk."

They walked to the end of the hangar. Patrice handed Jason a 9mm pistol and a TEC-9 semiautomatic rifle. "You're on your own for this."

"Yeah, I figured you'd say that."

"Hey," she said, holding up her hands, "it's not that I wouldn't want to see the Garden of Eden. . . . It's just, well, you know. . . Adam and Eve. . .you and Anna. . .me the third wheel. . ."

"No," Jason said, "I get it. It's okay. We'll be fine. I won't let anything happen to her."

"I know that, love." Patrice scratched her chin and said, "Tell you what. I'll stick around here and see if I can find out about anyone looking for you two. If I'm needed, I'll find you."

Jason smiled, gave Patrice a hug, and said, "Thank you. We'll be careful. I promise."

Jason joined Anna, who was already seated in the Jeep, still as silent as she'd been on the plane. Jason reached behind him and pulled his backpack into the front seat and handed it to Anna. "There's a map in there. I drew it while you were in the. . .you know. . .I drew it on the plane."

It felt awkward sitting there with her. He wanted to say something about their earlier conversation, but he didn't want to press the issue. It was Anna who brought it up a few minutes later as he drove away from the airport.

"So, I was thinking," she said, "what makes you so different from me?"

Jason could already hear the accusatory tone. He let it pass. If things went the way he thought they would, this would be the best conversation he and Anna would ever have in their entire existence. He sent up a silent prayer for wisdom.

Anna stared at him. "Well?"

"Anna, do you believe that Jesus Christ died on the cross for real, actual sin? And that God raised him again on the third day?"

"Yeah, I guess so."

"Well, so do demons. That doesn't mean that they are saved.

Believing that up here"—he tapped on the side of his head—"doesn't make someone right with God. It doesn't save them from their sin."

Anna rolled her eyes. "See, there it is! I don't get the whole 'saved' thing. Why can't I just say I believe and be done with it?"

Jason took a deep breath and let it out. "Anna, it's possible to believe in things that we don't care about. People do it every day. People believe that there is hunger around the world and lack of clean water, but they don't care. If they did, they would do something to change it. However, it is impossible to care about something you don't believe in. In other words, our lives will demonstrate what we care about and believe in. Simply believing in something doesn't mean that you'll ever care about it. You follow me?"

"Okay, you make a good point."

His fingers tapped the steering wheel. "Tons of people say they are believers in Jesus, but they don't actually care about Him. It doesn't affect their life, and that is not salvation. Anna, the Bible makes it very clear. Every person has sinned and fallen short of God's standard. God is perfect and holy, and if we want a relationship with Him, we must be holy. But we're not. Nobody is. And because of our sinful nature, we are separated from God. Nothing we do can ever earn a relationship with Him."

"I'm not perfect by any means, but I'm not that bad either," Anna said matter-of-factly.

"Compared to whom?" Jason asked.

"What do you mean?"

"Compared to me? Compared to the people who were trying to kill you? You see, the problem is, most people measure themselves against other people. Compared to some people in this world, you are right—you are not that bad at all. But you and I won't be measured by other people when we stand before God. God will judge us according to His holiness, not by other people. And that means we're in big trouble. But God, whose love for us is immeasurable, looked at us, a broken and sinful people, and gave His perfect Son for us. On the cross, Jesus took our sins on to Himself and paid the price that God requires for sin: death. On the cross, our sin, and the sin of all who come to Him to receive His righteousness, was put on Him. That means that those who accept that grace are no longer seen by God as sinners, but as people with perfect holiness and righteousness, and therefore are able to have a relationship with Him. All because of Jesus. *Only* because of Jesus."

Anna let a few seconds go by, seemingly trying to wrap her mind around Jason's words, then said, "So does that mean I have to become a missionary like you?"

Jason laughed. "No, Anna. It means that you give yourself to Jesus and serve Him wherever He leads you. You quit relying on the things of this world to be your source of joy. He gives grace freely to those who accept it. You merely need to accept it."

"Then what happens?"

"Anna, let me ask you something. Do you feel like God is drawing you to Him?"

"What does that mean?"

"It means exactly what it means. Do you feel like God is speaking to your soul? Calling you to come to Him?"

She sat silently, and a single tear ran down her cheek. "I think so."

Jason took her hand, keeping his other hand on the steering wheel. "You know so."

She nodded as more tears came.

They had been driving for a while now and were out of the

city. The road they were on was barely a road. It was more like a compacted dirt path in the middle of the desert. There weren't many cars going either way. Jason pulled over to the side. "Then, Anna, you need to cry out to God and tell Him. You need to give your life to Jesus, turn your heart over to Him. Tell Him that you don't just believe it, but you care about it. That you need Him."

She wiped her face and asked, "And how do I do that?"

"First we need to draw a pint of blood. . ."

"What?" She pulled her hand away from him.

He started laughing. "I'm just kidding. Give me your hand." She looked at him skeptically. He leaned in and put his arm around her. "Now, I'm going to pray for you, silently. While I'm doing that, I want you to talk to God. Tell Him that you know you have a sinful and broken heart. Thank Him for giving Jesus to die in your place. Ask Him for forgiveness, and tell Him that you accept His grace given through Christ's sacrifice. Ask God to change your heart so that you can live for Him."

Anna nodded. She watched as Jason closed his eyes and bowed his head. She did the same thing. She didn't know where to start, so she just started talking.

"God, you know how I have lived my life. I have done many things that I'm ashamed of, and I know that I do not deserve your forgiveness. But I believe that Jesus died for me—for my sins. I know I need His help. God, I give you my life. I'm putting You first from now on. It will no longer be about me. I want to follow Jesus. Please help me, God. I can't do it myself. Amen."

When she was done, she looked at Jason, who had tears in his eyes. "What's wrong?"

"Nothing, Anna. Not anymore!"

"I feel relieved," she said.

"Like how?"

"Like I've known that I needed to do that but I've been running from it.

"You have been," Jason said. "But you're His now and always will be."

"So that's it?" she asked hesitantly.

"No, it's only just the beginning. Now, and for the rest of your life, Jesus will continue to shape you to be more like Him and you will get to know Him better. That's the fun part. It's an amazing journey!"

They spent the next two hours of the drive talking about what it meant to be a Christ follower. Anna had a thousand questions. Jason tried to answer them the best he could but finally admitted that no one knew all the answers. The best advice he could give her was to read the Bible. He told her that he'd never had a question about God, or faith, that he couldn't find the answer to in the Bible.

The road finally ended in a small village dotted with a couple of shacks that looked like they would fall apart with the next sandstorm. A few chickens ran freely throughout the village, clucking around a handful of abandoned cars. The center of the village held a well, but it didn't look like it was used, since the rope from which a bucket would normally hang was rotted. A lone old man sat in a dilapidated rocking chair in front of one of the shacks. He stared at them as they got out of the Jeep.

"Excuse me," Jason yelled, as he started toward the man. "Do you speak English?"

The old man nodded.

"Could you maybe help me and my friend?" He stepped onto the porch.

The old man looked Jason up and down and in a thick accent asked, "Now why would I want to do that?"

It caught Jason off guard. "I'm sorry. It's just—"

"Only one reason you come out here," the old man pointed at him with a raised eyebrow. "You think you can find it?"

Jason looked back at Anna for help.

"Well, let me tell you," the old man continued. "Is nothing out there! Better men than you have tried. They're all dead. They spend their whole lives looking through that desert trying to find a fairy tale. Every one of them. And they all have fancy equipment. Look at you!" the old man spat. "You show up here with your beat-up Jeep and pretty girlfriend. You have no supplies! What! You just sniff it out? Go back to wherever it is you came from. Forget this fairy tale!"

"Thanks for your help," Jason said sourly.

He walked back to the Jeep, took out his backpack, got his map, and spread it out on the hood. Anna stood next to him, looking over his shoulder.

"If the map's correct," he said, "we should be here." He pointed with his finger. "According to where Thomas thought the garden should be"—he marked it with his other hand—"we need to walk that way." He pointed in the direction of the old man's shack. "It looks like it could be a long walk. Maybe a couple of hours."

"Well then," Anna said and slung her backpack over her shoulder, "let's get moving."

They could feel the old man's beady eyes watching them as they walked through the village. Jason was right. It took almost two and a half hours to get to their destination. The first hour they climbed over rocky terrain, stopping every so often to rub out a cramp or get a drink from the canteen. After that, they spent the next hour climbing sand dunes. The sand made breathing difficult, so Jason took an old shirt out of his bag and ripped it into strips that they tied around their heads. It wasn't the most brilliant invention, but it did the trick. The last half hour they walked across a barren strip of desert, the sun beating down on them and the temperature rising with every step. They both thought they would soon pass out when finally, on the horizon, they could see the dark waters of the Persian Gulf.

As they approached the beach, the waves crashed against the sand like cymbals in a performance of a John Phillips Sousa march. They stood at the shoreline, letting mist cool them off. Jason sat down in the sand and retrieved the map.

"Now all we have to do is find the river channel," he said.

"Oh right! There couldn't be more than a couple thousand miles of coastline here!" Anna said sarcastically. "Shouldn't take us but a couple of minutes."

Jason smiled and pulled out a small GPS device from his pack. "Actually, it may take about ten to twenty," he said, pushing a couple of buttons on the contraption.

Anna looked closer and said, "Where did you get that?"

"I found it inside a lamp in the study." He saw the questions on her face. "Don't ask! Thomas already has four places marked for examination. It's tracking right now to let us know exactly where we are in relation to those marks. If we followed our map and compass right, we should be right here." He pointed to the farthest southern point marked. "From here, we can work our way north."

Anna rubbed the sweat from her forehead. "Jason, this garden was lost how long ago?"

"Long, long, long time ago," he said.

"And how are we going to find a riverbed that has eroded away for the last however many years? We're talking thousands of years, right?"

"Yep! Pretty exciting, huh?"

"Pretty unrealistic!" She plopped down in the sand beside him.

"Seriously! How are we supposed to find a riverbed that's been buried by sandstorms?"

"We don't." He continued fidgeting with the gadget.

Anna threw up her arms in surrender. "What am I doing here! This is ridiculous!"

Ignoring her, Jason stood up and began walking down the beach. "Relax," he called over his shoulder. "We don't have to. Thomas already did it for us."

Now she was totally confused. What was he talking about? She grabbed her backpack and chased after him. "Hey! Wait up!" She jogged the twenty-yard gap between them. When she caught up, she said, "What do you mean?"

Jason removed his backpack as he kept walking. He took out a few photos and handed them to Anna.

"What are these?"

"Those are satellite imaging photos that your granddad had done right before he died. Also in the lamp. I already told you— Don't ask! I'm telling you, Anna, he knew. He had it figured out. All of it."

"Except the key."

"Yeah, but he knew where the garden is." He stopped walking. "It's kind of a shame, you know."

"What's that?" she asked.

"Thomas was a Christian. He should've been able to figure out what the 'key' was. He would've been the one to do this."

"I wish it were him," Anna said somberly.

Jason continued walking. "I'm sure he's looking down on you right now, gathering all of his friends and family around to watch you make the most significant discovery in the history of mankind." He stopped walking again. "This is the first one. We're here."

They both looked around. Nothing seemed special about the place. Just a stretch of beach. The shoreline was a mixture of rock and sand.

"So now what?"

"Well," Jason sighed, "I'm not sure. The scroll says that God will open the way like He did at the point of no escape. The only thing that makes sense to me is the Israelites and the parting of the Red Sea. Apparently God will open the sea and we'll find it."

Anna stood there looking dumbfounded at him. "You're serious."

"Pretty much."

"Okay. I know I'm new at the whole Christian thing, but parting the sea? Maybe back in Moses' day that kind of thing happened all the time. Not so much these days."

"And that's where the key becomes the issue!" Jason said smiling. "Believing in Jesus Christ is a faith issue. We're called to walk by faith, not by sight. And we have to have faith that it will happen. We need to pray."

He took her hand, and they knelt on the sand. They both began to pray that God would open the waters for them. Anna wasn't sure if it was because she was so new to this, but she found herself being distracted easily. Finally, she opened her eyes. Jason was still praying.

She sensed that there was something else vying for her attention. As she looked around, she saw a very strange thing. A dove sat perched atop a rock about a hundred feet away, looking straight at her. She didn't know why, but she needed to go to it. She let go of Jason's hand and started walking. She heard Jason stop praying, but he didn't say anything to her. She could sense him behind her. Finally, she felt him take her hand as he caught up. Neither said anything.

As they got closer to the dove, it fluttered and took to the air. But it only flew another couple hundred feet down the beach before landing on another rock that jutted out from the sand. It sat there, as if beckoning them to it.

Again they followed the bird. It did this five more times, each time getting farther and farther away along the beach. Jason felt like he needed to say something. Ask what they were doing. But Anna seemed to be in some kind of trance.

At last the dove found a resting place. It sat, of all places, on a limb of a small olive branch sticking out of the sand. When they got there, Anna stuck out her finger, and the bird climbed on to her hand.

"This is it." Anna said. "We're here."

Jason looked at her astonished. "You think? I mean a dove in the middle of the desert who leads us to a piece of vegetation that has absolutely no business growing here! Yeah, I'd say this is it!"

He checked his GPS system. They were directly on top of the third marked location. A sense of awe came over him. This was actually happening!

"So now what?" Anna asked.

Jason started to say something when the air all around them suddenly turned cool. Dark clouds whipped in from the east, covering the sky. The dove fluttered again, let out a squawk, and flew away. The atmosphere all around took on an ominous air.

"Jason," Anna said shakily.

"I have no idea," Jason said, stepping closer to her.

A small tremor shook the ground beneath their feet. The waves splashed all around them from the beach.

"It's an earthquake!"

"No," Jason shouted back. "Worse!"

The ground shook violently. They couldn't stand. She cupped

her hands over her mouth to yell something to him but never got the words out.

The blood drained from her face, and panic stopped her dead in her place as the ground suddenly split wide open. The crevice groaned. The earth tilted.

And into the crack in the earth, Jason vanished.

CHAPTER 73

Banks of the Persian Gulf

As suddenly as the tremors started, they disappeared, but the clouds remained and the air was still cool. Darkness had taken over the midday sun like an eclipse.

Anna had been violently thrown back against some rocks. Her ankle twisted, and she slammed her shoulder on the hard ground.

Shaking, she stood up and wiped the sand and dirt from her face. Her ankle immediately revolted against her, and she fell to one knee. The tears, she realized, weren't coming from the pain, but from fear. She crawled over to the edge of the crevice and looked over. Jason lay unconscious about four feet down, wedged into the crack. His forehead was bleeding and his left arm looked to be bent in a direction it was never intended to be. She choked back a few tears and called out to him. Nothing. "God, please don't let this be happening," she cried. Again she shouted down to him. She watched as his eyes fluttered and opened.

"Jason! Are you all right?"

"I can't move my left arm."

Anna ignored the pain from her ankle and swung her legs over the edge of the crack. There wasn't any room for a foothold, so she used the other side of the crack as a leverage point. Straddling the chasm, she bent down and grabbed hold of Jason's left arm, the only one visible. The second she took hold of his hand, he let out a cry.

"I'm sorry," she cried. "It's the only thing I can grab on to."

"It's all right. Just do it quick. I think it's already dislocated, so you can't do much more damage to it. Just do it fast."

"Okay. Here we go. One. . .two. . .three!" She pulled with as much strength as she could muster. Loose rocks, dirt, and sand fell on top of him as she pulled. Jason let out a blood-curdling scream. It scared her so much that she let go and fell backwards. She scrambled back to the edge to look. Jason was sitting up, holding himself with his right arm.

"Good work there, Hercules," he said. "Now help me out of here."

"Are you all right? Did I hurt your arm worse?"

"I'll live. Get me out of here."

She planted her feet again and grabbed hold of his good arm this time and hauled him out of the crevice. They both stood on their knees trying to catch their breath.

"Your head's bleeding." Anna pressed her cloth face covering to the gash.

"Yeah, I feel kind of woozy. Probably a concussion."

"What if it's worse?"

"We'll deal with it later." He sat and looked around.

"What the heck was that?"

"I think we'd rather not know," Jason said.

She narrowed her eyes, suspicious that he knew and just didn't want to frighten her. But on second thought, she was already frightened enough. "So, what now? If this isn't the place, then we've just plain lost our minds."

"You need to go in," Jason said.

"What do you mean?"

"When God parted the Red Sea, he told Moses to touch his staff to the water and the water would part. God could've told Moses to stick his toe in the water. Would've made no difference. It was then, always has been since, and will be till the end of time, about faith. Moses had faith that his staff would part the water because God said it would. Same thing with Joshua and the Jordan River. You need to walk into the water and believe that God is going to part it and give you entry to the garden."

"Yeah, I get all that," she said dismissively. "What about you?"

Jason looked somberly at her. "Anna, I wish more than anything that I could be the one who sets the first foot, since Adam and Eve, in that place. But I'm not the keeper of the scroll. You are. You have to go alone. You're the one who was chosen. I know Father Vin would say the same thing."

Anna panicked. "I. . .I can't! I can't do that by myself. Jason, you have to go with me."

He smiled at her and took her hand. "Living your life for Christ means living a life of faith. Walking into that water will definitely prove you have faith!" He chuckled.

"That's not funny!" She poked him in his dislocated shoulder.

"Ow!" He half laughed, half winced. "I know. But it's true."

Anna was scared, but she knew Jason was right. She'd known all along that when it came time to do this, she would have to do it alone. She wiped the tears from her eyes and nodded. She let go of his hand and walked into the water. She was waist deep when she heard a guttural moan and turned back.

Jason was lying on the ground struggling with a huge snakelike creature. It was squeezing the life out of him. His face was red and his eyes were bulging out. He saw her coming back out of the water toward him. He managed to shout, "No! Go! Right now! Go!" And then his eyes closed, and he slumped in the creature's grasp, unconscious. Or maybe dead.

CHAPTER 74

The Persian Gulf

Anna screamed as she splashed through the water back up onto the beach. Jason's motionless body lay in the sand. A massive white serpent coiled itself next to him. Its eyes were black and its tongue was forked. Its head was raised at her and moving back and forth in a weaving motion. It hissed as she got close. And then it spoke.

"Surely you would rather save his life than drown yourself in that ocean."

She should have been surprised. A talking snake! But somehow, it seemed natural. "What are you going on about?"

The serpent uncoiled itself and started to slither closer. "He's not dead, you know. Not yet. You could still save him."

"How?"

"Do you know who I am?"

"I think so," she said shakily.

"I see His mark on you."

"What do you mean?"

"No matter. Surely you don't think that after all this time,

He'll let you in. He banished your mother and father from here ages ago. They sinned against Him."

"I know."

"Well then, surely you can't think that all of a sudden He's just going to let you in. I mean you of all people, Anna," he hissed.

"What do you mean, *me*?"

"You are the worst kind. You've spent your entire life avoiding Him. He's called to you before and you've turned your back on Him. You've cursed His name. You've rebelled against Him. You've worshipped things other than Him. You are an idolater! You've betrayed Him! Haven't you?"

Anna started to cry as the weight of her sin hit home.

"I'm sorry," the serpent hissed, "was that a yes?"

"Yes," she squeaked. The tears came in a wave now.

"If you enter that water, Anna, you will surely die. You know you aren't worthy of the Garden of Eden. Now, if you leave here right now, you can save him. He needs medical attention. But if you go into that water, who's going to help him? He'll die right after you. And then you'll be no better than a murderer. A selfish one at that."

"But what about the garden?"

"Oh, don't worry. I'm sure someone far more qualified than you will eventually stumble upon it."

Anna felt a wave of emotion. If she went into the water to find the garden, would she be letting Jason die? Would she be no better than a murderer? "God, what do I do?" she whispered. "Please help me."

Peace filled her, and she understood at last. She looked at the serpent and smiled.

"So, Satan—I can call you by your name, right?—tell me why Adam and Eve were never allowed back into the garden," she said smugly.

The serpent slithered back into his coil. "I told you, they sinned against Him."

"No! They were not allowed back in because they couldn't pay for their own sin. Mine has been paid in full."

The serpent twisted in an evil hiss. "There is no forgiveness for what you are!"

Anna shook her head and looked sadly at him. "Yes, there is. And Christ died for it. For me! You have absolutely no authority over me anymore. I'm His now. And that makes me as qualified as anyone to enter that garden. So you just sit back and watch!"

As she turned to run back into the water, the serpent lashed out at her, coiling around her ankles. She fell face-first onto the rocky beach. Her fingers clawed at the wet sand, trying to pull herself away, but the serpent's grasp was too tight. She kicked and flailed, but it was no use. The serpent was pulling her back. She turned around to face him and swung a backhanded fist. She caught him in the head. The strike shot pain through her arm and into her shoulder, but it was enough to stun the serpent. For a moment, its grip loosened. She pulled a leg free and kicked the serpent again. Freedom. She crawled like a crab on hands and knees toward the water. She dove in headfirst and began to swim out into the deep.

The water was cold and bit into her skin like little razor blades. Her feet barely touched the bottom. She turned back to the beach. The serpent was gone. Jason lay lifeless on the rocky sand. She closed her eyes and prayed.

God, I believe that I was chosen to find this place. I believe that You have led me here. I know, deep in my heart, that this is what You called me to do. Please, Jesus, help me.

She treaded water, waiting. The chill numbed her body, and it was becoming hard to fight against the pulling current drawing her farther out.

She started to cry. Jason said she had to have faith. Didn't she? Wasn't she out here because of faith?

Her arms moved slower. She fought to stay above water. Her teeth clattered together. Maybe she should turn around, try to swim back.

A Voice.

Not an audible voice, but a voice nonetheless.

"Do you trust Me?"

"Yes," she said aloud.

"Then let go."

"You mean, just drown?" That made no sense. She was supposed to find the garden. Wasn't she?

"Do you trust Me, Anna?"

"Yes," she said again, crying. "I trust You."

"Then let go."

"I'm afraid."

"Do you trust Me?"

She took a deep breath and let it out again. "Yes, Father," she whispered. "I trust You."

She stopped kicking her legs and moving her arms. She didn't even hold her breath. She simply let go. Her body sank slowly under the water. When she opened her mouth, the cold sea overtook her. She shook violently as the cold water poured into her lungs. Burning, searing pain ripped through her body. Death was overtaking her, and she started to lose consciousness.

Then, as if she were dropped from a rooftop, her body crashed down onto the beach. She coughed and heaved violently, throwing the seawater out of her lungs. Her eyes burned and her head throbbed, but she could breathe. She could breathe! Didn't she just drown? What was going on?

She lifted her head and wiped her eyes, then rubbed them

again, for she couldn't believe what she saw. Walls of water standing at least a hundred feet in the air stood all around her. She was on a dry pathway about ten feet wide that stretched and sloped from the beach behind her to. . .

"Oh my!" She fell back to the ground. In front of her, a couple hundred yards ahead, was the most beautiful canopy of green she'd ever seen. Trees and vegetation she couldn't recognize stood before her. Every branch was weighted with ripe fruit. Birds, singing songs that sounded what could only be described as angelic, flew between the treetops.

She didn't know where the strength to move was coming from, but she found herself running. In seconds she was in the Garden of Eden. The vegetation was so thick she could barely see through it. But there was a path that led into the heart of the garden. She took a step to cross the line into it and heard a blood-curdling scream. When she turned, she was face-to-face with the serpent again. The serpent had dragged Jason's body with it. Jason seemed to be dead.

"Murderer!" the serpent hissed at her. "You've done this to him! Go on! Try to walk in there. See what happens. You've killed. You're no better than Cain!"

Anna was about to launch at the serpent when a brilliant flash of light shot down from the sky, fast as a bolt of lightning, slamming into the serpent and knocking him and Anna over. There was a huge ball of dust and smoke as if a bomb had been detonated. When it all cleared, Anna scrambled to her feet. The serpent was restrained by Michael, the archangel.

"Let go of me!" the serpent hissed.

"Not on your life!" Michael spat. "I've waited for this day for thousands of years." He turned to Anna. "Walk through that path." He pointed it out to her. "Take Jason with you. There is someone waiting for you there."

Anna did as she was told. She leaned Jason's body up and placed her arms underneath his shoulders. She started off down the path, backpedaling and dragging Jason along the way. She stole a glance back up the path and saw that the serpent had now transformed itself into a massive dragon. It spat fire at Michael, who slashed at its flames with his sword. Michael turned to catch Anna's stare. He winked at her and smiled broadly before returning to his battle.

Anna followed the path beside a stream with water as clear as finely polished crystal. A massive tree marked the end of the stream, light shining from its branches. Cherubim stood guard on both sides of the tree, and flaming swords flashed back and forth in front. Anna lay Jason's body down at the foot of the tree. She closed her eyes and prayed.

"Jesus, I am in so much awe right now, I don't even know what to pray. I am so at home in here right now. I feel like I've never been home before until now. Thank You for hearing my prayer and allowing me to come home. I love You and worship You."

The canopy of the garden slowly parted. The clouds lifted, and the sun shone brightly down on her. A booming voice from the heavens spoke.

"This is My daughter, My creation, with whom I am pleased."

The tree's branches swayed back and forth, applauding the voice. The stream bubbled and frothed. The birds sang one song.

Anna cried tears of joy but couldn't move anything else. A hand touched her shoulder and released her from her paralyzing grip. She looked up and saw a man clothed in white. His hands were rough, His face scarred. His robes were silk, and His beard was dark. His head was crowned with pure light. His feet were bare and bore holes in them. As He held out His hands, she saw the piercing there, too. When He spoke, His voice was like a warm blanket that gently caressed.

"Anna, welcome home."

She fell at His feet and cried more tears of joy.

"Stand, child."

She did. He took her by the hand and pulled her to Himself in a tight embrace. His smile was like nothing she'd ever imagined.

When He let her go, she stepped back a step and pointed to Jason. "Jesus, what about him?"

Jesus leaned down and touched Jason's hand. "Come forth, Jason!"

Immediately Jason opened his eyes and sucked in a breath. He stood and turned to see his Savior in front of him. He then fell back to his knees and cried out, "My Lord, Jesus!" as he laid his head at Jesus' feet.

"You may stand, My son."

Slowly, and with his head still bowed, Jason rose to stand before his King. "Thank You."

"You are My child, Jason. What else could I do?" Jesus explained.

Jason lifted his head to meet Jesus' gaze.

"Anna, Jason, this is the tree of life." He pointed behind Him. "Adam and Eve were banished from it because of their sin and rebellion. Their choice has led to a hurtful and broken world. Your faith and perseverance have brought this world to an end, and I will now redeem and restore it."

He waved His hand. The cherubim and flaming sword disappeared.

"You may take fruit from the tree and eat it. You and Jason may live here freely for a time. Eat from whatever tree you want. Now that the tree of life has been granted to you, My Father's plan is complete. I will go back to the world one last time and bring an end to all things. I will judge the living and the dead, and establish

My kingdom forever. And I will bring with Me those the Father has given Me, that they may also be where I am."

Then He reached out and pulled them in, so that they each rested in His arms. "Jason, Anna, I've loved you, even before you were born. Well done, good and faithful servants!" He let them go and motioned for them to continue into the garden.

They both walked a few steps in and turned to see Him once more, but He was gone. "Where did He go?" Anna asked.

Jason smiled. "To make all things new," he said. He grabbed Anna and pulled her to him. "Anna, you did it! Look at this place!"

Anna shook her head. "Uh-uh. *We* did it!" she said. Then she kissed him and said, "I love you, Jason Lang."

He brushed the hair out of her eyes. "I love you, too, Anna Riley."

EPILOGUE

The city of Cairo, Egypt, was alive and festive as they prepared to host their first ever FIFA World Cup soccer event. The opening ceremonies were some of the most spectacular visual displays the world had ever seen. Over a million people had come to the city to witness the tournament.

The stage was set for the first big game of the thirty-day event. For the first time in World Cup history, the Americans and the Egyptians were ranked as the number one and two teams in the tournament.

Cairo International Stadium swelled with the masses of people pouring in through the gates. Vendors selling trinkets and team paraphernalia lined the city streets all the way to the front gates of the stadium. The smell of food saturated the air for miles around, as the restaurants were filled to capacity. The entire city was bustling with preparations for this eagerly anticipated sporting event.

The players took the field as the officiating crew gave a final look over the team rosters. The crowd chanted and stomped their feet in unison on the concrete and metal floors, creating a cacophony of noise. Banners waved through the air with the different team logos. And then the ball was placed at center field.

As if in reverence for a spiritual moment, the crowd grew eerily silent as the referee raised his hand and waited to blow his whistle to signify the start of the game.

And then the ground began to tremble with a slow, soft rumble. The fans looked around in a bit of confusion, as if this were some kind of special effect saved by the opening ceremonies crew for the special match. Then the rumble grew.

But not from the ground. As the noise grew louder, people realized the rumble emanated from the sky. Slowly, but intensely, the sound crescendoed from a low-pitched hum to an earth-shaking rumble. People stood still, watching and listening, waiting for the noise to reveal itself.

Outside in the street, cars stopped. People came out of buildings and gave their attention to the sight above. Clouds had begun to streak across the sky, obscuring the sun.

Television and radio stations were already carrying the coverage of the strange noise and visual occurrences going on above the ground. The phenomenon, it seemed, was happening all over the world. The rumble was getting louder now and began to rise in pitch. People covered their ears to shield themselves from the deafening noise that now sounded like a thousand fighter jets at close range, as panic rose in the heart of every man, woman, and child.

Suddenly there was an enormous explosion in the sky, as if the sun had burst and shot its rays like giant fireworks. And then the sky changed. Both hemispheres were plummeted into almost complete darkness. People screamed and ran as the entire world seemed to be under attack.

A few moments later it stopped without warning as suddenly as it had happened. Either out of fear or curiosity, everyone stopped with it. And the inhabitants of the entire world stood still, collectively holding their breath, wondering what had just happened, or worse, what was coming next.

Then, as if a giant hand had reached down and pulled the lid off a canister, the sky was peeled back and an enormous crack filled the sky, encircling the entire globe. Then, from the crack, an ear-shattering trumpet blast sounded. And with it came the most brilliant, radiant white light ever seen. And it pierced the darkness.

The Guardian Discussion Questions

1. In the opening scene, Anna meets the young boy and is faced with a decision to act on faith. What situations or circumstances have you faced that have required you to act on faith?

2. When Anna is facing the decision to leave New Orleans and go to Pittsburgh, she is not yet a believer. However, God gives her the grace and mercy needed to act, which sets her on a course to meet God. In what ways has God shown you grace and mercy as you were on your way toward Him?

3. In a defining moment for Anna, she meets her parents to inform them of all she has experienced and learned about the family history, but she is met with their skeptical assertions that cause her to doubt everything. Describe how skeptical friends or family in your own life have caused times of doubt in your faith.

4. Anna felt a sense of betrayal from her parents because they had told her that her grandfather (Thomas Riley) had died when she was young. What situations or circumstances have you faced in life where you felt betrayed by someone, perhaps even close friends or loved ones? How did you deal with them?

5. Anna is told that it is her destiny to be the guardian of the scroll, and she wrestles over her ability and faith to do it. In what ways have you struggled with discovering God's plan for you? What doubts or insecurities have you faced in trying to accomplish it?

6. *The Guardian* is less about an adventure to unlock a scroll's secret and more about Anna's faith journey. At what point in the story do you believe her heart began to truly open to God? What examples or evidence bring you to this conclusion?

7. From Father Vin to Jason, God knew exactly what people to put in Anna's life and when to put them there. In what ways has God strategically placed people in your life at the right times and seasons? Discuss some examples.

8. How does Jason begin to have an effect on Anna's life? What are the different ways? What were some of the key moments that show this?

9. Cardinal Wickham in this story is in pursuit of the scroll as he works for Satan. What has brought Wickham to this place in his life? How has Satan deceived him and used him? In what ways do some of the things Satan does still happen in how he operates in our world today?

10. Joseph McCoy finds himself catapulted into the middle of this cosmic battle because of his misguided aspirations and dreams for fame and power. Have you ever fallen into temptation like this? How can our enemy use this against us and God?

11. Anna's last battle before achieving victory happens on the beach with Satan (who is in the form of a serpent). In this moment, Satan does his best to cause Anna to have

doubt by bringing up her sinful past. In what ways does Satan still attack you by bringing up your past? How can you combat this?

12. At the end of the book, Anna finally has to walk by faith and not by sight as she enters the water and is forced to trust God completely. What times or moments in your life have you faced "faith not sight" experiences that have required you to put trust completely in God's hands, not your own?

13. What feelings, thoughts, and emotions did the Epilogue stir in you?

14. As believers, it is easy to say to ourselves that if God called us to do something that required a complete change of direction in our life, or required us to leave behind everything that was normal for us, we would do it. But if you were put into Anna's shoes, how do you think you would respond? If God clearly called you to make some radical change in your life, what obstacles do you foresee in your life now that would make that change difficult?

15. What lessons or "take-aways" have you learned from *The Guardian*? How can this story be used to strengthen your own faith?

ROBBIE CHEUVRONT is the worship pastor of The Journey Church in Lebanon, Tennessee and cofounder of C & R Ministries with Erik. He is also a songwriter and formerly toured with BNA recording artists, Lonestar. Robbie is married to Tiffany and has two children, Cason and Hadyn, and is currently pursuing a theology degree.

ERIK REED is the lead pastor and an elder of The Journey Church in Lebanon, Tennessee. He graduated from Western Kentucky University with a B.A. in Religious Studies. He also graduated with his MDiv from Southern Seminary. Erik is married to Katrina, with two children, Kaleb and Kaleigh.

Acknowledgments

Robbie would like to thank...

First of all, I would like to give glory to my Father in heaven. Through His mercy and grace, this sinful creature has found redemption that I don't deserve, in Christ Jesus. I live to serve Him. I pray that He will be glorified in everything that I do.

I would like to thank my wife, who I also don't deserve, who tirelessly stands beside me in all things. She is my partner in all things. That God would choose for me a woman like her to share my life with, is mind blowing. Every day! I love you, Tiffany. To my children: For whatever reason, God has blessed me with you, Cason and Hadyn. I cherish each and every moment that I get to spend with you, and I pray with every ounce of my soul that God would save you. I beg that you would never take your eyes off of Him, and that you would trust Him for everything in this life. I love you two with all my heart. To my family: Thank you to my Mom and Dad for raising me and my sister, Crystal, in a good home. Though we were never rich, we had more treasure than I can count.

Lastly, to The Journey Church: As Erik has said, it is an honor to serve you. I thank God for calling me into a life of ministry and placing me here, at this church. I love you all and am in awe of all that God has chosen to do through you for this body and His Kingdom. You are an amazing group of people, and I count it as pure joy that I get to serve alongside you and see your witness for Christ. Let's never forget that this is His church, not ours.

Erik would like to thank...

There are so many people to recognize for their contribution to my life. First and foremost, God has been incredibly gracious to me. I am an undeserving sinner who has received the greatest gift of all—Jesus Christ. I have been so captured by His grace that it is my life's desire to love Him and live for His glory, for all my life.

Secondly, I want to thank my family. They are a tremendous encouragement and joy to my life. My wife, Katrina, is irreplaceable. She is the one God chose for me from the foundations of the world, and He chose well. My wonderful children, Kaleb and Kaleigh, are my pride and joy. They give me such pleasure in life. I love them in ways that I did not know existed. Third, I want to thank my parents, Billy and Ginger Reed, for raising me and my sister, Amber, in a loving and stable home. Thank you for working hard to support us and providing a home that was filled with wonderful memories and experiences.

Lastly, the Journey Church: What a privilege it is to serve you. We have witnessed God work in incredible ways among us, and as we seek to continue lifting Christ up, and proclaiming His Word, we will continue to see that work done. Keep clinging to Jesus. Keep your eyes fixed firmly on the Author and Perfector of our faith, and He will make your paths straight.

Robbie and Erik would like to thank. . .

Our agent, Literary Management Group LLC., Bruce "BRB," Barbour, & Lavonne Stevens. WOW! What a ride! The way that we came into contact with you in the first place, only serves as more proof of God's sovereignty. You guys have been incredible. I can only imagine that other authors are jealous of our relationship with you all. Thank you for believing in us and taking a chance.

Our Publisher, Barbour Books: When we decided that the manuscript was finished, we were only hopeful that a publisher would show a little interest and maybe give us a shot. You all have been unbelievable in your excitement and your hard work to see this book come to fruition. Your staff is top notch! And from the first moment we signed with you, you have taken us on a whirlwind of a journey. Thank you, too, for believing in us. We look forward to working with you again on our next book! Thank you, Rebecca and Mary, specifically for all you've done to bring *The Guardian* to life.

Our Editor, Meredith Efken, and The Fiction Fix-It Shop: This being our first published novel, we were completely ignorant of how the editing process happened. We won't lie. We were a little scared of you before we got started! But you quickly eased our minds. You are brilliant! And this manuscript would not be the book that it is without you. You brought life where there was lull, you brought coherence where there was disjointedness, and you brought depth to Anna where she was lacking. You are amazing, and we can't imagine having gone through this process without you. Get ready! The next one is coming!

Lastly, we would like to thank all of our extended families and friends who believed in us, encouraged us, prayed for us, and even read along as we wrote. So many of you have made the writing of this novel possible, and we are grateful to you for everything. Thank you, Michael Hyatt, for your article for new authors and the resources that you made available. This novel has been published as a result of that article. Thank you to Google. You wouldn't believe how much of a writing tool the Internet is! Thank you to Waffle House and Starbucks. Many hours were spent in your establishments brainstorming and writing. Thank you to our best friends and coworkers, Shawn Allen, John Griffin, Kendria Spicer, Miranda Allen, Philip Organ, Shelly Baker, and Josh Waggoner. You guys make serving in ministry such a joy. Thanks for all your help in taking care of the tasks that Erik and I couldn't, as we finished this book and got it ready for print. And finally, thank you Tom Hilpert for showing us how to even set up the template for writing in the first place.

CHAPTER 1

Hidalgo County Sherriff's Department, Edinburg Texas
July 2, 2025, 10:30 a.m.

Becky Sayers looked at the discolored flat-screen plasma TV and silently cursed her boss. "You'd think in this world of technology, we could find a TV that wasn't made before I was born," she mumbled to no one. "I mean, this thing's not even in 3-D. A rerun of *Everybody Loves Raymond* was playing—the one where Raymond fakes going to the doctor so he can play golf. She'd seen it at least four times, but it was one of her favorites.

She pushed back from her desk and stretched her legs. The switchboard had been pretty quiet so far. A few drunk-and-disorderlies and a domestic dispute. The holiday weekend usually meant a boring few days at the Hidalgo County Sheriff's Department.

The green light flashed on her board. She placed the earpiece in her ear and said, "Thank you for calling the Hidalgo County Sheriff's Department. This is Becky...."

The caller made her complaint and hung up abruptly. Her neighbors were setting off illegal fireworks; could a deputy come by and take care of it? All of south Texas had experienced a horrible drought these past few months. The governor had issued a decree suspending all fireworks throughout the entire state. Residents weren't happy, but they understood. Brushfires this time of year were common and could lead to billions of dollars in damage.

Becky keyed her microphone. "Roy, this is Becky. I need you to go out to Ms. Dobson's farm, out on highway 83. Neighbor kids are shootin' off firecrackers or something."

She waited for the grumpy complaint that was sure to come. Roy hated dealing with neighborly disputes. He always tried to pawn them off on one of the other deputies. Nothing.

"Roy, this is Becky—come in."

Nothing.

"Roy! I ain't playing! Pick up that radio or else!"

Still nothing.

She switched over to another channel. She couldn't figure out why one of her deputies would switch channels, and she was starting to get a little worried. Roy was dependable, if nothing else. He'd never gone without answering a call while he was out in the field.

"Roy, this is Becky. You change channels on me to try and get some R and R?"

Nothing.

Now she was getting worried. She switched the channel back. "Clay, this is dispatch. Check in—over."

Nothing.

"Marcus, check in—over."

Nothing.

She walked down the hall and found her boss, told him what was going on, and waited for a response. He told her not to worry. It was probably just weather-related. "Probably a sun spot or something messin' with the radios," he said. "Try again in a few minutes."

Back at her desk, she waited, watching the end of the show. As the credits rolled, she picked up her microphone. After five minutes of the same thing, she decided that this was no sun spot.

She grabbed the phone and called the Cameron County Sheriff's office—the next county over. She told them what was going on and asked if they were having any trouble. Gina, the dispatcher over there, said she had been experiencing the same thing for the last hour. None of her deputies had checked in or returned back to headquarters.

She immediately hung up and called Star, Zapata, and Webb

counties. All three reported the same goings on. At that point, she dismissed paranoia and hurriedly called the state police. They too had a few officers who weren't responding, but all of the state police vehicles were equipped with GPS systems and were being located. The young man at state police headquarters offered to send a few officers her way to check on her deputies, too. She thanked him and provided the deputies' last known whereabouts.

July 4, 2025, 12:00 p.m.

Becky stood in front of her fourth TV camera in the last hour and told her story again. This time it was Fox. NBC and CBS had already been by. The mysterious disappearance of her deputies two days ago was making national news. Several sheriff's deputies, border patrol agents, and state and local police officers had turned up dead all across the border towns of Texas. Over the past two days, New Mexico and Arizona had reported the same.

Becky was one of the first to discover the disappearances along the border, and therefore, she was a hot commodity with the news anchors.

The blond supermodel-looking reporter nodded intently as Becky told her story. The reporter was about to ask her fourth and final question before wrapping the interview up with her own summation of things, when her left ear bud beeped. An excited voice began to relay information. The reporter's expression faded and gave way to a look of disbelief, shock, then horror. Tears filled her eyes and her face turned ashen. Her arm dropped to her side, along with her microphone. Becky stopped mid-sentence and asked, "What's wrong?"

The reporter turned to her, eyes wide. She moved her mouth, but nothing came out.

Becky grabbed the woman by her shoulders and shook her. "What's wrong?"

The reporter looked at her blankly and said, "Bomb...they're all dead." Her knees gave out, and she slumped to the hard, dry ground.

Becky let go of the woman and ran back inside to the flat-screen TV.

CHAPTER 2

Following the directions he was given, Jonathan Keene pulled his car off the road and onto a dirt path. After a mile, he came to the fork in the road. Then up ahead, on the left, stood the house.

He parked the car, got out, and surveyed the area. Nothing. Walking into the house, he noticed a reflection of light coming from the hillside off to his left. He waited ten minutes. Then, as per his instructions, he left through the back door and walked slowly up the hill from toward the reflection's source.

At the top of the hill he knelt, placed his hands behind his head, and interlocked his fingers. This was the unsettling part. Out in the open. No cover. The sun blazing in his eyes. The wind blowing dust everywhere. It was hard to see anything more than twenty feet away. He did feel better though knowing that strapped to his back, under his loose shirt, was his Glock 9mm. It lay mere inches from his fingertips.

After nothing for five minutes, he finally heard the faint hum of motorcycle engines. Within seconds, he was surrounded by a half dozen armed Mexicans.

One covered with tattoos and a scar across his left cheek moved toward him. According to the description he'd been given, this was his informant.

"*Hola*, holmes," the young man said. "Welcome to *Mehico*."

Though the walk uphill was a short one, Keene knew that he had illegally crossed the invisible border into this gang-banger's country.

"*Gracias*," he replied. "You must be Hector."

"Do I need to search you?" Hector asked.

"Not unless you want to find the nine mil I got strapped to my back," he said flatly.

Hector laughed and said, "Stand up."

"Now what's so important, Hector, that you need to talk to the CIA?" he asked.

"Follow me," Hector said, walking down the hill toward the house.

Keene followed the men back into the house, thankful to be back on sovereign U.S. soil.

"I know what happened to those sheriff's deputies," Hector said.

"Yeah, so? Call the police."

"Nah, holmes—*la policia* don't want none of this."

"None of what?"

"That's a nice watch, CIA. Where was that made? China?"

"Yeah," Jonathan said quizzically. "What's that have to do with anything?"

"Lots of stuff in your country made by China."

"Yeah, so?"

"Funny thing. In the last two months, I been seeing lots of Chinese people 'round here."

"Maybe they like the food," Jonathan said.

"Maybe," Hector answered. "But these Chinese been coming in droves, holmes. In big military trucks. From down south."

"Interesting," Jonathan murmured.

"You want to know what's really interesting, CIA?"

"I give up," Jonathan said in mock anticipation.

"These Chinese, they got guns."

"So?"

"And tanks. And airplanes."

"What?"

"You heard me, holmes. They got an army down here. They been bringing it up here to the border for the last two months."

"Impossible. We would've known about it." Jonathan said, a little worried.

"You wanna know what happened to your cops, CIA? About

three hundred Chinese foot soldiers with automatic weapons crossed your border and took them out. I got boys all up and down the border saying they seen it, man. Now, I don't know what's up with a hundred thousand Chinese being in my—"

"What did you say? How many?"

"From what I hear, about a hundred thousand."

Jonathan's jaw went slack. There was no way that a hundred thousand Chinese soldiers were living across the border without the United States knowing about it. Something was wrong.

"You look like you seen a ghost, CIA."

"Why are you telling me this, Hector? Why now? Why not two months ago?"

" 'Cause two months ago, I couldn'ta cared less, holmes." Hector said. "You Americans don't know what goes on down here. You come to our fancy resorts and get treated like kings. Then you go back home and don't care what happens to the rest of us out here. Well guess what? These Chinese start showing up and doing nice things for our communities. Nobody says anything 'cause they like it. Then, without warning, they start taking over. And our policia don't care. They gettin' paid off. Next thing I know, I start seeing guns, tanks, and fighter planes. And then they come into town and line up five men and shoot them in the head. They say, anyone talks or tries to do anything, they kill the whole town!"

"This is—this is just ridiculous, Hector!" Jonathan said. "I don't know what your game is, but this isn't funny. You could get into a lot of trouble—"

"I ain't playin', holmes!" Hector shouted angrily. "They kill my little brother, man! And something bad is about to happen! I'm telling you as a favor." He hung his head and wiped his eyes. "I don't know why your government don't know about this, CIA, but I'm telling you. Someone had to mess up big to miss this."

Keene stood there dumbfounded. There was no way this could be true. An entire army couldn't march on the United States' border and not be detected. He had to call Langley. He reached for his phone and felt it vibrating in his pocket. He looked at the display. Funny, he thought.

"I was just getting ready to call you," he spoke into the mouthpiece.

"Get back here immediately," Kevin Jennings ordered.

"Yeah, about that," Jonathan said, "I think I need to stay here awhile. I need to check something out."

"No, you need to get back here immediately. Turn on the TV."

"What's wrong?"

"Just do it!" came the reply.

Keene glanced around and saw a small television sitting on a makeshift stand at the opposite end of the room. He pushed past the group of men and turned it on. It only took a few moments for him and the others to see what was happening.

Every channel had interrupted their programming, now covering the breaking news. Plumes of black smoke rose into the sky from devastated buildings. Bridges and highways melted into a pile of searing red metal. Ash and debris covered the entire landscape. Cars were turned over and blown to bits. Then the camera changed. A new city. Same result. Then another. And another. Finally, the images ended. The cameras returned to the news station. A disheveled looking man in blue jeans and a sweater sat in front of the camera. He opened his mouth and said the words that would change the course of history.

"Ladies and Gentlemen, less than ten minutes ago, the entire west coast of the United States of America was attacked. A full nuclear strike. Every major city from San Diego to Seattle. The death toll is in the millions. . . ."